The
Margaret
Trilogy

Other books by Bernice Thurman Hunter

Booky: A Trilogy
Amy's Promise
Janey's Choice
Two Much Alike
It Takes Two
The Runaway
Lamplighter
The Railroader
The Firefighter
Hawk and Stretch

The
Margaret
Trilogy

Bernice Thurman Hunter

Cover photograph by Shawn Hamilton

Scholastic Canada Ltd.
Toronto New York London Auckland Sydney
Mexico City New Delhi Hong Kong Buenos Aires

Scholastic Canada Ltd.
604 King Street West, Toronto, Ontario M5V 1E1, Canada

Scholastic Inc.
557 Broadway, New York, NY 10012, USA

Scholastic Australia Pty Limited
PO Box 579, Gosford, NSW 2250, Australia

Scholastic New Zealand Limited
Private Bag 94407, Botany, Manukau 2163, New Zealand

Scholastic Children's Books
Euston House, 24 Eversholt Street, London NW1 1DB, UK

Library and Archives Canada Cataloguing in Publication
Hunter, Bernice Thurman
The Margaret trilogy / by Bernice Thurman Hunter.
Contents: A place for Margaret -- Margaret in the middle --
Margaret on her way.
ISBN 978-1-4431-1391-5
I. Hunter, Bernice Thurman. Place for Margaret.
II. Hunter, Bernice Thurman. Margaret in the middle.
III. Hunter, Bernice Thurman. Margaret on her way.
IV. Title.
PS8565.U577M39 2012   jC813'.54   C2011-908107-5

Thank you to Paul and Donna Starr, of Five Point Clydesdales,
and Morgan.

6 5 4 3 2 1   Printed in Canada 116   12 13 14 15 16

The Margaret Trilogy

A Place for
MARGARET

For Anita Louise and Heather Anne.

Contents

Chapter 1

Starr

The first time we met he bit me. I held out my hand, straight and flat, just like Aunt Margaret said, but Starr snapped at it so excitedly with his big yellow teeth that he nipped my skin and made it bleed. It hurt like the dickens and I yelled blue murder, scaring the wits out of him. Then he turned tail and galloped across the meadow, disappearing into the woods on the other side.

The next time was just as bad. I was lying in the hammock feeling sorry for myself and missing the city noises. I wasn't used to the quiet of the country, where all you ever heard were bees and bugs and the odd cow mooing. My home in Toronto was on Jones Avenue right near Gerrard Street, where the air practically vibrated with the clanging of trolley cars, the squealing of sirens and the racket of a hundred screaming kids.

So at first I spent a lot of my time on the farm lying around pining for home. I did this in the hammock that Uncle Herb had slung between two poles in the front yard especially for me. There were lots of trees he could have slung it from but Aunt Marg said I wouldn't get enough sunshine under them. "Of all God's miracles," she said, and she could name them off by the peck, "sunshine is far and away the best. It cures nearly anything that ails you." Anything except loneliness, I thought dejectedly.

That day, as I was lazing in the sun talking to my imaginary friend, Emily (I had invented Emily so I wouldn't go crazy), I suddenly had this creepy feeling come over me that somebody was watching me. I swivelled my eyes around nervously, and there was Starr with his big brown head lolling over the fence staring straight at me.

We eyed each other curiously. I don't know what he thought of me, but I thought he was beautiful. He was chestnut brown with a white star the length of his nose, a thick tawny mane and the most peculiar long white eyelashes I'd ever seen on a horse. He batted them at me now, sweeping them down over his shiny dark eyes, which just happened to be the same colour as my own.

I got out of the hammock the quickest way I knew how, by rolling over and landing *kerplunk* on the ground. Startled, he flung up his head, gave a piercing whinny and went tearing across the field as if the devil himself were after him.

"What did you do to him?" called Aunt Marg from the porch. She set down the two pails of milk she was carrying and threw her floppy straw hat up on a nail.

"Nothing!" I pouted, close to tears. "He just doesn't like me, I guess."

"Well, never you mind," she laughed, holding the door open with her backside and lifting the pails into the kitchen. "I like you!" The door clacked shut behind her.

I already knew that! But I wanted Starr to like me. So the next time he hung his head over the fence I was ready for him. Instead of being in the hammock, I was sitting stock-still on the little bench that I had dragged down from the porch — the one Aunt Marg set her bread tins out on. Rising slowly to my feet, I tiptoed towards him, carefully balancing two sugar cubes on the end of a long, flat stick. But as soon as I got close to him he bolted.

"Dang!" I swore, throwing the stick at the fence. "Not even a *horse* will come near me!"

* * *

Boy, I was lonely those first weeks on Uncle Herb's farm. Every night I'd say to Aunt Margaret, "I want to go home." And she'd say, "But Margaret" — I was named after her — "if you go home the doctor will send you to the TB sanitarium. You don't want that, now do you?" And I'd say, "No, but at least at the sanitarium there might be other sick kids to play with."

That's why I had been sent to the farm. Because the doctor said I had TB, which is short for tuberculosis, and I had to be isolated. "It's either the san or the farm," he said, "take your pick." So my mother picked the farm.

In that summer of 1925, sunshine, home cooking and good nursing care were all that could be done for TB. My mother said I was bound to get plenty of all three on the farm. "My sister Margaret is the best practical nurse in Ontario. Maybe in the whole country," she declared proudly. "Why, she's nursed hundreds of sick folk back to health after the doctors had given them up for lost. And she's only buried half a dozen so far."

"How long will I be gone, Ma?" I was beginning to get suspicious. What if I was dying and they weren't telling me?

"Oh, just a few weeks at the most, Peg." That's what I got called at home — Peg or Peggy. I didn't like either one. "Don't worry your head. Margaret will have you fit as a fiddle in no time at all."

Next came the problem of how to get me there. The farm was sixty-odd miles from Toronto, and my father didn't own a car. And I was too weak to travel by train. So the doctor volunteered to deliver me himself. He said his folks lived in Shelburne, which was the nearest town to Uncle Herb's farm, and he owed them a visit.

So Ma packed my grip and slipped a snapshot of our whole family into the side pocket. "Just so you don't forget us," she said.

Then the doctor bundled me in a woollen rug and laid me out on the back seat of his Pierce Arrow. It had a lovely new-car smell and I would have enjoyed the trip if I'd been feeling better. On the other hand, if I'd been feeling better I wouldn't have got to go. So it was six of one and half a dozen of the other.

Curled up on the velvety seat, I soon fell fast asleep. The next thing I knew the doctor was calling, "Wake up, missy. We're here!"

I jumped up, rubbing my eyes, and stared out the front window as he steered the Arrow up the long lane leading to the green farmhouse. At least it used to be green, but now the paint was flaking off, letting the parched grey wood show through. A weather-beaten sign nailed to the fencepost read, in faded letters, *Green Meadows*.

My aunt and uncle were both on the porch to greet us.

Uncle Herb was a solid looking man, with wiry red hair, a friendly grin that showed the space between his teeth, and a farmer's burnt complexion. He had on grey overalls and a blue-checkered shirt. Aunt Marg was a stockily-built woman in a housedress that looked as if it had been cut from the same cloth as Uncle Herb's shirt. She had red hair coiled up in a bun, fair freckly skin and a wide sweet smile. They looked almost like twins.

The first thing I said was, "Am I going to die?"

Uncle Herb let out a hoot of laughter and the straw he had been wiggling between his teeth flew out of his mouth. "You do and your aunt will kill you!" he cried.

That made us all laugh. Then the doctor assured me that I was going to get well, and my aunt and uncle thanked him for dropping me off (like a sack of potatoes, joked Uncle Herb). I was soon tucked in under an afghan on the day-bed in the big farm kitchen.

I liked the kitchen. It was a homey room with a huge black iron stove, a long wooden table and six plain chairs. A washstand stood by the door with a graniteware basin on top and a pail of water underneath. The floor was made of wide boards with no linoleum. At the end of the room was a door that led upstairs to the bedrooms.

Both my aunt and uncle were nice, which in my experience is pretty unusual. Most often if your aunt is nice your uncle is awful — or vice versa.

* * *

Aunt Marg worried a lot about my loneliness because she said that pining would hinder my progress. But since I wasn't allowed within a mile of other people, especially children, what could she do?

Of course she spent as much time with me as she could spare. Every night before bed she'd play a game of dominoes with me or read me a story when the TB made me too tired to read to myself.

But because it was the haying season and Uncle Herb didn't have a hired hand, Aunt Marg had to help out. So she had to leave me on my own more than she really liked.

It was a small farm, with just one horse — Starr — two cows — Flora and Fauna — and a flock of black and white hens that Aunt Marg called her "ladies." They didn't have regular names like the other livestock. Uncle Herb said his farm was a one-man operation. "One man and one woman!" Aunt Marg reminded him dryly.

"You're right there, Mag." That's what he called her sometimes — Mag. She didn't like it because it rhymed with hag, but there was no use trying to stop him. "That man!" she wagged her finger in his direction. "That uncle of yours. Why, if I didn't love him so much I'd have sent him packing long ago!"

* * *

The second week I was there it rained cats and dogs so I had to stay indoors and rest on the daybed, with only my imaginary friend, Emily, for company. Sometimes I heard Starr neighing in the distance, which only made me feel more lonely.

Then one day Uncle Herb came in sopping wet; he slapped his hat on his knee and showered me with raindrops as he handed me a letter. I recognized the writing instantly. It was from my sister Josie, the one I was the closest to and shared the bed with at home. Squealing with delight, I ripped it open.

June 16, 1925

Dear Peg,

How are you? I hope you are lots better. We're all fine down here. We are having a swell summer so far. Do you know what we did last Saturday? We had a block picnic and all the families on our block went to High Park. All the mothers packed lunch baskets. Ma made egg and bologna sandwiches and gumdrop cake. There must have been a hundred people there altogether. Even Olive and Elmer went. (Olive and Elmer were the oldest in our family and they usually thought they were too grown-up to go on family outings.) *The minute we jumped off the trolley car we all trooped down to where the animals are kept and fed them carrot tops through the fence. Then we played games like Shadow Tag and Cowboys and Indians. That's lots of fun in High Park because there are so many big trees to hide behind. The big boys played Buck, Buck, How Many Fingers Up? Our Harry was at the bottom of the heap and he nearly got his back broke when fat Theodore Duncan landed on top of him. So Jenny begged him to quit.* (Jenny was Harry's twin so they were extra close.) *Gracie and Davey were good as gold and didn't fight once because they were having so much fun playing London Bridges and Here I Sit A-Sewing. Bobby wet his drawers once so Ma put him back in napkins, but she didn't spank him. Flossie Gilmore went with Zelma Speares because Mrs. Gilmore had the vapours and couldn't go.* (Flossie Gilmore was my best friend, but who the heck was Zelma Speares?)

At suppertime the men put the picnic tables in rows, end to end, so we could all sit down together. There was tons of food and oceans of lemonade. Afterwards we kids lay around on the grass moaning and holding our stomachs. Then we started telling jokes and stories.

When the women got the tables all cleared up and the men came back from their walk, the grown-ups played progressive euchre. The big kids, like Olive and Elmer, were allowed to play, too.

On our way home on the trolley car we flipped the wicker seatbacks over so we could ride facing each other. Then everybody sang "Hail, hail, the gang's all here, what the heck do we care, long as we got our carfare" and after that we sang "Show me the way to go home, over land or sea or foam." It was the most fun I ever had in my life. Even better than kids' day at the Ex and the rides at Sunnyside. Too bad you missed it.

I was so tired when I got home I went to bed without washing myself and Ma didn't even notice. I really like sleeping alone. There's no one to poke me when I wiggle my toes, and make me shove over. And it doesn't matter that the bed sinks down in the middle when there's only one person in it. But I miss you quite a bit, Peg, and hope you miss me too. Goodbye. Write soon.

> Your sister,
> Josie.

P.S. Ma and Pa want to add a line.

Hello there, daughter. I hope you're being a good girl and not giving any trouble. And I hope this finds you

*well. Write me a note when you feel up to it. I'll hand
the pen to your Pa now.*

Your loving mother.

*Well, Peg, we received your aunt's welcome letter a day
or two ago saying how much better you are. That's sure
good news to us. We'll be looking for you home at the
end of the summer.*

Lovingly, your father.

That night I went to bed early, but I didn't blow out the
lamp right away. Instead, I got the picture of my family
down off the washstand mirror and studied it for a long
time. We all looked so happy standing in a bunch on the
steps of our house on Jones Avenue. I noticed every little
thing — the welcome mat hanging crooked over the railing, Bobby's damp drawers drooping down, our old Flyer
wagon lying on its side on the weedy lawn. I remembered
what fun it was coasting down the hill on Jones Avenue. I
stared hard at each face, especially Ma's and Pa's, hoping
I could make myself dream about them.

Josie's letter had made me feel better and worse both at
once. I was glad to hear all the news from home, but how
come, I wondered, they never thought of having a block
picnic before, then all of a sudden when I'm not there, they
have one?

I sighed and stuck the snapshot back up on the looking
glass. Then I spread-eagled myself on the bed. It *was* nice
having a bed to myself. And my own room, too! At home
there were two beds in each room and two kids to a bed.
My bed on the farm was a double one that didn't sink in

the middle. And it was extra soft because it had a downy feather tick. And Emily never wiggled her toes and she didn't take up any space at all.

Now, if only I could win over that stubborn horse!

Chapter 2

The Secret Signal

Three more days passed before it was dry enough to go outside. Then I decided to get up the nerve to stand on Starr's side of the fence. Uncle Herb had just taken the bit out of his mouth and turned him loose after a hard day's work. He hadn't had his water yet and froth bubbled around his muzzle.

When he spotted me he stopped short and stood perfectly still, blinking with those long white eyelashes. He pawed the ground, tossing his head, then, ever so slowly, came ambling towards me. Suddenly I realized how huge an animal he was. With all my might I willed my hand to stay steady and my heart to stop its thumping. I held a big red apple out at arm's length on my sweaty palm. It must have looked refreshing, because he stepped right up and took it — *crunch!* — and the juice sprayed out and clung in sparkling beads to his whiskers.

Just then Uncle Herb opened the gate and came staggering over with a tub of freshly pumped well-water. He set it down with a grunt and a splash and Starr plunged his nose right in up to his snowy lashes.

"What are you doing here, youngster?" asked Uncle Herb, mopping his brow with his sleeve. "I thought you were afraid of Starr." Turning his head he spat an arc of tobacco juice over his shoulder.

"No. I never was. He was afraid of me. But he's not now. He took an apple right off my hand without biting. See?" I proudly displayed my uninjured palm.

"Well, by rights you shouldn't make friends with work animals, Maggie." That's what he had been calling me lately. "They aren't pets, you know. Why don't you go play with Mabel?"

Mabel was the cat. A mean old mouser.

"Eww!" I wrinkled my nose. "I don't like her. She's nasty and she's got spots all over her."

"*Hah!*" He let out a big guffaw. "That sounds like the pot calling the kettle black." He walked away, chuckling to himself at his own joke.

I knew he was only teasing. Uncle Herb wasn't the type to go around hurting other people's feelings. Aunt Marg always said he didn't have a mean bone in his body. But just the same it bothered me because I was extra sensitive about my looks. I had big brown freckles splattered all over my face and arms, and I had to wear thick, steel-rimmed spectacles for my nearsightedness. Then, to top it off, my black hair, which used to be curly before I took sick, had gone all straight and stringy. So Uncle Herb's little joke didn't set too well with me. And his disapproval of my friendship with Starr brought out my stubborn streak and made me all the more determined. But after that I made sure he was nowhere in sight when I was wheedling Starr with treats.

Little by little the horse came to trust me. Every day he let me get a step nearer, until one day he allowed me to stroke the star on his nose for about fifteen minutes. After that it was as easy as falling off a log (or out of a hammock). I'd walk along beside him through the tall grass patting his smooth brown belly and talking to him a mile a minute. And when he leaned down to munch a patch of sweet clover, I'd fling my arms around his broad neck and give him a huge hug. Then, when he raised his handsome head, I'd kiss him right on the lips. His muzzle was soft and warm, like a hairy velvet pillow.

The secret signal happened by accident. One day I saw Starr grazing on the other side of the meadow. He was so far away he looked no bigger than an ant. I thought he wouldn't hear me if I called his name, so I decided to whistle. I pursed my lips and curled my tongue and blew and blew and blew. I nearly blew my head off but no sound came — just air. Then the strangest thing happened. Starr raised his head and stared in my direction. It seemed that he had heard my soundless whistle . . . or felt it . . . or sensed it . . . or something.

Anyhow, after that, no matter where he was, when I blew he'd stop whatever he was doing, throw up his head, spot me and come galloping towards me, his tawny mane waving like wheat in the wind, his tail flying like a banner.

It was swell having a horse for a friend . . . and I wasn't nearly so lonely any more.

Chapter 3

My Dilemma

I had been on the farm for three whole months — June, July and August — when Doctor Tom (we called him by his first name because he and Uncle Herb had been boys together) announced that I was cured.

All summer long, whenever he was passing by in his horse and buggy (he said one of these fine days he was going to get himself a car), he'd stop in to take a look at me. Then at the end of August he gave me a thorough going over.

Aunt Marg stood anxiously by as he listened with his stethoscope, told me to cough, thumped me on the back and pronounced me sound as a dollar. "But just to be on the safe side," he said, snapping shut his black leather bag, "it wouldn't hurt if she stayed up here in the country for another month, or as long as the good weather lasts."

"Well, Margaret," Aunt Marg gave me a searching look, "what do you think? Do you want to stay a while longer? It's up to you, girl, because as far as your uncle and I are concerned you're as welcome as the flowers in May."

I didn't know what to say because I was taken by surprise. It suddenly got quiet in the kitchen. The only sounds were the ticking of the clock on the wall and the noise of a giant blowfly banging on the window.

If I stayed it would mean I'd be late starting school. I didn't mind that because I was smart. I knew it would be easy to catch up. (I always reasoned that God had given me extra brains to make up for my homeliness. Personally I'd have been satisfied with a little less of each.) Anyway, missing school didn't bother me, but missing my family did.

Every night I'd look at the snapshot stuck up on the mirror and "God bless" everybody. Josie had written me two more letters since the one about the picnic. And Ma and Pa each wrote me once telling me to behave myself and sending me a shinplaster to spend. But it wasn't the same as seeing them in person. Of course I knew they wouldn't miss me as much as I missed them because they had each other. There were nine kids in our family and I was the one in the middle. Sometimes I actually felt invisible. And I was perfectly at home with my aunt and uncle now.

For some reason that I hadn't gotten to the bottom of, they had no children of their own, so they treated me just as if I was theirs. Aunt Marg hugged me a lot and called me her "old sweetheart," even though I was only eleven, and Uncle Herb said I was a "corker." That's because I played tricks on him every chance I got. And being the only child in the house had its advantages. For one thing, I sure didn't feel invisible anymore.

All of a sudden my thoughts were interrupted by a high-pitched whinny from the paddock. "Excuse me!" I cried. "I think Starr's calling me." Then I bolted out the door.

Climbing the split-rail fence, I sat on the top rail and took Starr's smooth brown muzzle between my hands. I told him all about my dilemma, while he stared solemnly at me. Uncle Herb always said Starr couldn't understand long conversations, just short commands, but I disagreed. "What do you say, boy? Should I stay a while longer?"

He blinked his long white eyelashes thoughtfully. Then he nodded, the way horses do, swaying his head up and down.

"Thanks, boy!"

Jumping down, I ran straight back into the house. "Guess what?" I cried ecstatically. "Starr wants me to stay!"

"Well, for mercy sakes, so do I!" Aunt Marg grabbed me and hugged me so hard it hurt. "I'll get a letter off to your mother this very minute." Immediately she got the paper, pen and ink pot down from the shelf. And Doctor Tom offered to wait while she wrote it so he could drop it off at the post office.

* * *

By this time Uncle Herb had accepted the fact that Starr and I were a twosome. He said he didn't object just so long as I never interfered while they were working. Aunt Marg even credited the horse with helping to save my life. She said the minute I stopped pining I started on the mend. And she said next to God's good sunshine, Starr was my best medicine.

Aunt Marg was a special kind of grown-up, the kind a child could really talk to. And now that the hay was all piled safely in the barn she had time to listen. Uncle Herb

was a good listener, too, so I told them just about everything. Almost. The one thing I didn't tell them about was
my secret signal, the soundless whistle that only Starr
could hear. I thought they might think I was imagining
things (the way I imagined Emily; I had to stop talking to
Emily because it gave Aunt Marg the heebie-jeebies) or
that I was just being silly. Sometimes grown-ups, even nice
ones, think that way. So I kept that to myself. Besides, it
was fun having a secret with a horse.

Whenever Starr was free in the field I'd purse my lips
and blow, and he'd come to me at a gallop, stopping in a
shower of grass just inches from my toes.

I rode him bareback and combed his tangled mane and
brushed his smooth brown coat until it shone like a polished chestnut. I even tried to clean his teeth once with
Aunt Marg's scrubbing brush, but he wouldn't keep his
lips folded back long enough for me to get the job done.

One day, after catching my signal with those long, pointy
ears of his, he came limping, instead of running, across the
meadow. I nearly had a fit.

"What's the matter, boy?" I cried in alarm.

Lifting the hairy hoof he was favouring (his hoofs were
shaggy and tawny coloured, matching his tail and mane),
I saw that there was a sharp stone wedged between his
flesh and the shoe.

"You wait here, boy," I said. "I'll be right back."

I ran to the house, got a knife from the kitchen table
drawer, and ran back as fast as my legs would go.

I rested his injured hoof between my knees, in the hammock of my dress, and dug out the stone as gently as possible. His hoof began to bleed, so I washed it with soap and

water and doused it with a whole bottle of peroxide. When the peroxide stopped fizzing I knew the wound was purified. And the bleeding stopped, too. Through it all my brave stallion hadn't even flinched.

"Good boy, Starr!" I rewarded him with a kiss on the flat of his nose. "Does that feel better?"

In answer, he flung up his head, kicked up his heels and went tearing around in circles with hardly a sign of a limp.

"Nice work, Maggie!" Uncle Herb complimented me when I told them all about it at the supper table. "You're a natural with animals. I think you should be a vet when you grow up."

"Your uncle's right," Aunt Marg agreed, placing a hot slice of huckleberry pie, topped with clotted cream, in front of me. "You seem to have an affinity for God's creatures, Margaret. I've even noticed my ladies following after you."

"What's an affinity?" I asked, scooping up the cream which had juicy blue rivers wending through it.

"It means a special understanding," she explained. "Animals sense they can trust you more than most folks."

It wasn't long after that that my affinity was put to a real test.

Chapter 4

Fire!

One night in the middle of September we were wakened by a horrendous storm. A huge thunderclap shook the frame farmhouse from top to bottom and jogged us all out of our beds. We ran downstairs and Aunt Marg lit the biggest oil lamp.

Great bolts of lightning flashed across the sky and lit up the whole world as plain as day.

"That was close." Uncle Herb was standing in his night-shirt at the open door. Then he added, "Ain't it eerie how quiet it gets in between?"

"Get away from there, you foolish man!" Aunt Marg yanked him back by the shirt tail. "Sometimes, Herb Wilkinson, you've got no more sense than a dew worm. And don't say 'ain't'!" she added for good measure.

No sooner had she spoken than another charge, ten times brighter than the last, zigzagged earthward and struck the barn dead centre.

"The animals!" cried Uncle Herb, and without hesitating

for a second, he raced towards the barn, his shirt tail flying. Aunt Marg ran after him. And I ran after Aunt Marg. Suddenly the rain began.

"Go back, Margaret!" Aunt Marg screeched over her shoulder. "You'll catch your death!"

But the cloudburst had come too late to save the barn. Orange flames were already shooting skyward from the hayloft. And the stable was attached to the barn. And Starr was in the stable!

"*Starr! Starr! Starr!*" I screamed and kept on coming.

Uncle Herb ran straight into the smoke-filled barn and disappeared from sight. Then, one by one, he dragged the terrified, bellowing cows out by their horns. Aunt Marg grabbed up a switch and drove them into the safety of the paddock. Meanwhile, Uncle Herb had gone back inside for Starr.

Suddenly I was sobbing and crying out loud, "Oh, God, please don't let Starr die! Please save my horse."

Aunt Marg put her arms around me and sheltered me in her flannel kimono. The rain streamed down and the lightning flashed all around us. But we were oblivious to the danger. "Save my man, dear Lord," I heard Aunt Marg pray, "save my man." Her long red hair, which she had let down for the night, whipped around us like wet rope, plastering us together.

Our eyes were glued to the barn door. Smoke poured out, and over the noise of the cracking thunder and teeming rain, we could hear Starr's terror-filled cries.

"I'm going in there," declared Aunt Marg, just as Uncle Herb came staggering out.

"He's panicked," Uncle Herb coughed and gasped, his

face as black as a coalman's. "I can't get him out, even with a blanket over his head."

"I can do it!" I yelled. Then, before they could stop me, I broke free from my aunt's embrace and raced towards the barn.

"*Margaret! Margaret!*" I heard them cry above the tumult.

Through the doorway, all I could see was billowing black smoke and a wave of red flames. Turning my head to one side, I gulped my lungs full of fresh, rain-washed air. Then, closing my eyes tight, I stuck my head inside. It was like sticking my head in a furnace. Pursing my lips and curling my tongue, I blew with all my might.

Just as I was about to run out of breath, Starr — poor, wild, terrified beast — came stumbling through the doorway.

The end of his tail was afire, but the rain put it out instantly. Round and round the barnyard he galloped in total panic. Thank goodness Uncle Herb had the presence of mind to shut the barn door so the horse, in his frenzy, wouldn't gallop right back into the inferno.

At last he tired and slowed to a walk. Finally he stopped, snorting and whimpering and pawing the ground. Then he saw me. Slowly he came to me and nuzzled his head in my arms. "Starr! Starr! There now, boy. Everything's going to be all right." I stroked his quivering muzzle soothingly.

His tail and mane were burned and bedraggled. And his long white eyelashes were all singed off. But he was safe, my friend Starr.

* * *

Uncle Herb was still shaking his head in bewilderment long after the animals were safely sheltered and the fire was out and we were sitting around the table, dry and warm, sipping mugs of hot cocoa.

"I still don't believe what I saw with my own eyes," he blinked. "Tell me again, Maggie, what you mean by your secret signal."

"Well, that's all there is to it, Uncle Herb, what I told you. I tried to whistle for Starr so I could call when he was out of earshot. But no matter how hard I blew I just couldn't make a whistle. But Starr seemed to hear anyway. No matter how far away he was. I can't explain it any better."

"Well, I said it before and I'll say it again — you're a corker, Maggie. A dad-blamed, solid-gold corker."

"The Lord works in strange ways," Aunt Marg remarked, feeling my forehead for the umpteenth time. She always thought the Lord planned things out ahead of time. And who knows, maybe she was right. Because if I had gone home, the storm would have come and the barn would have burned, and Starr would have perished for sure.

"It was meant to be, Margaret. It was destiny."

"Maybe I really do have an affinity."

"I'll drink to both them things," laughed Uncle Herb. Then he downed his hot cocoa in one gulp, wiped his chin with his clean nightshirt and poured himself another mug.

Chapter 5

The Barn Raising

The barn was levelled to the ground. The next day, in spite of the torrential rains, it was still smouldering.

Starr and the cows were tethered temporarily in the driving shed along with the buggy and the cutter. The fire hadn't reached the shed or the hen house, so Aunt Marg's ladies were safe and sound.

They fluttered around us now as we came to gather eggs. "Come, my ladies!" Aunt Marg called to them politely. She never squawked, "Chook! Chook! Chook!" like other people did. With a wide swoop of her hand, she scattered grain from the folds of her apron.

"What's Uncle Herb going to do?" I worried, surveying, in dismay, the heap of steaming grey ash that used to be the barn.

"Oh, he'll have plenty of help rebuilding, never you fear. We'll have a new barn on that very spot before this week is out. And it'll mean lots of work for you and me, old sweetheart."

She wasn't just fooling. The barn raising was scheduled

for Saturday, and this was Monday, so after the wash was hung out we started into the baking. Hundreds of suet pies, baking-powder biscuits, raisin scones and seed cakes — enough to feed an army.

"Lucky my ladies are being so generous this week," remarked my aunt as she cracked a dozen eggs into a huge mixing bowl.

I must have filled a hundred tart shells with vanilla pudding. Then I stirred a big bowl of batter and poured it, without spilling any, into four huge, round cake tins with scrapers attached. When the cakes were cool all you had to do was twirl the scrapers around twice and the cakes came out clean as a whistle. Next Aunt Marg showed me how to make the icing.

"Are you getting tired, Margaret?" she looked at me anxiously. "You've been working like a Trojan this week, and after that soaking the night of the fire it'll be a mercy if you don't take a relapse."

"What the heck's a relapse?" I asked, licking chocolate icing off my fingers.

"It means the sickness might come back on you," she explained, leaning down to touch my forehead with her cheek, which was so flushed from the wood-stove fire that my forehead was bound to feel cold by comparison.

"Well, you don't need to worry, cause I never felt better in my life. I'm even getting fat." I patted my aproned stomach, leaving sticky brown prints on it.

Then something occurred to me.

"I guess that means I'll be going home soon."

The smile slid off Aunt Marg's face. "I hate to think what this house will be like without you, girl. You're just the best company that ever was. Why, you're my old sweet-heart!" She stopped kneading a pile of dough just long enough to give me a floury hug. "And your Uncle Herb will be lost without your tricks. I thought he'd split his overalls laughing at the last one."

Just for fun, the day before, I had covered his red jelly dessert with cellophane. I tucked the clear paper under the wobbly mound so neatly that he couldn't even see it. Well, when he went to eat it, his spoon kept sliding off. "This gol-dang stuff is tough as shoe leather," he com-plained, giving it a hard poke. "What's it made of anyway, Mag?"

Aunt Marg got up, stone-faced, to make the tea. But I couldn't control myself. I giggled and snickered until I gave myself away. "You're a corker, Maggie," Uncle Herb said, giving my nose a tweak, "a genuine eighteen-karat-gold corker."

I tried to think up a new trick to play on him almost every day of the week. He had such a swell sense of humour. And he always made me feel good about myself by insisting that when the Lord made me he threw away the mould. "Leastways, I hope he did," he would add, "because another one like you would be the end of me."

Remembering this, I said to Aunt Marg, "Let's not talk about me leaving, at least until after the barn raising."

"Good idea," agreed my aunt, her round face brightening up. "Sufficient unto the day —"

"What's that mean?" She was always quoting mysterious things, mostly from the Bible.

"No time to explain. I've got to get this baking done before that uncle of yours wants his supper. I swear —

you'd think that man's stomach was a clock, the way he tells the time by it."

She put four more raisin loaves into the hot oven, and we dropped the subject of my leaving for the time being.

On Saturday morning, while the rooster was still crowing, people began to arrive in droves: women and children and men . . . horses and wagons and lumber . . . saws and hammers and nails . . . and more food!

I was beside myself with excitement. I hadn't seen another kid in months. So I ran out to meet a skinny fair-haired boy who was carrying a covered tray across the verandah. "Hi!" I cried. "My name's Margaret. What's yours?"

"My name's Matty — short for Matthew — but my ma said I had to stay clear of you because you're germy." As he spoke he started backing away towards the verandah steps.

"*Germy!*" Boy, did I see red! "How the heck can I be germy when Doctor Tom says I'm all better? Does your ma know more than Doctor Tom?"

"What's this ruckus all about?" demanded Aunt Marg from the doorway.

"He says I'm germy!" I howled indignantly. Then, before she could settle it one way or another, I took a flying leap at Matty and blew my breath all over his startled face.

"*Halp! Ma! I'm poisoned!*" He stumbled backwards off the top step. The tray flew up in the air, raining sandwiches all over the place like leaves on a windy day.

"*Margaret, go to your room!*" ordered my aunt.

"But Aunt Marg, I'm all better now and he said —"

"Go, Margaret!" She pointed to the stairs with the maddest look I'd ever seen on her face.

By this time Matty's mother got wind of it and she dragged him, wailing all the way, over to the well. Shoving his head under the spout, she pumped ice-cold water all over him.

Peeking out from the bottom step of the stairs, I heard Aunt Marg yell, "Now you listen to me, Jessie Muggins! That girl is no more germy than I am. And I'll get a doctor's certificate to prove it! And stop dousing that boy! What are you trying to do, drown him, or give him pneumonia? Cold water won't wash off germs even if there were any, you silly article!"

Now Mrs. Muggins hauled Matty into the kitchen, and without so much as a by-your-leave, grabbed our towel and began rubbing his head furiously.

Suddenly, for some devilish reason, I jumped into full view and shouted, *"You silly article!"* Then I jumped out of sight again. Halfway up the stairs I was sent sprawling by a hard smack on my behind. I turned around and came face to face with my aunt's flashing green eyes and flaming cheeks.

"Don't you dare let me hear you sass your elders like that again, you hear me? Now get!"

I high-tailed it up the rest of the way and slammed my bedroom door. When Aunt Marg came up, about fifteen minutes later, my backside was still smarting and my grip was all packed.

She sighed as she sat down, and the little wooden bed creaked under her weight. Shoving the grip over, she pulled me down beside her. "Margaret . . . I'm sorry, my love, for striking you, especially since you're not my own. But it was the only thing I could think to do at the time."

"Uncle Herb wouldn't have hit me," I said defiantly.

Cupping my chin firmly in her hand, she made me face her. "Oh, yes he would, my girl. On important matters we see eye to eye, him and me."

I didn't dare answer back.

"Now, Margaret, there's something you need to know. Then, if you're still bent on going" — she glanced at the grip gaping open, a stocking hanging out, the family snapshot on top of my jumble of things — "I'll not stand in your way."

I waited for her to compose herself. I'd never seen her so agitated before, and I felt awful knowing I had caused it.

"Matty's mother, Jessie Muggins, was Jessie Hopkins before she wed. We were best friends when we were girls, and still are. At least I hope we are after this." I hung my head and noticed her hands twisting nervously on her lap. "Well, Jessie had a twin brother, Jonas, and two more brothers and a baby sister. All of them — all of them, Margaret — died in a smallpox epidemic within four months of one another. That left Jessie alone at the age of nine with parents who worried themselves into an early grave over her. I thought she was never going to be really happy again, but then when she grew up she married happy-go-lucky Zacharia Muggins. A year later she gave birth to twins. I helped bring them into the world — a healthy boy and girl, just like her and Jonas. She named them Matthew and Martha and she was beside herself with joy. Then an influenza epidemic struck and little Martha sickened and died. Now — can you understand why a woman who has suffered such dreadful loss could go plumb hysterical at the very thought of anything happening to her only child?" She paused, then murmured, as if to herself, "Why the Lord never saw fit to give her another one is more than I can fathom."

"Oh, Aunt Marg . . ." Tears were streaming down my face at the thought of all those poor dead children. "I'm sorry. I've never been so sorry in my whole life. I'll go straight down and apologize. Are they still here?"

"Yes, they're still here. Matty can't go outside until his clothes are dry. But the best thing you can do, my girl, until I get that health certificate for you, is to make yourself scarce. I'll apologize for both of us. I've got some crow to eat myself in this affair."

The bed creaked with relief when she stood up. She smoothed out her apron and tucked a strand of red hair into place. "Now you go rinse your face and clean your specs and watch out the window. Isn't it handy that your bedroom looks right out onto the barnyard? You won't miss a thing. And when I've got a minute I'll bring you up a tray fit for a queen."

I sighed with disappointment. And then I asked a question about something that was bothering me. "Aunt Marg, did you mean that, about being sorry you hit me because I'm not your own?"

"Well, now, I'm sorry as sin that I lost my temper, girl. I've got no use for grown-ups who beat children. But you are my own, Margaret. You're my everything!" Then she hugged me tight, let go suddenly and rushed downstairs.

True to her word, a little while later she brought me up a tray fit for a queen.

I ate hungrily as I watched out the window. I could see Starr teamed up with a dappled grey. Both of them were

straining in the harness, working their heads off along
with the men.

The framework of the barn had to be constructed on the
ground. Then each side was raised up with great long pike
poles. All day long the hammering and clammering went
on, until the last rafter was nailed to the roof. Uncle Herb
would have to finish the inside himself. But at least the
hard part was done. It would be a fine barn. Bigger and
better than the old one, with a separate stable.

I envied the kids, not only helping, but chasing each
other around the barnyard having lots of fun.

Suddenly Matty looked up at my window. I was just
about to turn away, ashamed because of what I'd called his
mother, when he grinned and waved at me. So I leaned out
the window and waved back.

"How does it look from up there?" he shouted.

The last rays of the setting sun glinted on the brand new
lumber, tinting it pinky gold. "It's beautiful. I've got a
bird's-eye view up here."

"I wish I could come up!" he yelled.

I laughed and nodded and he, reluctantly it seemed to
me, went back to join the other kids at play.

Later, when it was too dark to work outside, almost
everybody came inside. But I was puzzled about one man
who didn't. He was strange-looking, tall and skinny, with
a scraggly beard and raggedy clothes. As soon as the work
was done, he got on his horse without saying a word to
anybody and rode off in a cloud of dust.

Soon the house began to rock and ring with the air of a
party. I heard loud guffaws and high-pitched squeals, clat-
tering crockery and tinkling glassware.

With a loud sigh I unpacked my grip, stuck the snapshot back up on the looking glass, put on my nightdress, used the chamber pot under the bed so I wouldn't have to go downstairs, and climbed in under my cover.

After a while the door squeaked open and a familiar voice whispered, "Any corkers awake in here?"

Jumping up, I lit the lamp on the washstand. Uncle Herb set a tray beside the lamp. On it was a tall glass of lemonade and a huge slab of angel cake topped with fresh churned ice cream.

"I'm mighty sorry you missed it all, Maggie. But I'm mighty proud of you, too. Your aunt says you showed understanding far beyond your years."

"Thanks, Uncle Herb. But don't feel bad. I saw everything from up here and I love the new barn." I took a big gulp of lemonade to wash the cake down. "By the way, Uncle Herb, who was that scruffy-looking man who rode away on a big black horse? Why didn't he come to the party?" I couldn't imagine anybody missing the party on purpose.

Uncle Herb scratched his head with his thumbnail. "Oh, you must be referrin' to old Joe Boyle. He's a funny fella, that one, Maggie. A regular old recluse. He lives all by hisself in the bush. Got no friends or folks that I ever heard tell of. And don't have nothing to do with nobody. But, by George, he never misses a barn raising."

Then I asked him a more worrisome question. "What will Starr and Flora and Fauna eat this winter now that the hay's all gone? It's too late to harvest more, isn't it?"

"Way too late," he agreed, jiggling the straw between his teeth. He did this to help him break the tobacco-chewing habit, which Aunt Marg detested. "But our neighbours will see us through. You can bank on that. Everybody will bring a bale of hay or a bushel of oats or whatever they can spare."

"Will you have to pay them all?"

"Not a penny. That's how farm folk operate. We stick together in times of trouble. Not like city folk — present company excepted, of course." He patted my cheek affectionately. "Your aunt tells me you were as much help as a growed woman this past week, Maggie."

"It was fun. I really think it's swell how farm folk stick together. In fact, I think that's what I'm going to be when I grow up — a farmer, just like you."

"Well" — he twirled the straw around in thoughtful circles — "If I had my druthers" (Aunt Marg would have a fit if she heard him use that word. She said he was an educated man and ought to know better. Hadn't he graduated at the top of his class from Senior Fourth?), "I'd druther see you become a vet. That way you can live in the country, but never have a barn to burn. Now that's what I call eating your cake and having it too."

"Swell! And I'll have my animal hospital right near here so I can look after Starr and Flora and Fauna myself. And I'll never charge you a penny, Uncle Herb. Not a penny."

"Well, by gingoes, that's the best offer I've had all day." He leaned down and gave me a little whisker rub. "I'm a lucky man, Maggie. I must have been born with a silver spoon in my mouth."

Chapter 6

A Day in Town

The next Saturday morning Aunt Marg and I went to Shelburne in the buggy to get a health certificate for me and to do some shopping. Uncle Herb stayed home to finish the new barn.

"Can I drive?" I begged, as Aunt Marg was backing Starr between the buggy shafts.

"Part ways. But when we get near town I'll have to take over because there'll be automobiles to contend with and they scare the daylights out of Starr."

Climbing into the driver's seat, I took up the reins and waited until Aunt Marg got settled beside me. She was wearing her second-best dress and a wide-brimmed, flowered hat held on by two sharp hat pins piercing her thick red bun. I clicked my tongue and Starr twitched his ears and started off at a nice easy trot.

It was a lovely day. The leaves were changing colours, the air was fresh and crisp, and the sky was a brilliant blue. Starr seemed to be enjoying the outing. Every time I said his name he pricked up his velvety ears and swished his tawny tail across our feet like a feather duster. I'd trimmed the singed part off his tail, so it looked full and beautiful again.

Just outside town Aunt Marg and I changed places. Seeing houses and shops and people and horses and cars got me all excited. I had been isolated on the farm for such a long time, and having been born and raised in Toronto, I really missed the noises of the city. My father called Shelburne a one-horse town, but after the wide open spaces of the countryside it seemed almost like a real city to me.

The waiting room of the Main Street Clinic was filled with people with broken legs and bandaged heads and crying babies, but we didn't have to wait long because Doctor Tom had made me an appointment.

First I had to stand in front of a machine that took pictures of my insides. Next I had to go down a long hall to a toilet and wet in a bottle. (That was embarrassing, bringing back the bottle.) Then a nurse, who seemed very nice, said, "This won't hurt a bit, honey," and jabbed my thumb with a needle that hurt like the dickens.

"What's that for?" I asked curiously as she dabbed my blood on paper.

"It's to see if you're anemic."

"What's that mean?" I watched, fascinated, as she compared the colour of my blood with red splotches on another paper until she matched it up exactly.

"It means weak blood. But don't worry. If you have it, an iron tonic will fix you up in no time." I wasn't worried because I was already taking a tablespoon of Aunt Marg's herbal blood tonic every day and I felt strong as a horse.

After that we had to wait while the doctors tested everything. Aunt Marg started chatting to a lady she knew — she knew just about everybody in Shelburne — so I wandered around the room reading the doctors' diplomas on the walls and imagining my name on a veterinarian's diploma. Pushing my glasses up the freckled bridge of my nose, I leaned closer, trying to read the Latin words. The lady with Aunt Marg must have thought I was hard of hearing, because she said in a loud whisper, "She's not a pretty child, is she?"

"No," agreed Aunt Marg coldly, "she's beautiful!" Then she got up in a huff and moved to the other side of the room. The woman turned beet red and didn't know which way to look. I was just about to put in my two cents' worth when I caught my aunt's eye and decided to hold my tongue.

At last we were out on the street again, grinning from ear to ear. I wasn't anemic, and the four doctors in the clinic agreed with Doctor Tom that I was completely cured.

"Just wait till I show Jessie Muggins this!" beamed Aunt Marg, waving my health certificate triumphantly. Then she rolled it up and put it at the bottom of her straw satchel.

"All right, old sweetheart, let's go shopping."

Grabbing my arm, Aunt Marg pulled me across the busy street, dodging between a pickup truck and a Model T Ford that were stirring up the dust at about ten miles an hour. Aunt Marg didn't get to town very often, and when she did Uncle Herb said she was like a kid let loose in a candy store.

We had left Starr at the blacksmith's shop to get him

shod, so we had the afternoon to ourselves.

"Does it hurt horses to have shoes nailed to their feet?" I asked, wincing at the imagined pain.

"Not if the smithy's worth his salt. And there's none better than Wilbur Shankley, that's for sure. The Shankleys have been smithies in Shelburne for five generations, so they should know what they're doing."

We stopped in front of the dry-goods store to admire the new fall material. "I'll tell you a secret about Wilbur Shankley if you promise to keep it under your hat, Margaret," my aunt said, her eyes twinkling.

"Oh, I promise. Cross my heart and spit."

"Cross your heart, but don't spit. One spitter in the family is all I can bear."

So I crossed my heart and swallowed the spit and she went on. "Well, Wilbur and I were engaged once, and we had the date set and everything."

"Oh, my gosh! Does Uncle Herb know?"

"Sure. He's the reason I'm not Mrs. Wilbur Shankley this very minute. I met Herb at a barn dance a few weeks after I'd promised my hand to Wilbur, and he swept me right off my feet. We knew we were meant for each other from that very first reel. So we got married on the very day that Wilbur and I had picked. I couldn't see any sense in wasting all my plans. But it made Wilbur furious and I don't think he's forgiven me to this day."

Boy! I could hardly wait to meet Wilbur. (He hadn't been there in the morning when we left Starr.) I was dying to see the person who nearly became my uncle.

Inside the dry-goods store, Aunt Marg told me to pick out any material I liked and she'd make me a new dress to go home in. Then she frowned at the thought, squeezed my arm and said, "Never mind what for. Just pick out a nice piece of goods — and hang the expense." I chose red wool with white daisies all over it.

Next we went to the Emporium and bought Uncle Herb new overalls. "Now all we have to do is figure out a way to get him out of the old ones," joked Aunt Marg. "He's starting to look as raggedy as old Joe Boyle." Then she bought me two pair of red socks and two white hair bows to go with my new material.

By this time we were starved, so we jostled our way along the crowded sidewalk to the drugstore and sat on soda-fountain stools. Aunt Marg said I could have anything I liked, so I ordered a banana split and a butterscotch sundae. She had salmon sandwiches and a pot of tea.

"Why, Margaret Wilkinson! Fancy meeting you here!" A fat lady about Aunt Marg's age, wearing a hat with imitation cherries all over it, sat down on the stool beside her. "And who might this be?" She looked me up and down as if I was a heifer.

"This is my namesake, my niece, Margaret Rose Emerson. Margaret, this is Mrs. Wilbur Shankley." She gave me a broad sidewise wink. "Margaret has been staying with Herb and me over the summer, so we've stuck pretty close to home."

"I heard you had a sick girl on your hands. How is she now?" (Honestly, you'd think I wasn't even there!) "Did the sickness leave her with weak eyes?"

"Don't be ridiculous, Bertha. Margaret inherited shortsightedness from her father's side. And she suits glasses.

Everybody says so." She gave me a fierce, possessive hug, which helped a lot to keep my saucy tongue from disgracing her again.

Well, once Bertha Shankley knew I had a clean bill of health she lost interest in me, thank goodness, and she proceeded to tell Aunt Marg all the latest gossip. Aunt Marg had been out of circulation ever since I came to stay with her. She said nobody wanted you within a mile of them when you had TB in the house. So she listened, all ears, to Bertha's tales about who had died lately and who had got married and who had been born. Boring stuff like that. I started to fidget, so she ordered me a sarsaparilla to drink.

"Are you going to the Magic Lantern Show at the Town Hall?" Mrs. Shankley asked as she began gathering up her things. She consulted a fancy gold watch that hung on a black ribbon around her roly-poly neck. "It starts in fifteen minutes."

So off we went to the Magic Lantern Show. The admission was ten cents for adults and five cents for children and Aunt Marg said it was worth twice the price. We saw slides of the Eiffel Tower and the Taj Mahal and Buckingham Palace and dozens of other exotic places. It was nearly as good as a trip around the world.

By the time we came out into the dazzling sunlight the Town Hall clock was chiming four o'clock. "My, how time flies!" exclaimed Aunt Marg as we hurried along the main street to the blacksmith's shop.

Starr was all shod and harnessed to the buggy, looking none the worse for wear. Wilbur Shankley himself helped us up into our seats and I could tell by the way he looked at Aunt Marg that he still had a soft spot for her. I must admit he was a handsome man: big and brawny, with dark wavy hair and a handlebar mustache. At first it was hard to see how plain, paunchy little Uncle Herb had won out over such competition. But when Wilbur smiled . . . I saw. There was no twinkle in his coal-black eyes and no tenderness about his thin, pale lips.

I guess Aunt Marg knew what she was doing.

We were late getting away, so Aunt Marg cracked the whip above Starr's back and he took off at a trot.

About a quarter mile from home, we stopped in at the Four Corners post office.

"You stay right where you are, Margaret." Aunt Marg handed me the reins and hopped down, so I moved over to the driver's seat.

"Be back in two shakes of a lamb's tail," she said, disappearing into the post office.

When we were alone I said, "It's me, Starr. Did you have a nice day? I hope it didn't hurt to get your new shoes on." He twitched his ears and switched his tail and answered, "Nicker, nicker, nicker." He understood me, all right.

Aunt Marg came hurrying out, ripping open a letter. She hopped up beside me, not seeming to notice that I had taken her place, so I clicked my tongue and Starr trotted off towards home.

"Oh, for mercy sakes!" exclaimed Aunt Marg as she read. "Oh, my stars!" she declared on the second page. By the third page she was really upset. "Oh, good gracious me, what a terrible shame. How in the world will poor Nell ever manage?"

Fear clutched my heart. Nell was my mother's name.

"Is something wrong at home?" All those exclamations had me worried sick.

"Oh, Margaret, child, I'm sorry. I didn't mean to alarm you. Well, the letter's from your mother and she says Olive and Elmer and the twins all have diphtheria, and the whole house is in quarantine for dear knows how long until they see if any of the rest come down with it. No one is allowed in or out except your father to go to work. Well, that settles it, old sweetheart, you can't go home for a spell. Your uncle will be tickled pink when we tell him, but how do you feel about it, Margaret? Are you homesick, child? Four months is a long time for a girl to be separated from her mother."

I was quiet for a minute, thinking, and watching Starr's brown haunches moving rhythmically. Then I said, "I do get homesick sometimes, Aunt Marg, and I do miss my ma . . . and I feel awful about everybody being sick, but" — I hoped what I was going to say wouldn't sound too disloyal to my family — "I really love it here with you and Uncle Herb."

We were on our way up the long lane to the farmhouse. Uncle Herb was waving his red hanky from the porch. Suddenly Starr broke into a canter.

"Well, girl, it's like I always say," Aunt Marg hung onto her hat, her green eyes brightly fixed on home. "It's an ill wind that blows nobody any good."

Chapter 7

Four Corners School

"Well, Margaret, we can't put it off any longer or we'll have the truant officer at our door. You'll have to start school on Monday."

Saturday was a nice warm day, so Aunt Marg and I took advantage of it by washing our hair in rainwater from the barrel under the eavestrough, and sitting out on the bench in the sun to let it dry.

Aunt Marg's hair was a sight to see when it was freshly washed. It draped around her shoulders and rippled down her back like a shiny brass curtain.

She had cut my hair fairly short, and as she was rubbing it dry, she exclaimed, "Glory be, Margaret, your hair is coming in all wavy at the roots. If I wind it around my finger and you sit still until it dries, you'll have a head full of ringlets, just like you did before you took sick. Won't that be grand?"

Boy, was I glad! My dark curly hair, which I had inherited from my father, along with my freckles and nearsightedness, was my only claim to beauty and I had been broken-hearted when I thought I'd lost it.

I got up bright and early Monday morning and decked myself out in my new red dress and white hair bow. Aunt Marg had been looking forward to starting me off at school, but during the night she had come down with a sick headache so Uncle Herb had to do the honours.

I was nervous as a cat. I didn't know any of the kids at Four Corners except Matty Muggins. Mrs. Muggins had let Matty come over three times and I had been to their place twice since she saw my health certificate and was finally convinced that I wasn't germy. We had hit it off right away, Matty and me. But I hadn't gotten to know any of the other kids yet.

It was less than a quarter mile down the road to the little one-room schoolhouse, but Uncle Herb harnessed Starr to the buggy because it had turned cold and windy. Aunt Marg was afraid I'd catch my death if I walked, and Uncle Herb said I might as well start out in style.

We were late arriving, and the yard was deserted, so Uncle Herb knocked on the windowless schoolhouse door. After what seemed like ages, the schoolmistress opened it.

My heart sank when I saw her. She had a stern face with long, narrow lines that pulled her lips down at the corners. Her eyes were cold and dark, like the black beads in Aunt Marg's button box.

Removing his hat like a gentleman, Uncle Herb introduced me. "This here is your new pupil, Margaret Rose Emerson. Maggie, say how-de-do to Miss Maggotty."

"Hmmph!" snorted the teacher before I had a chance to speak. Her beady eyes darted a glance over the top of her spectacles to the big round clock on the wall. "Not only a whole month late, but ten minutes tardy the first day!"

Uncle Herb stiffened and tightened his grip on my shoulder. "The missus took sick in the night, Matilda, or we'd have been here on time. It's not the girl's fault, so don't you go blaming her or you'll have me to reckon with."

Jamming his hat back on his head, he said to me, "I'll pick you up at four o'clock sharp, Maggie." Then he left.

It was a bad start for me. Not only had Uncle Herb defied Miss Maggotty's authority in front of the whole class, but he had spilled the beans about her real name, too. I found out later that she always signed the report cards *Millicent* instead of *Matilda*.

"Oscar Ogilvey, move over and make room for her royal highness," she said with a twisted smile. The big, awkward boy sitting on the front bench right under her narrow nose glared at me and shuffled over. Wordlessly she pointed, and I took his place.

"What class were you in last year, miss?" she snapped the question out sarcastically.

"Junior Third," I answered promptly.

"Junior Third, *Miss Maggotty*!" she barked.

"Junior Third, Miss Maggotty!" I parroted.

"Very well, Miss Smarty, you can stay in Junior Third, since you've missed a whole month of schooling already."

"Oh, no! I passed with honours last year. And I'm very smart. I can catch up easy!"

"Easily!" She caught my mistake gleefully.

"Easily," I agreed.

The class snickered and she grinned her appreciation. "Very well, Miss Smarty, we'll test you out and see."

"Miss Maggotty," my stomach was in knots, but I had to

say it, "my name is Miss Emerson. Margaret Rose Emerson."

The class roared this time and she silenced them with a loud crack of the yardstick over her desk. I had won that round, but I could tell by the expression on her mean old face that I'd probably regret it.

While the other kids had recesses and lunch hour, I spent the time doing tests. They were all as easy as pie. During the afternoon I saw Miss Maggotty marking them, so at the end of the day I asked, in as polite a voice as I could muster, "Miss Maggotty, may I please go into Senior Third tomorrow?" I was sure I had passed all the tests.

"You will remain where you are until I deem otherwise," she answered smugly.

Uncle Herb and Starr arrived at four o'clock on the dot. Boy, was I glad to see them.

"How did it go, Maggie?" Uncle Herb asked, handing me the reins.

"I don't know, Uncle Herb." I clicked my tongue and Starr twitched his ears and started off at a brisk trot. I was both mad and bewildered about my first day at school. "Miss Maggotty gave me tests to see if I'm ready for Senior Third, and I'm sure I am. But she wouldn't tell me anything. And I know she doesn't like me."

"We'll see about that," he answered gruffly, spitting a long stream of tobacco juice into the bushes at the side of the road. "Matilda's got a grudge against your aunt and me ever since we opposed hiring her ten years ago. I didn't cotton to her then, and I don't cotton to her now, but since we had no young-uns of our own, nothing ever came of it before. You just leave her to me." He let loose another arc of brown juice, trying to get rid of it all before we got home. "How did it go otherwise? Did you make any new friends?"

"No. I didn't have time. Matty talked to me for a minute. But I had to stay in both recesses and lunch hour. I ate my sandwich while I worked. And tonight I have to write a five-hundred-word essay about schools. I think I'll do a comparison."

After supper Aunt Marg and I sat writing at the kitchen table in the circle of yellow lamplight. She let me use the best pen. I was doing my essay and she was writing in her personal diary. We both dipped from the same ink pot.

"Can I see your diary, Aunt Marg?" I asked curiously. I couldn't imagine what she found to put in it every night.

"Oh, pshaw, Margaret. It won't be half as interesting as what you're doing. Besides, it's not a diary, it's just a journal. But I'll let you read what I wrote if you'll let me read what you wrote."

Aunt Marg's entry for the day read: *Oct. 2, 1925. Our Margaret started school today. Herb had to take her because I had a sick headache. My, I was disappointed! I only hope Matilda Maggotty realizes what a gem our Margaret is. I've always found the woman a bit dim, myself, so I'll have to keep a sharp lookout in that direction. It rained in the afternoon. Then the sun broke through and my headache cleared up so I sawed some wood and stacked it along the east wall of the woodshed. Hard to believe winter's nearly upon us. Herb will have to get busy and chop down that dead elm. That'll provide plenty of firewood till spring. It would be nice if Margaret could stay all winter. She's such a blessing. Herb thinks the sun rises and sets on her.*

We exchanged books and our eyes met between the lamps.

"Your essay is fine, Margaret," Aunt Marg said.

"Yours, too," I said.

"How about some hot cocoa before we turn in?" suggested Uncle Herb, pulling off the earphones of his new crystal set.

"Can I listen while I wait for cocoa, Uncle Herb?" I loved to hear the faraway places drifting in and out on the radio. Two nights ago I had heard Al Jolson singing, "Mammy!" It almost made me cry.

"They just signed off the air, Maggie. I wish you'd spoke up sooner. I had WIP in Philadelphia as clear as a cowbell."

"That would have been a sight more enlightening than my dull old journal," said Aunt Marg, stirring cocoa and sugar into a smooth paste before she added it to the hot milk on the stove.

"Oh, no it wouldn't, Aunt Marg. I loved your journal."

"Go on with you," she laughed, setting the hot cups down and pinching my cheek with warm fingers. "Anyways . . . you're partial."

No wonder! I only hoped Miss Maggotty would be a bit partial to me. I had worked hard on my essay and I hoped it would be my ticket into Senior Third.

Chapter 8

The Switch

The next morning, realizing that I hadn't played a trick on Uncle Herb for at least a week, I thought up a good one.

"Aunt Marg, will you slice my egg exactly in half?"

She knew how to do it perfectly. Then I scraped the hard-boiled centre out onto my plate and put the two empty half-shells, round side up, in two egg cups shaped like roosters. Setting them carefully at Uncle Herb's place, I mashed the egg on my plate, saturated it with salt, pepper and butter, and ate it. Aunt Marg waggled her head as she served up the porridge.

Uncle Herb came in from the barn and began washing up. He filled the basin with a dipperful of rainwater and sluiced it noisily over his face and hands. (He stubbornly refused to use the warm water from the cistern at the end of the stove, saying cold water was good for what ailed him. Aunt Marg said stuff and nonsense. It was more likely good for pneumonia.) Reaching for the warm towel that hung over the stove on a bar suspended by wires from the ceiling, he dried himself with satisfied grunting sounds like a happy bear. Finally, he drew his chair to the table.

"Cold out today," he remarked as he brown-sugared his oatmeal. "You'd better dress warm, Maggie."

"I will," I promised, waiting impatiently for him to get to his eggs.

At last he pushed the bowl aside and drew the egg cups towards him. He whacked at one with his knife and the empty shell splintered and flew all over the place. Without batting an eye, he whacked the other one, sending bits of egg shell sailing through the air. Mabel, the cat, who had been dozing on top of the woodpile, yowled and spat and streaked under the stove.

"For two cents," growled Uncle Herb, "I'd make the dad-blamed upstart who et my eggs clean up the whole dad-blamed mess!"

Poker-faced, Aunt Marg reached up to the little shelf above the table, took down two pennies and placed them in front of me. Squealing with delight, I ran to the pantry for the corn broom.

"You're a corker, Maggie," grinned Uncle Herb, as Aunt Marg fished two more eggs out of the pot and I swept the little pile of brown shells into the dustpan, "a genuine ten-karat-gold corker!"

"Eighteen!" I cried, smart-alecky, as I raced upstairs to fetch my school bag.

* * *

The minute I entered the classroom I put my essay on Miss Maggotty's desk. Then I went and sat down on the front bench. Miss Maggotty had moved Oscar Ogilvey. Next to me now was a small, sweet-faced girl by the name of Eva Hocks. (Aunt Marg always referred to Eva as a little wisp of a thing.) I noticed she was having an awful struggle with her arithmetic and I wished I could help her, but I didn't dare.

At recess Eva and I ran for the see-saw. "I hate arithmetic," she sighed, climbing on one end of the board. "I like artwork best, but we hardly ever have it. I just wish I could draw all day long. You're lucky, Marg, that you're so smart. I saw how quick you got your problems solved."

"Sure," I pushed my feet and we started going up and down, "but I can't draw a straight line with a ruler."

That made her laugh. "What are you going to be when you grow up?" she wanted to know.

"A veterinarian." I got all excited at the thought. "I love animals, especially horses. My aunt says I have an affinity for animals. My horse Starr understands every word I say. And —" I almost told her about the secret signal, then I decided not to.

"I know what you mean," Eva agreed. "My cat Belinda is the same way. My mother says dogs and pigs are smarter than cats, but I don't believe it."

The conversation was really getting interesting, and I thought I might tell her about the secret signal after all, when Miss Maggotty appeared at the schoolhouse door clanging the bell. We both got off the see-saw at the same time so as not to dump each other.

The day was almost over before Miss Maggotty picked up my essay and began reading it. I could hardly wait for her reaction. But when it came you could have knocked me over with a feather.

"*Margaret Emerson!*" She shouted my name so loud the whole class jerked to attention. "Is this . . . thing," she flicked the pages disdainfully, "supposed to be amusing?"

"Nooo —" I was completely perplexed.

"*No, Miss Maggotty!*"

"No, Miss Maggotty!"

Needles of hatred darted from her flinty eyes. "I'll teach you not to make a mockery out of me," she snarled. "Nor will I tolerate you poking fun at this fine country school."

"But Miss Maggotty, I didn't mean —"

"Oh, I know what you meant, all right. I recognize sarcasm when I see it. And I see it in every line of this so-called composition. Your petty little jibes don't fool me."

"But Miss Maggotty —"

She raised her hand for silence. Then, smiling sweetly at the pupils as they squirmed uncomfortably in their seats, she continued. "I shall read it aloud and let your classmates be your judge."

So, in a silly, sing-songy voice, she began: "Schools: a comparison by Margaret Rose Emerson. I had no idea how different schools could be until I came to stay with my aunt and uncle on the farm. Last year I attended Leslie Street School in Toronto. It is a big, two-storey brick building with many classrooms. In the basement there is a huge coal-burning furnace that heats the whole school. It is attended by a janitor. The water closets are in the basement, which is very convenient in wintertime." The class snickered and Miss Maggotty allowed it — as if she herself had made a clever joke. "In the city school each boy and girl has a separate desk, and each desk has a built-in inkwell and pencil groove. And the desk lid raises up so you can put your books inside.

"You can imagine my surprise the first day I entered

Four Corners School and saw the long rows of benches and tables, and the piles of paper and ink pots that we all share.

"Another curiosity to me was the stove in the middle of the room. I was amazed to learn that it was the teacher's duty to arrive early on cold winter days to start the fire, and that the big boys were expected to keep the wood box full, and that all the parents contributed their share to the woodpile outside. But most surprising of all was the fact that all the children, from six to fourteen, were taught their different lessons by the same teacher. How could one teacher do so much? I wondered. She must be very, very —"

Here Miss Maggotty stopped, just when my essay began to praise her. Holding the pages up between her thumb and finger as if they were disgusting, she said icily, "I consider this . . . thing . . . to be pure trash, and not worth the effort of marking." Then she ripped my composition in half. "Tonight, Miss Smarty, you will write another essay, this time on the meaning of manners and deportment, which seem to have been neglected in your fine city school. And now, as punishment for mocking my name, you will be publicly switched."

"But, Miss Maggotty —" I could hardly believe a teacher would be so unfair, "if you'll read the rest you'll come to the part about the country school's rich heritage, and the teacher's great responsi—"

Rip! Rip! Rip!

Even as I spoke, she shredded the pages, lifted the stove lid and fed them into the fire. "Go outside and bring me a good, thick switch!" she commanded.

The whole class gasped. The little kids began to cry. Eva

Hocks reached out and squeezed my hand. Matty glared daggers at the teacher, and even Oscar Ogilvey looked sorry for me.

I got up, shoved my glasses up the bridge of my nose and walked calmly to the cloakroom. Ignoring my coat, I went out, slamming the door behind me.

I wasn't scared. Being the middle child in a big family makes you pretty tough. But I was mortified. And mad! How dare she burn my hard work to a crisp, the old witch!

I was tugging furiously at a stubborn hickory stick when I heard the clop and rattle of a horse and buggy. Turning, I saw that Uncle Herb and Starr had come early.

Leaping down, not bothering to tether Starr (who never wandered off like dumb horses do), Uncle Herb cried, "Maggie! What in tarnation are you doing? And where's your coat?"

"I have to get a switch to be punished with," I said.

"What for? What did you do?"

I told him, and his tender face hardened like a rock. With a quick twist of the wrist he snapped off the branch, took off his coat and threw it over my shoulders and marched with me towards the school.

He flung open the door and it banged against the cloakroom wall. Miss Maggotty jumped, and her face went white. A hush fell over the classroom. Then Uncle Herb did the most unexpected thing. He removed his cap, held it flat against his chest and spoke in a very polite voice. "What's all this about, Matilda? Are you putting on a play? Oliver Twist, mebbe? Or David Copperfield? Is it early practice for the Christmas concert?"

"I can explain, Mr. Wilkinson," jabbered the flustered teacher.

"Don't 'mister' me, Matilda. Just you tell me what this switch is for." He zinged it threateningly past her pointy nose. "Is my girl here playing the part of the wicked schoolmarm? Is that it?"

The blood rushed up from under Miss Maggotty's high collar, changing her face from dead white to blotchy red. Her hand shook as she clutched at her throat. "Margaret wrote a particularly scathing criticism of this school," she said breathlessly, "and she mocks my good name at every opportunity. She is a born troublemaker and I do not want her in my classroom."

"Well, now, that's odd," Uncle Herb pulled at his chin, "because the missus herself read that piece last night and was sure it would please you." He turned to face the class. "What do you say, boys and girls, is my girl here a troublemaker? Do you want to see her expelled from your school?"

Even Oscar Ogilvey hollered, "No! No! No!" Then Uncle Herb snapped the stick with a loud crack across his knee, and threw it contemptuously into the fire. "One more thing, Matilda, if this youngster catches pneumonia, or even the sniffles, you'll be running the roads looking for a new post, mark my words! Get your coat, Maggie; we're going home."

At the cloakroom door he turned back, as if he had forgotten something. "Oh, by the by, class dismissed!" he bellowed. Bedlam erupted as my classmates made a mad dash for freedom.

Well, I never became one of Miss Maggotty's favourites, but she never picked on me again either. Not even when I deserved it, like the times she belittled Matty.

Matty was smart enough, and he had no trouble with his paperwork, but when it came to answering out loud or writing on the slateboard he got all mixed up. And Miss Maggotty seemed to delight in making him squirm.

For instance, on the slateboard she wrote sixty-nine. "Matthew Muggins, read that number," she commanded.

Matty hesitated, as he always did, then answered haltingly, "Ninety-six?"

It happened every time. For some weird reason that he couldn't explain, Matty saw numbers backwards. But on paper he got his arithmetic perfect nearly every time.

Well, one day when the inspector was visiting, Miss Maggotty wrote forty-eight on the board and asked poor Matty to read it. As usual, he dragged himself to his feet and answered hopelessly, "Eighty-four?"

"There, you see!" Miss Maggotty squeezed her lips together as if she had just sucked on a lemon. "How can I be expected to teach such a dullard?"

That's when I exploded. Leaping up, I yelled out boldly, "Why don't you ever ask him thirty-three or sixty-six or ninety-nine?"

If looks could kill I'd be dead.

But the inspector, a kindly grandfatherly man with a grey moustache, asked to see some of Matty's written work. He examined it carefully as Miss Maggotty stood nervously by, wringing her hands.

"The girl has a good point," nodded the inspector sagely. "This boy is obviously not stupid. But he requires patience and understanding, not ridicule and shame. Remember the old adage, Miss Maggotty." He pointed an accusing finger at her. "What the pupil hasn't learned, the teacher hasn't taught."

She didn't speak to me for days after that. But she never made a fool of Matty in front of the whole class again either.

Another thing I did that annoyed Miss Maggotty no end was to speak when I wasn't spoken to. I was bored silly in Junior Third and I always had time on my hands, so I listened in on the older children's lessons. Then, if no one could answer her question and I knew the answer perfectly well, I'd forget myself and jump up and rattle it off.

"Thank you very much, Miss Smarty!" she'd say derisively.

That was one thing that her run-in with Uncle Herb hadn't prevented, her calling me "Miss Smarty." But since I deserved it half the time, I decided to ignore it.

In the end my being a smart-aleck paid off. By Christmas time she was so sick of me getting into mischief from sheer boredom that she promoted me to Senior Third. If she hoped that the new work would keep me busy, she was right.

Chapter 9

Lost

For a while there was talk of me going home for the holidays. But several ferocious snowstorms in a row made it impossible to get even as far as Shelburne. I wasn't too disappointed because I really wanted to know what Christmas would be like on the farm.

"When are you going out for the tree, Herb?" asked Aunt Marg one still, cold December morning.

Uncle Herb was busy poking a thick, dry log into the stove. Sparks glittered in the air and the fire crackled cosily. Steam rattled the lid of the teakettle. "This looks as good a day as any," he said, moving the kettle to one side.

"Oh, boy! Can I go with you?" I jumped up and flung my arms around him. But they wouldn't reach behind him because he was growing stouter every day. "It's my winter bear fat," he confessed, patting his barrel-shaped stomach.

"Matty's going to ski over for some help with his numbers," I said. "Can he come, too?"

"Sure, just so long as he learns his number work first. Jessie's mighty pleased that you're helping him, Maggie."

"Oh, he's catching on really fast. It's all I can do to stay ahead of him."

Matty came, and we finished the arithmetic in no time flat.

"Mind you get a perfect spruce now, Herb," Aunt Marg said as the three of us bundled up against the cold. "I won't make houseroom for a scraggly old pine."

"You're a bossy old cow, Mag Wilkinson," he teased. Then he kissed her just as if they were young. Right in front of Matty, too. Was I ever embarrassed!

It was a bright blue afternoon and we had to squint to keep from getting snow-blinded. Oh, but it was fun, gliding over the sparkling meadow in the cutter behind Starr. He was so glad to be out of the stable that he pranced and snorted like a circus horse. He must have been bored stiff with only Flora and Fauna for company while I was at school.

Deep in the woods, we came to a clearing, and Uncle Herb called, "Whoa, there!" Starr stopped in a flurry of snow. "This is as far as the cutter can go." Uncle Herb dropped the reins on the horse's back and hopped down. "Now let's see what we can find."

We searched all along the edge of the clearing, but we couldn't see a perfect spruce. "I'll have to go into the bush a ways," Uncle Herb said. "You two stay here in the clearing."

"Why can't we go, too?" I protested, disappointed.

"We might get separated, that's why. And it's mighty easy to get turned around in these here woods."

"How come you won't get turned around, then?"

"Because I know every inch of my land like the back of

my hand," he answered proudly. Then he slung the axe over his shoulder and disappeared into the forest.

Matty and I waited in the cutter. We talked about school and family and friends. I had shown him the picture of my family and rhymed off all their names.

"It must be great fun to have a bunch of brothers and sisters," he said enviously.

"Maybe sometimes." I felt a twinge of homesickness. "But we fight a lot."

"Well, that's better than having nobody to fight with. I hate being an only child."

"I don't. I like it." I had never admitted that before. Not even to myself. But it *was* nice in some ways. Like getting your own way most of the time. And always being the one to finish up the cake. And coming home from school and being listened to. Ma hardly ever had time to listen. She was always too busy bathing babies or refereeing fights or just trying to catch up on all the work that nine children made.

"It's nice being an only child," I said.

Matty shrugged. "I'm freezing," he said. "Let's get down and run around."

There wasn't much room to run around in the clearing, so after talking to Starr and brushing the icicles off his whiskers, we lay on our backs in the snow and stared up at the sky. We could see a patch of blue through the tree-tops about the size of Uncle Herb's Sunday shirt. Then a white cloud that looked like a woolly lamb floated by.

We both heard it at the same time — a crunch of crisp snow, a crackling of twigs. At first we thought it might be Uncle Herb coming back. But we hadn't even heard the ring of the axe yet. Exchanging jittery glances, we sat up without making a sound. And there she was, not twenty paces away, a lovely brown-eyed doe. She stood stock-still, looking at us. We didn't even breathe. Then Starr began vibrating his lips, making that airy, fluttery sound horses make when they're bored. That frightened the deer and she bounded to the edge of the clearing. There she stopped, her bobbed tail twitching, her luminous eyes gazing over her shoulder.

"Darn!" declared Matty under his breath. "I wish I'd brought my gun."

"Matty Muggins," I whispered, "how could you even think of such a thing?"

"Heck, there's nothing wrong with hunting. And there's sure lots of good eating on that deer." He actually licked his chops like a dog. "Mmmm . . . I love venison."

"Well, I love animals," I said as the doe disappeared into the woods. "C'mon, let's see where she goes."

I had only intended to go a short distance, keeping the horse and sleigh in sight. But the deer seemed to be playing peekaboo, tempting us to follow. Every time we thought we'd lost her, we caught a glimpse of her again through the thicket. But, finally, she vanished completely.

"Maybe we should turn back now," I suggested, looking around at the deep, dense bush that blocked out most of the sky. It was getting dark, and colder by the minute. The bitter air went right through the woollen muffler I had wrapped around my face. It stung my lungs with every breath I took. And my glasses were all smustered with frost, so I took them off and put them in my pocket.

I looked around, but I couldn't remember which direction

we had come from. The bush was so thick there was almost no snow on the ground and no footprints to follow back to the clearing. "I think we're lost, Matty," I said, my voice quavering.

"Nah! I know this bush like the back of my hand!"

He sounded so sure of himself with Uncle Herb's words coming out of his mouth that I followed him trustingly. A red tassel got torn from my scarf as we pushed our way through the brambles. About fifteen minutes later, breathless and freezing, I found the red tassel again.

"Now you've done it, Matty Muggins!" I shook the ragged tassel in his face. "We're lost and I'm frozen and Uncle Herb will be mad as a hornet!"

"Nah! Your uncle never gets mad," scoffed Matty.

"He does if it's serious. Remember Miss Maggotty and the switch?"

"Yeah . . . well . . . I musta made a mistake. It's this way." He pointed in the opposite direction. "Don't be scared, Maggie. I'm awful good at directions."

"You better be," I muttered, trudging after him. "And don't call me Maggie anymore."

"Why not? You call me Matty."

"Well . . . I'll promise to call you Matt if you promise to call me Marg."

"Promise," he said.

We plodded on, the woods pressing in all around us. Bushes and thorns grabbed at our coat sleeves, and burrs and pine needles stuck to our woollen stockings.

I was about ready to drop when Matty stopped suddenly in his tracks. He turned around and I nearly died when I saw tears in his eyes.

"We're lost," he admitted glumly.

"Well, damn you, Matty, I told you so long ago."

"You did it again!" he yelled.

"What?"

"You called me Matty. And you swore, too."

"Oh, shut up! What difference does that make now? Who cares if they put 'Matty' Muggins and 'Maggie' Emerson on our tombstones? And who'll know I swore when they find us stiff as statues?"

"I guess you're right. It won't make no difference." He collapsed on a crumbling log, banging his mitts together. "My fingers have gone all numb," he worried.

"I think my toes have died already." I couldn't even feel them, so I started jumping up and down.

"What'll we do, Marg?" he asked pitifully.

"I don't know. I can't even find the sun."

"We're lost for sure then." Suddenly he burst into sobs. "Oh, my gosh!" he blubbered. "Oh, my golly! This is gonna kill my ma."

I knew he was right about that. Mrs. Muggins *would* die if anything happened to her only child. And it was all my fault. It was my dumb idea to follow the deer in the first place.

Then, like a lamp being lit in a pitch-black room, an idea flashed through my mind. "I'll call Starr!"

"What the heck good will that do? We've been yelling for help for ages and your uncle hasn't come."

"No, but . . . I'll tell you a secret. Well, maybe I won't. You just watch and see." So I puckered up and curled my tongue and blew and blew and blew.

"You aren't whistling," Matty said scornfully. "Let me do it."

He pulled his mitten off with his teeth, stuck two fingers in his mouth and was just about to blow when I yelled, "*No!* Starr doesn't come for a whistle!" Again I cupped my hands around my mouth and blew with all my might. Matty looked at me as if I was crazy. But I just said, "Shh!" and didn't bother to explain.

I crossed my fingers inside my mittens, and we held our breath for about a minute, then Matt said, "Listen! I think I hear something." Sure enough, a high-pitched whinny came piercing through the trees. Next we heard a crashing of underbrush, and clumps of snow began raining down on our heads. Then a long nose with a white star on it pushed through the thicket. "Starr!" I screeched, lunging at him through the bushes.

Somehow we managed to climb up on his back and get him turned around. I hung onto his thick winter mane and Matt hung onto me, and my brave stallion crashed his way back to the clearing.

Uncle Herb had unharnessed Starr the minute he suspected we were lost. "I knew your best chance was the secret signal," he said in a trembling voice. I think that was the first time Uncle Herb was ever tempted to give me a whipping. But, thank goodness, he was so glad to see us, scratched and bedraggled, but safe and sound, that he settled for a good tongue-lashing instead.

The perfect spruce was already spread out on the cutter, so we headed straight for home. Matt unhitched our hero and led him into the stable. I filled his bin with oats and got him fresh water and kissed his nose a dozen times.

"You know, Maggie," Uncle Herb was leaning on the stable half-door, wiggling a straw between his teeth, "since you saved his life in the fire, and now he's saved yours in the forest, that means you belong to each other for better or worse."

"Really?" I held Starr's face between my hands and looked deep into his dark, mysterious eyes. "I love you, boy," I whispered. Down swept his snowy lashes as he nickered softly and nuzzled my neck.

All three of us agreed not to tell Aunt Marg or Mrs. Muggins what had happened. "What *they* don't know, won't hurt us," said Uncle Herb wisely.

Chapter 10

Christmas

Christmas was funny that year. Nice but funny. I had received a parcel from Toronto a few days before and that set me to thinking about home. I missed the hubbub of a houseful of kids getting ready for the big day. And I missed our messily decorated tree. At home on Jones Avenue, we put it up a week early, and all us kids were allowed to throw the trimmings on, willy-nilly. But here on the farm, Christmas was taken more seriously. In fact, so many things happened I completely forgot to hang up my stocking.

It started on Christmas Eve when we went in the cutter to a church service held in the schoolhouse. After the service everybody sang carols, led by Miss Maggotty waving a pointer. Then we schoolchildren put on a play that we had been practising for weeks. I was the leading angel, and Aunt Marg had made me a scintillating costume. I was the hit of the show — at least according to my aunt and uncle. Then we went home to trim the tree.

Uncle Herb had made a sturdy wooden stand, so our perfect spruce stood perfectly in the corner of the kitchen. (The parlour was too cold.)

Uncle Herb draped the tree with red and green paper garlands, and then Aunt Marg and I tied on the coloured glass balls.

"Here, Margaret." Aunt Marg handed me a box of carefully packed, much-used silver-paper icicles. So I started to throw them on willy-nilly like we did at home.

"No! No! No!" she cried, really upset. "You must hang each one individually so that it falls free — like this."

With work-roughened fingertips she daintily hung each glistening strand on the very outside branches. When all the icicles were on, Uncle Herb set up the stepladder and held it steady while I climbed up and fastened the Star of Bethlehem to the topmost branch.

Next — and I'll never forget this part as long as I live — Aunt Marg and Uncle Herb actually attached tiny white birthday candles in little tin sockets to the tip of each branch. And lit them one by one. With matches!

"I'm scared!" I said, backing away, the memory of the burning barn still blazing in my mind.

"Sit yourself down and hold your breath," whispered Uncle Herb. "This is a sight for sore eyes — believe me."

It was. Aunt Marg blew out the lamps and we sat in a row on the daybed, me between them, mesmerized by the glittering pyramid. "Squint," Uncle Herb said. So I did and the yellow lights merged and shimmered like stars on water.

"Well, Maggie?" he scratched my cheek with his stubbly chin. "Have you ever seen the like of that before?"

"Never!" I let out my breath in a big puff and the candles

flickered. Then Aunt Marg got up reluctantly and pinched out each little flame. Taking them off the tree, she meticulously packed them away.

"That's that for another year," she sighed. "I always wonder if it's worth the trouble. Then I always think it is . . . especially this year with you here, Margaret."

"I only wish I had a picture of it to send home," I said.

"I only wish I had a picture of your face," she lifted my chin gently, "with the reflection of all those tiny lights sparkling like fireflies in your spectacles."

"No camera could do it justice," said Uncle Herb with a catch in his voice.

Aunt Marg relit the lamps, and even without the candles the tree was beautiful with its wide bottom branches spread out on the floor like a skirt.

"Have we got time for hot cocoa?" I asked, shivering from the draft creeping under the door.

"Sure! Only tonight it's hot toddy for us. This is no ordinary night. It's the best Christmas Eve ever." Uncle Herb got the mugs down from the hooks in the pantry and set them on the table.

I had never tasted hot toddy before. It was strange. I had expected to be a bit melancholy on this particular night, especially at bedtime, but the hot toddy made me drowsy and sent me off to sleep before I had time to think about it.

On Christmas morning I woke to find a lumpy stocking hanging on my bedpost. It was filled with the usual orange and apple and candy and nuts. I jumped out of bed excitedly, not knowing what else to expect. I had slept late (Uncle Herb said hot toddy affected some folks that way) and I could smell bacon and eggs and wood smoke wafting deliciously up the stairwell. So I put my woollen kimono on over my nightdress and hurried down to the kitchen.

Besides the parcels from home, there were other packages under the tree now. One was a long box wrapped in white tissue paper and tied with a red ribbon. Out of the corner of my eye I thought I saw my name on the tag.

Uncle Herb came in, shaking the snow off like a polar bear. "Brrrr!" he shuddered, hanging his coat and cap on a nail and beginning his morning wash. "Well, I gave the animals their extra rations — not that they know it's Christmas." He rubbed his wind-reddened face briskly with the warm towel. "And I'm ready to tie on the feedbag myself now, Mag."

She gave him a poke, as she always did when he called her Mag, then she set a full, steaming plate before him on the oilcloth-covered table.

He looked at it warily, peeking under the eggs, which were done sunny side up, just the way he liked them. "No tricks today, Maggie?" he asked suspiciously.

"Oh, no, Uncle Herb. Not on Christmas Day. That would be sacrilegious."

"You don't say!" he declared.

I ate hurriedly, and when I was done I said, "Can I start now?"

"Sure!" they chorused, drawing their chairs closer to the tree.

The first gift I went for was the big long box. Tearing off the tissue, I found that it was wrapped in newspaper underneath. I tore it off, only to find more wrappings. Layer after layer of newspaper was tied securely with binder twine. My fingers were all thumbs, so Aunt Marg handed me the scissors. At last I came to a big red Eaton's box. I shook it and it rattled mysteriously.

"Mind you don't break it!" warned Uncle Herb.

So I lifted the lid ever so carefully and, lo and behold, the box was full of small stones. "What the heck!" I cried. Then I spotted a note among the pebbles. Opening it, I read: *Maggie Emerson, look instead . . . underneath ye olde daybed.*

Screeching with excitement, I dove under the bed and pulled out the most beautiful pair of snowshoes I'd ever laid eyes on. "Oh, Uncle Herb!" I knew instantly that he had made them himself. "It's the nicest present I ever got in my whole life. But you're a corker, fooling me like that. A dad-blamed, sacrilegious corker!" Jumping up, I kissed his bristly cheek.

"I thought you might need them to get to the barn when the snow comes deep," he explained, giving me a fierce hug. The thought crossed my mind that my own father had never hugged me like that, but of course he had so many children he wouldn't have time. And it was true, what my mother often said — he was a good father, as fathers go.

Next I opened a soft, lumpy parcel from Aunt Marg. Inside I found a red woollen sweater-coat and a toque and mittens to match. She must have made them after I'd gone to bed at night because I'd never seen a knitting needle in her hand.

I tried the whole outfit on, snowshoes and all. "Gee, thanks, Aunt Marg. Red's my favourite colour." I kissed her smooth round cheek and she kissed me back.

"It suits you to a T, Margaret," she said. "You look ever so nice."

Then I gave them *my* presents. They were completely surprised, because what they didn't know was that every time I got a letter from home there was a shinplaster in it, and I had saved them all, so I had quite a bit of money. I had bought them both new cocoa mugs because I'd noticed their were getting chipped. On Uncle Herb's was printed *To the man I love!* and on Aunt Marg's, in gold script, was written *To my other mother.* (I was a little worried about that inscription because I didn't want to be disloyal to my own mother.)

They both *ooohhhed* and *aahhhed* for about fifteen minutes, and Aunt Marg kept wiping her eyes and blowing her nose. Then she said, "Margaret, you haven't opened your presents from home."

A wave of guilt washed over me as I undid the forgotten parcels. The first one held a pretty doll with eyes that opened and shut; in the second one I found new clothes — a dress and a petticoat and bloomers. I didn't play with dolls any more, now that I had Starr. And I could tell at a glance that the clothes were too small for me. It gave me a funny turn, realizing that my parents didn't know how big I was now.

To cover up my feelings, I said, "Well, I think I'll go to the barn and give Starr his present now."

"I'll tidy the kitchen while you're gone," Aunt Marg said, jumping up.

I gave Starr the huge red apple I'd been saving for him since October. Then I braided his mane with a blue ribbon and tied his forelock in a bow. He looked beautiful, and as proud as Punch of himself.

Back at the house, I volunteered to do the dishes. Aunt

Marg had placed the new mugs, with messages conspicuously showing, on the shelf above the table.

I had no sooner got the oilcloth wiped and the dishpan hung up when Uncle Herb came in and plunked down two pullets, still warm, on the middle of the table. He had already plucked them and cut off their heads, thank goodness, so I didn't recognize them. (Even though Aunt Marg's ladies had no names, I knew them all individually.) Aunt Marg cleaned out their insides, saving the giblets for gravy, stuffed them with savoury dressing, tied them together like Siamese twins and popped them into the oven.

"Jessie and Zack and Matty will be here before we know it," she said, bustling about the kitchen. "Be a good scout, Margaret, and go down the root cellar and bring me up a nice rutabaga and some potatoes that haven't started to sprout. Your legs are younger than mine."

Normally I'd do anything willingly for Aunt Marg, but going down into that musty old root cellar was a real test. I went — but not willingly.

Lifting the trap door in the pantry floor, I leaned it against the pots and pans on the wall. Instantly the smell of earth filled my nose. I shone the flashlight down into the deep, dank hole. The wooden ladder glistened with damp. I had to force myself to grasp each mouldy rung as I descended. My secret fear was that the door would suddenly slam shut and I'd be trapped and eaten alive by giant grubs and potato bugs. I'd scream blue murder, of course, but no one would hear me. Not even my loving aunt, who was singing "Joy to the world!" at the top of her lungs in the kitchen.

I filled the basket with potatoes (to heck with looking for

sprouts!), grabbed a huge purple turnip and scurried back up the slimy ladder. Sighing with relief, I lowered the trap door. I hadn't even seen an innocent earthworm down there, let alone a giant grub, but just the same I felt all creepy and crawly, so I decided to have a good wash. I got my blue china jug from my washstand and filled it with the nice warm water from the cistern at the end of the stove. Then I took it back upstairs and poured it into my china basin.

I scrubbed myself fast because the room was cold, then I put on my best dress and tied my dark curls back with a white ribbon. Next I looked in the hazy mirror. The silver had worn off the back of it and Aunt Marg said she'd get it re-silvered one of these days. But I could see myself fine in the centre and I couldn't help but think that if it wasn't for my freckles (at least they were lighter in winter) and my thick, wire-rimmed spectacles that kept sliding down my nose (I adjusted them with my forefinger for the umpteenth time), I wouldn't be too bad-looking. And at least I was growing. Poor Eva Hocks was still a "little wisp of a thing."

"I think I'll give my new clothes that Ma sent me to Eva Hocks," I told Aunt Marg. "I bet they'll fit her perfect."

"Perfectly," corrected Aunt Marg. (She was a stickler for grammar. Sometimes Uncle Herb's sayings gave her fits.) "That's a nice idea, Margaret. Eva could do with something new. We'll wrap them up for her birthday."

When everything was ready, with the red candles bright against the snow-white tablecloth and the crepe-paper crackers beside each plate, I sat up on the window sill to wait.

"By the way, Aunt Marg," she was putting the mince pies

on the trammel at the back of the stove to keep them warm, "don't call Matty Matty anymore. He hates it. We have to call him Matt or Matthew from now on."

Aunt Marg's reddish eyebrows flew up and her green eyes twinkled like emeralds. "Have you got that straight, Herbert?" she asked her clean-shaven, spruced-up husband.

"I've got it, Margaret. Big Margaret that is. And what in tarnation do we call you, missy? Little Margaret? Is Maggie going to be taboo all of a sudden?"

"*You* can call me Maggie till the cows come home, Uncle Herb. But nobody else. *Nobody!*"

"Then what, pray tell, must I call you — Miss Emerson?" Aunt Marg did a good imitation of Miss Maggotty.

"How about 'old sweetheart'?" I said. "That's my favourite."

"Right you are, old sweetheart, and if my ears don't deceive me, here comes Master Matthew Muggins now."

We had a swell Christmas with the Muggins family. Matt and I exchanged presents. He gave me a wonderful book about horses. On the cover, in full colour, was a horse that looked enough like Starr to be his twin. "That's a Clydesdale," Matt informed me. "They're a special breed."

"Gee, thanks, Matt. I always knew Starr was special."

I gave Matt a game board with checkers on one side and Snakes and Ladders on the other. I thought the Snakes and Ladders might help him with his numbers, as well as being fun. But I didn't tell him that.

Dinner was delicious. The pullets were done to a golden turn. The pies would melt in your mouth. And after dinner we all snapped our crackers and put on our paper hats and read our fortunes out loud. "There's money in your future!" mine said. (Wow! Did that ever turn out to be prophetic!)

Matt and I played on the game board while the women did the dishes. Mr. Muggins and Uncle Herb tipped their chairs back and sat with their sock-feet on the oven door, patting their stomachs. Mr. Muggins took a packet of Old Plug chewing tobacco from his shirt pocket, cut off a generous chunk and offered it on the point of his knife to Uncle Herb. Uncle Herb darted Aunt Marg a guilty glance. He had promised her on a stack of Bibles that he'd never chew in the house again. But it was a gift — a Christmas gift from a friend — so what in tarnation could he do? He shrugged his shoulders helplessly and accepted the aromatic present. Then, every time one or the other of them lifted the stove lid and sent a brown stream sizzling into the fire Aunt Marg would clamp her hand over her mouth and gag noisily.

Matt and I played ten board games and won five each. Aunt Marg and Mrs. Muggins chatted happily at the table over dozens of cups of tea.

"It's nearly time we were making tracks," said Mr. Muggins, letting his chair down with a thump. "I've got the livestock to see to before bed."

"All right," sighed Mrs. Muggins, getting up reluctantly, "but my, it's been a grand Christmas. And Matt and Margaret are such good children. Never a speck of trouble." She smiled at us approvingly.

We two "good" children darted Uncle Herb a worried look and were relieved when he gave us a sly wink.

"Want to come to the stable and see how I decorated Starr for Christmas?" I asked Matt.

"Sure," he agreed. So we put on our outdoor clothes and headed for the barn.

Starr was thrilled to see us and whinnied his head off.

"How does he look?" I asked, as the vain Clydesdale bobbed his head up and down, making his ribbons dance.

"Like a prize winner at a horse show!" laughed Matt.

We both thanked Starr again for saving our lives. Then the Muggins family left for home and we stood at the door until their sleigh bells faded into the cold, still night.

We had hot toddy again before turning in. "It's been my best Christmas ever," I told my aunt and uncle as I sipped the steaming drink.

"Ours, too, girl," they said. Then we kissed and hugged good night and wished each other "Merry Christmas!" one more time.

Just before climbing into bed I held the snapshot of my family close to the lamplight so I could recognize all their faces. "Merry Christmas!" I whispered as I called them each by name. Then I kissed the image of my mother and father, in the middle of the group, blew out the lamp and climbed into my cozy bed.

Aunt Marg had filled the brown crockery pig with hot water and put it under my covers earlier. I touched it with my cold toes and shivered with delight. I had intended to think about home for a few minutes before I went to sleep. But I dozed off just as the house on Jones Avenue and my family all sitting around the long dining-room table started coming into focus.

Chapter 11

Old Joe Boyle

I got my snowshoes just in time because between Christmas and New Year's a ton of snow fell. Uncle Herb taught me everything he knew about snowshoeing. Then he said I was on my own.

So I bundled up, laced my snowshoes to my galoshes and headed for the stable.

"Hi, Starr!" I called the minute I got inside. He whinnied and bumped his flanks against the stall, snorting impatiently as I struggled to get my snowshoes off.

"You're getting awfully tatty-looking, boy," I said, running my fingers through his tangled, beribboned mane. "I think it's time you had a good going-over."

So I unbraided the ribbon and combed his mane and tail until they were as soft as rabbit's fur. Then I brushed his coat until it shone like a new penny. Next I cleaned the ticks out of his ears, and once again I tried to brush his big yellow teeth. But that's one thing he wouldn't put up with — tooth-brushing. He just rolled his cushiony lips down and clamped them shut, tight as a vise.

"You're a bad boy," I teased.

Batting his long white eyelashes at me like a big flirt, he nipped the toque right off my head and tossed it over into Fauna's stall. Startled, she mooed at us crossly, but Starr just nickered his head off. Talk about a horse laugh! We had more fun than a picnic, him and me.

* * *

On New Year's Day we were invited over to the Muggins' house for dinner.

"Did you remember to bring your snowshoes, Maggie?" asked Uncle Herb. He was pleased as Punch that I was so crazy about them.

"Sure," I said. "Matt and me might go for a walk."

"Matt and I," corrected Aunt Marg with a hug. She always did that so as not to hurt my feelings.

The second we turned up their lane we knew something was wrong. They were all standing around out in the cold stomping their feet and looking strangely excited.

"What's the matter, Zack?" called Uncle Herb.

"It's old Joe Boyle!" Mr. Muggins called back.

"He's dead!" yelled Matt. "Mr. Raggett just left here and he said he found old Joe Boyle —"

"Lying outside his shack in the snow," finished Mrs. Muggins, not to be outdone.

"Froze to death?" asked Uncle Herb, astounded.

"No, shot to death!" declared Mr. Muggins.

"Shot!" You'd think Aunt Marg had been shot herself, the way she screeched. "Who shot him, for mercy sakes?"

"Shot hisself," explained Matt importantly. "Isn't that right, Pa?"

"That's right," confirmed his father. "Shot hisself with his old war pistol. Tom Raggett said he stuck the barrel in his mouth" — he demonstrated with his finger — "and blew the top of his head clean off."

"Brains flew all over the place," cried Matt, flailing his arms in all directions.

"Can we go and see?" I asked, dying to be part of the gory drama, yet shivering at the thought.

"Sakes alive, no!" Aunt Marg dismissed my bloodthirsty request with a disgusted, "Tsk, tsk, tsk!"

"Let's go inside," Mrs. Muggins said, hugging herself. "It's cold enough to freeze a polar bear out here."

Well, we all sat down to the best New Year's dinner I ever ate, but even during the delicious meal we couldn't stop talking about the tragedy.

"How old is . . . was . . . old Joe Boyle?" I wanted to know. I hadn't gotten a good look at him the day of the barn raising.

"Oh, he wasn't really old," Mr. Muggins said while buttering the crust of his hot apple pie, "maybe forty-odd. But he looked old because of his dirty, scraggly beard and his raggedy clothes."

"He was a regular old hermit, and skinny as a scarecrow," added Matt, copying Mr. Muggins with the butter. I decided to try it myself. It looked heavenly the way it melted and ran around the crispy lumps and bumps.

"No wonder, living alone in that little shack in the bush, eating jackrabbits and berries, never talking to a living soul," put in Mrs. Muggins.

"Yep," agreed Uncle Herb, spreading honey on a baking-powder biscuit bursting with steamy plump raisins, "lived like a pauper, he did, though I heard tell he had a fortune hid away someplace on his land."

"Well, we'll soon know about that, Herb," said Mr. Muggins, wiping his greasy chin, "because that rumour has spread like wildfire and there's folks swarming all over his place like flies on a cowflap; and the poor fella not even decently planted yet."

"You mean he's still out there in the snow?" A ghastly picture of pure white snow splattered with blood and brains went flashing through my mind.

"Nope, he's been took away. He's at Weeper's Undertaker's Parlour in Shelburne. Doesn't that name beat all?" Mr. Muggins shook his head and couldn't suppress a smile. Then he continued soberly, "The man's got no family, and no home to be buried from, so I guess you and me better try to get in there and pay our respects, Herb."

"You're quite right, Zack," agreed Aunt Marg. "It would be downright sinful if nobody showed up for the poor soul's send-off."

So they went the day of the funeral, and sure enough they were the only ones there to see old Joe Boyle laid away in a pauper's grave. Everybody else was too busy digging up his property and tearing his shack apart, hunting for his fortune. They even went so far as to chop down trees and poke into squirrels' nests and groundhog holes, disturbing their winter naps. But after a few frantic weeks of searching, without finding a red cent, they all gradually lost interest. All except Matt, that is.

"I think I know where it's hid," he whispered to me one recess.

"Hidden." I was beginning to sound like Aunt Marg. "Where?"

"We'll go over Saturday and look around," was all I could get out of him. "Be ready about noon and I'll pick you up. And bring your snowshoes. We might need them."

Matt arrived on the dot in the sleigh, without the bells, drawn by their black gelding Bill. The Muggins had two horses, Belle and Bill. They were nice, but not nearly as intelligent or beautiful as Starr. Even Matt admitted that. "Starr's one in a million," he said.

Matt had told his mother he was invited to our place and I had told Aunt Marg I was invited to theirs, so, with no questions asked, we headed straight for old Joe Boyle's.

The shack was tucked so tightly in a tangle of trees and vines and bushes, that it couldn't be seen from the road. Matt took the sleigh in as far as it would go, then tied the reins to a sapling. You couldn't trust Bill not to run off. As I said before, he wasn't as smart as Starr.

We didn't need our snowshoes after all because the snow was packed down solid by the tramping of hundreds of anxious feet. But now the place was completely deserted.

The door to the tarpaper shack sagged open, creaking in the winter wind.

"Are we going in there?" I whispered, my spine prickling right up to my hairline. Matt's pale blue eyes grew dark with excitement. "Well, the fortune ain't . . . isn't . . . in there. But let's go in just for fun."

He crept up and propped the door open with a stick. I was right on his heels.

Inside, the place was a shambles. Broken crockery and furniture, patchy bear hides and chunks of rain-streaked cardboard that had been stripped off the walls — everything was in a heap in the middle of the floor. And on top of the whole mess, lying on its side, was a moth-eaten deer's head with one glass eye missing and the other staring at us eerily. The stove had been knocked over and the stovepipe dangled from the ceiling. There was black soot all over the place.

Suddenly, from underneath the rubble came a creepy whining sound. Matt and I grabbed onto each other. But it was only a scrawny old cat. It hissed at us, then scrambled over the heap and leaped out the broken window.

"Whew!" Matt blew out his breath as if we'd just had a narrow escape. "Let's get out of here!" His face had gone white as a sheet, making his light brown freckles look as dark as mine.

Once outside we both breathed easier.

"C'mon," Matt said. I followed him around behind the shack and down a weedy path. At the end of it stood a lopsided, smelly old outhouse.

"We're not going in *there*, are we?" I gagged, holding my nose.

"We got to," said Matt. "That's where it is."

"The fortune?"

"Yep."

I stopped at the door, pinching my nose, as Matt stepped gingerly inside. The rotting floorboards creaked under his weight.

Kneeling down by the hole, which was all chewed and splintered by porcupines, Matt turned his head away and gasped, "Ewww! Ahhhh! Ughhh!" He held his breath and his cheeks puffed out like a chipmunk. Thrusting his arm down the hole to the armpit, he began feeling all the way around under the cracked wooden seat. "I feel a ledge in the corner." He let his breath out in a big huff. "Ah! I think I've got it!" He withdrew his arm slowly, and in his hand he held a small, rusty tin box. He shook it over the hole and it made a clinking-clanking sound.

"Don't drop it!" I screeched.

"Shhh! Let's get out of here!"

We hurried to the sleigh, untied the reins and climbed breathlessly into the seat.

"Open it! Open it!" I demanded.

"Oh, no. It's locked!" cried Matt.

"Dammit!" I exploded, then clamped my hand over my mouth because I'd promised Matt I wouldn't swear any more.

"Dammit!" he agreed. "If only I had something to pry it open with."

"I know what!" I jumped down, ran to the shack, picked up a knife I'd noticed in the rubbish and ran back to give it to Matt. "How's this?"

"Swell!" He began prying all around the rusty lid. He worked and worked until the sweat stood out on his forehead. Then, *ping!* the lock broke and the lid flew open.

Suddenly our eyes were dazzled by a mass of silver coins sparkling like diamonds in the winter sun.

"Oh, boy, we're rich! My Christmas cracker was right!"

"Shhh!" Matt's eyes darted around as if the woods had ears. Shoving the box under my feet, he took up the reins and slapped Bill on the back. The horse took off at a gallop. I had to press my feet down hard to hold the jingling box steady on the floor.

When we were safely out on the road again, headed

towards home, I said, "How did you know where to look, Matt?"

"Ho, Bill!" he slowed the horse down to a trot. "Well, one day I was out hunting jackrabbits when I saw old Joe Boyle going down the path to his outhouse. I ducked behind a gooseberry bush because Pa always said you could never tell what old Joe Boyle might do. He'd likely shoot first and ask questions later. But this day he wasn't carrying a gun, just some kind of a box. He went in the dumphouse and I hung around until he came out. I noticed right away that he wasn't carrying the box 'cause his hands were swinging at his sides. I forgot all about it until the other day. Then I put two and two together."

"Hey, you're getting good at arithmetic," I teased. Then I said seriously, "The money's yours, then, Matt."

"Nope," he shook his head. "It's ours, Maggie, because I wouldn't have come here alone. And I don't trust nobody else. You won't tell Eva Hocks or any of the other kids at school, will you?"

"Cross my heart," I promised. That was twice he'd called me Maggie since we'd made our pledge. But I let him get away with it because I was pleased by his faith in me. Then I had a disturbing thought. "What the heck will we tell our folks?"

"I was wondering that, too. I guess we got to tell them the truth, because if we don't, and we hide the money, it'll be like stealing."

First we went to Matt's house. He told his mother and she went running to the barn to tell his father, then all four of us hopped into the sleigh and galloped over to my house. Now it was my turn.

"Great day in the morning!" exclaimed Uncle Herb as I lifted the lid and showed him the glittering treasure.

All four grown-ups looked perplexed as they passed the box around. None of them seemed to notice the bad smell coming from it. "First off, let's count it," said Uncle Herb.

So Matt poured the silver coins onto the table and I did the counting, first by twos and then by ones. Old Joe Boyle's fortune came to exactly one hundred silver dollars.

"Holy smokes, we're rich!" cried Matt.

"Now, hang on a minute." Uncle Herb scratched his head thoughtfully. "What do you say, Zack?"

Mr. Muggins shrugged uncertainly. "What do you think, Jessie?" he asked his wife.

She turned to her friend, "How do you feel about it, Margaret?"

Matt and I swung our eyes eagerly from one to the other. Then Aunt Marg said, "Doesn't that bush lot where Joe Boyle's been living belong to Delmer Pyatt?"

"That's right!" Mr. Muggins slapped his knee. "Old Joe Boyle was just a squatter — not even a tenant. He never paid a cent of rent, but Del let him stay on because he wasn't doing any harm."

"Then the money rightly belongs to him," said Uncle Herb.

"Heck, no!" cried Matt. "Finders keepers!"

"Yeah!" I loudly agreed. "Finders keepers."

"Well, leave it with me," said Uncle Herb. "I'll go in to Shelburne tomorrow and see Del. He's justice of the peace so he'll know what to do."

So that night Matt and I went to bed sorely disappointed.

The next afternoon Matt and his parents came back, and we all sat around the kitchen anxiously awaiting Uncle Herb's return.

When he finally arrived he kept his face purposely expressionless. But I thought I saw a twinkle in his eye. "Tell us! Tell us!" Matt and I yelled, jumping in circles around him.

"Keep your shirt on till I get my coat off," he said brusquely. Then he hung his coat and hat, with the ear-muffs attached, on the back of the stairwell door. He seemed to be moving in slow motion.

At last he spoke, "Well, my friend Delmer Pyatt — Mr. Justice of the Peace to you —" here he paused so long I thought I'd burst, "said . . . finders keepers!"

"Yay!" Matt and I screamed so loud the dishes rattled in the cupboard. "We're rich!"

"Just a dern minute," said Uncle Herb solemnly.

"Holy smokes, what next?" cried Matt.

"The money's yours on one condition. That you two never lie to us again about your whereabouts."

Matt and I glanced at each other guiltily. We'd both completely forgotten about that.

"We promise!" we answered seriously, and we crossed our hearts with a great big X.

Chapter 12

The Invitation

At the beginning of March the cold weather broke, so Uncle Herb and Mr. Muggins decided to go into town for supplies. During the long spell of bad weather we had run out of nearly everything — mash for the hens, oats for Starr and flour and sugar for ourselves.

Aunt Marg had even started churning again. "There's nothing like fresh-churned butter on hot biscuits," she declared, working the paddle of her grandmother's old wooden churn steadily up and down. "But I wouldn't go back to being a dairy maid for all the tea in China. No sirree! It took me years to wean that uncle of yours off homemade butter, and I'll be dashed if I'm going to start spoiling him again."

"You're a hard woman, Mag," grinned Uncle Herb as he got ready to leave for Shelburne with a list as long as his arm. He turned to me. "By the way, Maggie, your aunt and me and Matty's parents have been talking it over, and we all agree that the best place for that money you found at old Joe Boyle's would be in the bank for safekeeping."

"Why?" I rejected the idea instantly. "It's perfectly safe where I hid it. I'll bet you can't find it, Uncle Herb."

"Mebbe not," he wagged his wiry red head, "but money don't earn interest for future veterinarians stashed away in a hidey-hole in a horse's stall."

"Uncle Herb! Darn it! How the heck —"

"Watch your tongue, girl." Aunt Marg gave me one of her rare no-nonsense looks. "Besides, your uncle is right. You listen to him."

So, with a loud, disgruntled sigh, I went to the stable on my snowshoes and got my fortune. (Starr snorted his disappointment because I didn't stay.) Matt had to hand over his money, too, and when the two men came back from town they presented us with our bankbooks. Our names and account numbers were neatly written on the cover of each red book and fifty dollars was duly recorded inside. But it didn't look very impressive after having a pile of silver coins to gloat over and run our fingers through.

As a small consolation, Uncle Herb had brought me a long paper of button candies, two large-size blackballs and a little game you shook to see if you could get five tiny green pellets into five tiny red holes. On his way home he had stopped at the post office, too. But there was no letter for me. Just a small embossed envelope addressed to "Mr. and Mrs. Herbert Wilkinson and family."

"Mercy, what's this?" puzzled Aunt Marg. Slitting it open, she drew out a gilt-edged card. "Oh, my!" she exclaimed, then she began to read aloud, her voice rising in astonishment. "*Miss Matilda Maggoty, Schoolmistress, requests the honour of your presence at her marriage to Mr. Archibald Arbuckle, Farmer. The ceremony to take place at*

*Four Corners Schoolhouse on March 25, 1926, at 4 p.m.
Afterwards a reception will be held. R.S.V.P."*

"Archie Arbuckle!" Aunt Marg was flabbergasted. "Why,
that man's a blatherskite who drinks like a fish."

"Well, *he* sure isn't getting himself any prize package,"
snorted Uncle Herb, twirling a straw in the space between
his teeth. (He was finding it awfully hard not to chaw in
wintertime when he wasn't very busy.) "But if anybody can
straighten him out, Matilda Maggotty can. I'll say that
much for her."

"How in heaven's name did they ever keep their
courtship a secret, I wonder?" marvelled Aunt Marg. "I've
never known anybody to pull the wool over Jessie
Muggins' eyes before. She'll be fit to be tied when she finds
out."

"Well, I'll guarantee one thing. They didn't use the telephone," said Uncle Herb with a knowing grin.

We didn't have a telephone on our farm. But the
Muggins did. There were nineteen houses all strung
together on the same party line, including Mr. Raggett's
where Miss Maggotty was boarding. Every time the bell
jangled, no matter whose ring it was (the Muggins' ring
was one short and three long), Mrs. Muggins shushed
everybody in the room, then she stealthily lifted the
receiver. It was her favourite pastime, and the only thing
Aunt Marg criticized her for. Matt and I listened in sometimes, too. It was great fun. Some of the things you heard
you wouldn't believe.

"Am I invited, too?" I asked, feeling left out of the whole
affair. I didn't even know Archie Arbuckle.

"Why sure you are. What do you think '*and family*'

means, old sweetheart?" Aunt Marg gave me a reassuring hug.

While we were putting the supplies away she talked a blue streak. I just listened and sucked on a blackball. Every now and again I'd pop it out of my mouth to see what layer I was on. There were three layers of candy — black, pink and white — before you got to the aniseed in the centre. I liked to bite the seed with my front teeth and let the weird flavour explode inside my mouth.

"I wonder what I could make Matilda for a wedding present," pondered Aunt Marg as she dumped the flour into the bin. "If I've got enough wool handy and I get a move on I might have time to knit her up an afghan."

The wedding turned out to be Four Corners' social event of the year. The weather was fine, and everybody came from miles around, decked out in their Sunday best. Not only had Aunt Marg got the afghan done, but she had managed to make herself and me new dresses, too. Uncle Herb said we both looked nifty in our glad rags.

The snow was too deep yet for buggies and automobiles, so the schoolyard was littered with horses and cutters. Inside, the schoolhouse had been transformed. All the furniture had been shoved back against the walls, except the stove. The deep window sills were decorated with tissue-paper flowers and real spruce boughs. Red and white crepe-paper streamers, twisted like stripes on a barber pole, drooped from corner to corner of the high-raftered ceiling. And in the middle hung a white paper bell that opened like a fan.

Everybody stood near the walls on either side of the room, forming an aisle down the middle of the floor.

Mr. and Mrs. Raggett, who were best man and best lady, stood up at the front with the Reverend Mr. Booth, our itinerant preacher.

The wedding was wonderful. Ernie Paddison, Mr. Arbuckle's best friend, had come all the way from Orangeville to play the wedding march on his harmonica. Then, out from the cloakroom stepped the bride and groom. Everyone gasped as they came arm in arm down the aisle.

Miss Maggotty (as Uncle Herb admitted later) was a sight for sore eyes. She was all gussied up in a white lace gown and she carried a spray of pink silk roses. A white net veil covered her face, making her look almost pretty. And Mr. Arbuckle looked pretty smart, too. He wore a grey pinstripe suit, his black hair was slicked down and his moustache was waxed and pointed at both ends. I thought he was real handsome for a blatherskite.

"Dearly beloved . . ." A hush fell over the congregation as the ceremony began. Everything went along smoothly until Reverend Booth asked Miss Maggotty if she would promise to love, honour and obey Mr. Arbuckle. Up went her hand, palm forward. The preacher gulped in surprise and his Adam's apple bobbed up over his backwards white collar.

"Stop right there, Reverend!" cried Miss Maggotty in her commanding teacher's voice. "I shall promise to love and honour, but I shall promise to obey no one, least of all Archibald Arbuckle."

The congregation held its breath so as not to miss a word. Then Mr. Arbuckle, seeing the pickle the preacher was in, laughed out loud and came to his rescue. "That's all right by me, Reverend," he said, "if it's all right by you."

Mopping his brow with his hanky, Mr. Booth side-stepped away from the stove. Then he repeated the question, leaving out the objectionable word.

"Well, I'll be flummoxed!" whispered Uncle Herb.

"Shush!" said Aunt Marg.

"Tain't right, and tain't legal," grumbled Mr. Muggins.

"Hush your mouth, Zack!" hissed Mrs. Muggins.

I noticed that all the men were frowning, and the women were smirking behind their hymnals.

Then, right after the "I do's" were said, Miss Maggotty interrupted again. "And another thing, Reverend," she said with the voice of authority. "Archibald here has sworn off drink to me in private, but I want him to swear in front of this whole company. And I want it incorporated into the marriage ceremony."

Well, poor Mr. Booth, you could tell he'd never come up against the likes of Miss Maggotty before. But once again Mr. Arbuckle saved the day. Placing his right hand on the Bible and his left hand over his heart, he looked his bride straight in the eye, through the netting, and solemnly declared, "As part and parcel of this here ritual, and in front of all these friends and folks, I, Archibald Arbuckle, do swear by all that's good and holy that I'll never touch hard cider again, so help me!"

The whole congregation burst into applause, and Mr. Booth promptly pronounced the couple "man and wife." And Miss Maggotty interrupted *again*. "No! No! No, Mr. Booth!" She wagged her finger in his face as if he was ten years old. "Not 'man and wife.' Just think how foolish it would sound if you pronounced us 'man and woman.' We already know that, don't we? So, you must use the words 'husband and wife.' That makes a lot more sense, don't you think?"

Well, the poor man was so flustered he didn't know what to think. So, red-faced and sputtering, he finally blurted out, "I pronounce you husband and wife . . . wife and husband . . . oh, for heaven's sake, kiss the bride."

Almost coyly, Matilda Maggotty lifted her veil. Then Mr. Arbuckle grabbed her and gave her a loud, wet smacker.

No sooner was the ceremony over than everyone threw rice, and Miss Maggotty threw her bouquet, and it was caught by the widow Hocks, who blushed to the roots of her black hair.

After the rice was swept up, refreshments were served: crustless sandwiches, iced tea-cakes and ruby-red punch made by the women from their wild raspberry preserves.

As the newlyweds were being toasted, Matt leaned over and whispered in my ear, "Will you marry me when we grow up, Marg?" I blushed and poked him with my elbow and answered solemnly, "I will if I have time."

Next, Uncle Herb and Mr. Muggins and Ernie Paddison brought out their fiddles and began playing "Turkey in the Straw" to beat the band. Up until then I had no idea that my uncle was a talented musician.

When the dancing began, I shrank back against the wall because I didn't know how to dance. But Matt did. He had been going to barn dances ever since he could walk. "C'mon, Marg." He pulled me onto the floor. "I'll learn you."

"Teach me," I corrected, dragging my feet.

"Yes, Miss Maggotty!" he mimicked, making us both laugh.

Well, dancing turned out to be as easy as falling off a log. Matt said I was a natural.

"I've never had so much fun in my life before," I told Aunt Marg breathlessly between dances.

"I'm glad, Margaret." She smoothed the damp curls off my forehead, then took my steamy glasses from the end of my nose, huffed on them, polished them with her hanky and put them back on my face again. "Why don't you go and tell Miss — Mrs. Arbuckle what you just told me?" she suggested.

"Oh, gosh, Aunt Marg, I don't think I better." I looked across the room at the radiant bride. "She still doesn't like me, you know."

"Try it anyway," urged my aunt, giving me a little shove. So I weaved and ducked my way across the wide board floor.

Miss Maggotty was standing beside her old desk, which was covered with a white tablecloth. On it stood the wedding cake and the punch bowl. She and her new husband were sipping punch from stemmed glasses. At first they didn't notice me because they were busy making goo-goo eyes at each other. (I couldn't believe it — old people like them acting so silly.) Then she saw me and smiled. I was amazed at how nice she looked when she smiled. Even with the netting pulled back. I guess it was true what Aunt Marg said, "There's no such thing as a homely bride."

"Are you having a good time, Margaret?" she asked me nice as you please, just as if I hadn't caused her a speck of trouble all year long.

"Oh, yes, Miss Maggotty —" I clamped my hand over my mouth, embarrassed by my mistake. But her new husband put me at ease with a reassuring wink. "I mean, Mrs.

Arbuckle. It's the nicest wedding I've ever been to in my whole life." Which was true because I'd never been to a wedding before.

"Why thank you, Margaret." Miss Maggotty's voice was unusually kind.

Having done my duty, I was about to leave when she touched my shoulder. "Margaret, there's something I want you to know before we part." She took a deep breath, as if what she had to say was difficult. "To tell you the truth, as a pupil I've found you a trial" — I hung my head and bit my lip so I wouldn't blurt out something awful to spoil her wedding day — "but as a scholar you're a pure delight. It's a privilege to teach a child as bright and eager as you are." She tilted my chin until our eyes met. "This is my advice to you, my dear. Set your sights high. You can be anything you want to be. *Anything*. You might even become Canada's first woman prime minister some day."

Her praise struck me almost dumb. "Thank you, Miss Maggotty," I managed to say as I backed away, bumping into people.

"What did she say?" asked Matt curiously.

"Oh, nothing." I wasn't ready to share the wonderful prophecy with anybody just yet. Not even Matt.

Luckily the music started up again and Ernie Paddison began to call a square dance. "Doe-see-doe and away we go!" he hollered.

"C'mon, Matt." I hauled him onto the floor. "It's my favourite!"

* * *

The next morning, bright and early, I went down to the barn with a bag of oats for Starr. He hadn't had a good feed of oats for ages. We were alone, so I told him all about Miss Maggotty's prediction. He listened attentively, twitching his ears and munching softly. "So you see, Starr, Uncle Herb was right about putting my money in the bank to earn interest. I'm going to need all the money I can get. Gee, I wonder how much money a prime minister needs anyway?"

Tossing his tawny mane in the air, Starr fluttered his lips and blew through his nose, spraying my face with oats. "Eeehhh!" he whinnied. Which sounded like a lot to me.

Chapter 13

The Letter

Two whole months went by before I finally got a letter from home. The last one, from my father, had no money in it. Not even a five-cent jit, let alone a shinplaster.

I had written home twice in the meantime, once to Olive, telling her all about Miss Maggotty's wedding, and once to Josie. In both letters I had enclosed a note to my parents. But I hadn't got any answers from anybody.

Then one day a letter in a thick envelope came for me. It had scribbly writing on it, and I recognized my mother's hand, but it looked as if it had been written in a hurry because her writing was usually neater. The stamp was stuck on crooked, too, and the envelope was addressed upside down.

Ripping it open, I found two letters inside, one for me and one for Aunt Marg. I handed her the pages with her name on them and anxiously unfolded mine. Inside I found a wide snapshot, almost identical to the one stuck up on my washstand mirror.

It was a picture of the whole family, except me, standing

on the steps of our house on Jones Avenue. Ma and Pa in the middle, looking a bit older than I remembered. Olive, with her head turned to one side showing her kiss curl. (Aunt Marg said she looked like Clara Bow, the "it" girl.) Elmer, looking handsomer than ever. (Olive always said he was full of himself.) Harry and Jenny, the twins (though they didn't look alike), grown long and gangly. Bobby, the youngest, in a cute sailor suit with buttoned-on pants. I noticed the pants weren't sagging so I guessed he was out of napkins at last; he was wearing rompers in my snapshot upstairs. Davey and Gracie, scrunched together at the edge of the picture in front of the post with our street number on it. Then there was Josie right in the middle.

It was Josie my eyes kept coming back to. In her arms, wrapped in a shawl, she held a tiny baby. All I could see was a teeny face with eyes squeezed shut and miniature fists tucked under its chin. Josie was gazing down at it adoringly. It could have been a doll, for its size, but I knew it was a real live baby.

My heart skipping like a trip-hammer, I read my letter.

May 21, 1926
11:30 p.m.

Dear Peggy, (It was the nickname I always got called at home. It sounded strange now because Aunt Marg never used it.)

I hope you will forgive your mother for not writing sooner, but I have been up to my ears in work since the new baby came. Yes, that's right, you have a new sister, two weeks old in this snap, named Patricia. She doesn't have a middle name. Josie named her because I couldn't think of another name and your father said he didn't care if we gave her a number. He must be getting fed up with children because he never said anything that outlandish about the rest of you. Anyway, now that she's here we're all pretty taken with her, even your pa, though he won't admit it yet. Josie is just like a little mother to Patsy. I must say I don't know how I'd ever manage without her.

(The news of the new baby came as a terrible shock to me. And I was filled with rage and jealousy at Josie for claiming her before I even had a chance to see her. It seemed to me I wasn't even a part of the family anymore. In fact, I thought the snapshot looked complete without me. I had to take off my misty spectacles and wipe them, and my eyes, before I could continue reading.)

The older children weren't too pleased about Patsy's arrival. But they are coming around one by one. Elmer, who had his sixteenth birthday yesterday — you must have forgot because no card came from you — well, I caught him peeking into the cradle when he thought no one was looking. And Harry and Jenny take turns holding her. But Olive is just the limit; she won't even look at the dear little soul. She says none of her friends have baby sisters and it's embarrassing. I said fiddlesticks! Just you wait young lady until you get married and have one of your own. Then she says she's never getting married and goes off in a huff. Dear, dear. I don't know what to make of young folks nowadays. But I'm glad to report that Gracie and Davey are fond of her. But poor little Bobby's nose is out of joint and I have to watch he doesn't pinch her.

Anyway, I'm sure you'll like her, Peggy, because she has dark curly hair just like you and your father. Come to think of it, she puts me in mind of you when you were born, if I'm thinking of the right baby. It's hard to remember when you've had so many, but it must have been you because you were the only girl born on Rose Avenue. That's where your middle name comes from. (I'd rather have a number than a street name, I thought resentfully.) *I do hope she's not nearsighted like you and your father though because I don't like spectacles on youngsters. But they suit you to a T, Peg, I've always said that.* (She probably thinks freckles suit me, too, I thought, wiggling my speckled nose to work my glasses closer to my eyes. They were getting all steamy again and I had to keep swallowing a lump in my throat that hurt.)

In my note to your Aunt Margaret I told her you could stay a while longer. I'm so busy now I could do with one less. But later on you can come home. You're always welcome home, Peg, you know that. It's mighty nice that your aunt and uncle like having you. And I know you're happy there with your friends and Starr. Do you still make a pet of Starr?

Well, love, I must sign off since the baby's crying. She needs nursing and changing, and then maybe I can catch forty winks myself. Dear, dear, I just get one out of napkins and then there's another one. I told your father plump and plain that she'd better be the last because I'm at my wits' end. I don't have time to comb my hair,

*and I look like a dying duck in a thunderstorm. Please
excuse your cranky old mother for running on. I'm so
tuckered out I hardly know what I'm saying.*
                    Lovingly, Your mother.

I folded the letter and glanced up just in time to catch
Aunt Marg's eyes on me. She had handed her letter to
Uncle Herb and he was watching me, too. The snapshot lay
between them on the table.

Uncle Herb was twirling a straw in rapid circles between
his teeth, "Well Maggie, it seems like your ma's got her
hands full."

"Did you know about the baby?" I snapped.

"Not a word or we would have told you. Are you all right,
old sweetheart?" My aunt's eyes were soft and tender.

"Yes. But I don't feel like supper. I'm going to bed."

"I'll keep your supper warm," she said, reaching out to
stroke my hair.

Grabbing the picture from the table, I put it in the envelope with my letter and hurried towards the stairwell. I
turned just in time to see Uncle Herb about to load up his
tea from the sugar bowl. He always used three heaping
teaspoonfuls and Aunt Marg worried it would give him
diabetes.

"Uncle Herb —"

"What is it, Maggie?"

"Don't put that in your tea. It's not sugar. It's salt. I
thought it was a good trick, but it doesn't seem funny any
more."

"Corker!" he exclaimed, his voice breaking.

Chapter 14

Thief

If I hadn't been lying awake stewing about my mother's letter and the picture, I might not have heard it.

The picture bothered me the most. I had cut out my own face from the old snapshot and pasted it over Josie's in the new one. So now Josie wasn't in the family and I was. But instead of making me feel better, it made me feel worse. As if I'd murdered her or something.

For nights now, thoughts of home had been floating around in my mind: the soft pink baby, my mother knee-deep in soiled napkins, my father coming home from work swinging his lunch pail, the little kids running to meet him, searching the pail for tidbits. All over the room they floated — the faces of my family.

This particular night was warm and balmy. It reminded me of the poem "What Is so Rare as a Day in June?" My bedroom window was open because there were no mosquitoes yet, but Aunt Marg had sprinkled my pillowslip with oil of citronella just in case. Aunt Marg was away for the night in Shelburne, nursing Mrs. Plumb who was very sick with the ague. So Uncle Herb and I were alone.

We had a good time together, sharing the earphones of the crystal set, cheek to cheek. We listened to a ghost story all the way from WPG in Atlantic City. I asked Uncle Herb where on earth that was. He said it was way down south in the United States someplace. Then I made the cocoa before we turned in.

Josie's phantom face was just appearing on the ceiling when suddenly, through the open window, I heard a wild, piercing cry that made her vanish instantly. It sounded almost like a human cry — but I knew it was Starr.

Bounding out of bed, I leaned far out the window just as a shadowy figure dragged Starr through the open paddock gate by a rope around his neck. The horse reared and whinnied in outrage.

"Starr! Starr!" I screamed at the top of my lungs. But he didn't hear me over his own frantic cries.

"Uncle Herb! Uncle Herb!" I streaked across the hall, leaped on his bed and began pounding him awake.

"What in tarnation!" he muttered sleepily.

"It's Starr! Somebody's stealing Starr!"

"Corker!" he exclaimed indignantly. "I told you no tricks while your aunt's away and I'm all alone, defenceless."

"It's not a trick. Oh, please, Uncle Herb!" Finally he believed me and we raced down the stairs and out the door together, just in time to see the thief disappear down the lane on Starr's back.

"Oh, Uncle Herb, what'll we do?" I started to cry.

"There, there, Maggie. Don't take on." He squeezed my hand reassuringly. "We'll think of something."

His words gave me an idea. I ran like the wind to the

gate, clambered to the top and, cupping my hands around my mouth, blew with all my might.

Uncle Herb was standing behind me now. We both held our breath to listen. But the sound of Starr's hoofs gradually faded away.

Over and over again I puffed and blew my heart out. I filled my lungs with the warm night air and tried and tried again. I made long, breathy, hissing sounds, the closest I ever came to a real whistle.

"It's no use, Maggie." Uncle Herb patted my back consolingly. "We'll find him in the morning."

"*No!* I'll never give up!"

Again and again I sent the secret signal out into the starry night. But I finally had to stop because I'd run out of air and my throat was as dry as a blotter.

Then we heard something — a faraway whinny and the soft thudding of hoofs. As the sounds grew louder, my heart banged in my chest.

Up the road came Starr at a gallop, his wild cry mixed with the bellows of a screaming man. The horse thief bounced crazily on the stallion's back like a puppet on a string. He hung on for dear life until they reached the barnyard. Then Starr whirled and bucked like a rodeo horse and sent his captor sailing over the henhouse.

Aunt Marg's ladies, wakened so rudely from their cozy sleep, squawked and clucked their heads off. Even the white rooster started crowing.

"Be careful, Uncle Herb!" I shrieked, as he disappeared behind the henhouse after the horse thief.

Meanwhile, Starr tore around the barnyard in wild confusion, whinnying frantically. "Whoa, Starr! Whoa, Starr!"

I screamed. At the sound of my voice he gradually slowed down, and at last he stopped. I ran to him and hugged his frothy muzzle. "There, there, boy," I murmured, stroking him gently, "don't take on . . . good horse . . . my Starr."

Vibrating his lips the way horses do when they're scared, he sprayed hot air all over my face. The skin on his neck rippled under my fingers. Gradually he calmed down.

Then Uncle Herb reappeared, dragging the horse thief by the legs, face down. He wasn't hurt because he had landed in the manure pile, the wind knocked clean out of him. Pinning the man's arms behind his back, Uncle Herb shouted, "Get the rope from the shed, Maggie!" I did, and in seconds the mangy thief was trussed up like a roasting chicken. Then Uncle Herb hitched Starr to the wagon, threw the blubbering wretch in back like a sack of potatoes and delivered him to the constable at Four Corners.

The next afternoon the Shelburne newspaper sent out a reporter to interview me. "What's this about a secret signal?" he asked curiously.

"If I told *you* it wouldn't be a secret anymore," I answered warily.

He laughed and wrote that into the story. Then he got his folding camera out of the back seat of his Model T Ford and took my picture, cheek to cheek with Starr. The next day there we were on the front page under the headline: *City Girl Foils Horse Thief With Secret Signal!*

Uncle Herb bought twenty copies when he went to town to fetch Aunt Marg. (Mrs. Plumb's fever had broken and she was on the mend.)

I was an overnight sensation. Matt was proud as Punch of me, and maybe a bit jealous, too. Eva Hocks was thrilled to pieces, and all the other kids at Four Corners School, even the ones that didn't particularly like me, wanted to be my friend. Why, even Miss Maggotty — Mrs. Arbuckle (who had been allowed by the school board to finish the year even though she was married) — acted as pleased as if I was her favourite pupil. "I always knew you were special, Margaret," she beamed.

"What's the secret signal?" the kids all begged to know. But I wouldn't tell. And I darted Matt a warning glance. He clamped his mouth shut tight and pretended to button his lips with his fingers.

Finally the excitement began to die down and the horse thief went to jail — for fifteen years! I felt sorry for him until I remembered that it was my horse he stole!

* * *

On the last day of school we got our report cards and I stood first. Aunt Marg and Uncle Herb were proud as peacocks. But I wasn't surprised. I knew I would.

While all these exciting and wonderful things were happening to me, I forgot about home and the snapshot. But when it was over and life got back to normal, my heartache started again. And this time it wouldn't go away.

Then Aunt Marg, who was a very knowing person (Uncle Herb said she could read people like a book), spoke to me one day out of a clear blue sky.

"It's time you went home, old sweetheart," she said. And she made all the arrangements.

Chapter 15

Home Again

After a tearful goodbye, I was put on the train at Shelburne. That was fun because I'd never had a ride on a train before, only a streetcar. I sat next to a nice lady with silver marcelled hair, rimless spectacles and a powdered nose. (I decided to ask my pa about rimless spectacles. They didn't look nearly so owlish as mine.) She let me have the window seat.

I was so excited I must have talked her ear off. I told her my name was Margaret Rose Emerson and I had a pet horse named Starr. Then I showed her our picture in the paper (I was taking five copies home) and of course she asked me about the secret signal. I hesitated at first. Then I decided that she could be trusted, so I demonstrated my soundless whistle and she seemed very impressed. Next I told her about Aunt Marg and Uncle Herb and Matt and Eva and Miss Maggotty. I also told her silly things like how I loved to play tricks on my uncle. What sort of tricks? she wanted to know.

"Well, yesterday, for my last supper, Aunt Marg made my

favourite dessert, floating island. She cut green cherries in the shape of trees and planted them on the islands. So I said, 'Look quick, Uncle Herb, a bluebird on the window sill!' And when he jerked his head around I stole his cherry tree and popped it into my mouth. When he realized he had been fooled again he hollered, 'Corker!' That's what he calls me when I play tricks on him. And Aunt Marg calls me 'old sweetheart' just for nothing."

"You're a lucky girl to have such a nice aunt and uncle," said Mrs. Bates (that was her name). "Do you live with them all the time? And why are you making this trip to Toronto all alone?"

Her questions flabbergasted me. Here I was telling her all about myself and I left out the most important part: that I was going home. She probably thought I was an orphan child living on the charity of kind relations. And all the time I had a family of my own.

"Well you see, last summer I had TB and my mother sent me to the farm to get cured. Aunt Marg is my mother's sister, and she's the best practical nurse in the whole country, so my mother thought I'd be better off with her than in a sanitarium."

"And your mother was right, of course, because you look as healthy as a rose-red apple. It sounds to me as if you have two fine families. But when all is said and done, be it ever so humble, there's no place like home, is there, Margaret?"

"East, west, home is best!" I chanted. We laughed companionably and she gave me a stick of spearmint candy.

It seemed like no time at all before we pulled into Union Station in Toronto.

"I've made this trip many times before," said Mrs. Bates, "but never has the time gone so quickly and pleasantly. I hope we meet again soon, dear."

Just then a white-haired man appeared, kissed her on the cheek and picked up her suitcase. "Will you be all right, Margaret?" she asked kindly.

"Yes, thanks. I'm supposed to wait under the clock for my pa."

So they walked with me to the bench under the clock and then they waved goodbye.

I saw my father before he saw me. After such a long time, he looked different, somehow. Almost handsome, in spite of his freckly skin and thick, gold-rimmed glasses and unruly black hair. I couldn't think of the right word to suit him. Maybe it was charm, or personality. Anyway, I was suddenly glad I took after him.

"*Pa!*" I cried, jumping to my feet.

"*Peggy!*" He strode towards me and swept me up, hugging me like he never had before. Then he picked up my grip and we made our way across the crowded floor to Front Street.

The sights and sounds of the city came rushing at me: clanging trolleys, blatting horns, bicycle bells and the policeman in his helmet blowing his piercing whistle. People were bustling every which way like ants on a sand hill.

When we stepped off the Gerrard streetcar, I was surprised to hear foreign languages mixed in with the English. I'd almost forgotten what Toronto was like.

But Jones Avenue hadn't changed a bit. The houses were packed together like sardines in a can; hundreds of kids were milling around playing games like Giant, Step and Kick the Can and Cinderella Dressed in Yella. The baker's horse was standing patiently at the curb, or maybe not so patiently, since the heavy iron weight attached to his bit had been dropped at his feet to keep him from bolting. I thought of Starr, my handsome Clydesdale, running free in the meadow most of the livelong day. Boy, he didn't know how lucky he was!

Suddenly a jumble of familiar people came scampering up the street to meet us.

"Peggy! Peggy!" they cried. That name sounded strange to me now. Josie reached me first and threw her arms around me. Instantly I forgave her for stealing the baby. Bobby and Gracie and Davey tugged at my skirt. I dropped to my knees and tried to hug and kiss them all at once. I saw Harry and Jenny and Elmer and Olive waving to me from the verandah.

Then my mother came to the door, wiping her hands on her apron, her red face beaming. "*Ma!*" I raced up the stairs into her embrace. She smelled different from Aunt Marg — like soapsuds instead of hay. Leaning back, she held me at arm's length. "My, but you look fine, Peggy. So strong and big! Not like the poor sick little creature I sent away last summer. And don't you look nice! Is that a new dress?"

"Yes, Ma. Aunt Marg made it for me to come home in."

"Ahhh, she's a good scout, that sister of mine. Well, come in, come in. You'll be wanting to see our Patsy. And I've got your favourite supper baking in the oven. Josie, run up and get the baby. It's her feeding time anyway."

Josie took the long, narrow staircase two stairs at a time.

But on her way down she watched her step, carefully cradling the precious pink bundle in her arms.

"Oh," I sighed, reaching out for my brand-new sister. Gently, Josie placed her in my arms.

The baby, a tiny mite with dark sparrow's eyes and downy black curls, took one look at me and yowled her head off. You'd think I'd stuck her with a pin.

"I'd better take her," Josie said anxiously. "See how she stops when I've got her? She knows me."

I knew she didn't mean to hurt my feelings, but a wave of jealousy washed over me. Ma handed Josie the bottle and she began to feed her expertly.

"Never mind, love," Ma said to me. "In a few days' time she'll take to you like a duck takes to water."

"She ought to," put in Pa. "You're alike as two peas in a pod." That made me feel better.

The special supper for my homecoming was macaroni and cheese. Two huge bowls of it. Nobody could make that homey dish quite like my mother. Not even Aunt Marg. The top was crispy orangey brown with little scorched "elbows" poking up all over. The sight and cheesy smell of it made me feel more at home than anything.

We all sat down at the long dining-room table. My father had made two extra leaves for the table so that on special occasions, like Christmas and birthdays, we could all sit down together. So my homecoming must have been considered special.

I sat in the middle on one side where I could see everybody. The little kids were all lined up opposite me on a board stretched between two chairs. They darted me shy little glances. I'd forgotten how cute they were.

All my brothers and sisters had grown and changed, but Olive seemed to have grown right up. And she was the spittin' image of our mother, except for her newfangled wind-blown bob. Ma still wore her hair in the old-fashioned way, parted in the middle and drawn back into a bun. But it was the same bright auburn colour, and they both had beautiful, red-fringed, greeny blue eyes.

"Aunt Marg would say 'Your mother will never be dead while you're alive, girl!' I told Olive.

"Oh, Peggy," my mother laughed, "you sounded just like Margaret, then. My, how I'd love to have a real visit with her again. We used to be so close when we were young." The memory brought sudden tears to her eyes.

"I brought you a present, Ma!" I decided to change the subject. "You, too, Pa." He didn't hear me so I hollered over the hubbub, "*Pa!*"

"Yes, Peg, what is it?" He was eating hurriedly, as he always did, so he could make his escape to the cellar. He had a private little nook down there, with an easy chair and a mantle radio and an ashtray, tucked between the coal bin and the furnace. No one except Ma was allowed to go there. I remember once sneaking down and switching on the radio. I was just snapping my fingers to the tune of "Barney Google" when Pa caught me and sent me upstairs with a whack.

"I brought you a present." I had bought him a tobacco pouch because I knew he smoked down by the furnace. "I brought everybody a present. Uncle Herb took me to Shelburne to shop and he let me have the reins all the way. He says it's uncanny how Starr understands me. Aunt Marg couldn't come with us because she couldn't leave

Mrs. Tom Raggett's ulcerated leg. The warm-milk-and-mouldy-bread poultice had to be changed every fifteen minutes so blood poisoning wouldn't set in, then gangrene, then —"

"Peggy! You're making me sick!" giggled Josie, clapping her hand to her mouth.

"Me, too!" gagged Elmer playfully.

Then all the other kids followed suit. Ma said, "Not at the table, Peg, there's a good girl."

I couldn't for the life of me figure out why they carried on like that, even in fun, because on the farm such a conversation wouldn't even turn a hair.

The macaroni and cheese was delicious, and Ma had given me a crunchy helping right off the top, but I could hardly swallow for the fun and elation of being home again.

After supper, when the little kids had been bedded down, Pa came up from the cellar and we all sat together in the parlour. Josie and Jenny fought to sit beside me on the couch. I had never been that popular at home before. Matt was right about brothers and sisters.

"Tell us about Four Corners," demanded Jenny.

"Yeah, and horrible Miss Maggotty," urged Josie.

So I told them everything I could think of, except Miss Maggotty's prediction about my future. I thought that might sound a bit show-offy.

"In one of your letters you mentioned a secret signal between you and Uncle Herb's horse," Olive said, wetting her finger and twisting the kiss curl in front of her ear. "What's that all about?"

So I told them, sort of shyly, about our secret signal.

"Let's hear it then," said Harry, all ears.

So I cupped my hands around my mouth, puckered up my lips and blew and blew and blew.

"I don't think a horse would hear that," said Harry skeptically.

"Naa, especially not from a distance," agreed Elmer.

"Oh, yeah? Well I can prove it!" I ran and got the newspapers out of my grip and handed them around. Their stunned reaction was all I could have hoped for. They stared at me as if I was famous, like Jackie Coogan or somebody.

"I'll have to make a special frame for this," Pa said, proudly holding up the front-page photo.

"And we'll hang it over the sideboard," Ma beamed.

That first night home was a night to remember. I had always shared a bed with Josie and I knew it would be hard getting used to that again. But I didn't expect to have *two* bedmates. Now that there was another baby in the family we were more crowded then ever. But still, it was lots of fun, talking and joking with Josie and Jenny, until Pa yelled at us to settle down. Then they made me sleep in the middle and I didn't hardly get a wink all night. Jenny snored and Josie picked her toes. In her sleep! And there was a steady parade to the bathroom all night long. Then somebody pulled the chain too hard and the water closet wouldn't stop running and somebody else had to get up and jiggle it.

It must have been the middle of the night before I finally dozed off. Then suddenly I was wakened up again by the clatter of the milk wagon coming down our street. Through the open window I could hear the milkman whistling, "Can

I sleep in your barn tonight, mister?" as he clanked about a dozen bottles on our front stoop. Then I heard his horse neighing impatiently at the curb. So even though I was thrilled to pieces to be home, the milkman's song and that familiar horsey sound made me a bit homesick for the farm. I drifted off at last and dreamed I was riding Starr bareback through the meadow.

The next day Ma let me sleep in until noon. That night I asked Olive if I could sleep with her if I promised to cling to the edge of the mattress.

"Uh-uh!" She shook her head decisively. "That's the only good thing about being the oldest, having a bed to myself. I do most of the work around here, so I get the bed."

I can't say that I blamed her.

Chapter 16

Back to Normal

In no time at all it seemed like I'd never been away. The turmoil of our big family soon made me feel almost invisible again. And Patsy still hadn't taken to me. Every time I picked her up she howled. So one day I handed her over to Josie and said, "Here, you can have her. I like horses better anyway." Josie was horrified.

I was a bit disappointed in my pa, too. After his big welcoming hug at Union Station, I thought we were going to start a brand-new friendship. But soon he seemed to forget about me. Every night he'd come home from work, tired and grumpy, sit down and eat as fast as he could, then head straight for his nook in the cellar. And no wonder. It was so noisy at mealtimes that you couldn't even hear the bevy of flies buzzing around the flysticker hanging over the table.

My mother was loving but distracted. One day when I'd finished my house chores, she said, "Go outdoors, now,

Jen, and get some fresh air, there's a good girl." Sometimes she'd even say, "There's a good boy." Half the time she was so rattled she didn't know which one of us was which.

Another thing that bothered me was that my best friend, Flossie Gilmore, had found a new best friend while I was away. Her name was Zelma Speares, and when she learned that I had spent the past year on a farm she would hold her nose when I came near and cry, "Phew! You stink like a horse!" To which I would reply, "Thanks for the compliment." But the old saying, "two's company, three's a crowd," proved to be true. And I was the one left out in the cold. Of course there were lots of kids to make friends with on Jones Avenue, but I didn't seem to hit it off with anybody in particular.

August was half over and the kids were all talking about the Exhibition and how much money they had saved up for it. (I didn't have to worry about that because Uncle Herb had given me a whole dollar.) Then came talk about school: would they like their new teacher, and what would they wear for the first day. That got me to thinking about Four Corners School, and wondering who our new teacher would be — or, rather, *their* new teacher.

I had written Aunt Marg and Uncle Herb a long letter but I hadn't had a reply yet. Then one day Ma yelled up the stairs at me as I was dusting the banisters, "Mail for you, Peg!" (I still wasn't used to that old nickname.) Sliding down the banister, I grabbed the fat envelope out of her hand and ripped it open. It was from Aunt Marg and I practically devoured it.

Green Meadows Farm, August 16, 1926

My Dear Margaret,

Well, and how's my old sweetheart? Your uncle and I were tickled pink to get your letter with all the news of the family. We both miss you awfully but we know you are happy with your own folks and that's all that matters to us, your happiness.

I was sorry to hear that your best friend deserted you. However, that's only natural when you were gone so long. And you have such a winsome way with you, Margaret, that you'll make a new friend in jig time, never you fear.

It's a pretty day today here on the farm. This morning I caught sight of a deer with its white flag of truce flying. But we're so busy this time of year that I hardly have time to notice things like that.

I have a bit of bad news that I might as well get off my chest (my heart stopped!), *but don't worry, it's not about Starr* (it started again). *Poor Fauna choked to death on a turnip and there wasn't a blame thing I could do about it. I tried, believe me, because she was the best milk cow we ever had. But you know the old saying, every cloud has a silver lining. Well, Flora dropped a calf last month and we named her Fancy. I'm glad it's a girl-calf because we need the milk more than the meat.*

Have you heard from Matthew yet? Jessie says he talks about you non-stop. But not on the party line, you can bet your boots on that! Your uncle and I are

*thinking about getting the telephone hooked up, since
the poles are already out on the road. And it would be a
blessing when there's an emergency, like Fauna. Maybe
the vet could have saved her. But there's no use crying
over spilt milk. Now that's a queer thing to say over the
loss of a cow isn't it? Anyway, if we do get the phone
connected I have made myself a solemn promise not to
pick up the receiver unless it's our ring. I don't want to
become a busybody like Jessie. Bless her, I shouldn't
harp about that one little fault. She's the truest friend a
woman ever had.*

Well, I guess you want some news on Starr. (I thought
she'd never get around to him.) *He surely misses you,
girl. Every time he sees me he blinks those outlandish
eyelashes of his and snorts his disappointment. And
one day last week that uncle of yours left the gate to
the front yard wide open and, besides stomping down
all my red hollyhocks, Starr came right up to the
kitchen door and scared the daylights out of me. His
hoofs sounded like thunder and he splintered the porch
to pieces so now it needs mending. And that uncle of
yours just sat there grinning like a chessie cat and
said, "He's looking for our girl. Isn't he a corker!"* (I
laughed my head off when I read that. I could just
picture Starr, his long, star-decorated nose denting
the screen, his huge brown eyes peering in at Aunt
Marg.)

*Well, Miss Maggotty, or I should say, Mrs. Arbuckle —
will I ever get used to that — seems to have settled in
nicely on their farm. But I hear rumours that she orders
Archibald around like a schoolchild. However, your*

uncle says he's never seen Archie so happy, so that's what counts.

We had a general meeting of the school board and hired a new teacher for the coming year. Her name is Miss M. Nesbitt and she is just sixteen. Now how in the world will a young thing like that ever manage Oscar Ogilvey? It took the likes of Miss Maggotty to handle him.

Anyway, since your room is empty now I suggested to Herb that she might come to board with us. (Oh, no! My room!) *Herb said it was all right with him if I wanted company, but she couldn't have your room.* (Whew!) *So now I'll have to get busy and wallpaper that little chamber at the back where I keep my treadle and odds and ends. I guess I'll have to move those things to the parlour, but it won't look very nice I must say. So your room will be ready for you whenever you come home. For a visit I mean. I know you're home now, but you understand what I'm getting at, girl. It's as if you had two homes. At Green Meadows there'll always be a place for Margaret.*

When I heard the new schoolmarm's name was Miss M. Nesbitt I hoped and prayed her given name wasn't Margaret. It would stick in my craw, calling another girl Margaret. But it turned out to be Mary so I was glad of that. I hope she's nice and that she agrees to board with us because I need somebody to talk to and do for. (My heart thumped with jealousy.) *But nobody could ever take your place, old sweetheart, never fear.*

Your uncle keeps pestering me to hurry up so he can add his two cents' worth to the end of this letter. He's

*not much of a hand at letter writing himself. I told him
to hold still because I'm not through yet.*

*You'll be glad to hear that Mrs. Raggett's leg is all
better now. I was afraid for a while that it was going to
putrefy. But it seems to be completely healed. There's a
scar left, though, actually a hole you could bury your
thumb in. I felt bad about that but Sophie said as long
as she had her leg she wasn't complaining. Besides she
wears her skirts so long it won't show.*

*Doctor Tom gives me full credit for saving Sophie's leg.
He says he couldn't have done better himself. Sophie
wouldn't hear of him tending her because her trouble
was above the knee. Foolish woman! But I insisted he
have one quick look to be sure it had healed properly.
Poor Sophie, she was so mortified when he lifted her
skirt that she hid her face in her hanky.*

*The tinker came down the road yesterday so I got all
my pots and pans mended and my scissors sharpened.
Then I helped his wife birth a nine-pound boy in their
covered wagon. Poor soul!*

*My ladies aren't laying worth a cent these days,
and with Fauna gone — oh, I feel terrible when I think
of her — I haven't any milk or eggs to sell so I'm a
little short of cash. Flora took sick and went dry, so
we're having to buy our milk from Jessie for the time
being. Matt brings it over every day. He's a good boy,
Matt is.*

*Your uncle gets after me and says there's no excuse for
being short of money. He says all I have to do is hitch
Starr to the buggy and go to the bank in Shelburne.
But I told him that I'm saving that money for a certain*

veterinarian's education. Anyhow, if I get Miss Nesbitt's board it'll take the place of my egg money until those lazy ladies start doing their duty again. And Herb is going to buy one of Zacharia's cows so we'll soon be back in business.

Well, old sweetheart, the lamplight is beginning to flicker so I'll hand the pen over to this impatient uncle of yours and go make us a spot of cocoa before turning in.

Lovingly, Aunt Marg.

(As plain as day I could taste the frothy brown drink. Hot or cold, nobody could make it like Aunt Marg. The handwriting changed abruptly from neat to messy.)

Hello there, corker! How's my favourite trickster? Tied any shoestrings together lately? (Funny he should ask. I had been tempted to the other night when I caught my pa napping on the couch, but I thought better of it.) *I still turn my egg right side up every morning. I ain't too fond of empty eggshells. Well, I just thought I'd let you know I'm taking good care of Starr and not working him too hard. Whenever I mention your name he just about whinnies my lugs off.*

Here's a big hug from your Uncle Herb. (He had drawn an awkward circle with both our names printed in the middle.)

P.S. I mended your right snowshoe. One of the cords was broke. Just in case you come up for a winter visit.
XXXOOO H.A.W.

The A stood for Alfred. Some of Uncle Herb's men friends called him "Haw" just for fun. But not in front of Aunt Marg. She let them know plump and plain that she had no use for nicknames.

The mention of the snowshoes brought winter pictures flashing through my mind: Starr drawing the sleigh over the crisp white meadow; Matt's hair, light as glass, blowing up over his toque; grey smoke curling from the school-house chimney; Uncle Herb coming in from the barn in a snowstorm looking like a polar bear.

It made me want to laugh and cry all at once.

Chapter 17

Making Friends

A few days later I was slouched on our verandah swing, swaying myself lazily back and forth with the tips of my toes, when a big truck stopped in front of the empty house across the street. I perked right up and went and sat sidesaddle on the railing to watch.

A family was moving into the house and some of the kids were carrying boxes inside. Among them I noticed a girl about my own age who looked exactly the way I had always dreamed of looking. She had long, golden sausage curls, like Mary Pickford, and even at a distance I could tell that her eyes were big and blue. And she wasn't wearing spectacles.

Remembering Aunt Marg's words about making a new friend in no time, I went straight over after supper. The girl happened to be standing on the verandah, knee-deep in empty cartons, looking lost and forlorn.

"Hello!" I said with a big welcoming smile, hoping my winsome personality was showing. "My name is Margaret Rose Emerson. I live over there. What's your name?"

"Shirley Shoemaker." She had a lilting voice and a radiant smile and perfect white teeth and no freckles. "How old are you, Margaret?"

"I'll be twelve next month," I said. "How old are you?"

"I just turned twelve, so we'll both be in Senior Third in September. Is the school far?"

"No. It's just around the corner. We don't have to leave till quarter to nine." I decided this was the wrong time to tell her that I had passed with honours into Junior Fourth.

"Are there any moving-picture houses near here?" was her next question.

"Sure. The Bonita is right on Gerrard Street. It's only a hop, skip and a jump away."

"Let's go to the matinee on Saturday," she suggested.

"That sounds swell," I agreed, thinking that if my pa wouldn't give me a nickel I could always break into Uncle Herb's dollar. That would still leave ninety-five cents for the Ex.

On Saturday we went to see Charlie Chaplin. It was a swell picture. The only trouble was, Shirley couldn't read the dialogue at the bottom of the screen fast enough and I had to read it out loud. That made everybody around us mad and they hissed and booed at us.

Anyhow, that's how Shirley Shoemaker and I became friends. But she wasn't half as much fun as Flossie Gilmore, because she wasn't allowed to run for fear her sausage curls would all fall apart. And she wasn't nearly as interesting as Eva Hocks because she didn't like animals. She got tired of hearing about horses in no time flat. And she'd never even heard tell of a Clydesdale. Eva never got tired of horse talk. And I never got tired of cat talk.

When Eva's cat, Belinda, had kittens, I even saw the last one come out. And speaking of friends, nobody could hold a candle to Matt.

But at least I had somebody to play with besides my sisters. They had their own friends and didn't want me hanging around all the time. By this time Shirley knew that I was a year ahead of her in school. At first it made her mad. Then she said, "I guess that's because country schools are easier than city schools. Everybody knows that."

"That must be it," I agreed. About schools, unlike my looks, I was very confident. So I didn't care what she believed as long as it made her feel better. But I couldn't help thinking what a shock she would get if she ever tried pleasing Miss Maggotty.

One day we were coming down Jones Avenue hand in hand, sharing a bag of humbugs, when Flossie Gilmore came running up the street to meet us. "Mind if I join you?" she asked. Then, without waiting for an answer, she grabbed Shirley's other hand and started swinging it. Shirley gave her a humbug from our bag.

"You sure are pretty," Flossie told Shirley, pointedly ignoring me.

"So are you!" beamed Shirley.

From then on they were a twosome and they dropped me like a hot potato. "Two's company, three's a crowd," my mother philosophized, as if that explained their treachery.

So that was the end of that friendship. I was beginning to feel jinxed or something when along came Mildred MacIntyre. Mildred was nice, but dumb as a doornail. She actually thought babies came out of doctors' black bags.

"It would smother in there," I told her.

"No it wouldn't, because it doesn't start breathing until the doctor turns it upside down and spanks it," she insisted.

So patiently, thinking I was doing her a favour, I told her all about the birth of Belinda's kittens.

"But they're animals, not people!" she protested, all agog.

"Well, people are animals, too, Mildred. Everything on earth is either animal, vegetable or mineral."

The next day I went to Mildred's house to see if she wanted to come out to play, and when I knocked on the door, it flew open and out rushed Mildred's huge mother. She swooped down on me and boxed my ears before I knew what was happening. "You vulgar girl!" I heard her yell through the ringing in my head. "How dare you tell my innocent child such a pack of lies! Now go away and don't ever come back!"

Stomping back inside, she slammed the door, leaving me rubbing my ears in bewilderment. How come I couldn't seem to keep a friend?

"Peggy!" My mother was calling from across the street, waving something white in her hand.

"Yes, Ma!" Could she have heard already that I was in trouble with Mrs. MacIntyre?

"Guess who's coming?"

"Who?"

"Your Aunt Marg and Uncle Herb!"

My troubles vanished in a twinkling. Taking Mildred's verandah steps in a giant leap, I streaked across Jones Avenue without looking and nearly got run over by a horse.

"You crazy little fool!" bellowed the Eaton's driver, reining in the big black animal, whose churning hoofs came so close I felt them brush my shoulder.

"I'm sorry, horse!" I apologized.

"Oh, Peggy!" My mother slapped my bottom, causing me to sting at both ends. "You nearly gave me heart failure. No wonder your Uncle Herb calls you a corker."

Chapter 18

The Visit

The letter said they were due to arrive the very next day and planned on staying two whole nights if we could put them up. So Josie and Jenny and I happily volunteered our bed and said we'd be thrilled to sleep on the carpet in the parlour.

"One of you can use the couch," Ma said, her face flushed with excitement. So it was decided that Josie should get the couch because she picked her toes. Personally, I would have slept sitting up on a kitchen chair to make room for Aunt Marg and Uncle Herb.

After supper I helped my mother clean our bedroom from top to bottom. Not that it needed it, but Ma wanted everything perfect for the favourite sister she hadn't seen for two long years.

"You're a wonderful helpmate, Peggy," she said, as I scrubbed the linoleum on my hands and knees while singing "When You and I Were Young, Maggie!" at the top of my lungs. "No wonder Margaret was so willing to keep you for a whole year."

"Oh, I never did much work on the farm, Ma. Aunt Marg was too afraid of me overdoing it."

"Oh, mercy!" My mother hopped down from the chair in the corner where she had been dusting cobwebs. "I hope I'm not making you overdo." She felt my sweating forehead anxiously.

"Heck, no, Ma. I didn't mean it that way. Don't worry. Doctor Tom says I'm fit as a fiddle. I'm just excited, that's all."

"Well, we're done now anyway and I'm all tuckered out. You must be, too, so off to bed with you so you won't be too tired to enjoy their visit."

The next morning after breakfast Ma said, "If I knew what train they'd be on I'd send Elmer and Peggy to meet it. I wish that sister of mine had said."

The words were no sooner out of her mouth than Aunt Marg and Uncle Herb came waltzing in the door. As it turned out, they had driven all the way down in their new Ford pickup. Dropping the grip with a thud, Uncle Herb stretched out his arms. I whooped with joy and threw myself into them, nearly knocking him over.

Then Aunt Marg hugged me tight and whispered, "How's my old sweetheart?" Squeezed between them, I could smell chewing tobacco and lavender and new-mown hay.

They hugged and kissed everybody in turn except Olive and Elmer, who insisted they were too old to be hugged so they shook hands instead.

"Now all you kids skeedaddle out of here." Ma began swooshing her hands as if she was sweeping us out with the broom. "I want to have a good chinwag with my big sister." She put her arm around her sturdy sister's waist.

Seeing them side by side, I noticed how alike they were. Except their hair was a different shade of red and Aunt Marg's skin was smoother. I guess having all us kids had given poor Ma a few extra wrinkles.

"But I want to hear about Starr!" I protested.

"Oh, Starr's as right as rain, Maggie. I'll tell you all about him later," said Uncle Herb.

"And Matt, too?" I hung around the door.

"And Matt, too. Now run along before your mother skins you alive." He jerked his frizzy red head towards the door and gave me a meaningful wink.

I finally got the message. Ma and Aunt Marg needed time alone to catch up on the lost years. So I went with Josie to the playground at the end of the street. She pushed Patsy in our rickety old perambulator and I took Bobby by the hand.

We stayed away from the house for two hours, me pushing Bobby on the swing and Josie jiggling the carriage. By the time we got home Patsy was crying and chewing her fist and Bobby had soaked his drawers.

Ma and Aunt Marg had had a wonderful visit. I never saw Ma look so happy. And when Pa came home he and Uncle Herb got on like a house afire. Pa never once went down to the cellar the whole time they stayed.

Aunt Marg made a big fuss over every last one of us. She said Olive was pretty as a picture and Elmer was as dashing as Doug Fairbanks and Jenny and Harry were the handsomest twins she'd ever laid eyes on. She said Gracie and Davey were cute as a bug's ears and Bobby was a blond charmer. And Patsy . . . well, when she held Patsy in her arms and gazed down at her adoringly, I just got sick with jealousy. At that moment I thought I hated the baby. But the next thing Aunt Marg said made all the difference. "Oh, she's beautiful!" she breathed, sticking her little finger through a soft, black ringlet. "Why she's the spittin' image of our Margaret."

Hearing those words put out the jealous fire in me as quick as the wind blows out a candle.

"Who's taking care of the animals, Uncle Herb?" I asked that night when the little kids were all bedded down. The rest of us were sitting around the kitchen table having a repast (as Aunt Marg called it). Of course Uncle Herb knew what animal I was talking about.

"Matthew is tending to everything," he assured me. "Him and Starr get along just dandy."

"And Zack or Jessie could get there in two shakes of a lamb's tail, if need be," put in Aunt Marg, "because we've got the phone in now."

"You have?"

"Yes. And I must say it's nice. I have a chat with Jessie nearly every day. Just a short chat, mind."

"And are you keeping your solemn promise to yourself?" I asked mischievously.

"Absolutely!" she declared self-righteously.

"Well, now, hold the phone." Uncle Herb scratched his whiskery chin, his blue eyes twinkling. "There was one call when you weren't sure whose ring it was, and it took you a mighty long time to figure it out, Mag."

"Herbert Wilkinson, you're a prevaricator!" She thumped him on the head with her wide gold wedding band. "I hung up in an instant. One instant — that's all the time I listened."

Uncle Herb rubbed his damaged head, then we collapsed into each other's arms, laughing uproariously.

"Oh, you two!" Aunt Marg scolded. "You're a pair of corkers if you ask me."

"Eighteen-karat?" I squealed hysterically.

"No, ten, and not a speck more," she grinned.

Josie huffed impatiently, and the rest looked on bewildered. They didn't understand our "family" jokes.

The next day we all got up bright and early and went to the Ex. All except Patsy, who stayed with our next-door neighbour, Mrs. Murphy.

The first building Uncle Herb wanted to see was the Horse Palace.

"For pity sakes," fussed Aunt Marg, "don't you get enough of those creatures at home?"

"Nope. How about you, Maggie? You coming with your pa and me?"

So I went with the men, and Olive and Elmer had to take the middle kids with them to the midway, and Ma and Aunt Marg took Bobby and headed for the flower show.

The first horse we saw was a Clydesdale. I went straight up to him and was about to walk into his stall when his owner said, "Don't go near him, girlie. He's a kicker."

"Oh, he won't kick me," I replied confidently. "I've got a horse just like him."

Before the owner had a chance to stop me, I sidled into the stall, murmuring softly in horse talk.

"Well, I'll be —" declared the dumbfounded owner, and Uncle Herb chuckled when the ornery Clydesdale nuzzled my shoulder as if he'd known me all his life.

After the horses, we inspected the cattle. One of the cows

had a darling calf and I let it suck my finger. Then I remembered about Fancy and tingled with excitement. I decided I liked calves even better than babies.

Later we all met at the fountain and Uncle Herb insisted on treating the whole bunch of us to supper in the restaurant under the grandstand.

"It'll cost you an arm and a leg," Pa protested. But Uncle Herb wouldn't have it any other way. So we all crowded around one big table and I sat between Uncle Herb and Aunt Marg. I was marvellously happy. Flossie and Zelma and Mildred and Shirley could all go jump in the lake and go under three times and come up twice for all I cared.

We stayed until the Exhibition lights came on and the whole place turned into a fairyland. It was amazing how the day's litter seemed to disappear when the coloured lights of the fountain made rainbows in the sky.

The next day Ma and Aunt Marg packed a huge picnic hamper and the bunch of us headed for Centre Island. This time we took Patsy and she was as good as gold.

Little Bobby was beside himself with excitement over his first ferryboat ride. The only problem was getting him off on the other side of the bay. Pa had to pry his fat little fists from the wire mesh under the railing. Then it took Ma about ten minutes to persuade him to stop his bellyaching because he was going to have another boat ride home.

All us kids, including Olive and Elmer, wore our bathing costumes under our clothes so we could splash in the green water. The grown-ups sprawled on a blanket under a shady weeping willow.

I guess we were the happiest people on Centre Island that day. Uncle Herb kept saying, "Ain't life grand!" as he twirled a slender spear of green grass between his teeth. Aunt Marg had brought her new Brownie, and every time one of us kids hollered for them to watch, she snapped our picture. "For posterity," she said.

On our way home a full moon was riding in the inky blue sky. Bobby pressed his cheek against the wire mesh, mesmerized by the moonlight dancing in the wavy wake of the *Ned Hanlon*. He fell sound asleep on his knees. When Pa picked him up and laid him on his shoulder, there were crisscross marks on his sunburned cheek.

We were so tired when we got home that all us kids went straight to bed without a whimper. But the grown-ups sat in the kitchen, relaxing and talking over a cup of tea. The door was open a crack and a beam of yellow light ran along the bottom and up the side of the kitchen door.

I lay on the parlour floor, struggling to stay awake because I didn't want to miss a minute of Aunt Margaret and Uncle Herb's visit. I knew they would be heading home early the next morning.

Josie and Jenny were sleeping noisily, Jenny snoring steadily and Josie pick-pick-picking her toes. I strained my ears to eavesdrop, but all I could hear was quiet whispering, and once I thought I heard my name.

Try as I might, I couldn't stay awake another minute.

Chapter 19

Saying Goodbye

The next morning I was the first kid up and dressed. It was still quite dark, but there was a light underneath the kitchen door.

I opened it quietly and there was Aunt Marg standing at the stove, my mother's apron tied in a blue bow across her broad bottom. She was scrambling new-laid eggs from the farm. My mother was frying bacon alongside her, and their freckled arms were touching as they talked in whispers.

Coffee was perking on the back gas jet. The blue flames made dark streaks up the sides of the white enamel pot. The kitchen smelled as delicious as a restaurant.

Pa and Uncle Herb were sitting at the freshly laid table. Uncle Herb's face was red and shiny from shaving. Pa still had a stubbly black beard.

"Good morning!" I said, my owlish spectacles sliding down my nose. Automatically, I pushed them up again. (Pa hadn't taken to the notion of rimless. They wouldn't suit children, he said.)

When I spoke they all jumped and stopped talking and

stared at me as if I was a stranger. Their expressions were so peculiar that I looked down at myself to see if I was buttoned up properly.

"Maybe we better put it to her before the others wake up," Pa said.

"Maybe we ought," agreed Uncle Herb solemnly. Ma wiped her hands on her apron and turned off the gas.

"What's the matter?" I said. They were making me all jittery, looking at me like that.

"Well now, Peg —" Ma was twisting her apron nervously. "What we've got to say doesn't come easy."

"What have you got to say?" I was getting scareder by the second.

"Well, the four of us had a long talk about you last night ... " there was a strange catch in Pa's voice, "and. . . well . . . you tell her, Herb."

"Well, it's not my place," said Uncle Herb, twirling an imaginary straw between his teeth.

I was fit to be tied with all their well, well, welling. "What are you talking about? Am I sick again?"

"No, no, no, girl!" Aunt Marg grabbed me to her bosom. "It's nothing like that. But your mother does have something important to say. Now out with it, Nell, plump and plain."

Taking me by the shoulders, my mother turned me gently around. Her green eyes were moist and shiny. She drew in a deep breath. "Peggy," she began, "how would you feel about going to live with your aunt and uncle and being brought up the rest of the way by them?"

My eyes darted from one set of grown-ups to the other. "You mean for good, as if I was their own girl?" My voice had gone squeaky and my scalp prickled under my mop of black hair.

"That's right." Pa sounded relieved now that it was out. "They're willing to raise you and educate you better than we ever could. But that don't mean your ma and me don't want you, Peg. Or don't love you like the rest. We only want what's best for you."

"You'd always be welcome home, Peggy," my mother added quickly. "It wouldn't change our feelings."

"Your uncle and I would dearly love to have you, Margaret. And we'd see you got home whenever you had the need. Well, love, what do you say?"

I just stood there dumbstruck.

"Let the girl have time to think it over," my wise uncle said. "The final decision rests with her."

The prickly sensation had spread all over my body. I could feel little hairs standing up on my arms. There wasn't a sound in the kitchen except one last perk from the coffee pot.

I didn't know what to say. The last thing I wanted to do was to hurt my parents' feelings. But the thought of going home with Aunt Marg and Uncle Herb, to Matt and Eva, to Four Corners School, to my own little room in the farmhouse and to Starr! Thrills chased up and down my spine. But I knew I must answer carefully.

Facing my mother, I said, "I'd like to go back to the farm, Ma, because I'm going to be a veterinarian when I grow up, and being around farm animals is good practice. But Ma, Pa, it isn't because I'm not happy here, you know."

"We know, dear, we know!" Ma hugged me tearfully and Pa sat biting his lower lip. But they both looked relieved.

Then I thought of something. "By the way, Aunt Marg, is Miss Nesbitt going to live with us?" I tried to sound casual, as if I didn't care one way or the other.

"No, love, she's already settled with the Raggetts. She's going to earn her keep by helping Sophie with the chores. Sophie's leg still acts up when it rains."

Just then Josie came into the room carrying a wet, squalling baby. Pretty soon the whole family had assembled and there was such a hubbub in the kitchen that they didn't find out what was happening until after breakfast. When they were told, they all looked at me curiously, as if they didn't know whether to be envious or sorry.

I tried not to act too excited or in too big a hurry to leave, but my heart was beating like a hummingbird's wings as I packed my grip.

"I'll send the rest of your things by parcel post," Ma said, wringing her hands in agitation.

I looked up from my packing, "Ma, you know that snapshot you sent me of the family, with Josie holding the baby?"

"What about it, Peg?" She started refolding my clothes to keep her hands busy.

"Well, I ruined it by pasting my face over Josie's. I wish I hadn't done that. Can you get me another one?"

"I've got a better idea," said Aunt Marg. She was standing at the bedroom door, her hat already perched on top of her shiny bun. "There's two snaps left in my camera. Why don't I take a family portrait? I'll take two to be sure I get a good one."

So that's what she did. We all lined up according to size on the front steps of our house on Jones Avenue just as the sun came beaming over the housetops on the other side of the street. Josie let me hold Patsy and for once she didn't cry. "Smile, everybody!" called Aunt Marg. And we kept the smiles glued to our faces while she snapped us twice.

Pa started cranking at the front of the truck while Uncle Herb sat in the cab revving up the engine. Everybody kissed everybody goodbye. Then, before we all burst out crying, I climbed into the cab between my aunt and uncle.

As we drove up Jones Avenue, I kept waving out the little back window until the truck turned onto Gerrard Street and my family was lost from sight.

We passed the Bonita and I thought of Shirley and Flossie and Zelma and Mildred. I wished they had seen me leave. I would have liked to thumb my nose at them.

The smell of the upholstery in the new Ford pickup reminded me of the doctor's Pierce Arrow. Boy, was I glad I wasn't sick this trip.

"Whew!" breathed Uncle Herb, the sweat beading on his brow. "This traffic is wilder than a stampede." He wrestled the truck along Gerrard Street. "And these dad-blamed trolley tracks are enough to ruin a man's tires."

Aunt Marg and I grinned and kept quiet. "*Gee!*" commanded Uncle Herb to the truck as he made a right turn onto Yonge Street. Then, some time later, he hollered "*Haw!*" as he wheeled the truck left onto the dirt road called Eglinton Avenue.

"Drive faster, Uncle Herb!" The speedometer read only twenty miles an hour and there wasn't another car in sight.

"No sirree!" He was relaxing against the seat back, chawing like a contented cow, the city safely behind him. "If the

Lord had meant us to fly he'd of given us wings."

"Oh, fiddlesticks!" Aunt Marg grabbed onto her hat. "Get a move on. Our Margaret's in a hurry to get home."

So Uncle Herb speeded up to twenty-five miles an hour, but wild horses wouldn't make him go faster.

Every once in a while he sent a stream of tobacco juice sailing out the window. Sometimes a fine spray blew back in. "Herb Wilkinson!" Aunt Marg scolded, "you promised to stop that filthy habit. Why, there's brown specks all over our girl's face. Stick out your tongue, Margaret." I did, then she wet her hanky on it and scrubbed my cheeks.

"There's specks on my specs too, Aunt Marg," I giggled.

"Oh, pshaw, so there is. Stop it this minute, Herbert!"

"I promised not to chaw in the house, Mag, and this ain't the house. Ain't that right, Maggie?" He winked at me, then added, "Oh, sorry about them specks, but they won't do you a speck of harm."

I shrieked with laughter.

"You're a pair of corkers, both of you," declared Aunt Marg, pretending to be mad, "and not gold corkers either. Just plain tin."

"Oh, boy!" I squealed happily. "This is just like old times!"

Uncle Herb took a back road, skirting Shelburne, so I had no idea how close we were to home. Then, suddenly, like a vision or a mirage, there at the end of the long lane was a bright green farmhouse.

"You painted our house! You painted our house!" I screamed.

"Wait'll you see your bedroom, girl!" beamed Aunt Marg, hugging me.

As we pulled in at the gate I noticed a brand new *Green*

Meadows sign nailed to the freshly painted post.

"Matt must have done that to welcome you home," declared Uncle Herb. "It wasn't there when we left."

"How did he know I was coming?"

"A little bird must have told him."

At last he parked the truck in front of the driving shed where our dear old buggy sat idle.

"Hurry up, Aunt Marg. Get out! Get out! I can't wait to step on our farm!"

"Well, mercy me, Margaret, I'm not as young as I used to be, you know." She laughed as she struggled to get her short legs from the running board to the ground. Leaping past her, I ran like a jackrabbit to the split-rail fence.

Leaning against the top rail, I gazed all around the meadow, but I couldn't see a thing. The field seemed empty.

I filled my lungs, cupped my hands around my mouth, and blew with all my might.

Suddenly, on the far side of the pasture, a brown head shot up and swung in my direction. The big Clydesdale hesitated for a split second, then, with a tossing mane and a piercing whinny, Starr came thundering to welcome me home.

MARGARET
in the Middle

For my friend Margaret Rose.

Contents

Chapter 1

Visitors

"Marrrgaret!"

"What?"

"Soup's on!"

"I'm coming!" I jumped down from the fence and ran towards the farmhouse. I had been swinging on the gate for hours — ever since the rooster crowed at daybreak — waiting for my sister Josie.

But it wasn't soup. It was crispy brown potato cakes and scrambled eggs and toast.

"They won't be here for a couple of hours yet, old sweetheart," Aunt Marg warned me.

That's what she called me sometimes: old sweetheart. I thought it was the nicest nickname in the world. But she said it was more of a pet name.

"A couple of hours!" I groaned, looking up at the big round clock on the kitchen wall through my dusty, wire-rimmed spectacles. It was one o'clock and I'd been up since six.

Aunt Marg took my glasses off my nose, rinsed them in

the soft-water cistern at the end of the stove, polished them with a bit of crumpled newspaper and handed them back to me. All of a sudden the world was bright and shiny again.

I couldn't eat much because I was too excited. I hadn't seen any of my family for a whole year. I'd been living with Aunt Marg and Uncle Herb for over two years now. They had no children of their own and I was really happy being raised by them. But sometimes I got lonely for my family. They lived in Toronto on Jones Avenue. I was supposed to go home for the summer holidays, but I couldn't because Gracie and Davey had the whooping cough and Aunt Marg was afraid I'd catch it.

"With your weak chest, Margaret" — I was named after her — "we can't afford to take any chances."

That's why I'd been sent to the farm in the first place: because I was sick with tuberculosis. Aunt Marg had nursed me back to health, and ever since, I'd been as strong as a horse. But she still worried about me.

Anyway, Josie had already had whooping cough, so Pa was bringing her up in his new car for two weeks holidays. At least it was new to him, but Ma said in her letter that it was just an old flivver.

I could hardly wait to see Josie again. Of all the ten kids in our family, I think I missed her the most. And we were closest in age. She was twelve years old and I was thirteen. Actually, there was one month in the year when we were both the same age (April), so we had been raised together like twins.

We shared everything: baths and bicycles, slingshots and skipping ropes. We even switched plates at the dinner table sometimes when Ma made something one of us didn't like. You could do that in a big family and nobody would even notice because of the hubbub.

It was this sort of racket at supper time that drove poor Pa to wolf down his meal and make a beeline for his sanctuary in the cellar. He was a quiet man by nature, and Ma often said with a sigh that he wasn't cut out to be the father of such a gang.

"Give them an extra hour or so for flat tires and boilovers," Uncle Herb said as he wiggled a straw in the space between his two front teeth, "and they should be here in jig time. So away you go and swing on the gate, Maggie."

That's what he called me: Maggie. And his nickname for me was corker. At home I was called Peggy. I had so many names, it's a wonder I remembered to answer to them all.

Usually I did the washing up after meals. It was one of my chores. But this time Aunt Marg excused me by nodding her head towards the door. She looked like my mother when she did that. They were about the same size and they both had red hair done up in an old-fashioned bun, though Ma's was more of an auburn colour. Uncle Herb had red hair, too. His was frizzy around his ears and sparse on top. Folks said he and Aunt Marg could have passed for brother and sister, which was funny because they were only related by marriage.

It was nearly three o'clock when at last I saw a cloud of dust at the end of our long lane. Sure enough, it was an old Ford flivver. As it came closer I could see that both Pa *and* Ma were in the front seat. And Josie was beside Ma, with her long brown hair blowing straight out the open window.

Then, when the Model T swung into the barnyard and

came to a rattling stop in front of the driving shed, I saw to my surprise that the twins Harry and Jenny were in the rumble seat. It turned out that they'd had whooping cough, too.

"Peggy! Peggy! Peggy!" The twins clambered over the back fender and Josie leapt out the door, missing the running board by a mile, straight into my arms. We collided so hard we landed in a squealing heap on the ground.

The next thing I knew, I was in Ma's arms and she was kissing the top of my curly dark head. I had inherited my dark hair from Pa, as well as his freckles and near-sighted eyes. We both had to wear thick glasses, and Ma said we were as alike as two peas in a pod. We all hugged and kissed for about five minutes while Aunt Marg and Uncle Herb stood beaming on the porch. Then Ma and Aunt Marg embraced each other and Pa and Uncle Herb pumped hands and slapped each other's backs.

"Oh, it's a treat to see you, Nell," Aunt Marg said as she wiped a tear away with the corner of her apron. "I thought you wouldn't get away because of the whooping cough."

"Well, Gracie's nearly all better and Davy's on the mend, so I figured Olive and Elmer were old enough to take care of things for one night. And Mrs. Murphy next door was kind enough to take the baby. Lord knows, I needed a little respite. I'm just about worn to a frazzle."

"Well, come in, come in and sit yourself down. We'll have a nice cup of tea and a fresh biscuit. Margaret baked them herself only yesterday."

"Hey, Peggy" — Harry was acting kind of shy with me — "how about taking us to see Starr?"

"Sure!" He couldn't have asked me anything I'd rather do. "Let's go!"

So the grown-ups went indoors and we kids ran through the barnyard to the split-rail fence. We all climbed up and perched on the top rail like a row of sparrows.

"There he is!" Harry pointed an excited finger to a brown speck on the horizon.

"Here, Starr! Here, Starr!" screeched Jenny and Josie.

The horse didn't respond, so Harry put two fingers in his mouth and blew a shrill whistle that nearly pierced my eardrum. Starr didn't even glance up. He just kept right on munching the sweet clover that grows thickly at the edge of the bush.

It was my big chance to show off. Cupping my hands around my mouth, I blew with all my might. No whistle came out — just a rush of air — but Starr instantly flung up his tawny head and came galloping towards us.

"How could he hear you?" yelled Jenny over the noise of his thundering hoofs.

"I don't know," I yelled back. "That's why I call it our secret signal."

The big horse stopped in a shower of grass just inches from our knees. Josie nearly fell off the fence backwards scrambling to get away from him.

Starr came right to me and snuffled his snout into my lap. "Hold your horses, boy," I laughed, stroking his velvety muzzle. "I think I've got something for you." Feeling in my pinny pocket, I came up with two sugar cubes. I held one on the flat of my hand and he took it gently with his full soft lips.

"Here, Harry," I said, "you give him the other one."

Harry was about to feed Starr with his fingertips when I stopped him just in time. "No! Not that way! Do you want to lose your finger, for Pete's sake?" I flattened my brother's hand and placed the sugar cube in the middle of his palm. "Keep your hand straight and steady," I ordered. He did, and Starr took the treat as daintily as a lady picking up a tea cake from a china plate.

"Gee, Peg" — Harry's voice was filled with admiration — "you must know everything about horses."

"Just about," I agreed, pleased as Punch with myself.

"Can we go to the barn now, Peggy?" Josie was standing a safe distance from the fence. She was obviously nervous of Starr, and who could blame her? Starr was a 1,500-pound Clydesdale — about the biggest horse you could imagine. And the most beautiful. He had the tawniest mane and the fullest tail and the hairiest hoofs and the longest white eyelashes you ever saw on a horse. Aunt Marg said his eyelashes were positively outlandish. And my best friend Matt Muggins always said that Starr was in a class by himself.

The rest of the day we spent playing in the barn. When she first stepped inside, Josie held her nose and cried, "Phew! It stinks in here!"

"When you get used to it," I answered coldly, "it smells good."

First we climbed the wooden ladder to the hayloft and, squealing, jumped over and over again into the pile of hay below. When we got tired of that I took them to the stable to see Fancy's first calf. It was a boy calf, but I hadn't named him yet. Josie hung back, but Jenny stroked his downy head and Harry let him suck his finger.

After that, Jenny found the barn kittens. There were four of them. Three were black like their mother, with white paws, but the fourth was white with black paws. This was the one that took to Jenny. It clawed its way up the front of her dress, perched itself on her shoulder and began licking her face with its scratchy pink tongue. "I wonder if Aunt Marg would give me this one?" she asked wistfully, letting its silky tail slip through her fingers.

"Sure she would," I said, "but Ma might not like the idea. You'd better ask her first."

Suddenly Josie, who was sitting primly on a bale of straw with her feet up off the floor, leapt into the air with a bloodcurdling scream. "A mouse! A mouse! I saw a mouse!" she yelled hysterically. You'd think she'd seen a bear!

"For crying out loud, Josie, a mouse won't hurt you. He's more scared than you are. That's what the barn cats are for — to catch them." Good grief, I thought, what have I let myself in for? Two whole weeks with this squeamish city kid.

Next door in the stable the cows Flora and Fancy had started bawling and thumping around in their stalls.

"Now see what you've done. You probably scared them so bad they won't let down their milk for a week."

Just then Aunt Marg began clanging the triangular dinner gong which hung from the corner of the porch roof. "Soup's on!" she hollered.

Harry jumped over a bale of straw and out the door. "Last one there's a rotten egg!" he yelled over his shoulder. And, of course, with his long legs he won as easy as pie.

Before sundown the lot of us followed after Uncle Herb as he showed off his crops to Pa. Then one by one he took the kids for a ride on his new tractor.

Early the next morning, after a hearty breakfast of side bacon, eggs and baking powder biscuits, Pa got up from the table rubbing his lean stomach and said, "Well, let's get a move on. We haven't got all day."

Then Ma said to the disgruntled twins, "Maybe next year it will be your turn to stay." I sort of wished it was their turn this time, since Josie was such a scaredy cat.

"Can I take the white kitten home?" asked Jenny hopefully while Ma was in a sympathetic mood.

"No!" bellowed Pa. "Our house is full enough with nine youngsters. It would get stomped on as sure as shootin'"

I couldn't help but notice that he didn't count me as one of his youngsters anymore. It gave me sort of a funny turn, even though it had been my own decision to live at Green Meadows, and most of the time I was so happy I wouldn't call the King my uncle.

The car rattled off down the lane and Josie and I chased after it, waving at Harry and Jenny as they bounced in the rumble seat. Then the old Model T disappeared from sight in a swirl of dust.

We turned back, retracing our steps in the dirt. Josie was walking backwards, carefully placing her feet in the tread of her new running shoes. I was surprised to see a big tear drop off the end of her nose, making a damp splotch in the sand.

Suddenly I realized that this was the first time she'd ever been away from home. And she *was* a year younger than me. So I grabbed her hand and cried, "We're going to have lots of fun, Josie. You'll see!"

Then she laughed through her tears and we ran hand in hand back to the house to do the washing up.

Chapter 2

Josie

That night, after we'd had our hot cocoa, I led the way down the weedy path to the outhouse.

"I wish there was a bathroom," Josie complained, clinging to the back of my kimono.

"Well, there's a chamber pot under the bed, but it's just for emergencies," I explained.

"It's awfully primitive up here," she whispered as we sat side by side gazing out the open door.

"Look up there at the Milky Way." I pointed to the glittering sky, trying to take her mind off her fears. "It looks like a million sparklers on the twenty-fourth of May."

"What's that?" she whispered as a faint skittering sound came from the bushes.

"Probably just a skunk or a porcupine," I said, sounding braver than I felt. She was beginning to get on my nerves. We were both glad when we were back in the house, safe and snug in my feather bed.

It was strange having a bedfellow again. At home we slept three in a bed because there weren't enough beds to go round. But here on the farm I had my own room. Which made up for not having a bathroom. Double, I thought.

We talked nearly all night long and Josie caught me up on all the news of Jones Avenue. I have to admit, even though I loved the advantages of being an only child, sometimes it got lonely. Of course Aunt Marg and Uncle Herb were swell company considering they were way up in their forties! And Matt Muggins and Eva Hocks were my very best friends. And Starr was the centre of my life. But there is something special about your own flesh-and-blood sister.

The next morning we came staggering down the stairwell into the kitchen, yawning our heads off. Aunt Marg was kneading dough on the wooden table top. "Well, lazybones," she smiled at us, "I thought you were going to sleep the whole day away."

I rubbed my eyes under my glasses and looked up at the big clock on the wall. It was ten o'clock. I hadn't slept in that late since the time I was sick.

Aunt Marg wiped her hands on her apron and came and kissed us both good morning. She didn't even have to bend over to do this because both Josie and I were nearly as tall as she was. Aunt Marg said if she stretched her neck as far as it would go she could probably reach five feet — which was plenty tall enough for a woman whose husband was only five feet four! They both said they didn't mind being short, if only they weren't so wide. But I thought they were absolutely perfect.

We sat down to bowls of creamy oatmeal porridge smothered in brown sugar. Then Aunt Marg said, "How about some toast with my homemade billberry jam?"

Josie looked around, puzzled. "Where's your toaster?" Aunt Marg laughed and reached for the long-handled apparatus hanging on a nail behind the stove. Handing it to Josie, she winked at me. Josie examined it curiously. "How does this thing work?" she asked.

"Here, for Pete's sake, let me show you." I used my most know-it-all voice, took it from her, separated the two long handles and spread open the wire mesh squares at the end. Then I put a thick slice of yesterday's bread in between the squares and closed the handles. "Now hold it by the end and I'll lift the stove lid off."

The log in the stove was orange-red, just right for toasting. I showed Josie how close to hold the old-fashioned gadget and when to turn it over.

She ate six slices of the crispy brown toast smothered in thick purple jam. Then she rubbed her stomach and groaned, "Ohhh, I think I'm going to throw up."

"You'll do no such thing," said Aunt Marg briskly. "Just run outside and jump up and down. That'll settle your breakfast in no time."

So we jumped off the porch about a dozen times. Then I said, "What would you like to do today, Josie?"

"Do you think I could have a ride on Starr?"

"Sure! C'mon!" I was really surprised, considering how nervous she was of him. I grabbed her hand and we headed for the pasture. Uncle Herb had gone to Shelburne in the pickup for supplies, so I knew Starr wouldn't be busy that day.

The minute he saw me he let out a glorious whinny and flung his handsome head over the split-rail fence. I gave him an apple and he crunched it greedily with his big yellow teeth. Then he began bunting me with his nose, begging for more.

"That's all for now, boy," I said, stroking the wide space between his shiny brown eyes. "Are you all set, Jose?"

"I'm a bit scared," she admitted.

"Don't be. I'll go first and show you how."

As I climbed to the top of the fence, Starr automatically moved closer, making it easy for me to hop aboard. I leaned forward and hugged him around his thick neck and whispered in his sinewy ear, "Okay, boy, let's go!"

With a high-pitched nicker and a swish of his magnificent tail, we set off at a gallop across the meadow. Then I turned him around just by tweaking his ear and we cantered back again. I slid down his smooth belly and landed easily on my feet.

"See, Jose," I said, "there's nothing to it."

"Okay, I'll try," she answered with a quaver in her voice.

I intertwined my fingers to make a foothold and hoisted her onto his back.

The second he felt her weight, he knew it wasn't me. "Eeeehhh!" he cried, and rose up on his hind legs. He shivered his glossy coat the way horses do when they're chasing flies, and slid Josie off right over his rump.

She landed on the soft turf, jumped to her feet and scrambled over the fence. "He hates me!" she declared, rubbing her bottom. "And I hate him."

"Shhh, Josie," I warned her. "Don't ever say that. He understands every word. He's just not used to you, that's all. C'mon, try again."

"No!" she said irritably. "I'd rather go see the calf." Then she went stomping off towards the north pasture, where the cows and calf were grazing.

I decided not to rush her. "Okay, I'll show you around the farm some more until Uncle Herb gets back. He'll know what to do about Starr."

The pickup rolled into the barnyard right at noon hour. While we were eating our dinner of Boston beans and freshly made pork pies I told Uncle Herb just how bad Starr was behaving. "What'll I do, Uncle Herb? He's never acted so ornery before."

"Well, now, Maggie . . ." He didn't say anything more, but instead poured some tea in his saucer, blew little waves across it and supped it from the side.

"Herbert Wilkinson!" Aunt Marg rapped him on his bald spot with her gold wedding band. "Aren't you ashamed, using such bad manners in front of these youngsters?"

"Now, Mag" — he loved to tease her by calling her Mag because it rhymed with hag — "it's the only way I know to choke down scalding brew."

"Oh, bosh!" she declared. Then she sipped from her teacup properly to set us a good example.

"Well, Uncle Herb?" I shook his arm impatiently.

"Well, Maggie" — he felt his head for a lump — "you're always telling folks that Starr understands every word you say. Now's the time to prove it. Why don't you go out there and give him a good tongue-lashing?"

I thought over his advice while chewing a tender chunk of pork. "Okay, I will!" I said, jumping up from the table.

"Margaret! Your manners!" Aunt Marg never forgot such unimportant things.

"Excuse me, everybody. You wait here, Jose. I have to do this alone."

Starr was upside down in the middle of the field, gleefully scratching his back, his four giant hairy hoofs thrashing the air.

"Starr!" I hollered in my maddest voice.

He rolled sideways, struggled to his feet, and came gam-
bolling towards me as innocent as a newborn foal.

Placing my hands firmly on either side of his muzzle, I
said, "I've got a bone to pick with you."

He batted his long white lashes and fluttered his downy-
soft lips, baring his teeth. Then he sort of brayed like a
donkey. I could have sworn he was giving me a horse
laugh.

"It's not funny, boy." I pulled his head down closer.
"Josie's my sister and you've got to be nice to her. If you
don't let her ride on your back I'll never bring you another treat as long as I live. No more juicy apples. No more
crunchy sugar cubes. Do you understand?"

He snorted and neighed and quivered his nostrils. Then
he clamped his mouth shut and tried to pull away. But I
hung on. My face was so close to his that his whiskers tickled my nose and his warm breath steamed up my glasses.

"Starr!" I yelled.

"Eeeehhh!" he answered.

"Are you going to be good? This is your last chance."

He looked down his long nose and our eyes met. Then
slowly he began nodding his head and pawing the ground
with his right hoof. I knew from long experience that he
was apologizing.

"Good boy!" I cried, kissing his velvety muzzle. Then I
ran back to the house, hollering for Josie all the while.

She came out on the porch. "What?" she asked.

"Starr says he's sorry. You can ride him now. C'mon."

"Are you sure?" she asked skeptically as we ran.

"Sure I'm sure. You'll see." But I had my fingers crossed.

Starr was already pressed up against the fence, waiting dutifully. Josie was scared but determined as she swung her leg over his back and grabbed handfuls of his tawny mane.

He stood perfectly still for a second and Josie looked down at me with eyes as big as saucers. "It's all right, Jose," I reassured her. Then to Starr, "Easy, boy. Nice and easy."

He moved off at a walk, his brown haunches swaying. Then he broke into a gentle trot and made a wide circle of the pasture. As I watched them from a distance I realized with a pang just how huge the Clydesdale was and just how small was my sister.

When they came back to me, Josie swung her leg over and slid triumphantly onto the ground. Then she ran to his head and patted the white star on his nose. I slipped her a sugar cube and, nickering softly, he accepted the treat from the palm of her hand.

Suddenly, as if to say he'd had enough of our nonsense, he wheeled his powerful body around and galloped at breakneck speed across the meadow to the bush on the other side.

Josie was ecstatic. "I did it, Peg! I rode on Starr! Tonight I'm going to write a letter home. Boy, won't Harry and Jenny be jealous!"

Chapter 3

The Green-Eyed Monster

For the rest of the week Starr had to work every day, so he didn't have time for us. That's one thing Uncle Herb was strict about. When Starr was working he was not to be interfered with.

So I said to Josie, "I'll telephone Matt and see if he can come over." I lifted the black trumpet-shaped receiver from the wooden box on the wall and turned the crank on the side. The bells on top jangled and the operator at Four Corners answered, "What number, please?"

"Hello, Central," I said, tilting the mouthpiece down closer to my lips. Actually her name was Norah Wiggins, but everybody called her Central because all the party lines for miles around came together at the switchboard in her sitting room. "I want to speak to Matt Muggins, please." She knew everybody's number.

"Just hang on a minute, Margaret" — she recognized my voice instantly — "I've got an emergency on another line." Then I heard her say, "How far apart are the pains?" I perked up my ear, wondering who was having a baby. Then she said, "Hold on. I'll put you through to Doctor Wiley." Doctor Wiley was the local veterinarian, so I guessed it was a cow having trouble. That's why I wanted to be a vet: so I could help animals in trouble. I loved animals, particularly horses.

Norah came back to me. "I'll ring Matt for you now, Margaret. By the way, how's your uncle's hand?"

Uncle Herb had got a nasty gash on his hand while fixing Starr's harness. "It's on the mend now, Norah," I said. "Aunt Marg did a swell job sewing it up."

"Well, it's a mercy it wasn't a lot worse," she scolded. "And he can thank his lucky stars his wife is the world's best nurse, if you want my opinion."

"Thank you, Norah."

She rang two longs and two shorts. That was the Muggins' ring. Ours was just the opposite: two shorts and two longs.

She rang three times before Matt's mother answered.

"Hello, Mrs. Muggins. It's me, Margaret. Can I talk to Matt, please?"

"I'm sorry, Margaret, but Matt's out in the field with his father right now. I'll have him ring you the minute he comes in. Is there any message?"

"My sister Josie is here on holidays and I wanted him to come over."

"Well, now, why don't you bring her over here and take supper with us. Matt's been hankering to meet your sister but he didn't want to be a nuisance."

"Thanks, Mrs. Muggins. I'll ask Aunt Marg." I put my hand over the mouthpiece. "Aunt Marg, Mrs. Muggins has invited Josie and me to supper. Can we go?"

"By all means, Margaret, but you'll have to walk because I'm too busy to drive you today."

"Thanks, Aunt Marg." I took my hand away. "We can come, Mrs. Muggins. We're going to walk over."

"That's just dandy, dear. By the time you get here Matt and Zach should be in from the field." Josie and I raced upstairs to get ready.

A china pitcher filled with soft water sat in the middle of a matching basin on my washstand. That was another one of my daily chores: keeping the pitchers full from the cistern at the side of the stove.

Josie filled the basin with the amber-coloured water and began to wash. "What makes the soap lather up so much?" she asked as she slipped the frothy white cake to me.

"That's because it's rainwater from the barrel at the corner of the house," I explained. Josie hardly knew anything. "Even carbolic lathers up in rainwater."

When we were both clean and paid for — as Aunt Marg would say — we set off down the lane.

It was a two mile trek to Matt's house. Most of the way the road ran between fields of grain or corn. But the last quarter mile narrowed down to wagon tracks with grass growing between, and wound through a heavy bush lot.

On our way we stopped at Four Corners School. It was a red brick schoolhouse with a bell tower. The date carved above the door was 1867. Josie wanted to see inside, so we climbed up to the windows.

She cupped her hands around her eyes and said, "Country schools are funny. There are no desks —just long tables and benches. And only a stove to keep the place warm. Don't you miss Leslie Street School, Peg?"

"Heck, no," I said defensively. "That old stove throws out a heat that would roast you alive if you got too close."

We jumped down and continued our journey. "What's your teacher like?" asked Josie.

"Oh, Miss Nesbitt's swell, Jose. She's only a bit older than our Olive, so she's more like a sister than a teacher. And I'm one of her favourites. I've never been a teacher's pet before and I like it. Miss Maggotty always said I was too smart-alecky for my own good."

Josie laughed and asked, "What happened to Miss Maggotty?"

"She married Archie Arbuckle and retired to live on his farm."

"I remember in your letters you used to say how awful she was."

"She was at first, but Uncle Herb gave her heck for being mean to me. And when she found out how smart I was, she almost got to like me."

"I wish I was as smart as you, Peg."

I knew Josie had to struggle with her lessons, so I said — and I meant it — "Well, I wish I was as pretty as you, Jose. I'm the homeliest in our whole family."

"No, you're not. Ma says Patsy is," replied Josie. But her words were cold comfort, because everybody said that Patsy, the baby who had been born after I left home, was the spitting image of me.

By this time we were on the bush road and Josie got kind of skittish. Every time we saw a wild animal, like a jack-rabbit or a groundhog, or even a baby deer peeking through the ferns, she squealed and jumped behind me, scaring them all away.

But just the same, it was nice having company. It made the two miles seem more like one, and the next thing we knew we were heading up the lane to Briarwood Farm.

The screen door swung open and Jessie Muggins came out on the verandah, wiping her hands on her apron. "You're just in time. Matt's watering the team, then he'll be right in." She reached out her hand to Josie. "So this is your sister. My word, she's pretty as a picture. How are you, my dear?"

"Fine, thank you," beamed Josie.

Right then I got my back up. Never once had Mrs. Muggins paid me a compliment. Not even about my naturally curly black hair.

"We're having roast duck. Matt shot it this very morning. He does love to hunt, that boy." That's one thing I didn't like about Matt — his killer instinct. "And there's sweet 'taties and freshly shelled peas and billberry pie."

A funny look flitted across Josie's face at the mention of more billberries, but she smiled gamely and said, "Oh, I love all those things!" I never knew she was such a good actress.

Mrs. Muggins invited us inside. "Now then, dear, tell me all about yourself." She fluttered around Josie like a mother hen around a chick. "I hear you have nine brothers and sisters. My, aren't you lucky. Poor Matty is all alone in the world. Set yourself down and tell me everything. Mercy, what I'd give to have a girl like you!"

That remark really stung. I knew Mrs. Muggins wished she had a girl because Matt's twin sister had died when they were babies, but she never said anything like that to me.

A half hour dragged by and still no Matt. And Josie never shut up. She and Mrs. Muggins got on like a house afire. I was beginning to feel left right out in the cold when Matt and his father finally came in the door.

Matt saw us and grinned from ear to ear, wiping his sweaty fair hair sideways across his forehead. We hadn't seen each other for days.

"Hi, Matt! Hi, Mr. Muggins!" I jumped up to greet them. Matt said "Hi!" and then they both craned their necks over my shoulder.

"Well, well, well!" exclaimed Mr. Muggins as if he could hardly believe his eyes. "And who might this pretty young lady be?"

There was nothing for it but to tell him. "This is my sister Josie, Mr. Muggins. Jose, I'd like you to meet Matt and his father."

They both reached out at once to shake her hand. Matt, the silly article, blushed to the roots of his light blond hair.

Mrs. Muggins said, "Go wash up, you two, and be quick about it. Supper's on."

Usually Matt and I sat side by side at the table, but this time he plunked himself down next to Josie and I had to squeeze myself onto the bench at the back. Mr. and Mrs. Muggins took their places at either end.

The dinner was delicious and Mrs. Muggins insisted that everybody have two helpings.

"Eat up, Matty," she said. "You haven't even finished your first drumstick yet. Are you sure you're feeling well?"

"I'm fine, Ma. Never felt better," he said. I'll bet! I thought sarcastically. I couldn't help but notice how his pale blue eyes lit up every time he glanced at Josie, which was every chance he got. And he hung on every word she said, no matter how dumb.

By the time we had finished our billberry pie I was mad as a hornet. Matt hadn't paid me the slightest attention, and all Mr. Muggins had said to me was that my sister and I didn't look the least bit alike.

"What beautiful hair you have, my dear," gushed Mrs. Muggins. Josie's hair was long and smooth, not a curly mop like mine, and it draped around her shoulders like shiny brown satin.

"Them's pretty sky-blue eyes you got there, girl," teased Mr. Muggins.

"And you got the whitest teeth I ever seen!" blurted out Matt.

That's when I saw red! "The better to eat you with, my dear!" I snapped.

Josie darted me a horrified look and everybody else went dead silent.

I could have bitten my tongue off. Wait'll Aunt Marg hears about this, I thought, my cheeks burning. Aunt Marg and Jessie Muggins were best friends and I just knew that Mrs. Muggins would ring her up the minute we left. Then about ten other people would listen in, and by the time we got home everybody for fifty miles would know that Margaret Rose Emerson was sick with jealousy over her own sister.

I wished I could drop dead. Boy, would they all be sorry to see me laid out in my coffin in my best red dress, my black curls arranged exquisitely around my flawless white face (my freckles having miraculously vanished), a pink rose clutched in my bloodless hands. I only hoped Aunt

Marg wouldn't put my spectacles on me.

Matt's expression was sullen as he got the box of dominoes from the roll-top desk. We played six games and I beat them all hollow on purpose.

When it got dark, Mrs. Muggins lit the lamps and Mr. Muggins said gruffly, "Come along, girls. Time to be making tracks."

I didn't dare look at Mrs. Muggins as we said goodbye.

On the way home my mind was reeling as I imagined Mrs. Muggins burning up the telephone wires reporting my bad behaviour. Boy, was I going to be in trouble!

We were glumly silent all the way home. As we drove up our lane we saw Uncle Herb in the moonlight, standing on the piazza — that's what he called the verandah — having a chaw of tobacco. Mr. Muggins put on the brakes just as Uncle Herb sent a stream of juice sailing over the cab. We heard it splat about twenty feet behind us.

"Much obliged, Zach," he said. "Say thanks for the buggy ride, you two corkers."

That was the last straw, him calling us both *my* special nickname. That was one thing I didn't intend to share with anybody. We both muttered our thanks and went in.

Aunt Marg was sitting by the table, leaning towards the big oil lamp so she could see to mend the pocket of my play dress. I was always ripping it by stuffing big apples in it for Starr. I had begged Aunt Marg for boy's overalls just to wear on the farm, but I hadn't been able to persuade her yet.

She looked up with a welcoming smile. "Sakes alive, I missed you two today! It was so quiet I could hear myself think." Laughing at her own joke, she broke the thread with her teeth and handed the dress to me.

Her smile told us instantly that Mrs. Muggins hadn't phoned! I heard Josie sigh with relief, which surprised me because if the shoe was on the other foot, I didn't think I'd be so forgiving. We both started talking at once.

"Oh, we had a swell time, Aunt Marg," bubbled Josie. "We had a duck dinner and we didn't even have to help with the washing up."

"Ah, Jessie's a good sort," said Aunt Marg, sticking the needle into her pincushion and returning the wooden thimble to her sewing box. "Now, have a quick bite and off to bed with you. We're going to Shelburne bright and early in the morning."

We both said we were too full to eat and I lit the small oil lamp and lighted our way up the stairwell.

We undressed in silence and crept into bed. A few minutes went by. Then Josie reverted to her old bad habit and started picking her toes, so I gave her a hard poke.

"Stop that!" I barked.

"I'm sorry, Peg," she sighed. "I only do it when I'm nervous."

Suddenly I felt awful. "Don't be nervous, Jose. It was all my fault. I'm a jealous, disgusting pig, that's all."

She reached out and clasped my hand and we finally fell asleep with our fingers locked together.

* * *

I dreamed I had long blonde curls and big blue eyes like Mary Pickford. Then along came Matt riding on Starr, of all horses. "What in tarnation did you do to yourself?" he demanded. "I liked you better before."

I woke with a start. "Boys!" I murmured. "There's no

accounting for them." Then I noticed my fingers had gone to sleep, so I pried them apart from Josie's and rubbed the pins and needles out of them. I glanced at Josie. She looked sweet in the moonlight, her shimmering hair fanned out on the pillow. Suddenly I realized how much I loved my sister and that her feelings were even more important to me than Matt's.

"Blood's thicker than water," my mother always said. Now I knew what she meant.

Chapter 4

Shelburne

Aunt Marg and Josie and I left for Shelburne right after breakfast the next morning. Uncle Herb couldn't go because he was too busy making mash for the hens in the barnyard. The big iron kettle, full to the top, sat on a metal rack over an open fire.

"Phew!" exclaimed Josie, holding her nose as she climbed into the cab of the truck. "That stuff stinks!"

"My ladies don't think so," laughed Aunt Marg. That's what she called the hens: her ladies. Sure enough, they were flocking and flapping and squawking around Uncle Herb's legs, all excited by the smell of their dinner.

Uncle Herb stopped just long enough to turn the crank to start the engine. Then he waved goodbye with the stir stick he used for mixing the mash.

Aunt Marg handled the pickup as if she'd been driving all her life. Actually she had just learned to drive at the beginning of the summer, but already she was a better driver than her husband. Uncle Herb was the nervous type. One time he drove right into the ditch when he saw a car coming, but I would never remind him of it for fear of hurting his feelings.

"Roll up the window, Margaret, so we don't choke to death on the dust," Aunt Marg said as we sped along at twenty miles an hour. "I must tell Herb this road needs a good oiling." Uncle Herb was in charge of the roads in our district.

"What are we going to do in Shelburne, Aunt Marg?" asked Josie.

"That's for me to know and you to find out," came the mysterious reply.

Her secretive answer and the little smile that dimpled her round cheeks really puzzled me. "I thought we were going in to get me new school shoes," I said, "and maybe see a magic lantern show at the town hall." Moving pictures hadn't come to Shelburne yet.

"We'll see!" was all we could get out of Aunt Marg. So Josie and I gave up and started waving out the window at the farmers and their helpers in the fields.

Twice along the way we had to stop to chase stray cows off the road. Aunt Marg and I hopped out, waving our arms and shouting, "Coo, Bossy! Coo, Bossy!" Josie stayed inside the cab because she was still scared of cows. Once we had to pull over under a grove of trees to make room for Barney Duffin's haywagon. Two of his kids were riding on top of the hayload, bouncing and laughing and tossing hay in the air.

"That looks dangerous," worried Josie, turning her head to watch their antics out the little back window.

"Heck, no!" I piped up before Aunt Marg had a chance to agree with her. "It's lots of fun. Maybe before you go home

Uncle Herb will give us a hayride."

By the time we got to Shelburne six miles away — or four miles as the crow flies, Uncle Herb reckoned — we were nearly stifled by the heat of the cab. Aunt Marg parked on Main Street and we all jumped gratefully out into the fresh air.

Then off she trotted along the broken sidewalk, the yellow daisies bobbing merrily on her white straw hat. The only reason it didn't pop right off her head was because it was stuck fast to her red bun with two long hat pins. Josie and I had to scamper to keep up with her.

First we went into the dry-goods store, where Aunt Marg started inspecting material. "You've managed to outgrow every blessed stitch I made you last year, Margaret. You're sprouting like a weed." She held up a bolt of blue serge beside me to see what length she'd need to make me a coat.

"Well, gee whiz, Aunt Marg, I'll be in senior fourth in September, you know. That's nearly grown up."

She winced at the words. Then she held bolts of blue and green and brown fabric against my face to see how they suited my complexion. Aunt Marg was very particular about things like that.

Josie hung back, looking sort of left out, so Aunt Marg quickly picked up a remnant of royal blue cloth and draped it over Josie's shoulder. "That colour matches your eyes to a T," she said. "How would you like me to run you up a new dress to go home in, girl?"

"Oh, Aunt Marg, I'd love that!" Josie beamed. "Ma never has time to sew for all of us kids, so I always get Olive's makeovers."

"Well, your mother does her level best, and don't you forget it." With that Aunt Marg picked out matching blue thread and buttons and headed for the counter.

As she paid for everything, she had a chat with Mrs. Hoperaft, the storelady. Then off we went to the general store.

The sign above the shop read *Fenton's Fine Emporium* and a hand-lettered sign in the window said, *If you don't see it, we ain't got it*. In we went, jangling the bell above the door.

"How-de-do, Miz Wilkinson," said the storekeeper politely. "What kin I do you for?"

"I'm fine, Mr. Fenton, and how are you?" Aunt Marg answered pleasantly while giving him a free lesson in grammar. "I'll have a pound of tea, if you please, and five pounds of sugar."

He measured these on the scales in brown paper bags and tied them with a piece of twine from the spool suspended overhead. "And I'll need two cakes of P&G, six pairs of brown shoestrings and a tin of Simon's Stove Black," Aunt Marg added.

While she waited, she lifted the lids off the big wooden barrels on the floor. One was filled with green pickles floating in brine, which I always thought looked like frogs in a pond. Another held walnuts in the shell and a third was filled with golden sultana raisins.

Aunt Marg said she'd have two pounds each of the nuts and raisins.

"They'll go good in my spice cake," she said. Then to me, "Run down the back, Margaret, and try on some oxfords. Brown or black, whatever suits your fancy, just so long as they're a size too big so you can grow into them. Meantime,

I'll look for a flannel shirt for your uncle."

On our way out, Mr. Fenton lifted the lid off the jar of jawbreakers and invited Josie and me to help ourselves.

"Don't eat those until later," Aunt Marg said as she stopped us from popping them into our mouths just in time. "We're going to have our repast now."

We sauntered past the post office and the fire hall to the drug store. Mr. Adair was behind the soda fountain, wiping the counter with a wet dishrag. Aunt Marg hoisted herself up on the cracked leather seat of one of the stools and Josie and I hopped up on either side of her.

"I'm famished," declared Aunt Marg. "My stomach's fairly cleaving to my backbone. How about you two old sweethearts?"

Darn, I thought. I wish they wouldn't do that! First Uncle Herb calls us both corkers, and now Aunt Marg calls us both old sweethearts. I hated having to share everything with Josie, even my special nicknames.

"I'm so hungry I could eat a horse!" declared Josie.

I darted her a baleful glance. "You sound like a cannibal," I snapped. "Don't you ever let me catch you saying that in front of Starr."

Mr. Adair let out a big guffaw. "And who might this comely little cannibal be?" he asked.

Jealousy flamed up in me again. Then Aunt Marg said, "This is our Margaret's sister, Josephine."

Those words, "our Margaret," doused the fire instantly.

"Now then, girls," she continued with a warm smile, "what'll it be? You may have anything your hearts desire."

Aunt Marg always said this to me at the soda fountain, so I was all prepared. "I'll have a banana split with three scoops of chocolate ice cream, marshmallow sauce, cherries and nuts, and a sarsaparilla with two straws."

Grinning from ear to ear, Josie said, "Double it."

Mr. Adair returned Josie's grin, winking with his one good eye. The other eyelid was closed and sunken in. Matt said there wasn't a thing underneath it. He said Mr. Adair showed him once, and once was enough.

Aunt Marg had a pot of black tea and a cheese sandwich.

By the time we had finished our splits Josie looked sort of green around the gills, so we went straight back to the truck, which was parked right out front.

"Are we going home already?" I was disappointed. So far we hadn't done a thing out of the ordinary. "It's only one o'clock." The town hall clock had just gonged once.

"You'll see," Aunt Marg said again. Mr. Adair, who had followed us out, turned the crank three times and the engine started. "Much obliged, Albert!" Aunt Marg called over the roar of the motor. Then she threw it in gear and away we went.

Chapter 5

A Visit to the Past

At the corner of Main and North Streets, Aunt Marg stuck her pudgy arm out the open window and signalled a right turn. Then she rolled the window up to keep the dust out.

Minutes later we had left the town behind. "Who do we know up here?" I asked curiously. I had never been up this way before.

"Not a blessed soul," Aunt Marg answered with a mischievous grin.

"How come we're taking this road, then?" I was getting really miffed.

"You'll see," came her maddening reply.

I was so sick of that answer by now that I got sullen and stopped talking.

About two miles north of town Aunt Marg suddenly wheeled into a tree-lined driveway. Above our heads huge maples reached out and touched each other, forming a leafy green tunnel. At the end of the tunnel stood a big stone house with a wide wooden piazza.

For a minute we just sat there staring at the big old house. Suddenly I got the strangest, brightest flash. With a surge of excitement, I leapt out of the cab and ran up the wide steps two at a time. Cupping my hands around my glasses, I peered through the hazy window. It looked dark and empty inside.

"Nobody's home," I said, disappointed.

Then all of a sudden Josie blurted out, "*You* used to live here, didn't you, Aunt Marg?"

I could have killed her. I was just going to say that.

"My stars, Josie, how did you ever guess?" Aunt Marg gave a nervous little laugh. "Yes, it was our house. Your mother and I grew up in it."

"How come you never brought me here before, then?" I asked resentfully.

"Because folks were living here before. But when your uncle heard they'd moved, I decided to come up and have a look around while the place was empty."

She walked across the verandah and tried the door. It opened with a grating sound. We all stepped cautiously inside.

The entranceway was as big as my bedroom. Bigger! And a wide staircase curved up to a landing and disappeared around a corner. On our left, double glass doors opened into a huge, high-ceilinged parlour. Straight ahead down a long hall we could see the kitchen.

Aunt Marg led the way down the hall. The kitchen was empty except for a water pump mounted on a wooden counter over a rusty sink. I glanced at Aunt Marg and saw her eyes were misty and her chin was trembling.

"I can see my mother standing there," she whispered,

pointing to the sinkboard. Then she began to walk around. "The table was here." She spread her hands out in front of a window. "And the kitchen cabinet was here. Granny's rocker sat in that corner by the range." She sighed. "I can picture her plain as day, rocking to and fro with the baby on her lap."

"What baby?" whispered Josie as if the baby might still be sleeping somewhere.

"Our little brother Henry. Your mother must have mentioned him. Henry Marshall MacDonald. He died of summer complaint when he was just a toddler. He's buried right out in the back garden. My father dug the grave himself and made the tiny white coffin. After the funeral in the parlour he carried the little coffin in his arms and buried it himself. You could do that in those days."

"Why can't you do it now?" It would be nice, I thought, to be buried by Uncle Herb behind the house or maybe near the stable, instead of in Four Corner's crowded old cemetery.

"There's a law against it now, Margaret. It's modern times, you know — 1927. Things change."

Josie and I were respectfully silent for a minute. Then I noticed a door. I opened it and peered up a dark stairwell.

"I loved these old back stairs," Aunt Marg said as she started climbing them. "I never used the front ones if I could help it."

On the second floor, five huge bedrooms opened off a massive landing. They were all empty except for dust balls and yellowed newspapers.

Aunt Marg poked her head in one doorway.

"This was our room — Nell's and mine." Then she went

to the next door. "And this was Uncle Ira's."

"Who the heck was Uncle Ira?" One mystery piled on top of another.

"Don't say heck, Margaret. He was my mother's brother, Ira Marshall. That's where Henry got his middle name. Uncle Ira came to stay with us when Aunt Lucy died. Her portrait used to hang on that wall in an oval frame with gold leaves carved all around it. I wonder what became of that picture. I remember one night" — her voice dropped to a whisper — "when Nell and I heard Uncle Ira talking in the quietest of voices. We wondered who on earth he could be talking to so late at night, so we crept on tiptoes across the hall and peeked in through the crack of the door. There stood Uncle Ira in his nightshirt and cap, holding the lamp up close to the picture of his pretty young wife. 'Well, Lucy,' we heard him say, 'it's been a busy day. The wheat's all planted and the hogs are killed and salted. And we trimmed off fat aplenty to make a good batch of soap.'"

"Fat for soap?" interrupted Josie.

"That's right," nodded Aunt Marg. "My mother mixed the fat with lye and made her own washing soap."

"Was your Uncle Ira crazy, talking to himself like that?"

"Not crazy, Margaret. Just lonely. He only lived a few years after his wife died. My mother said he died of a broken heart."

She turned, as if to put the sad memory behind her, and pointed to a plank door off the landing. "That's the way to the attic," she said. "Nell and I used to play up there by the hour on rainy days."

The door creaked on its rusty hinges as if it had been

shut for years. At the top of the dark staircase was another closed door. I started up the squeaky steps with Josie right at my heels.

I lifted the latch but the door stuck, so I gave it a hard push. Just as it flew open a bat whizzed by.

"Yiii!" screeched Josie, and she went tumbling backwards into Aunt Marg's arms.

I didn't like bats much myself, but I wasn't terrified of them like my sister because I was used to dealing with all sorts of different creatures. I waited until the bat had settled himself upside down between the peaked rafters and then I crept inside.

At first I couldn't see a thing in the dim light coming from the little dormer windows, so I took off my glasses, huffed on them and polished them on the hem of my dress. Then I pressed them close to my eyes and peered around. Gradually, as my eyes adjusted to the gloom, a strange, ghostly thing took shape in a shadowy corner and my heart leapt into my throat.

"Aunt Marg!" I screamed.

"What's the matter, Margaret?" She came scurrying up the stairs to save me from heaven only knew what.

Shaking from head to foot, I pointed to the thing in the corner. It took a minute for her eyes to get used to the dimness. Then she drew in a sharp breath.

"Oh, my soul!" Her hand flew to her throat.

"What is it, Aunt Marg? Is it an animal? A dead animal?" The thing didn't move. It just leaned stiffly against the sloping rafters. I didn't feel so brave anymore.

"It's all right, Margaret. It's nothing to be afraid of. It's only an old hobbyhorse."

I crept closer to the creepy-looking thing. Sure enough, it was nothing more than a scruffy hobbyhorse with no rockers and only three legs.

"My father made that rocking horse for Henry," Aunt Marg remembered wistfully, "and the poor little fellow never lived to enjoy it. After we lost Henry, my mother couldn't bear to look at it anymore, so my father stored it up here in the attic. It used to be hidden behind a big steamer trunk."

"Awww!" I murmured sadly. Then I had an idea. "Let's take it home. Maybe Uncle Herb can fix it up for our Patsy."

"Oh, I don't know." Aunt Marg wiped her eyes and blew her nose. "It's such a wreck of a thing." She began swatting the cobwebs away with her damp hanky, sending sleepy spiders skittering up their ladders.

"Some kid must have been playing with it," I remarked, "or it wouldn't be all broken."

"You're right, Margaret. What a sorry state it's in."

"When are you two coming down?" hollered Josie.

"Right away, love!" called back Aunt Marg. "Here, Margaret, you take the head and I'll take the hind and we'll carry it down where we can see it better."

We took it downstairs and out onto the piazza and set it on its three legs. It looked awful with its patchy brown coat, flaky blind eyes and little tufts of hair where its tail and mane used to be.

"Tsk, tsk, tsk." Aunt Marg surveyed it in dismay. "I have my doubts that even Herb can mend that."

"Sure he can!" I had perfect faith Uncle Herb could do anything, especially if *I* asked him to. So we carried the dilapidated old toy out to the pickup and laid it on its side in the back.

"Let's rinse our hands in the spring and then we'll be off," suggested Aunt Marg. She led the way down a hill-path behind the house. We were almost there — we could hear the spring gurgling — when Aunt Marg suddenly dropped to her knees with a little cry and began scratching at a patch of weeds. She uncovered a stone about the size of a hubbard squash. Its surface was smooth and there were words etched faintly on it.

"What does it say?" asked Josie.

"I can read it with my eyes shut," Aunt Marg said. She closed her eyes and two tears squeezed out and ran down either side of her nose. *"Henry Marshall MacDonald. Born September 30, 1888. Died October 9, 1890. Two years, nine days. Not dead, but sleeping."* She didn't miss a word.

Aunt Marg quickly covered the stone with bracken. "We mustn't disturb his rest," she said as she hustled us on down the sloping path to the spring.

We washed tears away in the sparkling water and drank its cold clear goodness. Then we hurried back up the hill, jumped into the cab of the truck and sped off home as fast as the four wheels would go.

* * *

I was right about Uncle Herb. "I'll give it a whirl, Maggie," he said, scratching his bald spot with his thumbnail as he examined the tatty wooden horse, "but I can't promise no miracles." That was good enough for me.

The three of us spent the last week of Josie's stay rejuvenating the hobbyhorse while Aunt Marg got busy and made Josie her going home dress. Uncle Herb made new rockers and a new leg that matched the other three exactly. Then he scraped off the rotting brown felt, right down to the bare pine wood.

Josie was the artistic one, so she had the job of painting the horse. She coloured the body brown and the eyes black with white eyelashes. Then she painted a white star down the middle of its nose.

Next it was my turn. I ran out to the fence and called Starr with our secret signal. I thought he might be mad at me and not come because I'd neglected him a bit lately, but he wasn't. He nickered and nuzzled me so ecstatically that he nearly bowled me over. I hugged his whiskery muzzle and kissed him between his eyes.

"I need a favour, Starr," I said. "You see, we're fixing a horse for Patsy and —"

He flung up his head and whinnied reproachfully.

"No, no, no! Not a real horse, silly. It's just an old wooden hobbyhorse. Honestly, Starr, you're so jealous I think you're worse than me."

He calmed down then and hung his head, embarrassed — which proved once again that he understood every word I said. "I just need to borrow some of your hair. It won't hurt a bit, I promise."

I took the scissors out of my pocket and began snipping from his tawny mane — being very careful not to take too much from any one spot. Then I cut sixty-two hairs from his tail, all in different places so it wouldn't show and ruin his looks.

"Thank you, boy!" I cried as he galloped away. Then I ran back to the kitchen where Josie was putting the finishing touches on the horse's face. She had outlined the teeth and nostrils in white and painted a dark shadow inside each ear.

It took me four hours to glue the mane and tail on, but we all agreed it was worth the trouble. It was now the handsomest hobbyhorse I'd ever seen in my life.

"It does this heart of mine the world of good to see it beautiful again," said Aunt Marg with glistening eyes.

When the paint and glue were thoroughly dry, Aunt Marg wrapped it lovingly in an old patchwork quilt and Uncle Herb tied it up with binder twine.

Josie was getting a ride home with Doctor Tom. He was our country doctor and Uncle Herb's boyhood friend. He had to make the trip to check on one of his patients in the Toronto General Hospital. Well, when he saw the weird-looking bundle that was to ride in the back seat of his new Durrant, he burst out laughing. "I'll be lucky if I don't get picked up by the Mounties for carting a body around," he declared.

Just before Josie and Doctor Tom left, the Muggins family arrived to say their goodbyes to Josie. Mrs. Muggins gave her a lovely pinafore she'd made to keep her new dress clean, and Matt gave her a book called *Girl of the Limberlost*. I wasn't jealous this time because Josie was practically gone, and besides, Matt treated her like any ordinary girl. I guess he'd learned his lesson. Then everybody kissed her — except Matt, who shook her hand — and away they went down the lane in a cloud of dust.

"Ain't that a swell automobile?" said Matt as he watched it disappear.

"It sure is!" I agreed heartily as it bore my sister away.

That night, alone at last in my feather bed, I realized

that I missed Josie. The bed seemed too big and the room too quiet. But at least I'd have more time for Starr. I had noticed when I was collecting his hairs that he needed a good grooming. And this time I was determined to clean his teeth.

For years I'd been trying to do that with Aunt Marg's scrubbing brush, but I had never succeeded. I'll do it tomorrow if it kills me, I promised myself.

Then I curled up in the middle of my cozy nest and floated away on a cloud of contentment.

A week later we got a letter from Josie saying that both Patsy and Bobby, the second youngest in the family, were just wild about the horse. Bobby wanted to name it after Starr, but Ma said Patsy could name it and she had christened it Sparky because it had sparkly eyes.

Then Josie said what a swell summer holiday she'd had, and I was glad.

Chapter 6

A Fine Life!

"Tarnation!" Uncle Herb exploded. He'd been in a bad mood lately because he hadn't had a good chaw of tobacco for a week. "Who hid my cheaters? I can't find them nowhere and I want to read this here article." He poked his stubby finger at page one of the *Farmers' Journal*.

Aunt Marg and I exchanged an amused, secretive glance. Uncle Herb's cheaters, as he called his spectacles, were right on top of his head. I hadn't played a trick on him for ages, so I decided it was high time.

"I'll help you look for them, Uncle Herb. I've got plenty of time 'cause Matt's giving me a ride to school." Since Josie had gone, Matt and I were our old selves again.

"I'd be obliged to you, Maggie," said Uncle Herb, distractedly scratching his stubbly chin. Then he puckered his brow so hard his whole scalp moved and I thought for sure his specs would slide right down his forehead and land on his nose, but didn't. I guess they were firmly anchored in the frizz of his curly red fringe.

"Maybe they're upstairs," I said. "I'll go see." I just had to leave the room so I could let out a giggle.

"I could have swore I brought them down," I heard him declare through the open stairwell door. "And I know I wasn't wearing them when I was doing the milking, that's for dang sure."

"Herbert, mind your tongue!" Aunt Marg hated slang.

Ignoring her reprimand, he said, "Mag, are you sure you ain't seen my specs this a.m.?"

"That's not my job, looking out for your spectacles." Aunt Marg pretended annoyance. "Hunt them up yourself. It'll teach you not to be so careless."

"You're a hard woman, Mag." He was searching the pockets of his overalls for about the tenth time when I came down.

"They're not up there, Uncle Herb. I looked high and low." Aunt Marg and I didn't dare glance at each other for fear we'd burst out laughing.

The search went on for another fifteen minutes. Then we heard Matt's horse and buggy pull into the barnyard.

I put on my new red sweatercoat and Aunt Marg handed me my dinner pail. Halfway out the door I turned and said, "By the way, Uncle Herb, did you check the top of your head?"

His hand flew up and found his glasses.

"Corker!" I heard him yell as I slammed the door and ran. It was swell being called a corker all by myself again!

* * *

It was the first day back at school and most of the kids had brought Miss Nesbitt a polished apple from their orchards. Just for fun I had brought her a photograph of Starr instead. Aunt Marg had snapped the picture while Starr and I were deep in conversation. You could just see a bit of the back of my head, but Starr's face hanging over the fence was in perfect focus. His long ears were bent forward and his big brown eyes looked as wise as old King Soloman's. I had hand-tinted the black-and-white print with watercolours and it looked pretty good in the little wooden frame Uncle Herb had made, even if I do say so myself.

Miss Nesbitt was really pleased. "Why, thank you, Margaret," she said quietly. "It's lovely. I'll treasure it always."

Miss Nesbitt was such a nice teacher, it was unbelievable. I only ever saw her get mad once. That was at Oscar Ogilvey for bullying little Danny Duffin. But Oscar was gone now, thank goodness.

Miss Nesbitt had long brown hair tied back with a ribbon. She looked about my age, but was in fact nearly eighteen. When she smiled, which was often, she had deep dimples in both cheeks. I always wished I had dimples because I thought they would divert attention from my freckles.

Myrtle Robinson also had dimples, and she told me how to make them. She said you had to press little round buttons into your cheeks and suck hard until the buttons disappeared. Then you held your breath for as long as humanly possible. You had to do this twice a day, morning and night. Well, I did it for a whole month and nothing happened, except I got cankers on the inside of my mouth, so I gave up.

"How come you always do dumb things like that, Margaret?" Myrtle whispered, interrupting my thoughts.

She was sitting directly behind me at the second table. Aunt Marg insisted that I sit at the front because of my near-sightedness. I didn't mind, now that Miss Nesbitt was our teacher, but I used to hate sitting right under Miss Maggotty's pointed nose.

For a second I thought Myrtle had read my mind about the dimples. Then I saw she was eyeing Starr's picture on Miss Nesbitt's desk.

"Jealousy will get you nowhere," I hissed back at her.

Just then my second best friend, Eva Hocks, slid along the bench beside me. I only saw Eva once while Josie was visiting and I missed her. I was just about to tell her this when I noticed tears in her eyes.

"What's the matter, Eva?" I whispered, alarmed. Eva wasn't very strong. Aunt Marg always called her a little wisp of a thing, and I worried about her. So did Matt. He was very sensitive for a boy.

"I'll tell you after," Eva answered in a tremulous voice.

Miss Nesbitt gave us five more minutes to settle down and then called the class to order.

At recess Eva and I went off by ourselves and sat on a circular bench that was built around a tree trunk. When we were younger we used to hog the see-saw, but now we left it for the little kids.

"What's wrong, Eva?" I asked again.

"It's my mother," she said.

"What about your mother?" I had a premonition of bad news.

"She's sick, Marg, and she won't tell anybody. She's getting weaker every day and now she stays in bed a lot. I wanted to ask your aunt to come and see her weeks ago, but she's forbidden me to mention it.

Aunt Marg had explained to me, when I asked her why Mrs. Hocks was always breathless, that she had rheumatic fever when she was a child and it had left her with a bad heart. "I'll tell Aunt Marg the minute I get home, Eva. Don't worry, she'll know what to do."

Eva sighed with relief. It seemed to cheer her up just to have somebody to share the burden with.

In the afternoon Miss Nesbitt outlined the first term's work (there were only four of us in senior fourth this year: Matt and Eva and Billy Boyd and me). I could hardly wait to get started.

I really loved school, and since my ambition was to become a veterinarian, I knew I had to have extra-high marks. Matt wanted to be a vet too, but he had to work a lot harder than me. It was too bad, because his piles of homework took up time we'd rather spend with our horses.

The second I opened the door when I got home I told Aunt Marg about Mrs. Hocks. She looked very concerned.

"I thought Sadie looked a bit peaked lately," she said, "but I'd better wait until tomorrow — and I won't take my club bag along, so she won't suspicion anything." I *knew* she'd know how to handle it.

Aunt Marg had the reputation of being the best practical nurse in the countryside. She carried a black bag just like a doctor, only hers was full of remedies she made herself out of herbs and roots and bark. She had learned all about the concoctions from her grandmother, who had been a country nurse too. Doctor Tom said some of them worked as well as modern medicine, if not better.

Chapter 7

Eva

The next day Aunt Marg went straight over to see Mrs. Hocks. When she came back late in the afternoon, she said in a worried voice, "I'm going to ring Doctor Tom," and lifted the receiver right then, cranked the handle on the side of the wooden box, and asked Central to connect her.

"Tom, it's Margaret Wilkinson here. Yes, yes, we're all fine, and how's yourself? Good. Well, what I'm calling about . . ." She paused a minute, reflectively, then continued, "Could you drop by this evening, Tom? There's a matter I'd like to discuss with you."

She listened to his answer, thanked him and hung up. Of course I knew why she didn't tell him anything over the telephone. When Doctor Tom's phone rang — one long and one short — all the busybodies on the party line dropped whatever they were doing to listen in. Uncle Herb said that somebody even dropped her baby once, but I'm sure he was joking.

"How is the Widow Hocks, Mag?" he asked now, his voice soft with compassion.

"Poorly, Herb. This is no case for me to take on alone." That's all she would say in front of me, but it was enough to let me know it was serious.

Aunt Marg stayed to nurse Sadie Hocks all the following week, and Doctor Tom visited the sick woman daily. While Aunt Marg was away I took over her chores. In the morning, before school, I even had time to help Uncle Herb with the milking.

"You don't need to rise so early, Maggie," said Uncle Herb kindly as I came yawning down the stairwell at six in the morning. "I can manage the milking myself."

"I like going to the barn in the morning, Uncle Herb. Did you see the surprised look on Starr's face when he saw me? And Fancy seems to like me milking her. But you're welcome to Flora! She twitched the glasses right off my nose with her dirty old tail the last time I tried to milk her."

Uncle Herb laughed. "She's been ornery ever since poor Fauna choked to death on that turnip. Durned if she doesn't seem to miss her sister. And folks call animals dumb."

He served up porridge thick as glue, but I didn't say anything. I'd eat sawdust rather than hurt Uncle Herb's feelings.

We managed without Aunt Marg until she came home one night just after dark. The minute we laid eyes on her, we knew Mrs. Hocks had passed away.

"Poor little woman." A tear trickled unheeded down Uncle Herb's weathered cheek. "Worked herself to death, she did, and not a wooden nickel to show for it."

"Where's Eva?" I asked anxiously, choking on the lump in my throat.

"The Raggetts took her in for the time being." Aunt Marg unpinned her hat and handed it to me. I hung it on the hook behind the door. Then she slumped wearily at the kitchen table and Uncle Herb poured her a cup of strong tea. We sat beside her quietly and waited while she sipped it.

Studying her tired face, I noticed lines I hadn't seen before and some silver threads among the red strands that had escaped from her usually tidy bun. My heart turned over at the thought that someday Aunt Marg would grow old and die. Then it struck me: Eva's mother had died and she wasn't even old.

"The funeral won't be held until the fifth day," Aunt Marg explained when the tea had revived her. "That will allow time for Hector Hocks and his wife to come from Elizabethtown. They're Eva's only living relatives. I sent them a telegram this afternoon."

Aunt Marg and Jessie Muggins took on the job of getting Mrs. Hocks ready for burial. They laid her out in her own parlour. Uncle Herb managed to contact the Reverend Booth, our itinerant preacher, so he could come in time to give the funeral message.

After the graveside service, everybody came back to Eva's house for refreshments. The neighbour women for miles around had brought cold roast chicken, pickled ham, mashed potato salad, cakes, pies and raspberry preserves. While they ate, everyone chatted and laughed and had a lovely time. But when the food was gone they all went suddenly silent, as if they just remembered what they were there for.

They began to leave in mournful little groups. The men

chucked Eva under the chin and told her to keep a stiff upper lip. The women patted her head and told her how lucky she was to have had such a good God-fearing mother.

Eva just hung her head and cried. At last everybody was gone except Aunt Marg, Uncle Herb, me, Eva's Uncle Hector and his wife, Hortense.

"Stop your blubbering, lass," her uncle said, snapping his suspenders with his thumbs. "I'll do me duty by you, never you fear, even though I have six youngsters of my own to feed and clothe. Your mother, God rest her soul, never left a brass farthing."

When Hortense heard this, her pinchy face turned white and she blew her long red nose with a furious honk. "It'll be the death of me," she wailed. "So many children."

"There's only one alternative I can think of," said Eva's uncle quickly. "That's the girls' home in Shelburne." Funny he should have that right on the tip of his tongue, I thought. "I hear tell it's a fine establishment. You might be happy there, Eva, with all those other orphans to play with."

Eva screamed and threw herself into my arms.

"You silly fool!" I yelled, forgetting Aunt Marg's warning about my saucy tongue. "Now see what you've done!"

Then, instead of chastising me, Aunt Marg cried, "Well, I never! What you suggest, Mr. Hocks, is a shame and a sin."

Now Uncle Herb jumped up and stood so close to Hector Hocks that their two stomachs touched. "You needn't worry about your duty to your dead brother's only child, Mr. Hocks," he said in a cold, angry voice. "She's welcome to come home with us. We're not her kith and kin, as you are, but Eva is like a sister to our girl here."

Suddenly panic seized me. You're wrong, I thought, she isn't! I've already got lots of brothers and sisters. I don't want Eva for a sister. I want her to stay what she is — my second best friend.

I felt Eva's thin body stiffen in my arms, as if she'd read my thoughts. She held her breath on a strangled sob, waiting for my answer.

So I spoke up loud and clear, in my sincerest voice, "That'll be swell, Uncle Herb. Eva can sleep with me."

"Oh, thank you, Marg," Eva whispered in my ear.

"That's settled, then," muttered a red-faced Mr. Hocks. Then he and his wife scurried out the door while they were still pulling on their coats.

So Eva came home with us. I was determined to be extra nice to her to make up for my awful thoughts.

Three days went by and Eva cried herself to sleep in my arms every night. Then on the fourth night, after supper (Aunt Marg had made a savoury pork pie to try to tempt Eva's appetite, but she only picked at the pastry), Jessie and Zacharia Muggins arrived in their Reo pickup.

"Where's Matt?" I asked automatically.

"He stayed behind to nurse Daisy," Jessie explained. Daisy was their heifer, but I didn't know she was sick.

Jessie pulled Aunt Marg by the sleeve into the pantry and whispered something to her and I saw Aunt Marg nodding her head. Then she beckoned to me with her finger. "Take Eva down to the stable to visit Starr," she whispered.

All the whispering had upset Eva. "I think they're planning to send me to the girls' home after all," she said as we went down the path to the barn. For a split second I hoped that was true, and that Eva would *love* it there! But I knew darn well she wouldn't. My face burned with shame at such an evil thought. But Eva didn't even notice as she began to cry again. "Oh, if only my parents weren't dead," she mourned.

"Don't worry, Eva," I said, taking hold of her hand. "Aunt Marg would never allow you to be sent there."

"Are you sure?"

"Sure as my name is Margaret Rose Emerson."

"Why isn't your name Wilkinson, the same as your aunt and uncle's?" Eva asked, distracted for a minute.

"Because Aunt Marg is my mother's sister. Uncle Herb isn't even my blood uncle, but I love him just as if he was. I'll tell you something, Eva, if you promise not to repeat it to a living soul." She promised solemnly. "I love him even more than my own pa."

"You're so lucky, Marg." She heaved a big sad sigh. "You've got two families and I haven't got any."

"You've got us," I assured her, hoping my voice held enough conviction that she'd believe me. "And you've got Starr. He really likes you, Eva. It isn't everybody he lets come in his stall, you know. Once Oscar Ogilvey tried it and Starr pushed him up against the boards and I had to rescue him from being squeezed to death."

This made Eva laugh for the first time since her mother died. Then we both sidled in beside Starr and began stroking his long silky neck. He neighed and nuzzled first me and then her. I fed him a carrot and Eva gave him a sugar cube for dessert. Then Flora and Fancy started bawling jealously, so we had to go and see them too.

I began to wonder what to do next to keep Eva occupied.

"Let's find the kittens," I said.

At last Uncle Herb came to fetch us. Wordlessly we walked back to the house with his arms around our shoulders.

The first thing I noticed when we stepped into the kitchen was the radiant smile on Jessie Muggins' face. Suddenly I had a perceptive flash and I knew exactly what she was going to say.

"Eva," Mrs. Muggins said gently as she cupped her hand under Eva's pointed little chin, "Mr. Muggins and I have been discussing your future with the Wilkinsons and . . . well, my dear, we were wondering if you'd like to come and live with us."

"For how long?" asked Eva, bewildered by this new turn of events.

"For as long as you'd care to stay, girl," put in Mr. Muggins. "That would be up to you. And if everything works out for the best, we'd like to adopt you. That is, of course, providing your aunt and uncle will agree."

As if they'd care, the silly fools! I thought.

"What about Matt? What does he say?" asked Eva nervously.

I'd been wondering the same thing.

"Oh, Matt's as pleased as Punch with the idea," declared Mrs. Muggins. "He's always wanted a sister or brother. He had a twin sister once, you know. Her name was Martha. She died when they were just little babies. You wouldn't think Matt could remember, but I've always felt deep down inside he still misses her."

"What do you think, Marg?" Eva turned to me with a helpless, searching look.

The kitchen went very quiet as I thought about my answer. The clock *tick, tick, tick*ed about a hundred times before I broke the silence.

"I think it's a swell idea, Eva, and I'll tell you why. If I couldn't live with Aunt Marg and Uncle Herb anymore, and I couldn't go back home to my ma and pa either, then I'd want to live with Matt and Mr. and Mrs. Muggins."

I heard the men chuckle and the women draw in their breath. Then Eva gave me a long hard hug.

"When can I come?" she asked Mrs. Muggins.

"Now. This very minute."

So Eva went home with Mr. and Mrs. Muggins and I was alone again with Aunt Marg and Uncle Herb.

That night I couldn't sleep for the pricking of my conscience. I couldn't help but wonder if Aunt Marg suspected the mean thoughts I'd had about Eva. Uncle Herb always said Aunt Marg could read people like a book. I sure hoped she hadn't turned the pages of *my* mind!

Chapter 8

Confessions

Mr. and Mrs. Muggins were so crazy about Eva that Matt got really jealous. "I wish they'd treat her like an ordinary kid," he complained to me one day when we were alone. "They're always hanging over her and buying her stuff. And Ma makes special foods to fatten her up."

"Well, Matt" — I slid off Starr's back and he slid off Bill's and we hopped up on the top rail of the fence — "you're always grumbling about your mother smothering you and treating you like a baby. Maybe it's good that she's got another kid to pay attention to."

"Maybe. I dunno." We mulled it over for about fifteen minutes until Matt whistled for Bill, who had wandered off, and climbed up on his back. "Bye, Marg," he said in a disgruntled voice. "See you next time I can sneak away." Then he and Bill went cantering down the lane.

Whenever I tried to give Matt advice about Eva I felt like a hypocrite. How could I teach him about caring for his new sister when I didn't want to give her houseroom myself? The problem bothered me so much it put me off my food. This was so unusual that it didn't go unnoticed.

"Eat your greens, Maggie," Uncle Herb urged as I shoved them to the side of my plate.

"It looks like seaweed," I said, turning up my nose.

"Well, a blind man would be glad to see it!" declared Aunt Marg. She always had such good arguments!

"It'll curl your hair," persisted Uncle Herb.

"Don't need it." I pointed to my curly black mop.

He tried again. "It'll sharpen your sight."

"Too late," I said, working my glasses up closer to my eyes by wiggling my nose.

"Well, then" — Uncle Herb tipped his chair back on its hind legs to make more room for his stomach and began to pick his teeth with a straw — "it'll put hair on your chest."

"Herbert Alfred Wilkinson!" Aunt Marg cracked him over the knuckles with her table knife and he yelped like a puppy.

I piled the greens on my fork, popped the mushy things into my mouth and washed them down with a tumblerful of water as if they were medicine. Then Uncle Herb and I went into an uncontrollable laughing fit.

"Oh, you two," scolded Aunt Marg. Soon her lips began to twitch and she couldn't help but join us.

That's the kind of family we were. And that was one of the reasons I didn't want anybody to butt in. Not even my own sister, let alone Eva.

Still, I was really worried about what made me so mean. I recalled Ma telling the story of her great-grandma Marshall and how she'd had a mean streak a mile wide. And whenever her name was mentioned long after she was dead and gone, her nastiness was always remem-

bered. What a terrible legacy to leave behind, I thought.
And I had a dreadful suspicion that I had inherited her
nature.

All of a sudden I realized that my aunt and uncle had
stopped drinking their tea and were watching me. So I
kept my head down and started counting the little blue
flowers around the edge of my willow plate. I was hoping
this would give me time to swallow the lump in my throat,
but it was harder to swallow than the greens.

"Come now, Maggie." Uncle Herb reached out and
clasped my hand, his calloused palm scratching my skin.
"You've got a face as long as a wet week." He tried to make
me laugh again, but when I didn't he became serious. "Tell
us what's troubling you. Mebbe we can help."

"I — I — can't!" I cried. I pulled my hand away and covered my face. To my surprise I burst into wracking sobs
and big hot tears leaked out between my fingers.

Instantly Aunt Marg took hold of my arm and drew me
to her, pulling me down on her lap. I was way too big for
her lap now, but I was glad to be there. Burying my face in
her soft shoulder I cried myself out while she patted my
back and rocked me to and fro.

"There, there, old sweetheart," she murmured lovingly.
"Things are never so bad they couldn't be worse.
Whatever's wrong, your uncle and I will put it right
again."

When I was finished crying I got up and went to the
washbasin and rinsed my face with soothing soft water.
Then I washed my glasses, dried them on the flannel and
hooked them around my ears again. Finally I went back to
the table and sat down between them.

"I have a confession to make," I said. My voice had gone all shaky. They didn't speak. They just waited.

"When Eva came home with us that night —the night of her mother's funeral — I was petrified she was going to stay. I even hoped she'd get sent to the girls' home in Shelburne. Anything, just so long as she didn't come to live with us. And it's not as if I don't like Eva — I do. But I wouldn't even want Josie to stay forever, and she's my own sister. I like our family the way it is. Just the three of us and Starr and the cows and chickens. I hate things to change. I know I'm a selfish pig and I'm sorry, but I can't help it. I don't want to share you with anybody." Tears started trickling down my cheeks again.

Aunt Marg fished her hanky out of her apron pocket and handed it to me. "Now wipe your eyes and blow your nose and let's get this settled once and for all."

Uncle Herb shoved all the dishes to the back of the table and they each clasped one of my hands. "There's no denying your thoughts were selfish, Margaret," my aunt agreed, and I hung my head in shame, "but I think your uncle and I can understand. You see, when you first came to stay with us over two years ago we had some misgivings ourselves."

I looked up, flabbergasted. That was the last thing I expected to hear. "What do you mean?" I asked suspiciously. My heart began to hammer and cold chills started running up my spine.

"Well" — Aunt Marg shifted uneasily in her chair and cleared her throat several times — "I have to admit that your uncle and I had some second thoughts about keeping you with us permanently."

I gasped and stared at them both. "You mean you weren't sure you wanted me?" I demanded.

Uncle Herb's grip tightened on my hand so I couldn't pull it away. "Not right off the bat, we weren't," he conceded reluctantly. "You see, Maggie, for twenty years there was just the two of us, Mag and me, and we was pretty set in our ways. So taking on a child to raise was a mighty big decision. And a mighty big change, too, for us as well as you."

"But that change was the best thing that ever happened to us, Margaret," Aunt Marg rushed on, squeezing my other hand so hard it hurt. "And you must remember you had to go home yourself before you were sure that you wanted to stay."

That was true. It had been hard choosing between my home in Toronto and the farm.

Gradually my heart calmed down and my stomach muscles relaxed. But I still needed reassurance. "Are you sure now?"

"Sure as the sky is blue, Margaret," whispered my aunt.

Then Uncle Herb, who had parked his specs on top of his head to dab his eyes, added huskily, "Sure as shootin', Maggie."

I was finally convinced. But there was one more thing I had to know. "Would you have kept Eva if Mr. and Mrs. Muggins hadn't wanted her?"

"Yes, Margaret," Aunt Marg answered decisively.

"I wonder if I ever would have accepted her?" I worried.

"Sure you would, Maggie." Uncle Herb reached out and tousled my head as if I was a kid. "Like I always say, you're an eighteen-karat-gold corker — and that includes your heart."

I decided I'd better leave well enough alone. Maybe they knew me better than I knew myself. I hoped so.

* * *

Well, *my* worries were over, but Matt was more confused than ever. I'd never seen him act so strange and sullen before. The only time he was the least bit natural was when he was alone with me, which wasn't often.

One day, during recess, Eva and I went down to the outhouse at the end of the weedy path behind the school. It was a two-holer, so we could sit side by side and talk. Eva turned to me with tragic grey eyes. "I don't think Matt likes me," she said.

"Sure he does." I decided to fabricate a little. "He's just crabby because he's having trouble with his senior fourth arithmetic."

"No, that's not it." Eva wasn't so easily fooled. "I don't think he wants a sister after all."

Matt's attitude was the only reason that Eva wasn't perfectly happy. She didn't even seem to miss her mother anymore. Mrs. Hocks had been a cold sort of woman who hardly ever smiled. I once told Aunt Marg that I thought Eva's mother didn't love her, but Aunt Marg said I was wrong about that. It was just Sadie Hocks' peculiar way.

Jessie Muggins was the exact opposite. She was always kissing and hugging Eva and calling her dear and pet. And Eva soaked it up like a parched garden soaks up rain.

Just as we were unlatching the door to let ourselves out of the outhouse the bell rang.

"Don't worry, Eva," I panted as we ran up the path. "I'll think of something."

She gave me such a grateful smile that it scared me.

What if I couldn't think of anything? Why, Eva might even get sick and die of a broken heart. I had heard Aunt Marg say that that was entirely possible. She had actually seen people die of broken hearts, so I knew I had to act fast.

I decided the best thing to do would be to go over and have a talk with Matt's mother. I rode Starr over to Briarwood Farm three times to speak with her, but I couldn't seem to catch her alone. Then one Saturday I finally did.

"Where is everybody?" I asked casually as I let myself in the kitchen door and hung my coat on the hook.

"Matt and his father went to town today, Margaret," Mrs. Muggins said, "and Eva's down at the barn seeing to the new batch of kittens. She'll be up shortly. So you can go on down or wait here with me."

She was sitting at the kitchen table snipping open the stitches of her pincushion. When she dumped the sawdust stuffing onto the oilcloth I sat down and began helping her find the needles that had been swallowed up in the fine beige dust.

"Be careful not to prick yourself," she said as she cautiously spread the stuffing with her fingertips.

"Mrs. Muggins, can I talk to you about something important and private?" I decided to plunge right in for fear we'd be interrupted at any moment. I kept my eyes down, busily searching for the bright little slivers of steel.

"Certainly, Margaret. What is it?" Her fingers came to a standstill. "There's nothing wrong at Green Meadows, I hope?"

"Oh, no, Mrs. Muggins." I glanced up into her concerned blue eyes and couldn't help but notice that they were exactly the same colour as Matt's. Then I hesitated, trying to find the right words.

"Come, dear, out with it. You know you can tell me anything." She gave my arm a reassuring pat.

"Well, it has to be kept absolutely secret, Mrs. Muggins." I hoped she wouldn't take offence at that, but Aunt Marg always said (and she ought to know because the two were lifelong best friends) that it was as hard for Jessie Muggins to keep a confidence as it was for Herbert Wilkinson to give up chewing tobacco.

"My lips are sealed," Jessie promised, pretending to sew them together with a long-lost darning needle.

I took a deep breath so I could say it all at once. "Well, it's about Matt, Mrs. Muggins. And Eva. You see Matt feels awfully left out these days, now that you've got the daughter you've always wanted. He thinks you don't particularly need a son anymore. Of course, I know that's not true," I hurried on, seeing her face stiffen with shock, "because Aunt Marg always says that Matt is the apple of your eye. But lately you've been giving all your attention to Eva and Matt feels he's lost his place. And it makes him jealous of Eva, so he takes it out on her by ignoring her and even being a bit mean sometimes. So now they're both upset and miserable." As I talked I kept sifting through the sawdust, adding to the glinting little pile of needles.

It got so quiet when I stopped talking that the kettle boiling on the woodstove sounded like a steam engine. When I dared look up I saw that Mrs. Muggins' azure eyes were brimming with tears and her chin was jiggling pitifully.

"I'm sorry, Mrs. Muggins. No offence intended," I murmured. Oh, my gosh, what have I done? I thought.

She stood up abruptly and said, "None taken, Margaret." Then she got the brown-betty teapot down from the cupboard, poured hot water into it, swilled it around and dumped it into the washbasin. She scooped a handful of tea from the caddy into the warmed teapot and filled it to the top with boiling water.

Silently she brushed the sawdust off the table into her cupped hand and threw it, crackling, into the fire. I gathered up the needles and put them in an empty matchbox. She laid the table with her best cups and saucers and a plate of freshly baked raisin scones. At last she sat down again and I could see she had gotten hold of herself.

"Thank you, Margaret, my dear young friend." She spoke very quietly. "My father, God rest his soul, used to say, 'There are none so blind as those that will not see.' Well, you've opened my eyes today, Margaret, and I'll always bless you for it."

Just then Eva came in. When she saw me, her thin little face stretched into a smile. "Marg! Why didn't you come down to the barn? Didn't Mother tell you where I was?"

Mother! I'd never heard Eva call Mrs. Muggins that before. No wonder Matt was jealous. "I just got here this minute," I lied. I was getting good at telling little white lies.

"Sit down, love," said Mrs. Muggins. "Let's have a cup of tea together, just we three ladies, before that father and brother of yours get home from town."

* * *

I soon noticed a change in Matt. But Eva wasn't convinced until the day that Billy Boyd cracked her over the head in the schoolyard with his big thick geography book. Matt seemed to appear out of nowhere. Roaring with rage, he spun Billy around, knocked him flat, jumped on him and pinned his arms to the ground. "Give up?" he snarled ferociously.

Billy was so surprised at his even-tempered friend turning so suddenly vicious that he gave up without a struggle.

Matt let him up and they both brushed off their clothes.

"Say you're sorry," commanded Matt.

"I'm sorry," Billy said.

"Not to me, dummy. Say it to my sister."

"I'm sorry if I hurtcha, Eva," Billy apologized sheepishly. "I was only trying to get your attention."

I burst out laughing and turned to Eva, but she had eyes only for her hero brother.

Then Matt grabbed both our hands and said, "C'mon, you two. We better get going. Bye, Bill. See ya tomorrow!"

Chapter 9

Silky

One Saturday late in October I was on my way home from Briarwood Farm, where I'd been doing my homework with Eva and Matt, when I decided to stop at the post office. I knew Uncle Herb was anxiously waiting for the 1928 *Farmers' Almanac*. He swore by its predictions, though Aunt Marg said they were just a lot of rubbish.

Emmet Hooley was behind the wicket, counting a big page of two-cent stamps with a new portrait of King George V on them. I waited so he wouldn't lose count.

"Hello there, Peggy," he said when he was finished. He was the only person outside of my city family who called me that. Once I asked him why and he told me he used to have a sister Margaret who was nicknamed Peggy and who died of a ruptured appendix when she was just six years old. So I never did tell him I didn't like the name.

He reached behind him to the wooden pigeonholes on the wall and handed me a sheaf of mail from number twenty-seven. I was glad to see the almanac had come, but I decided not to give it to Uncle Herb for at least a week because

I hadn't played a trick on him for ages.

"Are you all by your lonesome today?" Mr. Hooley inquired.

"Nope. Starr's outside waiting for me."

Mr. Hooley raised his green eyeshade, which he wore whether it was sunny or not, just to prove he was postmaster. He peered out the window at the untethered horse grazing alongside the fence. I never tied Starr to the hitching post, even though Uncle Herb had told me to. He said horses should always be tethered away from home just in case they got spooked and decided to bolt. But I knew Starr would never do that.

"That Clydesdale's far too big an animal for a girl your size to handle, as any fool can see," muttered the postmaster.

His words made the black hairs rise up on the nape of my neck. "Well, my uncle's no fool, Mr. Hooley. He knows I'm a lot safer with Starr than without him." Grabbing the mail out of his hand, I marched to the door, where I turned around and dared to add, "And some horses are smarter than some people I know!" With that I darted out the door before my saucy tongue took over completely. As it was, if Aunt Marg got wind of what I'd said I'd be milking Flora — the only farm job I hated — for a whole week for punishment.

Starr ambled along beside me as I shuffled eagerly through the post. And sure enough, there was a letter addressed to me in my mother's handwriting. My heart skipped a beat. I always got a special thrill when I heard from home. It was hard to explain, because I wouldn't trade my home at Green Meadows for room and board at

Buckingham Palace, let alone our old row house on Jones
Avenue. Still, heart pounding, I stopped in the middle of
the deserted road and tore the envelope open.

October 29, 1927 10:45 p.m.

Dear Peggy,
    *This will have to be short and sweet because I'm so
busy packing I don't know which way to turn.* (Packing?
Where would Ma be going?) *Just last week that father
of yours* (that's how she always referred to Pa when she
was mad at him) *sold this house right out from over my
head and bought a bigger one on Rose Avenue —
without so much as a by-your-leave, mind you. Well, the
house itself isn't a lot bigger, but it is detached and the
parlour has wide windows that will need new curtains.
The main thing is, the cellar is a lot larger, and that's
all your father cares about. He says he needs a room of
his own down there where he can meditate. I wish I had
time to catch my breath, never mind meditate. Besides,
as I told him, he's got that nice cubbyhole down by the
coal bin all fixed up with his easy chair and mantle
radio and stand-up ashtray, so what more could a man
want?*
    *But he says the cellar on Rose Avenue has a foot more
headroom and it's dug right out from one end to the
other, and he's going to make a real den for himself
underneath the kitchen. And woe betide anybody that
sets foot in it. He means the children, of course — he'd
never dare say that to me!*
    *I guess I can't really blame him, because he was never
cut out for such a big family. Much as he loves them all,*

they do get on his nerves. But that's neither here nor there. He won't lift a finger to help with the move, and if it wasn't for Olive and Elmer pitching in, I'd be at my wits' end.

So that's the news for now, Peg. Our new address is 149 Rose Avenue. I think I'll like it once I'm settled in because the kitchen has cupboards built right over the sink and the floors downstairs are all hardwood. Tell your aunt and uncle all about it. I'll be looking for the lot of you to visit as soon as the dust settles.

Lovingly, Your mother.

P.S. The new house is just a hop, skip and jump from the house you were born in, Peg. That's why your name is Margaret Rose.

Ta, ta, Mama.

I hated being reminded I was named after a street!

I folded the letter up, stuffed all the mail in my school bag, and decided to hurry home with the news. I jumped up on a stump, climbed onto Starr's back and set off, being careful not to jerk the reins, since Starr had his bridle on and the bit was in his mouth.

"How would you like it if you had to eat around an iron bar?" I had asked Uncle Herb once. He had laughed and said it would probably break him of the tobacco-chewing habit, and for sure it would interfere with his spitting. But he still insisted that I use the bridle when I rode Starr off the farm — so I would have better control if something unexpected happened, which it never did. My uncle could be stubborn about some things, especially when they had anything to do with my safety, so I had to give in.

It was a crispy autumn day and Starr's hoofs sounded nice crunching through the fallen leaves. We were just passing under an almost-bare oak tree with a few scarlet leaves still clinging to it, when I thought I heard something.

"Whoa, boy," I said. Starr stopped instantly and I heard the sound again — a thin, pitiful mewing coming from far above our heads. I pressed my glasses close to my eyes and peered upwards, and sure enough there was a little kitten stranded near the tip of a branch, crying its head off.

"What are you doing up there, you silly article?" I called, and directed Starr over to the tree trunk.

"Now stand still, boy, and give me a boost up," I said. I was pretty good at climbing trees, even in a dress, which was all I ever wore because Aunt Marg said overalls weren't ladylike. She could be stubborn, too, when she felt like it!

"Hold your horses, I'm coming!" I called up to the kitten.

"Eeeehh!" whinnied Starr.

"It's not you I'm talking to, Mr. Smarty," I laughed, giving his brown flanks a slap. Honestly, he was so vain that every time he heard the word horse he automatically thought it referred to him. Uncle Herb said that was because I spoiled him absolutely rotten.

I climbed up easily from branch to branch until I was level with the kitten. I tried to coax it to me in that whiny voice cats love, but it just spat and trembled with fright, so I unbuttoned my coat to give myself more leg room and began shinnying along the branch. I heard my dress rip

and I skinned my knee. Then the scrawny tree limb started bending under my weight.

"Here, kitty, kitty!" I wheedled, but she just arched her
back in terror and meowed at the top of her lungs.

Suddenly she lost her grip and the next thing I knew she
was hanging upside down like a squirrel. I shinnied faster
until I was within arm's reach, but just as I grabbed her by
the scruff, my dress snagged on a sharp twig and tugged
me sideways. I held on for dear life, with the cat clawing
and squirming frantically, and tried to think what to do. At
that moment the branch broke with a crack like a rifle
shot and I went plunging downwards, hanging onto the cat
with one hand and grabbing wildly for branches with the
other. In a split second I landed with a crash at Starr's
feet.

At first I thought I'd been killed. The wind was knocked
clean out of me and a searing pain rent my chest as I
gulped for air.

When at last I could breathe again, I whispered to Starr,
who was leaning over me neighing pitifully, "Go get Uncle
Herb, Starr!" But he wouldn't leave me. He just pawed the
ground and nipped at my coat sleeve. "Please, Starr," I
pleaded. "Prove you understand. Go for help."

He moved off a few feet, then swung his head back to
look at me uncertainly. "Go!" I commanded with all the
strength I could muster. Finally he took off in a flurry of
flying gravel.

I had never experienced pain like that before. My whole
body was wracked with it and my head and chest
throbbed. I managed to raise myself onto my elbows and
stare down at the rest of me. Suddenly I realized that my

right leg was on backwards. I tried to move it and immediately cried out. Gingerly I tried the left one. It seemed all right — just a bit sore. I must have fainted then, because the next thing I knew my splitting head was being cradled in Aunt Marg's lap.

"Where's the kitten?" I spoke so unexpectedly that she gave a little jump.

"Oh, Margaret, my old sweetheart, you're back! Thank the dear Lord!"

"Where's the kitten?" I repeated. Aunt Marg's worried face was just coming into focus.

"Right here, love." She put the fluffy troublemaker on my chest and it crept up and licked my face. Then it circled around three times, swept my cheek with its silky tail, curled up under my chin and began to purr. I couldn't help but smile — and even that hurt.

"Is my leg broken, Aunt Marg?" I asked.

"Yes, Margaret, it is. Your uncle's gone to fetch Doctor Tom. We didn't dare move you for fear of making it worse."

Suddenly I had another awful thought. "Where's Starr? Did I land on him and break his neck?" For a minute everything that had happened had gone completely blank.

"Mercy no, he's right as rain. He came whinnying up the lane as if the devil himself was after him. You sent him to us, didn't you, Margaret?" I nodded, remembering, and she shook her head in amazement. "It's uncanny how that horse understands you," she said. "It just plain baffles me. He led us right to your side. There he is by the road."

I turned my head and yelled "Ow!" as a pain shot through my neck. Starr was staring at me with a sad, helpless expression. I pursed my lips and blew. He came and stood within inches of my crooked leg, leaned down, neighing softly, and nuzzled my leafy hair. His big nose scared the wits out of the kitten, so Aunt Marg picked her up and tucked her inside her coat.

"You're a good boy, Starr," I said, rubbing his muzzle.

"You are that, old fellow," agreed Aunt Marg. Just then Uncle Herb and Doctor Tom arrived in the pickup. Uncle Herb leapt from the truck and knelt by my side, his dear sweet face puckered up with worry. "Well, Maggie, how's my girl?" he asked, forcing a smile.

"I'm fine," I said, determined not to cry as the doctor examined my leg. "But you know, Uncle Herb, if I had tied Starr up like you told me to, he couldn't have gone to my rescue."

"You're a corker, Maggie," he said, as he whisker-rubbed my forehead.

In spite of all the pain, I decided I might as well bring up one more thing. "You know, Aunt Marg, if I'd been wearing overalls, none of this would have happened. You see, it was the dress getting caught that made me fall."

"Hush, now, child." She wiped the sweat off my brow. "We'll talk about that later."

Then Doctor Tom said, "Grit your teeth, girl!" I did, and he and Uncle Herb lifted me as gently as possible onto a feather mattress in the back of the pickup. Aunt Marg climbed in beside me and put the cat on my chest. Starr followed faithfully behind us.

That very night I ended up in the Hospital for Sick Children in Toronto.

By straining my ears I had managed to hear Doctor Tom explaining to Aunt Marg and Uncle Herb that it was the worst break he'd ever seen and he wouldn't touch it for all the tea in China.

My aunt and uncle rode with me in the ambulance, sitting on little fold-out canvas chairs. They held my hands and murmured encouraging words, trying to hide their fears.

Suddenly I remembered something. "Where's the mail?"

"We found it in your schoolbag," said Uncle Herb.

"Did you see the new almanac?"

"Yep. I'm mighty glad to get it, too."

"Well, lucky I broke my leg or you wouldn't have. I was going to hide it on you for a week."

"You're a caution, Maggie, which is ten times worse than a corker." His lips began to twitch and he couldn't suppress a grin.

Chapter 10

Sick Kids' Hospital

My leg was broken so badly — a compound fracture, the doctors at Sick Kids' said — that it needed an operation to fix it. It was my first experience in a hospital and I'll have to admit I was scared. But I didn't let on because Ma and Pa and Aunt Marg and Uncle Herb looked worried enough already.

By the time I was wheeled away to the operating room I couldn't have got upset if I tried. The nurse had given me a needle in my hip, which hurt though she said it wouldn't, and I felt myself floating down the long corridor to the operating room as carefree as a king billy in a meadow.

On the operating table under the bright white lights I managed to mutter groggily, "Promise you won't start until I'm asleep?"

The gauze-covered face leaning over me gave a muffled laugh and promised. Then a mask was held over my nose and a gassy smell made me gasp for air.

The next thing I knew, I was coming to, sick as a dog and upchucking all over the bed. I slept some more and when I woke up again it was nighttime.

Ma and Aunt Marg were on either side of the bed holding my hands.

"How are you, pet?" Ma said. She'd never called me anything so sweet before.

"I'm fine," I said, which wasn't true at all. I felt awful. "When can I get out of here?"

"You'll have to stay in the hospital for a few weeks, Margaret, because you've got a bad break," Aunt Marg said, squeezing my hand. They both had tears in their eyes.

"A few weeks! I'll miss school!" Raising myself shakily on one elbow I threw back the bedsheet. What I saw nearly gave me a conniption. My right leg was in plaster of Paris right up to my hipbone. "Oh, my gosh! How long will I be in this thing?" I fell back, dizzy, on the pillow.

Just then a woman came through the door wearing a white coat and a stethoscope around her neck. "I think I can answer that," she said, smiling. "I'm Dr. McIntyre. That 'thing' will be part and parcel of you for the next six weeks."

"Six weeks! Oh, no! I've got a horse to take care of."

"A horse!" The doctor laughed out loud and the gold filling in her front tooth glittered in the light of my bedlamp. "I've heard of some fancy excuses for getting out of the hospital in a hurry, but that one takes the cake."

"Margaret lives on a farm," Aunt Marg explained, "and our big Clydesdale is her responsibility."

"I see." Doctor McIntyre was examining the blue toes sticking out of the white cast. "Well, you could leave the hospital in about three weeks, but you'll need to come back regularly for X-rays. And of course, once the cast is off we'll have to remove the stitches."

"Stitches? How many?" This was getting interesting.

"Oh, about twenty," the doctor said as she continued her scrutiny of a set of toes that seemed oddly detached from my body. "Is there somewhere she could stay here in the city?" She directed this question to Aunt Marg.

"Well, for mercy sakes, yes! She'll be coming home with her pa and me." Ma's face got red with vexation. "You'll like that, won't you, Peggy? You'll get close to your brothers and sisters again."

It had been a long time since I'd been home, and I was torn between needing to get back to Green Meadows and wanting to see the new house on Rose Avenue. But the hurt look in my mother's eyes made up my mind for me. "That'll be swell, Ma. I can hardly wait to see everybody." Then I glanced at Aunt Marg and she nodded her head in approval.

Aunt Marg and Uncle Herb got special permission to visit me early the next morning.

"We'll have to be shoving off, Maggie," Uncle Herb said. "It's started to snow." I turned my stiff neck towards the window. Sure enough, big snowflakes were floating by. "We daren't stay any longer. There's too much work for Matt to do alone."

Matt always saw to our animals when we were away.

"What about Silky?" I suddenly remembered the culprit who had gotten me into this mess. "Maybe we can keep her now that Mabel's gone." Mabel was the mean old mouser who used to wag her tail like a dog. She had died of old age. Ever since she'd been gone, the mousetrap in the pantry had snapped shut regularly. I felt sorry for the tiny brown field mice with their bright beady eyes. I could never bear to watch as Uncle Herb carried their lifeless little bodies out by the tail.

In spite of the trouble she'd caused me I'd taken an instant liking to Silky.

"If no one claims her, she's yours, Margaret," my aunt promised me.

"And you'll take good care of Starr, Uncle Herb? He saved my life, you know."

"I'll treat him like the hero he is, Maggie," promised my dear uncle, giving me a whisker rub on the nose and a goodbye kiss on the forehead.

I cried a bit after they left. Then I was distracted by my breakfast tray. The oatmeal looked lumpy and the toast felt cold, but I suddenly realized that I was famished. The tall dark nurse who had brought it leaned down and cranked up my bed. Then she grabbed me under the armpits and hoisted me into a sitting position.

"Ow!" I couldn't help yelling out from the searing pain that ripped through my leg.

"Sorry, love," the nurse apologized. "I'll bring you something for that."

She brought a big needle and said it was going to hurt. At least she told the truth. It put me right to sleep and when I woke up again there was another kid in the bed next to mine. He was a boy about my own age — thirteen or maybe fourteen — with a bandaged left eye. He reminded me of Matt.

"What's your name?" I asked in a friendly voice.

"None of your beeswax!" he snapped.

"Go jump in the lake!" I snapped back. He wasn't like Matt at all.

In the afternoon a nurse brought me a tattered copy of *Tom Sawyer*. I had read it before but it was such a good story I didn't mind reading it again. Besides, it would have been a lot harder to read if it had been the first time because my spectacles had been broken in the accident and it was hard to see past the crack where Uncle Herb had mended them with mucilage. Pa said he had already ordered me new ones.

That night as the visiting hour approached I kept my eyes glued to the door. I was hoping against hope that Pa would bring my new glasses. But instead it was Elmer who arrived. I didn't really know my big brother very well, so at first we were pretty tongue-tied. Then he handed me a tissue-wrapped parcel. I ripped off the paper and inside was a book called Basic Animal Husbandry.

"Gee, thanks, Elmer!" I cried. "It's a swell present."

He grinned, really pleased with himself. "Uncle Herb told me all about your ambitions to be a veterinarian, so I thought the book would suit you. We must be a lot alike, Peg, because I'm nuts about animals, too."

"Why don't you be a vet, Elmer?"

"Can't." He shrugged his broad shoulders. "I'm not smart enough to go to college. Anyway, I've already quit school. I'm a Simpson's driver now. Didn't Ma tell you?" I shook my head and he went on, "It's a very responsible position. You have to take care of both the horse and the wagon, just as if they were your own."

"It sounds like a nifty job," I said excitedly. "Tell me about your horse."

"His name is Midnight because he's pure black. He's really a beauty. You'd like him, Peg."

"I sure would." Just talking about horses made me miss Starr like the dickens. "Tell me everything."

Elmer and I got on like a house afire. After he left, the night nurse, who was young and pretty like Miss Nesbitt, plumped up my pillow and asked with a twinkle in her eye, "Who's your boyfriend?"

"He's not my boyfriend. He's my big brother," I answered, a bit embarrassed, but proud as Punch.

A few minutes later the boy in the next bed said, "Sorry."

That was all, but I could tell by the tone of his voice that he really meant it, so I closed my book and pulled my glasses down my nose so I could see him above the crack. "You're probably in a lot of pain," I said to help him save face.

"Yeah," he agreed gratefully, his one good eye twinkling. It was pale blue like Matt's.

"How did you hurt your eye?" I asked.

"I fell and poked it with a stick," he replied. "How did you bust your leg?"

"I fell out of a tree trying to rescue a kitten."

We both laughed and then talked non-stop after that until the nurse came in, popped pills into each of our mouths and turned out the lights.

It was three weeks to the day before Doctor McIntyre let me go home. I had learned to walk on crutches in the hospital corridors, so I was dying to show off to my younger brothers and sisters. They hadn't been allowed to visit me in the hospital.

Pa picked me up in the flivver and my right leg took up

the whole back seat. By this time my cast was covered in autographs. All the nurses and doctors and visitors had signed it. Albert Coombs, my roommate, had even written a verse: *XXO and HO, HO, HO, from the crabby guy next door.*

I was going to miss Albert. He had finally lost his eye, so he had to stay in the hospital until the hole healed and he could be fitted with a glass one. I only hoped he got a good match. Boy, was I glad I still had my leg!

Chapter 11

The New House

The new house was gorgeous. The front room had a cornice around the ceiling and a gas fireplace in the wall, and Pa had bought a wine velour chesterfield with two matching chairs. I was to sleep on the chesterfield because Josie or Jenny might kick my cast. That suited me fine because Josie still picked her toes sometimes and it nearly drove me crazy.

Everybody was swell to me. The little kids hung around, fascinated by the hard cast. I let them sign their names on my hip, which was the only space left. Even two-year-old Patsy tried to scribble her name. Then she dragged the hobbyhorse in from the kitchen and rocked beside me, yelling in her squeaky voice, "Giddy-up, Sparky! Giddy-up!"

Ma couldn't get over how much Patsy and I looked alike. We had the same black curly hair and brown freckles and she squinted her dark eyes just the way I do when I'm trying to see without my glasses. "I think she's going to need spectacles, the same as you and your pa," Ma lamented, "and I'm none too fond of spectacles on children." I knew exactly what was coming next. "But they suit you to a T, Peg. I've always maintained that." She did always maintain that, and I hated it. Yet I knew she didn't mean to hurt my feelings. Anyway, the very next night Pa brought home my new glasses.

"Rimless!" I screamed with joy!

"It goes against my grain, youngsters wearing rimless," Pa said stubbornly as he hooked the gold wires behind my ears. Then he stepped back to inspect me through his own thick lenses. "Well, by George, they look fine on you, Peg. Nell, come in here and see what you think of this girl."

Ma came hurrying in from the kitchen, her face as red as her hair. "Oh, my!" she exclaimed. "Why, they're practically invisible. You look lovely, Peg."

"Let me see! Somebody get me a looking glass, quick!"

Harry came running with the mirror from over the kitchen sink. I stared at myself critically. I didn't think I looked lovely, exactly, but it sure was an improvement. "Gee, thanks, Pa. I can see ten times better without rims."

"Not to mention the crack!" Pa grinned and went to wash up for supper.

Ma and Pa were both being extra kind to me. Ma made all my favourite dishes and Pa helped me get used to my crutches. Pretty soon I was swinging my stiff heavy leg up and down the stairs and all over the house.

Pa seemed a lot happier here than he had ever been on Jones Avenue. Every night he went downstairs and started hammering away in his den. We even heard him whistling "There's No Place Like Home" once. He had always been a quiet sort — Elmer called him an introvert — so it was a treat to hear him whistling a happy tune.

The twins Harry and Jenny set the crokinole board up on the kitchen table nearly every night after supper and we had a game or two. Even Olive sat down to talk to me sometimes. Ma always said Olive was the different one in the family. She was a beautiful eighteen-year-old who kept to herself a lot. Ma shook her head over Olive and said she didn't know what to make of her. I liked my big sister once I got to know her. I sensed something was troubling her but didn't dare ask what.

Some of my old friends from Jones Avenue dropped over. Flossie Gilmore, who had been my best friend for years, until I moved to the farm, stopped by one Sunday after church. "I'll bet you won't want to go back to that old farm after living here," she remarked, staring enviously around at our newly furnished parlour.

"Oh, yes I will." I was immediately on the defensive. "I love the farm. And I'll bet my horse Starr is nearly dying of loneliness without me."

"Yes, but you don't even have electricity up there, do you? How can you stand it without electric lights and a radio?"

"We've got a huge oil lamp that throws enough light to blind you," I exaggerated. "And Uncle Herb's got a swell radio. Every Saturday night we listen to *The Saturday Night Hockey Broadcast*."

"How can it work without electricity?" she asked skeptically.

Her smart-alecky questions were beginning to make my neck prickle. "It's a crystal set. It doesn't need electricity. You listen to it through earphones."

"What makes it work?"

"Well, Uncle Herb attached a wire that goes out the window and wraps around a ground rod. It works terrific. Sometimes we even hear Philadelphia and Atlantic City. They're in the United States," I boasted.

"I know my geography," she sniffed. "But it must be an awful nuisance having to take turns with earphones."

"Sometimes we take turns and sometimes we stretch the earphones over both our heads and listen together. That's the most fun of all. Other times, when we've got company, Uncle Herb puts the earphones in Aunt Marg's big glass fruit bowl and it magnifies the sound so we can hear it all over the room. Just the night before I fell out of the tree, Matt and Eva and I listened to *Amos 'n Andy* from the fruit bowl."

"Who are Matt and Eva?" She sounded a bit jealous.

"They're just my very best friends in the entire world, that's who."

After that, she changed the subject to hairstyles and fashions and the latest colours in lip rouge. Flossie knew all about those things and I didn't. Besides, I knew Aunt Marg would never allow me to wear lip rouge, so I wasn't sorry when Flossie said she had to leave.

* * *

The highlights of my days were letters from Four Corners. The latest one was from Aunt Marg.

Green Meadows Farm, November 26, 1927

Hello there, old sweetheart. (The words made my heart go thump.)

You'll never guess what your uncle won at the Four Corners Fiddle Contest. A piglet! The fat little creature was first prize and Herb's rendition of "Turkey in the Straw" put all the other fiddlers to shame. We haven't named our new baby yet, so you'd better put your thinking cap on. (I think I'll name it Flossie, I thought maliciously.)

Your cat Silky is a treat to have around the house, Margaret. She must be yours because nobody's come to claim her. She's so pretty, a real tortoise-shell, and a good mouser too. The trap in the pantry's been empty ever since she came.

By the way, I'm enclosing lessons prepared by Miss Nesbitt. You are to send your work back for her to mark. She says she doesn't want her star pupil to fall behind. (I'd been studying from Olive's old high school books, so there was no fear of that.) *Everybody at Four Corners keeps asking for you. Mr. Hooley sends his regards.* (Whew! What a relief. That meant he hadn't snitched on me.)

I'll sign off now, love, and go let miss miglet out for a frolic. Right now she's penned in the chicken coop until your uncle gets the pigsty finished. He's building it downwind of the henhouse, and a finer pigsty you've never seen. Something tells me we won't be eating pork this winter. Your uncle treats her like a puppy dog. Whoever heard of a pig for a pet, I ask you?

Right now Herb is over at the Muggins' place helping Zach mend their cookhouse roof. So he's not here to add his usual two cents' worth. But I'm sure I don't need to tell you how much he misses his girl. Give our love to

*all the little scallywags — and the big ones too. And
especially to my old sweetheart.*

> *Lovingly, Aunt Marg.*

*P.S. Starr's gone all moody and restless since you left. I
guess he's wondering whatever became of his best pal.
Every time I come into the barn he swings his head
around expecting you. Then he snorts and glowers at me
with those white-fringed orbs of his as if I was a
stranger, for heaven's sake.*

*P.S. 2: Eliza Hicks just dropped in on her way home to
Shelburne. She wanted a bottle of my winter tonic
because her youngest boy, Morry, has the croup and she
wants to ward off bronchitis, or worse, before it takes
hold. She offered me fifty cents for the large bottle but I
said it wasn't for sale. I only hope it works.* (It will, I
thought. After three years of Aunt Marg's winter tonic
— sulphur and molasses and gosh knows what else — I
was living proof that it worked. Ugh!)

*P.S. 3: I might as well enclose this snap of Matt and
Eva while I'm at it. Jessie took it with her new camera.
They're both growing like weeds, those two. I won't be
able to call Eva a little wisp of a thing much longer. She
says to tell you she'll write soon. And Matt says he
wishes you would hurry home.*

> *XXXOOO*
> *A.M.*

It seemed like forever before Matt's wish came true.

Chapter 12

Olive

Sleeping on the chesterfield was becoming more and more difficult every night because my cast wouldn't let me turn over. I was often awake when Ma and Pa thought I was fast asleep. Sometimes I overheard their late night conflabs. It was the only chance they got to talk in private. The rest of the time the house was in such a hubbub, with all us kids, they couldn't get a word in edgewise. That's why Pa gulped down his supper every night and escaped like a grumpy bear to his den. Then Ma would sigh and repeat once again, as if to excuse him, that he wasn't cut out for such a big family.

On this particular night I was wide awake because I was excited about getting my cast off and the stitches out the next day.

That darn cast had been driving me crazy. The hairs on my leg had been shaved off for the operation and were now growing back in. The itching was enough to make a preacher swear, as Uncle Herb would say. Pa had sanded smooth a long thin stick so I could slide it down inside my cast to scratch. I don't know what I would have done without it. I just hoped I hadn't broken any stitches.

I could hear Pa now in the cellar shaking the furnace down. The clinkers clattered noisily through the grates — Ma said it was enough to waken the dead. Then Pa scraped up coal from the bottom of the pile, causing a little avalanche to come rattling down from the top. Three times he shovelled up the coal and threw it into the hungry mouth of the furnace.

Meantime, in the kitchen, Ma had put the kettle on to boil. Then she began slicing toasting bread on the cutting board with *Waste Not, Want Not* carved on it.

Pa came upstairs and they sat at the kitchen table to have their nightly repast while they waited for the coal gas to burn away. Once the blue flames had disappeared and the fire was glowing bright red through the black anthracite, it was safe to check the damper off. Pa was religiously careful about this ritual, because every winter you would read in the paper about a father who had checked the furnace off too soon and the whole family had ended up dead from asphyxiation. But we never had to worry about that.

The smell of the toast made my mouth water. It was all I could do to keep quiet. I didn't dare let on I was awake because I wanted to hear what they were going to talk about. The door was always left ajar so the heat could circulate, and I heard every word without really trying.

This night it was about Olive. She had gone out early to the picture show with Raymond Colbeck, her steady beau. It was now past eleven o'clock and she wasn't home yet.

"I don't like it," grumbled Pa as he crunched his delicious-smelling toast. "She's only seventeen."

"She's eighteen, Will," Ma gently reminded him. "That's the very age I was when we tied the knot."

"It was different then."

"That's what my father said about us," Ma said, slathering crabapple jelly — I could smell it! — on another piece of toast. "You just feel that way because Olive's our first and she's always been your favourite. (I felt a twinge of jealousy. I wished I didn't have that jealous streak in me.) But don't fret yourself, Will. Olive's got a good head on her shoulders and Raymond's a fine boy. She could do a lot worse."

"I had plans for her to go to normal school. Especially since Elmer's dropped out," Pa complained.

"Well" — I heard Ma stacking the dishes in the sink — "it's not as if they were our only children. Surely with a gang like ours one of them will amount to something."

Pa was silent for a moment. Then he said, "Young Harry's sharp as a tack."

"And our Gracie's at the top of her class," put in Ma.

"What about Davey and Bobby and Jenny and Josie?" Pa showed a sudden interest in the whole brood. Generally, he left the children's progress up to Ma.

"They're all doing fine, Will. There's not a one of them below the line."

Then Pa added proudly, "I heard wee Patsy say her ABC's from start to finish without a miss the other day. She's quick as a cricket, that little nipper."

I was listening intently for the mention of *my* name when the front door opened quietly and Olive slipped in. But instead of going straight upstairs as usual, she tiptoed through the dining room into the kitchen. Then darned if she didn't shut the door! I had to sit bolt upright and strain with all my might to hear a word.

"I've got something to tell both of you," Olive said nervously.

"Out with it!" I had no trouble hearing Pa.

"Look at my finger. See, Ma?"

"Oh, my stars, it looks like an engagement ring."

"It is. Ray and I are planning to get married in the spring."

"I forbid it!" roared Pa. "Do you hear me? I forbid it!"

"You can't, Pa!" cried Olive. Now it was easy to hear everybody. "This is a free country, you know!"

"It's free to them that's over twenty-one. And you've got a ways to go yet, my girl. So take that thing off your finger and give it back where it came from. That's an order!"

"I hate you, Pa!" Olive sobbed out the awful words and I could hardly believe my ears.

Suddenly the kitchen door banged open and I was caught craning my neck, eavesdropping. Pa stomped right past me as if I wasn't even there.

Ma shut the kitchen door again and I could hear only murmuring after that.

Upstairs I heard the water closet chain being pulled and water gurgling down the pipes, echoing all over the house. When everything was quiet again, the kitchen light clicked off and Ma and Olive crept through the dark so as not to disturb me.

From then on, the Christmas spirit, which usually ran riot at this time of year in our big family, was dampened by the tension in the house. Ma and Pa tried to hide their feelings for the sake of the little ones, but you could still tell something was wrong. Also, it was my first Christmas at home in ages and they didn't want to spoil that.

Pa set the tree up on Christmas Eve as usual and fastened the Star of Bethlehem, lopsided, on the top. His job done, he quickly disappeared down the cellar stairs.

Then all us kids began decorating the tree, flinging the icicles and garlands on willy-nilly. It was loads of fun, but I couldn't help thinking what Aunt Marg would say. She was so particular — persnickety, Uncle Herb called it — about the trimming of the tree. Hers was always the talk of the whole countryside. Folks would come for miles around to admire it while sipping hot toddys and munching on mincemeat tarts.

By comparison, this tree was a mess. Even the new red glass balls Pa had bought didn't help much. But the thing I missed most were the tiny white candles set so carefully in little tin sockets at the tip of every branch. Aunt Marg would light them one by one and Uncle Herb would blow out the lamps. Then the three of us would snuggle close together on the daybed and gaze as if hypnotized at the flickering pyramid.

"Squint your eyes, Maggie," Uncle Herb always said. I did, and the tiny white flames would merge together like stars shimmering on water.

* * *

I could hardly wait until Christmas morning to open the huge parcel that arrived from Four Corners. The gifts from Aunt Marg and Uncle Herb had been thoughtfully chosen to suit our personalities. Mine was a nifty set of blue denim overalls — or overhauls, as Uncle Herb would call them. Pinned to the wide shoulder strap was a note which read: *These overhauls are guaranteed for climbing trees and such and riding bareback on a horse who misses you so much!*

I went straight upstairs to try them on. They were about two sizes too big (Aunt Marg always bought things too big for growing children), but I was glad of the bagginess because it helped to hide my injured leg. For some reason it seemed to have shrunk while it was in the cast, but Doctor McIntyre had assured me that if I exercised it regularly it would soon be good as new.

On Christmas night Olive slipped out the front door while Pa was down in his den. He came up later, lit the gas fireplace and played a few parlour games with us. If he missed Olive, he never let on. Then Ma lugged all the tired little kids, clutching their new dolls and teddy bears, up to bed and Pa went back down to the cellar.

All of a sudden I took a notion to follow him. I hadn't seen his den yet, because the steep wooden steps had been too hard for me to manoeuvre before my cast came off.

Well! I couldn't get over it — Pa's den, I mean. It looked like a picture in a magazine. It had dark panelled walls, red-shaded lamps and a little potbellied stove to keep it warm.

Pa was sitting hunched in his easy chair, facing the stove. He didn't turn his head, so I knew he hadn't heard me. Over his shoulder I could see that he was holding a silver-framed picture of Olive when she was a baby.

"Pa." I spoke right up so he wouldn't think I was spying. He jerked around, startled, then quickly slapped the picture face down on a little side table.

"What're you doing down here, Peg?" he asked in a grouchy voice.

"I just came to see your den," I answered innocently.

He brightened up then and began showing it off. "This here wall is going to be all bookshelves. And this spot in the corner is for my radio. And I'm thinking of having that other old easy chair recovered for your ma. Well, how do you like it so far?"

"I think it's swell, Pa," I said, and I really meant it. "It's like a different world down here."

"That's why I like it," he asserted.

"Pa . . ." I dared pick up the picture and turn it over.

Scowling, he knelt down and began feeding the fire from a little black coal skuttle beside the stove. "Pa . . ."

He left the small iron door open and the orange flames danced and crackled cosily.

"Well?" His voice had become suddenly surly.

I was starting to lose my nerve, so I blurted out,

"Did you ever stop to think she's a lot like you, Pa?"

"Who?" he snapped, as if he didn't know.

"Olive."

"She looks like her mother."

"I know she *looks* like Ma. But in her ways she's more like you, Pa. It's the same as you and me. I *look* like you — everybody says so — but Aunt Marg always says I'm my ma all over again."

His forehead creased in a frown. "Your ma says what she thinks and hang the consequences," he admitted.

"I know," I said.

He sat down with a sigh, which was more like a grunt, and reached for the photograph. "In what way is this one like me?" He traced the baby face with half a finger. He'd lost the other half in the Great War.

"Promise you won't get mad if I tell you?"

"No, I won't get mad."

"Well, she's stubborn like you, Pa. And she needs to be alone a lot. That's why she won't share her bedroom, no matter what. And she keeps her feelings all bottled up inside, same as you. Elmer says you're a couple of introverts."

"He does, does he?"

Uh-oh. I hoped I hadn't got Elmer into hot water. Then, to my relief, a slow smile began to spread across Pa's face. "Introverts, are we?" he murmured thoughtfully. "'Ornery' might be a better word."

"Well, maybe a bit ornery — but not mean. Aunt Marg says there's a world of difference."

"Your Aunt Marg's quite a woman," Pa said, setting the picture upright on the table, "and so's your ma. And as for you, young lady" — he took hold of my chin and we stared at each other through our thick lenses — "your Uncle Herb's right about one thing. You're a corker if there ever was one."

Just then we heard voices from upstairs. Olive had come home and she and Ma were talking. Slipping my hand into Pa's, I said, "Let's go up."

Olive and Ma both looked shocked when we appeared in the cellar doorway. Ma shot me a quick, questioning glance. Olive looked straight at Pa.

Suddenly she leapt the space between them and threw her arms around his neck. "It's okay, Pa," she cried in a tremulous voice. "I gave the ring back, see!" She held out her bare left hand and wiggled her fingers.

"You didn't need to do that for me, daughter." Poor Pa sounded all choked up. "You were dead to rights. It's a free country and you're old enough to make up your own mind."

"But that's exactly what I did, Pa." Olive laughed triumphantly. "I gave Raymond Colbeck his ring back tonight because he said that once we were married he'd be the boss. And I just told him I'm my father's daughter and nobody's going to boss me. So there!"

"See, Pa? I told you! I told you!" I was proud as Punch with myself.

"Like I said before, Peggy, you're a corker." Then, turning to Ma, he said, "C'mon, Nell. Don't just stand there gawping. Let's have some tea and Christmas cake to celebrate."

Chapter 13

Back to Green Meadows

In the afternoon on New Year's Day, Ma and I were alone in the house. Well, not exactly. Little Patsy was upstairs in her cot having her afternoon nap. Ma was in the kitchen baking about a dozen raisin pies and I was at the dining room table doing some lessons Miss Nesbitt had sent me.

The older kids had all gone bobsledding with their friends on the Riverdale slides and Pa had taken the little ones ice-skating on the corner rink.

Suddenly the telephone rang and Ma and I nearly jumped out of our skins. It was still hard for me to realize that every time it rang it was for us.

"You get it, Peg," Ma said from the doorway. "My hands are all over dough."

The phone was a newfangled black handset. A cradle phone, it was called. It sat on a wicker table in the dining room. The mouthpiece and earpiece were combined all in one and I was never sure which end to talk into.

"Hello!" I said, hoping I'd picked the right end.

"Happy New Year, old sweetheart!" Aunt Marg's voice came in as clear as if she was right next door.

Suddenly, without a speck of warning, I burst into tears and the words leapt right out of my mouth: "I want to come home!"

When I saw my mother staring at me with shocked green eyes, her sticky hands held high in surprise, I dropped the handset with a clatter and ran up the stairs as fast as my bad leg would let me. Jumping into Josie and Jenny's bed, I burrowed under the counterpane and bawled my head off.

When I was all cried out, I felt sick with shame. Poor Ma. What would she think? I decided I'd better get up quick and go downstairs to explain, or try to. I threw back the cover, and there was my mother standing quietly in the doorway. She was rubbing her hands nervously together, scattering little doughballs on the linoleum.

"Why didn't you tell us you wanted to go," she said in a hurt tone. "Your pa and I would have sent you."

"I don't know what came over me, Ma. It was hearing Aunt Marg's voice, I guess. I do that on the farm sometimes too. Like when I get a letter from you. Or when I look at the snapshot of our family."

"Well, now" — my words seemed to appease her — "if you're sure it's not because you're unhappy here."

"Oh, no, Ma. Just the opposite. I'm really glad I broke my leg and had to come home. But, you see, there's Starr to worry about. Aunt Marg says he's gone all moody since I left. I'm afraid he might get sick with melancholy. And then there's Aunt Marg and Uncle Herb. They really get down at the mouth when I stay at the Muggins' for even one night. You know, Ma, you and Pa have nine other kids, but they've only got me."

"It's all right, Peg." Ma smiled a little bit sadly. "You don't have to say any more."

"Is Aunt Marg still on the line?"

"No, she rang off. But Herb was there when she called and he said there's been an early thaw and the road to Shelburne is wide open, so we should pack you off before the next snowfall."

"Oh, thank you, Ma!" I jumped up and gave her a big hug. "But what do you think Pa will say?"

She looked perturbed for a second. Then she answered, "We'll tell him Margaret got so lonely she phoned for you to come. And it's not really a lie because I've a notion that's exactly what she had in mind."

Right then and there I got the grip out from under the bed and started packing. I put my new overalls on the bottom and a nice green dress Olive had given me on the top. It was a bit big, so Aunt Marg would have to alter it to make it fit me. Olive insisted that she'd outgrown it, but actually I think she considered it too childish now that she was a woman of the world who had already turned down one proposal of marriage and was off bobsledding with a new fella this very minute.

We had a swell New Year's supper in the dining room. The little kids — Davey and Gracie and Bobby and Patsy — were all perched opposite me on the ironing board set between two chairs. They were being good as gold, not poking at each other like they usually did. I don't think they quite knew what to make of this strange sister who went in and out of their lives so mysteriously. At bedtime I kissed them all goodbye. I would be leaving on the train early in the morning before they woke up.

* * *

"Take care of that leg now, Peg!" Pa shouted above the noise of the shunting engine. Then we both had to smile at the funny little rhyme he'd just made.

"I'll be fine, Pa." The conductor shut the folding gate as the train began to move. Suddenly I leaned over it and yelled at the top of my lungs, "I love you, Pa!"

I don't know whether he heard me or not, but he swung his lunch bucket above his head as the train steamed out of Union Station.

No sooner had we left the city behind than heavy black clouds began to fill the sky. Wind rattled the window panes and snow began to fall. Pretty soon I couldn't see a thing outside for the thick white flakes plastered on the glass. It got dark as night inside the coach and the conductor had to switch the lights on.

It was a cold, damp, gloomy trip and my leg was paining like a toothache. Minutes dragged by like hours. After demolishing the delicious lunch Ma had made me, I started dozing like all my fellow passengers. By the time we pulled into Shelburne station the snowstorm had become a full-blown blizzard, but I wasn't too worried because I knew Aunt Marg had arranged that if I got held up in Shelburne I was to stay with Mr. and Mrs. Rabbit Hare.

Rabbit wasn't his real name. I think it was Roger, or Robert, but everybody called him Rabbit because he could wiggle his nose and ears at the same time. That was his favourite way of entertaining children. It never failed to send us into hysterics. And, of course, his name *was* Hare.

The Hares' yard backed right onto the railway tracks, so they could hear the train whistle plain as day. Mr. Hare was the Shelburne postmaster and he had to collect the mailbag no matter what, so it wouldn't be much trouble for him to collect me too.

But the first person I saw standing on the platform, looking like a red-headed snowman, was my Uncle Herb. I took a flying leap right into his arms and we hugged so long and hard that the snow started melting between us. Then we went into the station house because the wind was howling so furiously that we couldn't hear a word either of us was saying.

Rabbit brought my grip in along with the mailbag. "You'd best plan on staying over with us, Herb," he said, giving his red nose a wiggle and a blow, "because it's bound to get worse afore it gets better."

"Thanks just as much, Rabbit, but Mag's alone and if I know her she'll be fit to be tied if we don't show up."

"Give her a ring on the blower, then, and set her mind at ease," suggested Rabbit.

"That's a good idee," Uncle Herb agreed, and he went into the station master's office to use the telephone. When he came out he looked really worried. "Lines must be down," he said. "I couldn't raise nobody. I tried the Muggins' place too."

"Well, then, let's get going!" I cried impatiently. "Where did you park the pickup?"

"Pickup? No mechanical vehicle could navigate these roads today. No sirree! I brung Starr and the cutter."

"Starr! You brought Starr! Why didn't you say so? Where is he?" I began to jump up and down like a kid.

"He's out back. So let's get a move on, Maggie, before he gets snowed under. I brought plenty of blankets for him and us, so we should be all right."

Starr stood by the hitching post, his plaid horse blanket already layered with a three-inch snowdrift. Whooping with joy, I screamed his name and threw my arms around his steaming muzzle. His long white eyelashes, spiked with icicles, blinked at me in amazement. Then he threw up his head like a frisky colt and whinnied louder than the wind.

"Up you get, Maggie," urged Uncle Herb, tossing my grip in the back. "There'll be plenty of time for carrying on once we're safe at home."

When we were wrapped in blankets up to our eyes, Uncle Herb grasped the reins and hollered, "Gee up there, Starr!"

I yelled, "Attaboy!" and my wonderful, gallant Clydesdale took off in a shower of snow.

We were halfway home when it happened. Right out of nowhere a red fox streaked across our path. Rearing with fright, Starr plunged sideways and immediately sank to his knees in the ditch. Uncle Herb leapt down from the seat and worked his way along the shafts to the horse's head. Tugging hard at the halter, he yelled, "Get up, Starr! Dagnab it, get up!"

Starr tried. Oh, how he tried! He heaved and strained, his mane tossing and pitching, his whinny as wild as the storm itself. But the sleigh wouldn't budge. Again he began the awful struggle. I was afraid his heart would burst, so I jumped down and, to my surprise, found that the icy crust was strong enough to bear my weight. I clung to the shafts and slid along to his head. Because I was on top of the drift and he was sunken into it, our eyes were on a level.

He gazed at me helplessly through thick, snow-laden lashes and gave a mournful sigh. I knew he was trying to tell me that he was sorry, but he just couldn't go on. Then he lowered his head and buried his snout in my arms. Holding him tight I spoke right into his ear. "Listen, Starr," I said, "it's me, Margaret. Listen hard because this might be our last chance." Then I staggered backwards against the wind until I was in the middle of the road. Cupping my mouth between my snow-clogged mittens, I blew with all my might.

The secret signal seemed to fill the stallion with a sudden miraculous power. With a wild, frightful whinny, he reared up on his hind legs and plunged desperately forward. Uncle Herb and I had to leap for our lives as the huge horse tore himself out of the gully, dragging the cutter behind him.

"Good boy, Starr!" we both yelled at once as we clambered up onto the icy wooden seat.

Flapping the frozen reins, Uncle Herb hollered, "Gee up there, fella!" and I screamed, "Home, boy!" As if he needed to be told.

* * *

Aunt Marg was standing in the doorway, heedless of the bitter cold, her arms outstretched. I threw myself into them and we hugged and kissed until she begged for mercy. Then Silky, who recognized me instantly, leapt from the woodpile onto my shoulder and wrapped herself around my neck like a furry purring collar.

Over steaming bowls of meaty broth, Uncle Herb and I

told Aunt Marg all about our horrendous journey.

"Starr is an honest-to-goodness hero, Aunt Marg. He actually saved our lives, didn't he, Uncle Herb?"

"He did that, Maggie," he said, sopping up gravy with his bread. "No doubt about it."

After supper I insisted I *had* to go to the barn. "Let your uncle take care of Starr tonight," pleaded Aunt Marg. "You can see him first thing in the morning."

"No," I said. "He'll be expecting me."

She sighed resignedly and off I went to spend the rest of the evening rubbing the tired horse down with warm flannels. All the while I worked, we talked to each other. Everything I said, he answered in soft neighing sounds.

When I was finally finished, his coat shone like a polished chestnut and my arms were nearly dropping off. The last thing I did was spread a thick bed of fresh straw all over the floor of his stall.

"It's time to turn in, Maggie." Uncle Herb had appeared at the stable door with the big lantern gleaming in his hand.

I turned to Starr and he batted his long white lashes at me. "See you tomorrow, boy," I said, and I kissed him goodnight on his hairy velvet muzzle.

The farm kitchen seemed like the most heavenly place to be. The three of us sat around the big black cookstove sipping hot cocoa, but not talking much because we were all so tired. Silky perched on my shoulder, scratching my cheek with her pink tongue. Pretty soon I began to yawn uncontrollably and my eyelids just wouldn't stay up. Aunt Marg said, "It's off to bed with you, old sweetheart."

Boy, it was good to be in my feather bed again! Every bone in my body ached, especially my broken leg. Snuggling under the patchwork quilts, I curled my toes around the earthenware pig that Aunt Marg had filled with hot water.

The wind howled down the chimney pipe that ran through my room and I could hear the stove lids dancing in the kitchen. I scrunched down deeper like a hibernating hedgehog and just had time before I fell asleep to thank God for teaching me the secret signal.

Chapter 14

Just Like Old Times

The next morning I woke with a cough, so Aunt Marg installed me on the daybed by the stove and covered me with afghans. "Just to be on the safe side," she said, "you're not to put your nose outside the door today." Then she served me breakfast on a tray — coddled eggs and over-the-fire toast (a hundred times better than any old electric toaster could make) smothered with country butter and gooseberry jam.

"Why don't you write a letter home to keep yourself occupied?" suggested Aunt Marg as she plumped up my pillows and felt my forehead for the umpteenth time. "You can't ring Matt and Eva because the lines are still down."

"That's a swell idea," I agreed, and she brought me a writing tablet and a pencil so I wouldn't slop ink on the daybed.

I wrote the family an open letter, using my breakfast tray for a desk. I told them the whole story, not leaving out one lurid detail. It took twelve pages, back and front, to get it all down.

The next day my cough was still sort of hacky and Aunt Marg started worrying that I might catch pneumonia. To ward off the dreaded illness, she rubbed my chest with goose grease and made me drink pots and pots of yara tea. Then she pulverized a chunk of camphor with a mallet, wrapped it in a scrap of sugar bag and tied it around my neck with a string.

When Uncle Herb came in for his noonday meal, he began sniffing around like a dog and his nose led him straight to me. "Whoo-eee!" he cried, burying his face in his hanky. "There must be a dead polecat around here somewheres."

Well, I let him get away with that because all I wanted to hear about was Starr. "He's strong as a horse, Maggie. Stop your fretting. He'll keep till tomorrow."

As soon as he finished eating, he went out again to help clear the roads. After he left, I decided to get back at him by playing one of my tricks. I didn't do that so much anymore now that I was thirteen.

Aunt Marg had Uncle Herb's hand-knitted work socks drying in the oven with the door open so they wouldn't scorch. I offered to fold them for her.

"That'll be grand, Margaret, if you're sure you feel up to it," she said as she carried a pile of mending into the back room where she kept her treadle sewing machine.

That was my chance. As the socks dried, I snatched them hot from the oven and began folding them into balls. But instead of matching them, as I was supposed to do, I hid a red sock inside a green one, a blue sock inside a yellow one and a grey one inside a brown cable-stitch. Then I quickly took them upstairs and stacked them neatly in Uncle Herb's stocking drawer.

That afternoon the phone lines were back in operation and I got through to Matt and Eva. We talked so long, squealing and laughing with excitement, that Central finally had to break in and order us to hang up because she was getting complaints right, left and centre.

The next morning I felt fine and was all set for school, but it turned out the school was still closed because the roads were fence-deep in drifts.

After the morning milking, Uncle Herb came in and did his ablutions, as he sometimes called washing himself. Then he sat down to breakfast.

"I'm fairly famished, Mag," he declared, tucking his checkered table napkin under his stubbly chin. "If I had some ham I'd have ham and eggs. If I had some eggs." Aunt Marg just raised her reddish eyebrows at his tired old joke and piled his plate full of sizzling ham and eggs. After making a "Scotch plate" with a thick heel of fresh bread, he hitched his chair up to the stove to enjoy his tea.

"Ahhh!" he sighed contentedly as he supped from his saucer, his stockinged feet crossed comfortably on the oven door.

Suddenly Aunt Marg cried, "Herbert Alfred Wilkinson! Have you all at once gone colour blind?" She wasn't fooling either, because the brilliant sun reflecting off the pure white snow can do that to a person.

Startled by her peculiar question, Uncle Herb let his chair tip forward, slopping his tea, and stared where she was pointing.

"What in the cock-eyed world!" he exclaimed, scratching his fuzzy red head as he gazed at his mismatched feet.

It had been a long time since I'd played a childish trick on him, so at first he didn't catch on. Then I went and gave myself away by snickering.

"Why, you corker, Maggie!" he exploded. "You genuine eighteen-karat-gold corker!"

"I thought I was a polecat," I said, smart-alecky.

"That, too," he grinned.

"You're a pair of corkers, if you ask me," Aunt Marg joined in. "You're both tarred with the same brush."

"Oh, boy!" I cried, flinging my arms around first one and then the other. "This is just like old times!" I was incredibly happy.

* * *

The next morning I finally got to the barn.

"Bundle up good, Margaret," Aunt Marg warned. "With your bronchial weakness you can't be too careful."

"I've already got two pairs of long drawers underneath my overalls," I assured her, "and the camphor bag still makes me stink like a polecat. And I've got so many sweaters on that I can hardly button up my coat."

"Good!" she said.

I laced my snowshoes over my galoshes and headed out the woodshed door. But I didn't need my snowshoes after all, because Uncle Herb had cut a narrow path from the house to the barn. It was so straight it looked like a giant brick of vanilla ice cream sliced in half lengthwise. And it was so high on both sides, I couldn't see over the top.

When Starr and I saw each other, we just about went crazy. At first he seemed perfectly normal, nickering and nipping and nuzzling my pockets for treats. But when I stretched my arms around him and leaned my head against his broad chest, I thought I heard a wheezy sound inside. So I pushed back my toque and pressed my ear flat against his breastbone.

"Shh!" I said, and he stood perfectly still.

Yep, I thought. I hear a funny rattle in there.

Aunt Marg was in the barn, clucking to her ladies. She always brought them inside in wintertime because they laid more eggs when they were kept warm. I hollered for her to come quick.

"What is it, Margaret?" She hustled to the door that connected the barn to the stable and set her egg basket down.

"Listen to his chest," I said anxiously.

She pressed a practiced ear against him and listened intently. "I don't hear anything amiss," she said.

"Oh, thank goodness!" I sighed with relief. "I guess I must have imagined it."

But just the same I was glad Uncle Herb had decided not to take Starr out to help with the snow ploughing. Matt's horse, Bill, got the job of ploughing our road. It would probably take him twice as long, because Bill wasn't half as strong as Starr. Of course, he wasn't a Clydesdale either.

On Sunday, the Muggins family skied over unexpectedly and I was so excited that I forgot all about Starr that day. Aunt Marg was right. Both Matt and Eva had shot up like weeds. I was still taller than Eva, but Matt could look down on both of us.

Not seeing Matt for months and then suddenly being together again gave me a funny turn. He seemed to have changed a lot. His pale blue eyes were darker now, and his fair hair, which used to be as light as glass, had grown browner and thicker. His skin was darker, too, and his voice had changed. It cracked nearly every time he spoke. I also noticed a thin red cut on his chin.

"How'd you cut yourself?" I asked.

"Shaving," he answered, as if it was the most natural thing in the world.

"Hmph!" sniffed his mother. "Serves you right. You're much too young to be shaving, let alone with your father's razor knife."

"Your mother's dead to rights," agreed Mr. Muggins cheerfully. "You should have a knife of your own. I don't hold with nobody sharing my razor. Not even my own son."

We all laughed, except Mrs. Muggins, who pretended to be mad. And Matt, the silly article, puffed up his chest as proud as a peacock.

"I think my brother's handsome, don't you, Marg?" Eva got the chance to ask me this when I took her up to my bedroom to show off the stitch marks on my right leg.

"Do you think this leg's skinnier than the other one?" I ignored her question on purpose.

"Just a bit. Not enough to worry about," she assured me, and switched the subject back to Matt. "I hope you two get married soon so you'll be my sister, Marg. I've always wanted a sister. And just imagine, I'll be your children's aunt."

"*Eva!*" I rolled the leg of my drawers down and tucked it into my ribbed stocking. Then I pulled my overalls back on. "I'm only thirteen and a half for gosh sakes. I've got to go to school for at least ten more years to be a veterinarian. I probably won't get married until I'm thirty."

"Soup's on!" Aunt Marg called up the stairwell. Boy, was I glad of the interruption.

But when we came downstairs, Aunt Marg sent me straight back up again. "You're not sitting down at my table smelling like that!" she declared, wrinkling her noise.

"Well, I told you I needed a change of overalls!" I was so embarrassed I took the nerve to sauce her back.

"Don't be cheeky, Margaret!" my aunt chided me.

"The girl's right, Mag." Uncle Herb jumped to my defence. "It's doggone near impossible to smell like a rose after mucking out a horse's stall in your overhauls."

"A dress will do nicely," Aunt Marg asserted. So I went up and changed into my oldest, ugliest dress.

Anyhow, we had a swell visit with the Muggins, though they had to leave early because more storm warnings were coming in over the wireless.

At bedtime I asked Aunt Marg if Silky could sleep with me, and to my surprise she said yes. I was getting more and more fond of the cat. Of course I'd always love Starr best, but one thing a cat could do that a horse couldn't was sleep at the foot of your bed.

That night I dreamed I sneaked Starr into my room and my cot crashed through the floor when he lay on it and we all landed in a screaming heap in the kitchen.

By Monday morning I was fairly chomping at the bit — Uncle Herb's expression — to get back to school. But the weather stayed so foul that Central telephoned every house on the party line and announced importantly that classes had been cancelled again.

After I'd helped Aunt Marg with washing up and making beds and cleaning lamp chimneys — boring stuff like that — I was excused to go to the barn.

Chapter 15

Starr's Down!

I hadn't done more than glance at the new piglet. I didn't really want to get to know her personally because I was pretty sure she would be pork chops in the spring. Still, it seemed mean to ignore her altogether. After all, it wasn't her fault she didn't give milk or draw a hay wagon. So I decided to visit her today.

Even though the weather wasn't as cold as the day of the big storm, freezing sleet still blew across the pasture, icing up my spectacles. Inside the barn I took them off, huffed on them to melt the ice and wiped them with my hanky.

As I passed Starr's stall on the way to the pigpen I noticed that his head was down and he didn't fling it up to greet me. So I went in beside him, rubbing my hand along his flanks and up his withers to his head. He didn't make a sound and his skin trembled under my fingers. When I tried to lift his head he resisted, his eyelids drooping dejectedly.

"What's the matter, boy?" A wave of apprehension washed over me. I cupped my hand around his muzzle. It was hot and dry. "Don't you feel so good?" He didn't answer, so I lifted his long white lashes between my thumb and finger and peered into his big dark eyes. They looked sort of glazed and there was no lively sparkle at the sight of me.

"Maybe you need a drink," I said. "I'll bet that uncle of mine forgot to fill your trough." I ran to the barrel and fetched him a pail of water. Usually he drank about ten gallons all at once, but this time he just took a couple of shallow slurps.

"Maybe you're hungry then." I brought him a fresh bucket of oats, but he just blew them around with his nostrils and turned his head away.

All this time he hadn't made a sound: not a neigh or a snort or a snuffle.

"What is it, boy?" I pleaded, fear clutching at my heart.

In answer he rested his heavy head on my shoulder and gave a shuddering sigh. I hurried back to the house to tell Aunt Marg.

"Is he taking water?" she asked anxiously.

"Yes . . . some."

"Well, that's a good sign. We'll make him his favourite dish — molasses and oats cooked together. That ought to tempt his finicky appetite. Then if you're still worried, Margaret, I'll come down and have another look at him."

She cooked up a huge cauldron of the sticky mixture on the kitchen range. When it was done to a golden turn it smelled good enough to eat.

After it was cool and crumbly I carried a basinful (covered in oilcloth to keep it dry) down to the stable.

"Here, boy, try this. It's just like crackly corn."

Scooping it up with both hands, I held it right under his nose.

Parting his soft lips slightly, he took a nibble, as if to try to please me. Then he turned away and hid his head in the corner of the stall. Suddenly, without warning, he sank to his knees. I dropped the basin and flattened myself against the boards just as he rolled on his side with a whistling groan.

"Starr! *Starr!*" Kneeling beside his head, I began stroking his nose and caressing his ears and calling his name over and over. But he didn't seem to hear me. His eyes had gone all hazy, as if he'd left them open and gone to sleep.

My heart pounding now, I stared at his midsection. It heaved slowly up and down. At least he was alive, but I also knew he was in trouble. I stepped carefully over the sprawled legs that took up all the space in the stall and ran like the wind to the house, screaming at the top of my lungs.

I nearly scared Aunt Marg to death. "Mercy, Margaret, what's got into you?" she cried.

"It's Starr! He's down and he can't get up!" Without another word she threw on her coat and we raced down the path together.

First she lifted his eyelids, which were closed now as if he were sleeping. Then she grasped his muzzle in both hands and pried his teeth apart to examine his throat. This would be a good chance to brush his teeth, I thought. How could I think such a stupid thing at a time like this? I must be going crazy.

"I'm pretty sure it's pneumonia," Aunt Marg said gravely. "Get all the blankets you can find, Margaret, and cover him up. Then start bathing his head with cool water. We've got to get his fever down. I'll go and telephone the vet, then I'll be right back."

I tucked horse blankets and a canvas tarpaulin all around his shivering body and sat in the straw, somehow managing to lift his hundred-pound head onto my lap. The tawny forelock that hung down between his closed eyes was wet with perspiration and his quivering nostrils were hot and running. I talked to him soothingly as I bathed him.

It was at least another half-hour before the vet arrived with Uncle Herb. My weak leg was paining something awful under the huge head, but I didn't budge. I just kept on bathing and commiserating.

Doctor Wiley lifted the blankets and knelt between the horse's legs. He put his stethoscope to the big brown chest and listened carefully. Then he peered into both eyes, as Aunt Marg and I had done.

"We need steam in here, Herb. Can you manage that?"

"I'll set up the coal-oil stove," Uncle Herb said.

Aunt Marg hurried to the house and returned with her large preserving kettle. Soon steam began to swirl all around the stable.

* * *

Doctor Wiley came twice a day for a week and treated Starr with Doctor Bell's Patent Horse Medicine, but it didn't seem to be doing any good. Starr just lay there, getting weaker and thinner by the day. And his breathing became more and more laboured.

On the seventh day, the doctor took Uncle Herb aside

and whispered something to him. Then they both looked strangely at me with a pained expression in their eyes. Suddenly I knew what the doctor had suggested.

"No!" I screamed, tightening my hold on the horse's motionless head. "You can't put him down. I won't let you. I'm not leaving him for a single second, so you'll have to shoot me first!"

Uncle Herb came and knelt down beside me. "He's suffering, Maggie," he said.

I looked at him reproachfully. "He saved our lives, you know," I reminded him.

"All right, girl." He sighed and laid his hand gently on my head. "You win. We'll give him a little more time."

Of course, I blamed myself for Starr's illness. "If only I hadn't been such a baby, begging to come home," I wailed helplessly, "then he never would have been out in that terrible storm and none of this would have happened."

"What's done is done, Margaret. And it won't help Starr if you wear yourself out tending him. Go to bed now and let your uncle and me take over."

"No!" I yelled stubbornly.

"Yes!" She used her no-nonsense voice and I knew I had no choice.

"I'm going," I said glumly from the bottom stairwell step, "but I won't sleep a wink." Strangely, the instant I laid my head on the feather pillow I went out like a lamp and slept like a log until morning.

I wanted to go straight to the barn, but Aunt Marg insisted that I take time to eat a good breakfast. "You need to be well fortified," she stated firmly.

Once I started eating, I discovered I was starving, so I

had a second bowl of oatmeal. "Aunt Marg," I said as I scraped the bowl clean, "if I had pneumonia, what medicine would you give me?"

She went into the pantry and came back with a bottle of dark green liquid with a cork stopper in it. "This is my grandma's secret recipe for lung fever, Margaret. It's made from a dozen roots and herbs. When all else fails I still use it. It's been credited with saving many a life."

"What else would you do?"

"The same as we're doing for Starr. Keep you warm, with plenty of steam in the room. I'd probably add a few teaspoons of Friar's Balsam in the water to mix with the steam. It helps open up the passages."

"Can I have this medicine for Starr?"

She looked doubtful at first, then she shrugged her shoulders. "It's worth a try," she said. "Dr. Bell's Patent Medicine doesn't seem to be working."

It took both of us to get the thick, syrupy liquid down Starr's throat. Aunt Marg held his mouth open while I poured the whole bottle down his gullet through a funnel. Aunt Marg massaged his throat to make him swallow. Next I dumped half a bottle of Friar's Balsam into the big iron pot boiling on the coal-oil stove.

At about ten o'clock that night, Aunt Marg came with the lantern and begged me to come in and go to bed. "No," I said. And this time she gave in after I promised her I'd come for her if there was any change. Then I bedded down in the straw beside Starr and fell asleep with my hand resting on his nose.

The next morning I woke to a faint nickering sound and soft lips nipping at my hair. "Starr?" Hope sprang into my heart for the first time in days. "Starr?"

He raised his head and snorted. Then he began to struggle, his hairy hoofs thrashing in the straw. I leapt to my feet and clambered up the boards out of harm's way.

He was on his knees now, his huge body swaying drunkenly.

"Attaboy!" I yelled encouragement. "Up, Starr, up! You can do it!"

Suddenly the muscles tensed over his rib cage and with a mighty effort he rose up on all fours.

Screaming like a banshee, I ran pell-mell up the slippery path. "He's up! He's up!" I practically fell into the kitchen.

Aunt Marg and Uncle Herb both leapt to their feet and ran with me to the stable. And there he was, my brave stallion — large as life, his legs wobbling under him, but definitely up.

"By George, Maggie, you did it!" Uncle Herb rubbed Starr's matted coat excitedly. "You're a born horse doctor if there ever was one. Just wait until Jim Wiley hears about this. He was sure this fella was a goner."

Starr whinnied weakly, as if to prove the doctor wrong.

"The Lord works in strange ways," murmured Aunt Marg, combing her fingers gently through the horse's tangled mane. Then she put her arm around my shoulder. "You're as stubborn as a mule, old sweetheart, but your uncle is right. You're a born veterinarian."

Leaning my head on Starr's chest, I heard his big heart thudding in my ear. Then, for no reason at all, I began to cry.

Chapter 16

Back to School

"Hurry up, Uncle Herb. I'll be late for school!"

"Late, my eye," burbled Uncle Herb, his face almost submerged in the basin of rainwater on the washbench.

"He'd sluice that whiskery physiognomy till the cows came home if we'd let him," joked Aunt Marg, dishing up the porridge.

Uncle Herb grinned his gap-toothed grin and rubbed his dripping red face on the drying flannel.

"Humbug!" came his muffled voice from the towel. "A man ain't got no rights around here with all you bossy womenfolk."

"That's right! And don't you forget it!" I agreed, pouring his cold water into the slop pail and refilling the basin with warm water from the cistern. Aunt Marg would only allow a slop pail in the kitchen in wintertime. She said the scummy thing was a disgrace and a slipshod way of keeping house.

Because my leg wasn't strong enough yet to snowshoe or

ski to school, Matt and Eva came to fetch me in the sleigh drawn by old Bill.

Miss Nesbitt and I were so glad to see each other that we hugged and kissed. I never thought I'd live to see the day I'd kiss a teacher.

"Well, Margaret Rose" — she was the only person who ever called me by both my names, and they sounded nice coming from her — "it's such a treat to have you back."

Like Matt and Eva, Miss Nesbitt had changed in the months I'd been away. She looked more grown and womanly in her starched white blouse and plain black skirt. And now she wore her hair pinned up in a shiny brown whorl on top of her head. She used to let it hang loose like Josie's.

"My, how you've grown, Margaret," she said as I took my old familiar seat on the front bench.

"You too, Miss Nesbitt," I answered.

"Well, now, we'll get the rest started on their daily work and then I'll give you a few tests to see where you fit in after such a long absence."

I really enjoyed the test papers. She gave me one a day for a week. I found them quite easy because I had faithfully done the lessons she'd sent me while I was recuperating at home. On top of that, I'd learned a lot from Olive's middle-school books. It was only in the last two weeks I'd neglected my studies to take care of Starr. So I wasn't too surprised when Miss Nesbitt told me that I had done really well, but I *was* surprised when she said my work proved that I was ready to skip into first form high school.

"Oh, good," I said, "because I'm in a hurry to get through school so I can start my veterinary practice."

Miss Nesbitt laughed and said, "Well, you'll have to work like a Trojan, Margaret, since half the year's gone by already. But I'm sure you can do it if you put your mind to it."

All the kids seemed glad to have me back except fat-faced Myrtle Robinson. At recess she said sarcastically, "Look who's here! Miss Gimpy, the teacher's pet." Then she nearly split her sides at her own joke and her dimples, which I used to envy, looked like knotholes in her moony face.

"Why don't you stick your head in the rain barrel?" Eva snapped before I had a chance to stand up for myself. Eva had the nerve of a canal horse now that she had a big brother.

"What the heck does gimpy mean?" It made me mad that Myrtle used a word I didn't know, because I was a lot smarter than she was.

"It means somebody who limps, Marg. She calls poor little Sidney Sawyer that all the time because of his polio leg."

"The stupid imbecile," I said, shooting one of my black-eyed looks at Myrtle through my thick spectacles. That was one advantage of thick glasses: they magnified your eyes and made them look twice as fierce as normal.

"Anyway, Doctor Tom said I'd better stop favouring my right leg or I *will* end up with a limp, so if you see me doing it, Eva, be sure to tell me."

"I will," she promised.

Every night I did homework at the kitchen table while Aunt Marg wrote in her journal. She was on the fourth thick volume and it was chock full of country news and daily doings. That might not sound very interesting, but

Aunt Marg had such a lively way of describing things that they seemed to jump right off the page. She could even make the price of butter sound exciting.

Once in a while I had time to listen to the crystal set with Uncle Herb, but not often, with so much extra work. I just hated missing my favourite programs: *Radio Ribs* and *Jimmy and Dad* and *The Saturday Night Hockey Broadcast*. But it would be worth the sacrifice, I thought, if I got to be a vet a whole year earlier.

"I hope you're not straining your eyes in this lamplight, Margaret," worried my aunt. "If you find you've got too much on your plate, catching up so late in the year, don't be afraid to say so."

"Oh, no. It's fine, Aunt Marg. I can read really swell through my rimless."

"I'll see about getting a Coleman," Uncle Herb interjected, glancing up from the *Shelburne News*. "They burn naphtha gas. Just one lamp hung up on the middle rafter there would illuminate this kitchen like the northern lights."

"Are they safe, Herb?" asked Aunt Marg.

"Safe as coal oil, if you know how to handle them," he assured her.

That satisfied Aunt Marg. She had perfect faith in her husband's judgement about such things.

I had to admit to myself, if not to Aunt Marg, that skipping a year did make it really tough going. I tried not to let it show, but Aunt Marg knew just the same. On some flimsy pretext, she'd often clap my books shut and send me on a wild goose chase down to the barn. Her strategy worked like a charm. The pungent smell of musty hay, and just being with the animals — especially Starr — seemed to refresh me like a drink of spring water.

On these trips back and forth from the house to the barn with my galoshes flapping open, I noticed the snow tunnel was gradually melting away.

"It says here in the weather report," remarked Uncle Herb, pointing with his chewed-up straw at the front page of the *Farmers' Journal*, "that this here's the mildest April we've had in nigh on 50 years."

I was sure that was true, because wildflowers were popping up amidst the snow patches all over the hills and fields. And when the first little daffodil unfurled its yellow head in Aunt Marg's front garden, I caught such a bad case of spring fever that the only way I could concentrate on my lessons was to stay after school and ask Miss Nesbitt for help.

* * *

There were rumours buzzing all over the countryside that Miss Nesbitt had a steady beau — a young man from out of town. Almost every Sunday, according to gossip, an unknown bay horse was tied up in front of Mrs. Raggett's house, where Miss Nesbitt was boarding. Some said the horse belonged to a teacher called Mr. Knickerbocker who taught several miles away, in another country school.

On Monday mornings, Mrs. Raggett would phone Jessie Muggins and report the news. Then Mrs. Muggins would phone everybody else, starting with Aunt Marg.

"Rachel says they're thinking of tying the knot, come June," she whispered to Aunt Marg.

"Well, there's no use whispering over the blower, Jessie. Don't forget there are nineteen hookups on this party line, so maybe we'd best just button our lips." Aunt Marg laughed as she related the conversation to us. "The minute I said that, I heard about fifteen clicks."

"I don't know how you can stop yourself from being nosy, Aunt Marg," I said. She made it a rule never to pick up the receiver unless it was our ring. "I think I'm going to be just like Mrs. Muggins. It's so much fun. And you hear things you'd never read in the papers. That's what Mrs. Muggins says."

"But most of it is downright gossip, Margaret, and I've never heard a word of gossip that did anybody any good."

"Still, it's fun," I insisted.

Then it happened! On the last day of June, Miss Nesbitt eloped with the mysterious Mr. Knickerbocker.

"We haven't had an elopement in Four Corners since Bessie Tonks ran off with the tinker!" declared Aunt Marg when Jessie Muggins came over with the news. She had to come over, because the telephone lines were all tied up and she couldn't get through.

"Does that mean she won't be our teacher anymore?" I asked. The news came as a real shock to me.

"I'm afraid so, Margaret," answered Jessie. "Now that she's Mrs. Knickerbocker, she'll be obliged to resign. Married ladies aren't allowed to continue teaching."

"Well, that's not fair!" I said, disgusted.

"It might not be fair, but it's the law, Margaret," Aunt Marg conceded.

"Well, whoever that feller was that said the law is a ass was dead to rights," asserted Uncle Herb.

"Herbert, watch your language!" Aunt Marg said.

"I don't know what I'll do without Miss Nesbitt," I

mourned. I gave my teacher most of the credit for helping me pass into second form with honours.

"Oh, you'll do fine, Maggie," Uncle Herb assured me. "There're no flies on you. Next thing we know you'll be off to Shelburne Continuation School. And after that comes veterinary college."

"I don't want to hear another word about our Margaret going anyplace," Aunt Marg interrupted in an agitated voice. "We'll cross that bridge when we come to it."

"I'm glad I've got another year at Four Corners School. The kids who are going on have to board in Shelburne and only get home on weekends. In the wintertime, when the roads are bad, they might not get home for a month. I don't much like the idea of boarding."

"Well, don't think about it right now, old sweetheart. Sufficient unto the day, I always say."

A week later, I got a beautiful postcard from Miss Nebitt.

Dear Margaret Rose,

I'm so sorry I had to leave without saying goodbye, but that's the way Mr. Knickerbocker wanted it — no fuss or bother. Anyway, we're having a lovely honeymoon. I'll write you a proper letter once we get settled in Ottawa. My husband (oh my, I wonder if I'll ever get used to that word?) has been offered a principalship there. I know you'll do well with your new teacher, whoever she might be, because you're the kind of girl who's bound to succeed, come what may. Good luck for the coming year, Margaret Rose.

Your loving ex-teacher,
Mary Knickerbocker.

Knickerbocker! What a name for Miss Nesbitt to have to lug around for the rest of her life!

* * *

After that, the summer months rolled by so quickly that I had no time to worry about teachers, or continuation school, or boarding.

In July, the Muggins family went down east by train to visit Mr. Muggins' sister, and that meant Uncle Herb, Aunt Marg and I were run off our feet taking care of both farms for a whole month. Then in August I went home to spend some time with my other family on Rose Avenue.

Pa took us everywhere. One day we went across Lake Ontario to Port Dalhousie on a big boat called *The Northumberland*. We were good sailors — all of us, that is, except poor Ma, who turned green as grass and upchucked over the side for the whole trip. She looked so bad, we kids were terrified she was going to die. But Pa, who wasn't even woozy, promised she'd be fine the minute she set foot on dry land. And sure enough, she was.

On the hottest day of the year, we motored all the way to Niagara Falls in the Ford flivver. Packed together like sardines in a can, we nearly suffocated. We were actually steaming by the time we finally slithered out of the automobile. But it was worth all the discomfort. Standing in the cool, cool spray, right at the spot where the water tumbles over the precipice, I felt as though I was being swept away into the billowing mists below.

Later in the month, Aunt Marg and Uncle Herb came down and we all went to the Exhibition together. I got a green Heinz-pickle brooch and two tiny pop bottles to take back home to Matt and Eva. Also, I collected fifteen blotters — five pink, five blue and five white — for the three of us to share.

Before we knew it, it was Labour Day and the beginning of the new school year.

Chapter 17

Changes

I walked to school the first day because the weather was fine and my leg was better now. It only acted up if it rained. When that happened, Aunt Marg made me take a good dose of her rheumatism medicine. It tasted like rat poison, but it worked like a charm.

Matt and Eva were waiting for me at their gate. We'd all been so busy during the summer that we hadn't given a thought to our new teacher, but we had taken it for granted that it would be a woman.

Imagine our surprise when the bell was rung — clanged would be a better word — at the schoolhouse door by a huge man with a big red nose and a bushy brown moustache.

His name turned out to be Elias Edgar Crabb, and it didn't take us long to find out that it suited him to a T. Right off the bat, I got into hot water with him.

"How old are you, Emerson?" he bellowed, even though I was sitting right under his bulgy nose.

"I'm fourteen," I said, the hairs on my neck bristling up.

278

He glanced down at a paper on his desk. "Then you belong in first form, not second." He scratched something out with his pen.

"Oh, no, sir." It seemed like a good idea to call him sir. "Miss Nesbitt tested me and I skipped a year. So I'm in second form now."

"You don't say! Well you can just skip right back again," he answered sarcastically. "My time's far too valuable to be wasted trying to drum second-form work into the head of a flibbety gibbet *girl*."

"Well! That's not fair!" I knew my saucy tongue was heading me straight for trouble, but I couldn't seem to control it. "I'm not a flibbety whachamacallit. I'm a serious scholar, studying to be a veterinarian. And my name is *Miss* Emerson. And I'll ask Miss Nesbitt to write a letter to the school board. She'll prove I passed into second form."

I guess it was the threat of going over his head that made him explode. "Veterinarian be damned!" he swore, his beady eyes glittering with contempt. "You must fancy yourself some kind of a crackerjack! Who ever heard tell of a female veterinarian?" The sneer on his lips tugged the corners of his moustache down, and blue veins popped out all over his mottled face. "One more word out of you, Emerson" — he wagged his fat finger just inches from my nose — "and I'll knock you back to senior fourth so fast it'll make your head spin."

Suddenly Matt leapt to his feet, sending his books crashing to the floor. "You ain't got no right to do that!" he dared to yell at the tyrannical teacher.

"Why, you — you —" Mr. Crabb sputtered with rage and his spiky eyebrows locked together like horns. "Get yourself back to the cloakroom, boy! I'll show you what rights I've got."

Then Eva jumped to her feet and I bounced up beside her. "You leave my brother alone!" she screamed.

But Matt lowered his head and whispered, "You two stay out of this. I can handle it." Then he spun around and marched to the cloakroom, his back as stiff as a ramrod.

The thick leather strap sounded like thunderclaps in the still, small schoolhouse. Eva and I plugged our ears and cringed at every whack. Billy Boyd held up his hands and counted ten thunderclaps on his fingers. But Matt never uttered a sound.

The rest of the day passed in deadly silence. At four o'clock we all hurried home to tell our families about our terrible new teacher.

"He sounds like a schoolmaster right out of *Oliver Twist*," declared Aunt Marg angrily. "What can be done about it, Herb?"

The soft lines of my sweet uncle's face had hardened like a rock as he listened. "Leave it to me, Mag," he said. Then he lifted the stove lid and shot the straw he'd been wiggling furiously in the space between his teeth straight as an arrow into the fire. It flared and hissed and turned to ash.

* * *

The news travelled like wildfire. Everybody for miles around agreed that Mr. Crabb would have to go. So, within a week, the school trustees called an emergency public meeting and the whole countryside turned out. I could hardly wait for my aunt and uncle to come home that night to tell me what happened.

Well, Uncle Herb was so mad he stayed outdoors on the

piazza and chewed and spat for an hour. Aunt Marg told me all about it.

"Butter wouldn't melt in that man Crabb's mouth," she fumed. "First he fell all over himself apologizing to Zach and Jessie for what he'd done to Matthew. Then he managed to sweet-talk the rest of the assembly into giving him another chance. A vote was taken by a show of hands and that mealymouthed varmint won! That's when your uncle stood up and faced the lot of them." She was so flushed and agitated she had to stop for breath.

"Oh, my gosh!" I cried. "What did Uncle Herb do?"

"He fixed everybody with a stony glare until you could hear a pin drop. Then he said, 'Well, you lily-livers might be willing to trust your precious younguns to this Simon Legree here, but I ain't. I'm pulling my girl out of this here school!'" I felt a thrill of pride and a tingle of fear.

* * *

It was decided I should attend Shelburne Continuation School and board with Rabbit and Dora Hare. Uncle Herb would come and pick me up on weekends.

"I hope the noise of the trains shunting back and forth won't interfere with your rest, Margaret," Aunt Marg fussed.

"Oh, don't worry. I'll get used to it," I assured her. "Besides, I like the sound of train whistles, especially at night. They make me shiver and feel cozy in my bed. And I like Rabbit and Dora. Rabbit's a barrel of fun."

"He is that," smiled Aunt Marg. "And Dora's a kind, good-hearted soul. I trust Dora."

On Sunday afternoon Aunt Marg and I began my packing. I had spent all day Saturday with Matt and Eva. I'd planned it that way so that Aunt Marg and Uncle Herb and I could have this last special day to ourselves.

"Take plenty of fleece-lined bloomers and undershirts, Margaret, and remember to wear clean underthings every day just in case, God forbid, you should have an accident." She shuddered at the thought and touched the wooden washstand for good luck, even though she vowed she didn't believe in such superstitious nonsense.

I had been terribly excited about going to school in Shelburne, but now that it was actually happening, I was beginning to get cold feet. "I hate changes!" I said suddenly. "I wish there was a magic pill we could take that would make things stay the same forever."

"Well, it's a fact, Margaret, that there have been a lot of changes in your young life. But mostly for the better, wouldn't you say? We can't turn the calendar backwards you know. We'll just have to hope for the best and look upon this as one of life's many vicissitudes."

"That's a swell word, Aunt Marg. What does it mean exactly?"

"It means change, Margaret. Variation, an alteration in one's circumstances."

"Well, I ain't too particular about this vicissitude," said Uncle Herb gruffly, "but if it's right for our girl, that's what counts."

"Don't worry, Uncle Herb. I'll be home every weekend to drive you crazy."

"And I'll be there to get you, come hell or high water."

"But not in a blizzard, Uncle Herb."

"No, not in a blizzard, Maggie. We won't make that mistake again."

"That reminds me. I must give Starr a good grooming. I might not have another chance for a long time."

"Away you go then, Margaret." Aunt Marg straightened up, wiped the mist from her eyes and blew her nose. "I'll start supper. What would you like, tea or cocoa?"

"Cocoa," I answered promptly. "Just like the good old days." Ever since I turned fourteen I had had my choice.

* * *

Starr gave a loud snort when he heard me open the barn door. He moved over in his stall and swung his head around so our eyes met.

"Eeeehhh," he whinnied.

"Eeeehhh yourself," I teased.

Then he nipped the toque right off my head and tossed it into Flora's stall.

"You big galoot!" I laughed as I reached for the currycomb.

"You won't be seeing me so much from now on, Starr," I explained as I worked, "because I'm off to Shelburne to start my higher education. It takes years and years to become a veterinarian, but it'll be worth it in the end because I'll be able to take care of you and Flora and Fancy myself. I'll be such a good doctor that you'll probably be the oldest horse in history."

He whinnied with delight at the idea of setting a world record. Then he began to flutter his lips the way horses do when they're excited, baring his teeth in a silly, horsy grin.

That reminded me that I still hadn't succeeded in brushing his teeth.

"Today, Starr," I told him sternly as I put away the currycomb, "I'm going to scrub those yellow choppers of yours if it's the last thing I ever do. Do you understand me?"

He understood all right. He poked his head into the corner of his stall and pretended not to hear. So I went away and came back with a bucket of rainwater, a bar of carbolic soap and Aunt Marg's scrubbing brush. I plunked the pail of water at his feet and he eyed it warily.

I watered the brush, soaped it into a creamy lather and brought it, dripping, to his rigid lips. "I'm waiting," I said.

He quivered his muzzle, flared his nostrils, twitched his ears and finally, looking at me with big trusting brown eyes, rolled back his velvety lips, baring his huge square teeth.

Quick as a wink, before he changed his mind, I began scrubbing up and down and sideways. The foam around his mouth made him look as if he was having a slobbering fit, so I dipped the brush into the clear water and rinsed it away. Then I dried his sparkling whiskers with the flannel.

"There!" I cried triumphantly. "Now, that's a change for the better!" I hugged his star-decorated nose.

One more time I ran my fingers through his shining tawny mane. Then I decided to leave before I started to cry, so I retrieved my toque, said goodbye to the cows and made a dash for the house.

Aunt Marg had just stepped out onto the porch to call me, her sweatercoat pulled tightly around her stout little body. The chill of autumn was in the air.

She had prepared a special going-away supper. Roast chicken (I was glad I didn't know which of the ladies had been sacrificed for me), fluffy potatoes, mashed hubbard squash and a big basin of giblets and gravy. Uncle Herb served me the left drumstick because, as everybody knows, chickens are right-footed creatures, so the left leg is tenderest.

For dessert, Aunt Marg had made my all-time favourite — floating island. As usual, she had fashioned little spruce trees out of green cherries to inhabit the island. I remembered a trick I used to play on Uncle Herb when I was young. I wondered if I could still get away with it.

"Uncle Herb, look! Quick! A bluebird on the window sill!"

He spun his head around to catch sight of his favourite bird and I snitched the tree off his island and popped it into my mouth.

He turned back, disappointed, and immediately spied the empty island. Then he looked at me with the tenderest of smiles. "You're a corker, Maggie," he said with a catch in his voice.

"Gold?" I asked.

"Solid!" he answered.

* * *

Early the next morning we set off for Shelburne in the pickup, Aunt Marg at the wheel. The three of us were squeezed into the cab — me in the middle. My trunk and grip were bouncing around in the back.

None of us spoke until we were almost there. I guess we were all lost in thought, wondering what the future had in store. Then, almost at the same moment, they each put an arm around me. I sighed and laid my head first on one shoulder and then the other.

"Well, Margaret, old sweetheart," Aunt Marg whispered huskily, "you're on your way."

MARGARET
on Her Way

For Barbara, Jean, Sonja, Vancy, Pat and Kathy.

I would like to thank Dr. C.A.V. Barker, Doctor of Veterinary Science and Professor Emeritus, University of Guelph, for his invaluable help and advice in the field of veterinary medicine.

Contents

Chapter 1

Great News

The phone was ringing off the hook when I dashed in the door. I dropped my schoolbooks on the table, raced through the kitchen to the parlour and grabbed the receiver.

"Hello!"

"Is that you, Margaret?"

"Sure, it's me, Aunt Marg. Can't you tell?"

"You sound all breathless. Are you all right?"

"I'm fine. I just ran to get the phone."

I was surprised to hear from Aunt Marg, because it wasn't her usual day to phone me at the Hares' house in Shelburne. I'd been boarding there during the week for two years now while I attended continuation school, and Aunt Marg phoned me regular as clockwork every Wednesday night. Today was only Monday. In fact, I'd spent the weekend at home on the farm as usual and Uncle Herb had brought me in from Green Meadows only the night before, so why was Aunt Marg calling me now?

"What's the matter, Aunt Marg? Is Uncle Herb sick? Is Starr hurt? Why are you phoning on a Monday?"

"Don't worry your head, Margaret. Everything's dandy here. It's just that I got a letter from your mother and I couldn't wait till Wednesday to pass on the news."

My father and my mother — Aunt Marg's sister Nellie — and my brothers and sisters (nine kids in all, not counting me) lived in Toronto on Rose Avenue, but I lived with my aunt and uncle on their farm. It was complicated having two families, but we tried our best to stay close.

"What news?"

Aunt Marg sounded tickled about something, so I was sure it wasn't bad news.

"Well, you'll never guess what I'm holding in my hand right this minute," she replied teasingly.

"No, I'll never guess, so for gosh sakes tell me."

"It's a gold-embossed wedding invitation that says Olive Eleanor Emerson is to be married July 5, 1930. Your mother wants us all to come down. I've spoken to Jessie about it already, and she says Matt's willing to take care of things here."

Jessie and Zacharia Muggins, their son Matthew and their adopted daughter Eva were our nearest neighbours and best friends.

"Oh, my gosh! Really? Olive's getting married?"

Olive was my oldest sister. She was a nurse at the Sick Kids' Hospital. I didn't even know she had a steady fella, never mind a fiancé.

"Who's she marrying, for Pete's sake?"

I felt sort of put out about being the last to know.

"Well, your mother said she took everybody by surprise, so you don't need to feel bad."

Aunt Marg could read me like a book.

"It seems she's been secretly engaged for three months now, but you know Olive. She might look the spittin' image of your mother, but she's close-mouthed like your father. And maybe it's just as well, because if the hospital gets wind of it they might let her go. They're so strict about married women working, you know. Anyway, Margaret, she's marrying a young intern by the name of Andrew Webster. Your mother says he's lovely."

"What does Pa think about it?"

Olive was Pa's favourite. I knew he wouldn't give her up willingly.

"Your mother says your father is resigned. I guess that means he's happy."

"Resigned doesn't mean happy, Aunt Marg. More likely he's just accepted it."

"Well, be that as it may, Margaret. But you haven't heard the best part yet."

"The best part? You mean there's more?"

"Yes. Olive wants you and Josephine to be her brides-maids. Now what do you say to that?"

"Really! Me and Josie? It sounds swell but . . . well . . . you know how pretty Josie is . . . and you know what I look like."

"Yes, old sweetheart, I certainly do. You're as handsome as a black-eyed Susan. You're as bright as a morning-glory. You're as —"

"Aw, you're just prejudiced," I laughed. But being compared to her favourite flowers made me feel better just the same.

"Well, love, I must ring off now. I've promised your uncle popovers tonight. Say hello to Dora for me, and tell her I've got lots of scraps saved up for her new quilt."

Dora Hare was an incurable quilter. Aunt Marg said her work was art in its purest form.

"I will, Aunt Marg. Give Uncle Herb my love, and tell him not to be late on Friday. I can hardly wait for the summer holidays. Take care of Starr and Silky for me." They were my horse and cat.

"I will. Never fear. Ta, ta, dear."

"Bye, Aunt Marg."

Just as I hung up, Dora came in from shopping. She was carrying a huge carton of tin goods. On the top was balanced a sack of biscuits and two loaves of bread. Dora was a town woman and didn't do her own baking and canning like Aunt Marg did.

I shoved my books aside and she hoisted the heavy box onto the table with a loud grunt.

Dora was a tall, muscular woman with a deep voice like a man. Her husband Rabbit — his real name was Roger, but everyone called him Rabbit because he could wiggle his ears and nose, and because of his last name — described her as *strapping*, so she got back at him by calling him a pipsqueak.

It took me quite a while to get used to Dora because her loud voice made me think she was mad all the time. But once I got accustomed to it, I came to really like her. As Aunt Marg always said, Dora was a good scout.

"Here, let me help you," I said, and we began putting the staples in the larder off the kitchen. While we worked, I told her about the scraps Aunt Marg had for her, to get that item out of the way, and then I told her the big news about Olive.

"Well, land's sakes, what a nice thing to look forward to, Meggie."

That's what she and Rabbit called me — Meg, or Meggie. At home I got called Peg or Peggy. Uncle Herb called me Maggie. It's amazing how many variations could be made out of just plain Margaret.

"A wedding in the family! And a pretty young bride to boot. The last wedding Rabbit and I went to was Jasper and Beulah Streets. They tottered up the aisle as if they were on their last legs."

I laughed at the picture that flashed through my mind of the funny old couple who'd kept company for forty years and had finally tied the knot. Then right after the ceremony they'd gone back to their respective houses. Even now, they still only visited each other once a month.

"It's a peculiar arrangement, and that's a fact." Dora knew what I was thinking.

"But if it works for them, then it's no skin off our noses."

That's the way Dora was. Nothing anybody did ever fazed her.

It'll be fun, I thought, going home to Olive's wedding. But that didn't stop me from feeling a bit leery about being a bridesmaid. I wasn't used to the limelight — except when I got in Dutch at school, that is.

Some of my teachers considered me a troublemaker. That's because I always caught them up on their mistakes instead of keeping my mouth shut. Sometimes they complained about me to Dora.

Mr. Draggett, our physics teacher, said I was too big for my britches. Honestly, what a dumb thing to say about a fifteen-and-a-half-year-old girl!

And Miss Needle, our mathematics teacher, whose nose suited her name to a T, called me a smart-aleck know-it-all.

Dora always stood up for me, though, and said I had a right to speak my mind. And as it turned out, when the report cards came out at the end of June I was vindicated. I stood first in third form — and was the youngest student by a full year, too.

Anyway, I only hoped that this Andrew Webster person was good enough for my beautiful and sensitive big sister.

Chapter 2

Wedding Jitters

Aunt Marg made my bridesmaid dress. It was sleeveless. I begged her not to put frills around the neck and armholes, but she said it had to be the same style as Josie's. Ma had sent up the pattern and material — mauve georgette (ugh!) — so we'd both look exactly alike.

According to her, that is.

"*Nothing* could make us look exactly alike, Aunt Marg," I complained. "Josie hasn't got a freckle on her face, she doesn't wear glasses and her hair is as smooth as corn-silk."

Lately my hair, which I used to be sort of proud of because of its natural curliness, had become as coarse as a horse's tail. I couldn't do a thing with it.

"You'll both be beautiful," Aunt Marg assured me through a mouthful of pins. "Now turn yourself around."

I revolved slowly on the kitchen chair I was standing on while Aunt Marg tacked up the hem of the dress.

* * *

We arrived in Toronto right at noon hour to find poor Ma in such a state that I didn't dare complain about the dress. We'd never had a wedding in the family before and Ma was beside herself. Aunt Marg pitched right in and made us all a bite to eat.

"I don't know why you're so all-fired upset, Nell," my father complained. "I've rented the Legion Hall. They're taking care of all the jollifications."

"You did, Pa?" I'd no idea there was going to be a reception and everything.

"You betcha," he answered proudly, his thumbs hooked under his suspenders. "We've invited a hundred folks, give or take a few. We can't fit them all in here."

Not many people could afford a big wedding for their daughter in 1930 because of the depression. But my pa was luckier than most because he had a steady job at General Steel Wares. In fact, he was a boss. Ma always boasted that the factory would grind to a halt without her Will.

* * *

When the dishes were done, Josie looked at me and said, "C'mon, Peg. You and Jenny and I have an appointment at the Elegance Beauty Parlour."

"We have?" I squealed.

Boy, that raised my hopes. Maybe a professional hairdresser could do something spectacular with my unmanageable mane.

And she did. She took a long look at me and then went to work.

First she cut all the crisp, sun-dried ends off. Then, with thick, green waving lotion she marcelled my mop into deep black furrows, like a freshly ploughed field. After that she sat me under the drying machine. When I emerged, hot as a fire-cracker, she combed and brushed my stiff black hair into wonderful, flattering waves.

"You've got a lovely head of hair," she told me as she did magic things around my face with her fingertips.

Twirling the chair around, she held a looking glass behind me to show me how nice the back looked.

"Oh," I sighed with relief. "Thanks a lot!"

It was worth every jitney of the twenty-five cents it cost.

"You're welcome," she said with a satisfied smile. "Now you can go on your way rejoicing."

When we got home and I changed, with my new hair style even the frilly dress seemed to suit me better.

The contrast between me and Josie wasn't nearly so startling now.

In addition, I had brand-new rimless glasses. Jenny said she could hardly notice them at all. Uncle Herb had insisted that I have them, even though my old ones were perfectly good. Aunt Marg said it was outlandish how he spoiled me, but she smiled when she said it.

Olive fixed her own hair in a wind-blown bob. It was shingled up the back, so all she had to do was set two big auburn kiss curls in front of each ear with bobby pins. When she combed it out she looked just like Clara Bow in the moving pictures. And she was every bit as pretty, too.

In the end, everything turned out almost perfect. Nobody tripped going down the aisle, and the best man, Rodney Gallaugher, who was handsome as the day is long, managed not to lose the ring.

Even the little kids in the family were good as gold. All

except four-year-old Patsy, that is. She was the youngest — the spitting image of Pa and me, spectacles, freckles and all.

Aunt Marg had had the foresight to tuck a bag of humbugs into her special occasions chain link purse in case Patsy should get fussy. Every time the baby opened her mouth, Aunt Marg popped a humbug into it. But instead of sucking quietly and contentedly as Aunt Marg had hoped, Patsy crunched and gulped and kept hollering for more.

Then when the clergyman said, "Who giveth this woman?" Pa looked at Olive and I knew exactly what he was thinking — what woman? This here's my little girl — and he was rendered speechless.

Two big tears trickled down the creases in his blue-shadowed cheeks and his Adam's apple bobbed up above his shiny white celluloid collar.

Ma gently put a hanky in his hand.

Dabbing under his specs and wiping his face, he finally got a hold of himself.

But instead of saying what he was supposed to, he suddenly turned on the nervous young groom and said fiercely, "Young man, do you swear you'll be good to my girl?"

Everybody in the congregation sucked in their breath and held it. You could've heard a pin drop. Only the sharp cracking of a humbug broke the silence. Poor Ma nearly died of embarrassment. Her face flushed as red as her hair.

"Will!" she hissed at Pa's back, but he just ignored her and waited for his answer.

Young Andrew Webster, who was about to become my

brother if he said the right thing, looked Pa straight in the eye with the kindest expression I'd ever seen.

"You have my word on it, sir," he said.

As if that wasn't enough breaking with tradition, when she saw the look on Pa's face, Olive went into his arms with a little cry and laid her white-veiled head on his shoulder. Her bouquet got crushed between them, but she didn't seem to care. Then, with green eyes glistening, she stepped back into place beside her husband-to-be.

The solemn words were repeated by a bewildered clergyman, and Pa managed to say, "I do."

There wasn't a dry eye in the church. Afterwards, everyone said it was the most beautiful and touching ceremony they'd ever witnessed and they wouldn't have missed it for the world.

* * *

The reception at the Legion Hall was really something. The ladies of the Legion had prepared a splendid repast, and Ma herself had baked and decorated the three-tiered wedding cake.

Later, when all the toasting and kissing and congratulating was over, Uncle Herb and two other uncles brought out their fiddles and the music began.

Dancing was one thing I knew I was good at. Matt had taught me years ago to barn dance and square dance and polka. There wasn't a step I couldn't pick up in a minute, so I wasn't the wallflower after all. To my surprise, Josie was. She only danced once or twice and then hid behind a post and said her feet hurt. I think she was just plain scared.

As I went twirling by the ladies sitting in a row along the

wall, Aunt Marg threw me a mischievous *I told you so!* look. Then, as I two-stepped merrily past the fiddlers, Uncle Herb cocked his fuzzy red head over his bow and gave me an exaggerated wink. And guess who caught the bride's bouquet? None other than yours truly!

It's funny, I thought, how things turn out exactly opposite to what you expect sometimes.

Chapter 3

Gracie's Turn

Gracie came home with us for her summer holidays. We took off up Rose Avenue leaving the three youngest — Davy and Bobby and Patsy — standing on the sidewalk howling their heads off as Gracie waved triumphantly out the window of our brand-new Model A Ford. It was Aunt Marg who had insisted on buying the new car for the trip. She said it would be a pure disgrace to go to a wedding in a pickup.

Gracie never stopped talking the entire way. My head was spinning by the time we passed Four Corners and bumped up the long lane leading to our green farmhouse.

"Aunt Marg says I can sleep with you, Peg," she cried as she gleefully wiggled off our long-suffering aunt's lap and bounced from the running board to the ground.

"Oh, thrills!" I answered.

"Margaret! That's not nice," reprimanded Aunt Marg as she rubbed the numbness out of her knees.

She'd been holding my plump sister on her lap for sixty

miles — three long hours — just so the little imp could see out the front.

"Sure, Gracie, that'll be swell," I said, trying to sound pleased.

I don't know what made me so mean sometimes. I'd been living with Uncle Herb and Aunt Marg for five years and I still didn't like to share them, especially now that I spent most of the year in Shelburne. I just wanted to keep them and Starr and Silky and everything else on the farm all to myself.

Of course, the first thing Gracie wanted to do when we arrived was learn the secret signal that only Starr and I understood. So right after supper we went out and sat on the split-rail fence together — Gracie's short fat legs pumping the air, my long spindly ones almost touching the ground.

We could see the small brown hump that was Starr's back far away on the horizon. Gracie watched fascinated as I cupped my hands around my mouth and blew with all my might. No sound came out, just a rush of air, but the big Clydesdale responded instantly.

He flung up his head, tossed his tawny mane and came streaking like the wind across the meadow. Aunt Marg always said that it was positively uncanny how he picked up the almost silent signal.

Day after day Gracie tried to copy the soundless whistle. But like all the other kids before her, she failed. So she just had to be satisfied with a ride on Starr's broad brown back while I guided him with the flat of my hand on the side of his nose.

* * *

Two weeks is a long time to spend with your eight-year-old sister, and I have to admit, I soon found myself doing things to avoid her.

I helped Uncle Herb with the haying and mucked out the stalls in the barn and mended broken fences. I even did the milking for Aunt Marg.

Our two cows, Flora and Fancy, hated that because I didn't have Aunt Marg's special touch. They'd switch my glasses off with their tails and try to kick the bucket over when it was full. I swear they even broke wind on purpose in an effort to get rid of me.

The second week of Gracie's stay seemed endless. I thought her prattle would drive me crazy. So I spent most of my time on the roof with Uncle Herb, helping him replace the cedar shingles that had been blown off in a windstorm. I was in my glory up there in my overalls, "overhauls," as Uncle Herb called them, hammering away as we discussed everything from potato bugs to politics.

All this time, Aunt Marg was alone with Gracie. She taught her how to make baking powder biscuits and to embroider a pretty sampler and to slop the pigs — Pauline the sow had had four pink babies recently — and to "chook, chook, chook" at the chickens (better known as Aunt Marg's ladies).

It finally dawned on me that the two of them were becoming thick as thieves.

One day I came into the house unexpectedly and caught Aunt Marg giving Gracie a great big hug as she declared, "You're an old sweetheart, if there ever was one."

Instantly I saw red! *Old sweetheart* was a special nickname Aunt Marg had given me when I first came to stay on the farm. I never thought I'd live to see the day when she'd use it for anyone else.

Even though I was going on sixteen years old, I still wanted to be exclusively Aunt Marg's "old sweetheart" and Uncle Herb's "corker."

I could feel my aunt's eyes following me as I strode fuming across the kitchen and up the stairwell, slamming the door behind me. I marched into the bedroom and slammed that door too.

I propped the bedroom chair under the doorknob and flopped on my bed and stared gloomily at the ceiling.

Just then, a daddy-longlegs came prancing boldly down the wall. I waited until it was within arm's reach — and then killed it with a swat of my bare hand.

Right away I regretted my action. After all, only last week I'd had a big fight with Matt for stepping on an ant.

Now I felt even worse.

About a half-hour later, I heard a tap, tap, tapping on my door.

"Go away!" I moaned, thinking it was Gracie.

"Open up, Maggie!" ordered Uncle Herb.

Reluctantly, I got up, moved the chair, and flopped back on the bed again. He sidled in, wiggling a straw in the space between his two front teeth.

He drew the chair over and sat down next to my bed, his heavy workboots barely touching the floor. He and Aunt Marg were both short and stocky.

"Your aunt tells me you're riled about something," said Uncle Herb, pushing his specs up on top of his frizzy red head with his thumb.

He always did that when he was puzzled. He said he

couldn't look and think at the same time.

"Not riled, exactly, Uncle Herb. Jealous, more like it. And I'm not very proud of myself for being jealous of a kid half my age either."

Uncle Herb stroked his stubbly chin thoughtfully.

"There ain't no age limits on feelings, Maggie," he said.

He might not know proper English, I thought, but he sure knows a lot about people.

"You must've objectified by now, Maggie, that nobody is about to take your place with your aunt and me. But that don't mean we can't take to a bright little gaffer like Gracie. She's a born mother, Mag is, and the Lord never seen fit to give us younguns of our own, so she took to mothering her sister's brood. Seems natural enough to me."

"Aunt Marg would've made a terrific mother," I agreed.

"She's been just that to you, girl," he pointed out.

"I know, Uncle Herb, and I'm sorry if I've been a disappointment. It's just that I was born with this mean streak in me. Ma says I inherited it from my Grandma Marshall, who was as mean as an old billy goat."

"Now hold on there, Maggie. You can't go blaming your grandma. We all have to shoulder our own load."

Uncle Herb worked the straw back and forth between pursed lips, then added solemnly, "You mustn't deny your aunt the pleasure of Gracie's company. There's always room for one more in a heart as big as Mag's."

"You're right, as usual, Uncle Herb."

I sat up on the edge of the bed.

"But don't let me catch you calling her 'corker,' if you know what's good for you."

With that I gave him a playful punch in the paunch.

"Oof!" he grunted, and the straw flew out of his mouth and speared itself in my hair. Then he said, "What's that there mess on the wall?"

"Oh, that. It's a poor defenceless spider that I ruthlessly murdered instead of murdering my sister. I'll scrape it off when it dries."

"You're a corker, Maggie," he chuckled, retrieving the straw from my tangled curls. "A dad-blamed solid-gold corker."

Chapter 4

Dora

Gracie ended up staying at Green Meadows indefinitely.

When we took her home after a month's stay, she cried and carried on like a maniac until we promised to bring her back again. So in a way she did take my place after all.

At first I continued to resent her presence, but when I saw how happy it made Aunt Marg to have a little girl to do for again, I couldn't stay mad. And when I returned to Shelburne in September to continue my education, I was glad Aunt Marg had the company.

"Boys, oh boys, I'm glad you're back!" cried Dora as she helped me unpack my things.

"Rabbit's been complaining all summer long that the house is like a morgue without you. He hasn't wiggled his ears for a month of Sundays."

"I missed both of you, too, Dora," I said as I lined my books along the shelf that Rabbit had built over my bed.

Suddenly she leaned down and gave me a quick peck on the cheek. Dora rarely ever showed any outward sign of affection, so I was touched.

"I'll run down and finish supper while you freshen up," she said, flustered by her own display of emotion. "I've got a nice gooseberry pie from Rachel's bakeshop just for you. It'll go good with the cream you brought."

She turned abruptly and left the room.

On my washstand stood a blue porcelain pitcher with purple flowers embossed on it. It was full of warm water and it stood in a matching bowl. A flannel towel and face-cloth were neatly folded over the wooden rung on the side of the washstand. The small frame house had running water downstairs. Dora's pride and joy was her indoor water closet and bright copper bathtub. But upstairs in the attic rooms, we still used washbasins and chamber pots.

When I came down, I saw that the kitchen table — there was no dining room because the house was too small — had been laid as if for company. Dora's bone white china-ware and silver candlestick sparkled on the green linen tablecloth.

"The table looks beautiful, Dora. Just like a picture in *The Ladies' Home Journal.*"

Dora beamed at my praise.

The reason I was so thrilled with the table setting was because of the amazing contrast between that day's table and any ordinary day.

It was all I could do not to laugh out loud at the every-day table. Dora had some funny eccentricities and one of her most hilarious was her habit of using newspaper tablecloths.

Every meal, she'd spread fresh newspapers over the bare wooden table. Then when we were finished supper, she'd roll them up, crumbs, spills and all, and stuff them into the stove.

"It saves a lot of fuss and bother," she explained.

I had to agree with that, but it did take me a while all the same to get used to eating off newspapers. However, once I got used to it, I found I really enjoyed it. The best day of the week was Monday. That was the day Dora used Saturday's coloured comics.

Aunt Marg nearly had a fit when she got wind of it. She said it was bad enough eating off newspapers, let alone perusing them at the table. But I didn't care. I enjoyed reading the tablecloth.

Just then, Rabbit came in from meeting the evening train. Part of his job was to pick up the mailbag and drop it off at the post office.

He grinned at me, wriggling his nose, and shot me a riddle. "How many buckets of dirt in Blue Mountain, Meggie?"

Quick as a wink I shot back, "That depends on the size of the bucket."

"Tarnation, girl, you done it again," he hooted, slapping his knee as he made his way to the tin sink to take his teeth out and wash up for supper.

Rabbit always greeted me with a riddle instead of a hello. And I think he'd have been really disappointed if I didn't always have an answer for him.

After a delicious supper of pork hocks and gooseberry pie, I helped Dora with the washing up. Then we joined Rabbit in the parlour to listen to the gramophone. He'd bought a packet of new needles and a brand new record just for me. It was my favourite singer, Al Jolson, singing "Keep Your Sunny Side Up."

Rabbit sat right next to the Victrola in a reed chair he'd made himself out of boiled bulrushes instead of bamboo. Every time the record slowed down and Mr. Jolson began to sound like a dying soprano singing through her nose, Rabbit would lean over and crank it up again. He played the same song over and over.

* * *

Dora's parlour was another of her eccentricities. Every inch of space was crowded with knick-knacks. There were china figurines, glass snowstorms, stuffed birds, pink seashells and miniature lamps with real silk shades Dora had made herself. Uncle Herb said she was a dab hand at sewing.

On a shelf that ran all around the room just below the ceiling were dozens of fancy plates standing precariously on edge. And the walls themselves were so cluttered with pictures and samplers and calendars that you could hardly see the pattern on the wallpaper.

Aunt Marg said Dora's parlour was a hodgepodge. And Rabbit called it a mess of gewgaws. But I thought it was downright interesting.

One of the samplers, signed in the corner by Dora, aged eight, particularly intrigued me. Embroidered on grey silk in neat black stitches were the words, *I wept because I had no shoes . . . until I met a man who had no feet.* The first time I read that, it made me cry.

But the sampler that hung beside it made me laugh out loud. All bordered in vines and roses, the verse read, *Women's faults are many. Men have only two. Everything they say, and everything they do.*

Dora and I sat on the cracked leather davenport that

was so filled with fancy cushions you had to hold some on your lap to make room for yourself. Dora had to keep her elbows raised so her hands were free to sew the brightly coloured squares together.

We finished up the evening by having tea and pie in the kitchen.

"What's the best thing to put in a pie, Meg?" cracked Rabbit, gooseberries dripping out of the slice in his hand.

"Your teeth!" I answered triumphantly.

"Dad blame!" he chortled, his false teeth with the orange gums clicking merrily. It was a game we played, and I was good at it.

"Well, Meggie," Dora interrupted (I guess she was sick of riddles), "how do you feel about your little sister living at Green Meadows?"

Her sudden question took me off guard. I'd always thought of Gracie as *staying* at Green Meadows, not *living* there. The more meaningful word brought me up short. A bright picture flashed through my mind of Gracie's copper-coloured hair and Uncle Herb's frizzy red curls intermingled as they shared the earphones of his crystal set the way we used to do.

My heart constricted and I was engulfed in a wave of jealousy again. Then ever so slowly, it subsided.

"I'll get used to it, Dora," I said, holding back a sigh. "I'm going to be so busy this year with four Maths, plus Latin and French, that I won't have time to think about it. Besides, I'm almost a grown woman now and Aunt Marg needs a little kid to do for. And Gracie never had so much attention in her life. They really need each other."

Chapter 5

New Friends

My friend Eva Muggins also boarded in Shelburne — with the Stromberg family — and I spent quite a bit of my free time there. Apart from a married daughter who lived in Parry Sound, Mr. and Mrs. Stromberg had two sons — Philbert, nicknamed the nut by his enemies and Bert by his friends, and Elliot, a fifteen-year-old cut up.

Bert was nice-looking, but not handsome. He had slick black hair with a white part down the middle that was so straight it looked as if it had been drawn with a ruler. His eyes were greeny blue, and his wide smile was only a bit spoiled by the way his two front teeth lapped over each other. But most important of all, he was taller than me!

One snowy afternoon in November, I was invited to stay for supper. Mrs. Stromberg set my place right next to Philbert. After supper, we all circled the dining room table to do our homework.

"Need any help?" offered Bert.

He was in fifth form and planning on going to university the following year.

"No, thanks," I answered cockily. "I can manage."

At nine o'clock, Mrs. Stromberg insisted that Bert walk me home, even though I said it wasn't necessary.

"Can I come too?" begged Eva, shutting her book.

"Have you finished your assignment?" asked Mrs. Stromberg.

"No, but . . . "

"Isn't it due tomorrow?"

"Yes, but . . . "

"No buts about it. Get to work. You, too, Elliot."

"Rats!" said Elliot.

I got my coat on quickly.

"Goodnight. Thanks for everything," I said. Then Bert and I left.

We strolled along — self-consciously, now that we were alone — taking little slides on icy patches of the road. It was really cold for November.

Uncle Herb said the *Farmer's Almanac* predicted a long hard winter.

"Want to go to the pictures Friday night?" Bert suddenly asked as he caught his balance at the end of a frozen puddle.

Shelburne didn't have a real cinema. Instead, movies were shown at the town hall on Friday nights. They were always silent films because, as Bert explained, they didn't have the sophisticated equipment needed to show the new talkies yet. All the young people went to the "flicks" on Friday night to celebrate the end of the school week. Afterwards, everybody got together at the ice cream parlour on Main Street.

"I can't," I answered reluctantly. "I go home on Friday nights."

"Why don't you go home on Saturday morning for a change."

"Gee, I never thought of that. Maybe I could. I'll ask Dora."

"Okey-dokey," grinned Bert. "Let me know tomorrow."

The minute I stepped inside the door, I broached Dora on the subject.

"Well, Philbert's a fine fella 'n all," she said, frowning, "but you'll need to get permission from your aunt. I'll be blessed if I want to take on that responsibility."

I dropped my books with a plunk on the bare kitchen table and made straight for the parlour phone.

The Hares' telephone was the long-stemmed table type with the flared mouthpiece that looked like a black daffodil in bloom. It sat grandly on a crocheted doily in the middle of a reed table. I picked up the horn-shaped earpiece from the hook on the side of the stem and gave Central the number. Then I heard the bells on top of the wooden phonebox in the farm kitchen jangle two shorts and two longs.

"Who might this be, calling at such an ungodly hour?" shouted Uncle Herb.

He always thought you had to yell over the telephone to breach the distance.

"Oh, Uncle Herb," I laughed, "what a way to answer! Suppose it was somebody important?"

"Sounds like somebody mighty important to me," he said. "What can I do you for, Maggie?"

"Tell Aunt Marg I have to talk to her right away. Then you come back on the line, okay?"

"Okay, corker," he answered.

I heard him shout, "You're wanted on the blower, Mag."
Then I heard a muffled, "Ouch!"

I knew Aunt Marg had cracked him on his bald spot with
her wide gold wedding band. She hated being called Mag,
because it rhymed with hag.

"What is it, Margaret?" Aunt Marg always sounded slightly worried at an unexpected phone call, especially at night.

"Well . . ." I paused for a few seconds and then rushed
ahead. "I need your permission to do something because
Dora says she can't take on the responsibility."

Aunt Marg waited patiently for me to continue. Then
when I didn't say anything after several seconds, she said,
"For mercy sakes, Margaret, out with it!"

So I told her. She hemmed and hawed for about five minutes.

"You're only fifteen," she muttered at last.

"Nearly sixteen," I reminded her, but she paid no attention.

"I don't know if your father and mother would approve,"
she hedged. "And your uncle's going to be sorely disappointed if you don't come home until Saturday."

She knew that would make me think twice.

"And Gracie wants you to have a look at Silky's ear. She
thinks it's infected, but I can't see a thing wrong with it."

"Gee whiz, Aunt Marg, if *you* can't find anything, how am
I supposed to?"

Aunt Marg was the best nurse in the whole countryside.
People trusted her even more than Doctor Tom, our country physician.

"Well, you know how Gracie looks up to you. She thinks
you're a veterinarian already."

"Good grief, I'm a far cry." I was getting frustrated. "Just say yes or no and I promise I won't argue."

"Oh, I guess it'll be all right this time. But you tell that Philip Stromberg —"

"That's Philbert, but his friends call him Bert."

"Well, tell that Philbert — what an outlandish name — that you can't make a habit of it. You're needed here on the farm."

"Thanks, Aunt Marg. You're an old sweetheart."

She laughed and said, "None of your soft soap with me, my girl."

"Tell Uncle Herb to come back on the line now."

"He's standing right here beside me, 'eavestroughing,' as he would say."

The receiver changed hands and Uncle Herb bellowed, "Hello, again, Maggie. I just want to put in my two cents' worth."

"I'm ready," I sighed, expecting a bit of a lecture.

Instead he just chortled and said, "Don't do anything I wouldn't do!"

Chapter 6

My First Date

I was pretty excited about going out with Bert. It was my first real date with a boy. Of course, I'd been out with Matt lots of times, mostly to picnics and barn dances and hayrides, but something told me this was going to be different.

"What'll I wear, Dora?" I had my whole wardrobe spread out on the bed. Dora leaned on the doorjamb, her long face stretched in a grin.

"Wear your best bib and tucker," she advised.

"I can't wear overhauls to the town hall," I joked.

"Now you're pulling my leg," she laughed, poking a dangling hairpin into her salt-and-pepper bun. "You know I meant your Sunday-go-meeting dress."

"No. That's too fancy. Besides, I don't like frilly things. I'm too tall and gawky. I guess I'll just wear my wool jumper and middy blouse. We won't be taking our coats off anyway, because everybody says the hall is as cold as Harper's Icehouse."

Well, as it turned out, the jumper was perfect. It was so

cold in the town hall you could see your breath. Not only did I not take off my coat, I didn't even unbutton it! The films were an old Laurel and Hardy comedy followed by a Felix the Cat cartoon.

I'd seen them both years before at the Bonita in Toronto, so it could've been quite boring. It wasn't, though, because Bert held my hand the entire time! Of course, we both kept our gloves on, so there wasn't much contact, but every once in a while his fingers would give mine a little squeeze. This made my heart do funny flip-flop things it had never done before.

After the movies, we went to the ice cream parlour. Mr. Blackacre made his own chocolate and vanilla ice cream in a wooden bucket outside in the snow especially for Friday nights.

Bert ordered a big chocolate soda with two straws. In order to share it, we had to put our foreheads together so that our breath steamed up my glasses. I took them off and put them in my pocket.

"Want another soda?" Bert asked. "Vanilla this time?"

I didn't really, but I did want to stay head to head with him for a while longer, so I said yes. By the time we were finished, my stomach was heaving and I quickly told Bert I thought it was time to leave.

The temperature outside must've dropped about ten degrees, but I welcomed the icy air on my face. I decided to say no to a second soda next time.

As we hurried down Rail Street, aptly named after the tracks behind it, the thin layer of snow squeaked under our feet. I slipped and almost fell, so Bert grabbed my hand — and didn't let go.

When we reached the house we lingered awkwardly for a moment outside, still holding hands. The porch light, shaped like a railroad lantern, gave off a soft amber glow.

Then as I was about to thank Bert for the swell time, the late-night train went roaring by, blowing its crossing whistle. Rather than shout, we just smiled at each other.

What a treat it was, looking up to a boy. I was as tall as, or taller than, most of the boys my age. Of course, Bert was eighteen, so I guess he was full-grown already.

Anyway, he looked nice in the dim orange light, his hazel eyes shining like a cat's, his black patent leather hair glittering with snowflakes.

Suddenly, without a speck of warning, he bent down and kissed me full on the mouth. I was so surprised, I didn't know which way to turn, so I closed my eyes — and he did it again!

All at once I felt bashful, so I lifted the latch and the front door creaked open.

Grinning, Bert jumped down the porch steps backwards and waved goodbye from the road. Then he broke into a loping run and disappeared up the dark street.

Rabbit and Dora had gone to bed and left the hall bulb burning. I was glad they were asleep, because I knew I was blushing. Rabbit could be a terrible tease sometimes.

Chapter 7

A Revelation

The next day there was a terrible ice storm, so I didn't get home until the following weekend.

On the Saturday, Gracie had her little friend Luella Raggett over to play. Then, later on in the afternoon, Mr. Muggins brought Eva over and together we worked on our geometry at the kitchen table while Gracie and Luella played old, familiar games at the far end of the room.

"Here I sit a-sewing, in my little housie," they sang in shrill, tremulous tones. "Nobody comes to see me, except my little mousie."

Eva and I exchanged nostalgic glances, sighing for our lost childhood.

"Can Luella stay all night if her mother says so, Aunt Marg?" begged Gracie.

"That might be nice, but where would Margaret sleep?"

"With me," suggested Eva. "I'll ring up Mother. I'm sure she'll say yes."

So she got Jessie's permission, and Uncle Herb let me drive to Briarwood Farm in the cutter. Starr got so excited when he saw us that it took me twice as long as usual to put his harness on.

"Sorry, old boy," I said as I put the bit in his mouth. I always apologized when I had to do that, because it seemed like such an insult, to shove an iron bar between the jaws of your best friend. But the horse didn't mind. He whickered happily, tossing his mane and batting his long white eyelashes at me like the big flirt that he was.

I couldn't resist throwing my arms around his huge head and rubbing my cheek against his smooth brown jowl. Then with velvety lips he nuzzled my hair. A lump came up in my throat and I felt like a kid again.

I climbed up on the seat beside Eva and took the reins. Starr moved off at a brisk trot without being told, steam streaming back from his flaring nostrils. It had taken me so long to set off that Eva was already shivering with the cold.

"Sorry, Eva," I said, "but I haven't seen him for a whole week and we really miss each other."

"I've never known a horse to act so human," Eva said. "He actually seems to love you."

"He does. And I love him, too, just as much as if he was a person. That's the main reason why I absolutely must become a vet. I've got to keep Starr alive as long as possible."

The Clydesdale pricked up his ears and switched his tail at the mention of his name, so I lowered my voice.

"He's eighteen years old, you know, Eva, and horses don't live much past twenty-five. I honestly don't know what I'd do if anything happened to him."

As we skimmed over the silvery snow and up the

Muggins' lane, we saw Matt coming from the barn.

"I'll take over, Marg," he said in his warm, amiable way.

He unharnessed Starr and led him to the stable while Eva and I headed for the cozy farm kitchen.

After supper, Eva and I were helping Jessie with the washing up when Matt said, "Will you come down to the stable, Marg? I want you to take a look at Bill's right front hoof. He's been favouring it lately and I can't figure out why."

Matt, too, thought I was a vet already because of the way I had with animals. Aunt Marg called it an affinity.

"You two run along," Jessie said. "My daughter and I can finish up here."

Jessie was so pleased to have a daughter — she'd lost Matt's twin sister to the terrible influenza epidemic during the Great War when they were babies — that she never missed a chance to use the precious word. So I hung up the dishtowel on the wooden spokes spread out like umbrella ribs above the kitchen range and went with Matt to the barn.

Bypassing Starr, who snorted his disapproval and fanned our faces with his bushy tail, we sidled into Bill's stall. Matt lifted the black gelding's hoof and I took my mitts off.

I closed my eyes and murmured soothingly as I prodded around the horseshoe with my bare fingertips. I sometimes found that my fingers were more sensitive with my eyes closed. Besides, coming in from the cold outside, my spectacles were steamed up, so I couldn't see anyway.

Suddenly I let out a yelp of pain. Bill gave a high-pitched whinny and jerked his hoof out of Matt's grip. I cleaned my glasses and peered at my finger. There was a sliver of glass no thicker than a pin poking out of a bright red bubble on my fingertip. Matt removed it gently.

Meanwhile, Bill had put his hoof down and now seemed to be standing comfortably on all fours.

"I think that's it, Marg!" Matt sighed with relief. "I'll walk him to make sure."

"It has to be disinfected first, Matt," I insisted.

Obediently, Matt fetched a bucket of well water, a brush, a cake of carbolic and a bottle of peroxide.

This time he held Bill's hoof tightly between his knees while I scrubbed and cleaned and doused it with disinfectant until the peroxide had stopped fizzing.

Then I dried the hoof with a clean flannel and finally let Matt walk my patient around the barnyard. There was no sign of a limp. Matt brought the horse back to his stall and gave him a good feed of corn and oats.

He treated Starr, too, of course, which helped to assuage his jealousy.

"Thanks, Marg," Matt said as we stood side by side stroking Bill's glossy black flanks.

I turned to tell him he was welcome and found that our noses were only inches apart. We were approximately the same height, so our eyes were on a level. His pale blue ones were shining into my dark brown ones.

Without a speck of a warning, he kissed me!

I was so startled I stumbled backwards, wiping my mouth with the back of my hand.

"For Pete's sake! What'd you do that for?" I snapped.

Matt's face turned beet-red and he yanked his peaked cap down over his windburned forehead to hide his embarrassment.

"Let's get out of here," I muttered, and made straight for the barn door.

There was a definite strain between Matt and me for quite a while after that, and I was truly sorry. When we were kids, Matt always used to say that we'd probably get married when we grew up, and I'd always answer, "Oh, sure!"

But now I knew we never would. Matt was more like a brother to me than a beau.

Chapter 8

S.W.A.L.K.

P.O. Box 37
c/o R. Hare
Shelburne, Ont.
January 7, 1931

Dear Josie,

I haven't heard from home since Christmas, so I thought I'd write. This way you'll be forced to answer.

Everything's fine at Green Meadows. Gracie is happy as a lark and doesn't seem to miss home a bit, not even on Christmas day. What a weird kid! Of course, Aunt Marg and Uncle Herb love her to pieces and she laps it up like a kitten with its nose in a saucer of warm milk, so no wonder.

I like it here in Shelburne, but I miss Starr a lot. Dora and Rabbit are really good to me. Their only son, Angus, whom I haven't met yet, lives in Toronto now, so I guess they're lonely.

You've simply got to come up in the summertime and spend a couple of days here, Jose. You'll die laughing at

Dora and Rabbit. Dora has the funniest habits. For instance, she uses newspapers instead of tablecloths on weeknights. We read yesterday's news while we eat! Sometimes we even trade pages.

Speaking of the news, isn't it awful lately? Imagine all those men out of work and having to ride the rails to Ottawa! Boy, with so many mouths to feed, I sure am glad Pa has a steady job. Aunt Marg always says we should thank our lucky stars that the depression hasn't hurt any of us personally.

Besides growing and canning everything they eat, Aunt Marg told me that Uncle Herb has a nest egg stashed away for a rainy day. His great-uncle Samuel left it to him when he went home. That's what Aunt Marg calls dying — going home!

Speaking of eggs, every Sunday when I come back from the farm I bring Dora a dozen white ones. She doesn't like brown ones even though Aunt Marg insists they're more nourishing. She always puts an extra half dozen brown ones in for me.

I also bring a gallon of milk, a quart of cream and sometimes a pie or cake if Aunt Marg has done lots of baking. I like that. Dora isn't such a good cook. For dessert she usually makes sago or tapioca pudding. I especially hate tapioca. It's like swallowing fish eyes. Ugh!

Besides all the foodstuffs, Uncle Herb also pays five dollars a week for my keep. This gives Dora some pin money.

Rabbit's nice, but he's not generous like Uncle Herb. Aunt Marg never has to ask for money. Uncle Herb says she's the boss, so she doesn't need his by-your-leave.

Rabbit is lots of fun, though, and he's always trying to baffle me with riddles. So far he hasn't succeeded. I'll pass one of them on to you now.

"What's the best way to keep a skunk from smelling?"

Send me your answer when you write back. Well, I've been saving my most important news till last.

Are you ready? Hold onto your hat, because here it comes.

I think I have a boyfriend! His name is Philbert Ashley Stromberg and we've been going around together quite a bit lately. Isn't that romantic? Aunt Marg thinks it's outlandish. But of course, she's a bit old-fashioned. Also, she still calls boyfriends beaus. Isn't that funny?

Philbert is called Bert by his friends and, for obvious reasons, the nut by his enemies. He has straight black patent leather hair that he slicks down with brilliantine, inscrutable hazel eyes and a wide sweet smile that's only slightly spoiled by one front tooth overlapping the other.

The best thing about him is his height. He's six feet tall. Isn't that marvelous? I'm five feet seven inches in my stockings, so I tower over most of the boys I know. You're sure lucky you took after Ma instead of Pa in that department. Anyway, it's a real treat not to have to hunch over all the time.

Bert and I go to the pictures at the town hall every other Friday night, and then I go home to the farm on the Saturday morning. Uncle Herb doesn't like that much, but I can't help it. Come to think of it, Uncle

Herb's been a bit cranky lately, and quiet, too. I wonder what ails him?

Bert and I also go bobsledding and ice-skating. Bert made a terrific bobsled out of two small sleds — the kind children use with runners close to the ground — and a long plank and the steering wheel from an old Model A Ford. We go around the curves on Harper's Hill about fifty miles an hour!

Aunt Marg doesn't know a thing about it, so don't tell Ma. They worry about the most stupid things. Bert says it's perfectly safe. Well, almost. We've flipped over once so far, but we didn't get hurt — except for a few bruises on the derrière. *At least, that's where mine are!*

Have you got a boyfriend yet, Josie? Will Pa let you have one? If not, don't tell him about mine, because even though I don't live at home any more, Aunt Marg says that where Gracie and I are concerned, Ma and Pa's word is law.

Write soon and tell me all the news. Does Patsy still look the spitting image of me? I hope not, poor little thing.

Your loving sister, Peg.

* * *

Just before I licked the envelope, I decided I'd better include a note to my mother and father so they wouldn't ask to see Josie's letter. Then I stuck on a two cent stamp and got Rabbit to send it for me. It would go quicker than mailing it at the post office because Rabbit would put it right on the train.

I had to wait quite a while for Josie's reply.

149 Rose Avenue
Toronto, Ontario
January 30, 1931

Dear Peg,

It was swell hearing from you. Especially about you-
know-who. I told Jenny, but nobody else in the family.
She's good at keeping secrets. You can't tell the boys
anything.

Yes, I've got a boyfriend as well, and Ma still calls
them beaus, too. Isn't that quaint? Anyway, the most
coincidental thing is that my boyfriend's name is
Gilbert, which rhymes with Philbert. Get it? Otherwise,
there seems to be no resemblance.

Gilbert is short and cute. He's got fair hair and
freckles. He reminds me a lot of Matt Muggins.

(For some unfathomable reason I felt a stab of
jealousy that made me feel ashamed. Perhaps it was
because I knew I'd hurt Matt's feelings a lot lately on
account of Bert. As far as Matt was concerned, I was
like a dog in a manger. Then again, maybe it was just
Grandma Marshall's nasty streak coming out in me.)

Gilbert walks me home from Parkdale Collegiate every
day and we go ice-skating on Riverdale Rink on
Saturday afternoons. Pa won't let me go out after supper
with boys yet. You're only eleven months older than me.
I'll bet if you were home you wouldn't be allowed to go
out at night either. So you can thank heaven you live in
Shelburne.

We had a good Christmas, but we missed Gracie a lot
because she's been gone only such a short time, unlike
you. Of course, there were just as many of us at the

table, anyway, because of Andrew.

    Oh, my gosh, Peg, I haven't told you the most wonderful news of all. Our Olive is in the family way. We'll soon be aunties. Can you believe it? I'm hoping for a girl, but Elmer hopes it's a boy and Jenny hopes it's one of each because she wants twins like Harry and her. Ma and Pa both say it doesn't matter a fig as long as it has all its fingers and toes.

    Speaking of fingers, I hate to have to tell you this, but our Davey lost half of one of his in an accident. Mr. Gossard across the street — I don't think you know him — was cutting down a tree with a buzz saw and Davey was helping.

    Well, you can picture the rest. There was blood all over the place. Poor Ma was hysterical. Too bad Aunt Marg wasn't here. She'd have known what to do. Pa was furious. He said Mr. Gossard was entirely to blame because Davey was too young to know better.

    Anyway, Davey won't have a right index fingerprint any more, so it's good he's left-handed. Ma used to worry that it would be a hindrance to him all his life being left-handed, but now she says, "The Lord works in strange ways."

    Patsy looks more like you every day. Pa says the two of you are cut from the same bolt — smart and sassy! Ma says the resemblance is so uncanny that she hardly misses you any more, but she doesn't mean it how it sounds, so don't take it to heart.

    I'm doing okay in school. I still wish you were here to help me, though, because I find high school hard.

    Rabbit sounds like fun. With a name like that he

ought to be. I give up on his riddle. What is the best way to keep a skunk from smelling?

Tell Dora I can hardly wait to meet her and that my favourite comics are Freckles and his Friends *and* Tillie the Toiler.

I'll sign off now, Peg. I have to pare the potatoes for supper. Harry's sitting right here twiddling his thumbs but Ma says he doesn't have to help with supper because he's a boy. What a dumb reason!

Give my love to everybody, especially Uncle Herb. I can't imagine him being cranky. Maybe he's just getting old.

Everybody sends their love, especially Ma and Pa. Pa just came in the door from shovelling the sidewalk.

Uh, oh, he just said he's about had enough of shovelling snow, so I asked him why he didn't make Harry do it. If looks could kill I'd be dead!

Jenny says she'll write soon and Patsy kissed the corner of this page.

As ever, Josie.

Sure enough there was a lip-shaped jam splotch on the right-hand corner that made me forgive Patsy instantly for taking my place at home.

Chapter 9

Double Trouble

"Why don't the corn like the farmer?" asked Rabbit with a twitch of his knobby nose.

"Because he picks their ears!" I shot back.

"Dag-nab it, girl."

He scraped the chair back from the table, his ears going a mile a minute. "One of these days . . . "

"I'll have to remember to ask Josie that one," I said with a smile.

"Well, if you want my opinion, I think it's disgusting," snapped Dora as she rolled up the newspapers and stuffed them into the fire. "It's just a mercy we're done eating."

Laughing, I got the graniteware dishpan down from the nail on the wall and set it in the tin sink. I filled the pan with dipperfuls of warm water from the stove's reservoir, then swished the wire soap-cage around to make some suds.

"Just leave the dishes to soak," Dora said with a sharp edge to her voice. "I want a word with you."

The minute Rabbit caught her change of tone, he beat it

out the back door, muttering something about unfinished business at the railway station.

I sat down opposite Dora, my mind flitting around like a butterfly, trying to settle on what I'd done wrong.

Dora wasn't one to mince words.

"Your exams begin soon. Isn't that right?"

"Yes."

I was immediately on the defensive.

"Well, miss, it's one thing to outwit Rabbit and his foolish riddles, but that means nothing when it comes to school work. They don't give marks for that on your report card. Don't you think it's high time you started knuckling down?"

"What for?" I answered boldly. "I'm not behind in anything."

"That's as may be. But sometimes it's them that thinks they're so clever that gets their comeuppance."

Dora kept her eyes down, drumming her fingers agitatedly on the table.

"Your aunt and uncle would be dastardly disappointed if you let spooning interfere with your school work."

Spooning? Good grief!

"Oh, Dora, don't worry," I said, relieved and offended simultaneously. "I'll go over my notes on the weekend."

"You'd better do more than just go over your notes," she huffed as she got up and started washing the dishes.

* * *

The following Friday night I was due to go to the picture show with Bert, and I wasn't about to let school work get in the way of my biweekly entertainment at the movies. This time they were playing a Rudolph Valentino film that was so old-fashioned that everybody roared with laughter at the sad parts and hissed and whistled through the love scenes.

Then right in the middle of the show the screen went black and the lights came on. Everybody began to stomp their feet and yell in protest and a boy named Horace Barwinkle pulled a beanshooter out of his windbreaker pocket and started blowing BBs in all directions.

Suddenly one of the little metal pellets creased my forehead. Then, before I had time to even yell, another one hit my right lens dead centre. The sharp *CRACK* so close to my ear sounded like a window breaking.

Outraged, I took my broken spectacles off to examine them — and found blood all over the frames. More blood began to trickle down my face, and with a little cry I clutched frantically at my forehead.

Instantly, Bert lunged at Horace and the two of them landed in a thrashing heap on the floor. Mr. Stromberg, who'd volunteered to be our chaperone and to run the projector, grabbed the two of them by the hair and yanked them apart.

As it turned out, I'd shut my eyes in the nick of time, so I'd actually received nothing worse than a bruise to my forehead and a minor cut over my right eye. Still, Dora was mad as a hatter when she saw me.

"Serves you very well right," she grumbled as she tore a strip off an old bedsheet and wrapped it none too gently around my throbbing head. "You never pay me no mind."

She was so crotchety that night that I was thankful when Mr. Muggins came to pick me up the next day.

Aunt Marg nearly had a fit.

"Oh, Margaret!" she cried as she carefully unwound the makeshift bandage. "Another half-inch and you might've been blinded."

After cleaning the cut with a carbolic acid solution, she daubed it with iodine. It stung like anything, but I didn't let on.

"I don't think you should go to that town hall any more. You don't belong with those hooligans."

"They're not hooligans, Aunt Marg," I assured her as she applied a neat patch. "It was just an accident."

Uncle Herb peered over the top of his specs and tried his best to look severe.

"You'd better hightail it into Arnold Sparkes' shop first thing Monday morning, Maggie," he said. "Tell him I'll settle with him on Friday when I come to fetch you."

Arnold Sparkes was the town optometrist.

"Oh, golly," I said, turning my head away. "That'll be my third lens this year. I'm sorry to cause so much expense, Uncle Herb."

"Speak up, Maggie. I can't hear you when you mumble like that," Uncle Herb said, cupping his right ear towards me.

I thought I'd spoken perfectly clearly, but nevertheless, I repeated what I'd said in a louder, clearer voice.

When Uncle Herb realized what I'd said, he brushed my lament aside with a smile and a wave of his hand and I thought the whole affair was forgotten and done with.

* * *

I didn't miss my glasses too much until I went to school on the Monday. Then I discovered that I had to settle for just listening to the lessons. It was useless to even try to read what was on the blackboard. And at the supper table that night the Saturday comics were just a colourful blur under my plate.

To make matters worse, it took a whole week to get my special prescription made. Mr. Sparkes said he had to go all the way to Toronto for them. And it was lucky for me he had other business there, or it would have cost Uncle Herb and arm and a leg.

Chapter 10

Comeuppance

The following Sunday night, Bert phoned and asked me to go bobsledding.

"*NO!*" barked Dora before I even had a chance to speak. She must be clairvoyant, I thought miserably as I turned my back on her and made a face into the phone. Bert had heard her answer, too, so after a whispered conversation we hung up.

As soon as I put the phone down, Dora asked in icy tones, "Don't your examinations start on Wednesday?"

"Yes."

"Then get at your books!" she snapped.

Sulkily I unstrapped my books and set to work. About an hour later, Dora silently set a cup of strong tea and a buttered scone beside my algebra book. I thanked her and she took herself off to bed.

I hate to admit it, but Dora was right. They don't give marks for solving riddles. All that week I crammed belatedly for my exams, but it was too little too late. To my shame, I received the lowest average of my life — seventy-two percent.

Not only that, but I was tenth in the class, a placing that I considered a pure disgrace.

"That's not so bad," commiserated Eva, "when you think how long you had to go without your glasses."

"Shoot!" exclaimed lackadaisical Elliot Stromberg. "If I got a mark like that, I'd think I'd died and gone to heaven."

But their words were cold comfort to me.

* * *

It was the first time in my life that I was ashamed to hand my report card to Aunt Marg and Uncle Herb. They studied it together in silence.

Finally Uncle Herb said quietly, "You'll need to do better than that if you plan on being a vet, Maggie."

The disappointment in his voice nearly killed me.

"No more Philip Stromberg for you, my girl," ordered Aunt Marg.

Gracie looked from one to the other, dumbfounded. Wordlessly, she placed Silky on my lap.

The cat crawled up my sweater to my shoulder and began licking my face with her pink, sandpaper tongue. Then she curled herself around my neck like a soft fur collar and started to purr. I scratched between her ears. Even though she belonged to Gracie now, I still think she remembered the time I risked my neck and broke my leg to save her when she was stranded high up in a tree.

"Don't worry," I assured them, "it won't happen again."

And it didn't. I worked like a Trojan for the rest of the school year and never so much as glanced at a boy. In fact

I was so busy that I hardly even noticed when winter turned into spring. One minute the meadow was covered in snow, then the next thing I knew it was sprinkled with purple violets.

The final exams lasted a solid week. When they were over, I knew I had outdone myself. But the results surprised even me. I had actually earned my junior matriculation with a ninety-five per cent average.

Dora was flabbergasted.

"I thought my Angus was clever," she said, staring at me as if I'd been transformed like a chameleon overnight, "but beside you, girl, he don't hold a candle."

"Oh heck, Dora, anybody can do it if they work hard," I said.

I tried not to sound too proud of myself, because I knew it wasn't all my doing.

When I had told Bert that I couldn't date (the newest word for courting) until the end of June, he had dropped me like a hot potato. Then I started to hear rumours through the grapevine that he had been seen lollylagging all over town with a blonde girl by the name of Belinda Barwinkle, Horace Barwinkle's sister.

Belinda was a cute little thing with big dimples and round blue eyes. She was only five feet tall, so she stared up at Bert adoringly. And he loved it, the silly article.

So, to keep my mind from thinking about them, I studied like mad, so in a way, Bert helped me get my high marks.

And I got my comeuppance, as Dora would say, twice.

Chapter 11

Summer, 1931

Gracie and I only spent one week of the summer holidays at home in Toronto. Uncle Herb and Aunt Marg were too busy to leave the farm, so we went by train.

Ma was tickled pink to have us. And the nicest thing happened while we were there. Olive had her baby! It was a boy weighing eight pounds.

Olive was lying in at the Women's College Hospital. They had very strict regulations. No one was allowed to visit the new mother except *her* mother and her husband. Pa was fit to be tied when he heard that.

"After all," he growled, "Andrew isn't even a blood relation."

Anyway, by telling her I'd come from out of town, Ma sweet-talked the head nurse into letting me see Olive. She managed to make it sound like I'd just flown in from Timbuktu.

I was amazed to see that motherhood hadn't changed my oldest sister the least little bit. In fact she seemed more beautiful than ever.

"Did you see the baby?" she asked, her face all aglow.

We'd stopped at the nursery on the way in.

"Isn't he gorgeous? He's just like Andrew, except for my red hair."

"He's pretty as a picture," Ma agreed, thrilled to pieces with her first grandchild.

"He sure is. He's going to be a real lady-killer when he grows up," I said. "Have you named him yet?"

"Yes. William Emerson, after Pa," Olive announced solemnly. "And I want him called William, not Will."

She looked pointedly at Ma when she said this, because Ma always called Pa "Will" for short.

"William Emerson Webster. That's a swell name. Pa must be proud as Punch."

Just then a woman wearing a white smock over a blue checkered housedress came breezing into the room. She looked like any ordinary woman except for the stethoscope around her neck.

Olive introduced us.

"This is Dr. McIntyre, Peggy. My husband is studying under her. This is my sister, Peg — I mean, Margaret — Emerson."

The doctor's eyes lit up.

"Aren't you the girl whose broken leg I set in Sick Children's Hospital? The girl who wants to be a veterinarian?"

I was thrilled that she remembered me.

Popping a thermometer under Olive's tongue, she pressed Olive's wrist with her fingertips.

"My father, God rest his soul, was a veterinarian. When I showed an inclination towards medicine, he backed me all the way — against a great deal of opposition, I might add."

She removed the thermometer and read it with satisfaction, then snapped it down repeatedly.

"I know what you mean," I sighed. "Nobody takes girls seriously when they say they want to be a doctor. My teachers are always trying to discourage me."

"Well, don't let them!"

Her eyes sparked with indignation. Then she added briskly, "I must be on my way. I've got twenty babies to attend to, including one beautiful red-headed boy."

Ma and Olive fell for that line like a ton of bricks.

Before she left, the doctor turned and looked me straight in the eye.

"Margaret," she said. "A word to the wise. You must ignore the doomsayers and forge full steam ahead. Remember, it's your life. Good luck!"

And with that, she whisked out the door and down the corridor, her white coat billowing out behind her.

"There now, Peggy," declared Ma proudly. "You see. You can be anything you want to be. And a plague on those who say you can't."

Knowing a full-fledged woman doctor was certainly an inspiration to me. But seeing Olive's radiant face made me want to be a mother, too. I didn't know how I was going to do it, but I was determined to be both.

* * *

The day before Gracie and I went back to Four Corners, Olive came home with William. She was going to stay with Ma for a week or so until she got on her feet.

The whole family was ecstatic. The little kids hung over

the cradle, sticking their fingers in the baby's tiny fist and touching his downy red hair. Even Elmer, who was shy of babies, held him once or twice.

I thought Ma and Pa would've had their fill of kids, what with ten of us, but they seemed overjoyed to have a grandson. Mind, I noticed Pa still made his escape down to his den in the cellar right after supper, just like always.

Anyway, I was glad Gracie had seen William before we left, or she'd have been mad all the way home.

Davey came back with us for his holiday because it was his turn. And Bobby and Patsy yelled their heads off at being left behind again.

When we got back, it was the funniest thing to see Gracie showing off to Davey as if she was a veteran farmer. She even pretended not to be afraid of Starr.

And there was another thing I noticed about her. She didn't get upset every time Aunt Marg hugged Davey or called him pet names like *bright eyes* or *sunny boy*. Gracie didn't seem to have a jealous bone in her body.

She was so good-natured that Uncle Herb nicknamed her his sweet patootie. The difference between *sweet patootie* and *corker* was pretty obvious. I guess that unlike me, Gracie hadn't inherited Grandma Marshall's nasty streak.

Chapter 12

Another New Babe

Right at the beginning of the summer, Uncle Herb's hired man quit all of a sudden and went out west to seek his fortune. Uncle Herb said that was about as dumb as going to the north pole for a suntan!

Anyway, since he was shorthanded, I pitched in with everything. I even helped Dr. Wiley with the calving.

Aunt Marg thought it might be too much for me — seeing Fancy in distress, that is — but I managed to soothe the young cow's fears and keep her calm while Doc Wiley did the work.

Oh, what a thrill it was to see that helpless little creature come slithering into the world. I watched fascinated as her skinny wet legs unfolded. She reminded me of a fern uncurling in springtime, so I instantly christened her Fern.

All our cows had names beginning with the letter F. There was poor Fauna, who'd choked to death on a turnip back in 1926, and Flora (Uncle Herb referred to her as the old girl now, but she still gave plenty of milk) and Fancy,

Flora's daughter. And now, pretty doe-eyed Fern, Flora's granddaughter.

While Doc took care of Fancy, I gently wiped the calf down and then gave her to her mother.

About a half-hour after the birth, both mother and daughter were on their feet. The little brown heifer stood on trembling legs, leaning on her mother. Then she began to bunt under Fancy with her pink wet nose in search of sustenance.

"She's pretty wobbly yet," laughed Dr. Wiley as he washed up in the bucket of soapy water Aunt Marg had brought out for him, "but she's a fine calf and it won't be long before she's as strong as her mother."

"How did I do, Doc?" I asked anxiously as he packed his instruments carefully into his worn leather satchel.

"You're a regular trouper, Maggie," he answered. "I just hate to think what'll become of my practice when you hang out your shingle."

I blushed with pride.

"Aw! I'll never be as good a vet as you."

But I knew I would. My heart was set on it. And Uncle Herb always maintained that when I made up my mind about something, I was as stubborn as McGogerty's mule.

I was flattered at the compliment, but not terribly thrilled with the form it took!

That night after supper I started to help with the washing up, when Aunt Marg took the dishrag out of my hand.

"You sit yourself down, girl. You've done enough for one day. Here, Gracie, you dry. And, Davey . . .

"For mercy sakes, child, what're you doing?"

Davey was standing on his head against the wall, his straight brown hair spread out like a fringed mat on the floor.

"I'm seeing if my supper will come back up," he replied cheerfully.

"Well if it does, guess whose job it'll be to mop the floor?"

At that, Davey did a quick backflip and was on his feet in a second.

"You put the dishes in the cabinet, Davey. There's a good boy. Your sister looks all done in."

"Thanks, Aunt Marg. I sure am tired."

I collapsed into the rocking chair, my legs as wobbly as the newborn calf's.

"I think I'll listen to the crystal set for a while. It'll help me relax."

I reached behind me for the earphones that hung on the knob of the chair.

"That set ain't worth a hoot any more, Maggie," remarked Uncle Herb, twirling a straw in rapid circles between his teeth.

I adjusted the headset over my ears and listened. To my surprise I picked up WIP in Philadelphia just as plain as if it was coming from Shelburne.

"It sounds swell to me, Uncle Herb. There's a man talking to Colonel Charles Lindbergh about his solo airplane ride across the Atlantic. Come and listen."

He sat down and I put the earphones over his fuzzy red head and kissed his bald spot. I used to do that a lot when I was a little kid.

He puckered his brow, concentrating. Then he began to jiggle first one earphone and then the other. After about five minutes, he yanked them off impatiently and handed the headset back to me.

"It's faded out again, Maggie. Mebbe it'll come back in tomorrow night."

I put the headset on again and found to my surprise that the station was still perfectly clear. Now a high tenor voice was singing a slow melody.

* * *

Right about then, I must've fallen asleep sitting up, because the next thing I knew it was morning and I was in bed beside Gracie.

"How did I get here?" I wondered aloud.

Gracie laughed her high-pitched giggle.

"We sleepwalked you up to bed and Aunt Marg put your nightshift on over your underwears."

"Swell!"

I flung back the summer quilt and bounded out of bed.

"That'll make it all the easier to get dressed. C'mon, Gracie, let's get Davey and go check on Fern."

We went down to the barn and spent the whole morning coddling Fancy and her baby.

On our way back to the house, Davey said, "Peggy, Gracie says that when you were our age, you used to play tricks on Uncle Herb. Will you show us how to play a trick?"

"Hmm," I pondered, "I'll have to think about that, Davey. Uncle Herb knows all my old tricks, so we'd have to think up a brand-new one."

"Did you ever play a trick on Aunt Marg?" asked Gracie.

"Once."

I grinned at the memory that popped back into my mind.

"Ma had sent me two celluloid eggs full of jellybeans for

Easter. When I'd eaten all the candies, I wondered what to do with the eggs. They snapped together in the middle and looked like real eggs. Then I got an idea. I sneaked out to the henhouse and tucked them under two of Aunt Marg's ladies. Well, when she gathered the eggs that day she must've been preoccupied about something, because she didn't even notice the difference in weight. It wasn't until the next morning at breakfast when she tried to crack them open on the edge of the frying pan that she realized she'd been fooled."

"What'd she do?" squealed Gracie.

"Was she mad?" grinned Davey.

"No, she wasn't mad. She laughed her head off. But she didn't let me get away with it. She made me gather the eggs every day for a whole week."

Gracie and Davey were still laughing when we walked in through the woodshed door.

"Wash your hands at the basin," said our practical aunt, ignoring the giggles.

But Uncle Herb said, "What's the big joke?"

"That's for us to know, and you to find out," I said, giving Gracie and Davey a conspiratorial glance.

They snickered and snorted all through dinner, but they didn't tell.

Chapter 13

A Brand New Trick

That night after supper, Uncle Herb went out to sit on the piazza. Tipping back a weather-beaten old kitchen chair, he balanced it on its wobbly legs, propped his feet up on the railing and began to chew to his heart's content. It was downright fascinating to see him spit through the space between his two front teeth and hit a yellow daisy right in the eye at ten paces.

The next day while he was still out in the field haying, Aunt Marg came back from the barnyard after feeding her ladies. I was in the kitchen laying the table for supper when I heard her let out a screech that made me jump a mile.

"What's the matter, Aunt Marg? Did you get stung by a bee?"

"My daisies! My glads! My delphiniums!"

Aunt Marg had dropped to her knees and was cupping wilted flowers in her hands.

"For mercy sakes, what ails them?" she mourned as the petals came off in her fingers.

"Why, they're all over brown spots. They look like they've got the blight."

She held a sickly flower to her nose and sniffed. Suddenly she knew.

"That man!" She rose up to her full five feet, giving her apron an angry shake. "That husband of mine. Just wait until I get my hands on him."

When supper was ready, Gracie and Davey fought over who'd ring the dinner gong. Then Uncle Herb came whistling in the door as innocent as a spring lamb.

"HERBERT ALFRED WILKINSON!"

The second Uncle Herb heard Aunt Marg use his full name like that, especially in such a stentorian voice, he knew he was in for it.

"What in thunder did I do now?" he growled defensively.

"You've killed my whole flower bed, that's what you've done. You and your vile tobacco habit."

I was on her side this time, because I hated to see anything killed, even flowers.

We ate our stew in stony silence. Even Gracie kept quiet. Davey studied his finger stub the way he always did whenever he was perturbed about something, almost as though he thought it might be about to sprout.

Uncle Herb hurried through his supper and went skulking off to the barn.

"Aw, poor Uncle Herb," I said to Aunt Marg, my heart melting. "I'm sure he didn't mean any harm."

"I know you think he's a paragon, Margaret. And bless my soul, so do I most of the time. But he's got to be taught a lesson."

I'd been thinking about the problem all through supper,

and I'd finally come up with an idea.

"Do you still want to play a trick on Uncle Herb, Davey?"

"Ya! Ya!" cried my mischievous little brother. Aunt Marg was filling the dishpan with dipperfuls of warm water.

"What've you got up your sleeve this time, Margaret?"

She sounded like her old self again.

That was the nicest thing about Aunt Marg. She never stayed mad for long.

"Let's make an imitation tobacco plug that looks so real Uncle Herb won't know the difference until he starts to chew. One that'll taste so bad he'll never get over it."

"What'll we make it out of?" squealed Gracie, hopping from one foot to the other.

"I know!" Davey dove headfirst into the woodbox and came up with a piece of wood about the right size.

"Davey! D'you want to break Uncle Herb's teeth?"

"Well, what'll we use, then?"

He plunked the wood back into the box, scaring Silky, snoozing under the stove. She yowled and spat at him.

"How about a chunk of carbolic soap smeared with brown shoe polish and wrapped in Old Plug paper?" I suggested as I dried the spoons and dropped them clinking into the spoon jar in the centre of the table.

"That's no good. He'll smell it!" cried Gracie, almost dropping a dish in her excitement.

"That's right. He will," agreed Aunt Marg. "Shoe cream would be a dead giveaway."

The problem nearly had me stumped. Then I got a flash of inspiration.

"I think I've got it," I said, pausing dramatically.

Gracie and Davey waited impatiently for me to go on,

nearly beside themselves with expectation.

"We'll rub real tobacco into the soap until it's completely camouflaged."

Instantly there was a chorus of agreement. Quickly we cleared the table. Aunt Marg fetched the cake of carbolic while I went to the woodshed and snitched a plug of tobacco from the pile.

I cut the soap and showed Davey how to roughen the smooth surface with a fork while I carefully unwrapped the tobacco plug so as not to rip the paper. Then Gracie and I took turns rubbing it into the soap. When we were finished, it looked and smelled exactly like the real thing.

Following the original creases, I wrapped our fake tobacco plug neatly in the paper and hid what was left of the genuine plug in the woodbox. I just had time to set the fake plug on top of the pile when Uncle Herb came sidling into the house through the woodshed door.

He took himself straight off to bed.

The next night at the supper table, we all acted perfectly natural. Gracie and Davey jabbered a mile a minute, Uncle Herb and I discussed the crops and Aunt Marg declared proudly that her ladies had produced a record number of brown eggs.

Then Aunt Marg and I started the washing up. That was Uncle Herb's cue to sneak out to the woodshed, grab a plug from the top of the pile and head for the piazza.

This time he placed his chair on the opposite side of the porch, facing the trellis of morning glories.

"Well, for land's sakes," sputtered Aunt Marg indignantly as we all peeked through the curtains. "Now that scoundrel's going after my glories."

We watched breathlessly as he began his ritual.

First he peeled the paper off, then he drew the plug under his nose to savour the aroma.

"If it passes the sniff test," chuckled Aunt Marg, "we're home free!"

Our soapy plug must've passed, because he snapped open his penknife and proceeded to carve off a corner.

"Oh, my gosh," I hissed. "He'll notice it's white inside."

Gracie and Davey sucked in their breath. The suspense was killing us all, but we needn't have worried. Uncle Herb was too busy daydreaming to pay any attention.

From the dull side of the knife, he popped the soap into his mouth and began to chew.

Suddenly he leapt to his feet, toppling the chair, and began frantically hacking and spitting over the railing.

"Argh!"

He gagged and coughed and choked and spat, wiping his mouth furiously on his shirt sleeve. The four of us dissolved into stitches. Then the screen door banged open and a red-faced, outraged Uncle Herb exploded in.

"WHY YOU . . . YOU . . . YOU . . . DODGASTED, COLD-BLOODED, ORNERY CRITTERS! YOU'RE OUT TO POISON A MAN!"

Gracie and Davey danced around him like whirling dervishes.

"We did it, Uncle Herb! We did it! Are you mad?"

Aunt Marg and I didn't hear his answer because we were laughing so hard we both had to race down the path to the outhouse. When we came back, Uncle Herb was gargling and gurgling at the basin.

Suddenly I felt remorseful, so I gave him a squeeze from behind.

"It's for your own good, you know," I said affectionately. "Dr. Tom says chewing tobacco is bad for the digestion."

"Well, carbolic's a dang sight worse."

Uncle Herb's voice was muffled by the flannel as he scrubbed his tongue.

"I'm sorry, Uncle Herb."

Gracie's face was all puckered up, as if she was going to cry.

"Me too!" agreed Davey, giving Uncle Herb's leg a bearhug.

"Well, you're a passel of no account corkers, the lot of you. Especially that one."

He glared ferociously at me.

"Don't look at me!" I protested innocently. "It wasn't my idea to play a trick on you."

"You can't bamboozle me, Maggie Rosie Emerson. A prank like that's got your stamp all over it."

Still wiping bubbles from his bewhiskered chin, he went on muttering to himself, "Dad-blamed no-karat corkers."

It was the last childish trick I ever played on my sweet uncle, and the meanest. It would've been worth it, too, if it'd worked, but all it did was put a cramp in his style.

Anyway, Davey had some swell stories to take home to tell the family.

Chapter 14

A Chat with Starr

"Well, Starr, I'm off to school again," I said as I rode the big Clydesdale into the bush lot on the far side of the pasture.

Matt and I had gotten lost in the bush lot once when we were kids, and Starr had saved our lives. It'd been dead of winter and we would've frozen to death for sure if my beloved horse hadn't responded to the secret signal. Now I knew every link and chain that made up Green Meadows farm like the back of my hand and I couldn't lose my way if I wanted to.

"I'm really anxious to get started on my senior year, because after that comes the Ontario Veterinary College in Guelph. Then I'll be on my way to becoming a real animal doctor. In the meantime, don't you dare get sick."

I scrunched down and ducked my head as we passed under some low-hanging branches.

"Are you listening to me, boy?"

Starr craned his neck around, twitched his long pointed ears and swept his snowy lashes over his shining dark eyes. Then he puffed out his velvety lips and blew a low vibrating whicker.

Oh, how I love that shimmying, horsy sound! Stretching myself full length along the crest of his strong neck, I clasped my hands under his smooth brown jowls and buried my face in his golden mane. After working and playing with him all summer long I was sure going to miss him.

* * *

Uncle Herb drove me into Shelburne on Labour Day. The pickup trundled down bumpy Rail Street and soon we could see Dora outside stooped over her bit of a flower bed.

The truck came to a stop with a squeal of brakes amidst billowing dust. Dora straightened up, rubbing her long spine as she did so, a bunch of purple zinnias in her hand.

"Well, speak of the devil!"

She laid the flowers on the porch steps and wiped her muddy hands on her pinafore.

"I just now said to my Angus, 'I hope Meggie gets here before you leave.'"

"Angus is here?"

I'd been dying to meet her only son.

"Yep. Been home nigh on two weeks. He's away again right after supper. I've got pot roast, string beans and bread pudding. Would you care to stop and have a bite with us, Herb?"

"Don't mind if I do!" declared Uncle Herb, licking his chops as if he hadn't just polished off a full course dinner at noon hour.

"I'll just give Mag a ring on the blower."

He hopped down from the cab and got my grip from the

back. Then he hoisted two big boxes of books over the side and set them on the grass with a grunt.

Just then, the screen door clacked open and out onto the porch stepped the living image of Gilbert Roland, the moving picture star.

"This here is my son, Angus," Dora said proudly.

"Angus, this is my star boarder Margaret Rose Emerson. 'Course, you two men know each other."

Uncle Herb shook his head in amazement.

"I never would've knowed you, boy. You've changed and growed so much, I'd have passed you on the street."

Angus ignored Uncle Herb's observation.

"How are you, sir," he said, clicking his heels and bowing from the waist.

I'd never seen anyone do that before, so I was impressed.

"Now, don't you go calling me sir, young fella. You know my name and I ain't been knighted by the king since last we met."

Dora's son didn't even so much as *hint* at a smile in response to my uncle's cheery admonition.

Darn, I thought, gazing at Angus's incredibly handsome profile. If only I'd worn a decent dress! And my hair. I should've been fixing it instead of combing Starr's tail. And my freckles! Aunt Marg warned me about not wearing my straw hat in the hayfield.

"How do you do, Miss."

Angus offered me a limp, lily-white hand and my heart did somersaults. Beside him, Bert Stromberg looked like a bucktoothed beaver.

"Pleased to meet you, Angus," I said in a breathy voice. "Your mother's told me all about you."

Our fingers had barely touched before he drew his away. I guess my hand felt rough compared to his.

He didn't say any more, so Dora and I picked up the boxes and Uncle Herb carried my grip into the house.

Angus didn't offer to help.

Rabbit was sitting on a stool beside the Kitchen Queen range, contentedly carving himself a chunk of Old Plug. He cut off the kitty-corner and tendered it to Uncle Herb on the dull side of the knife. Dora allowed chewing in the house. They even had a spittoon in the parlour next to the Quebec Heater, though I'd never seen Rabbit actually use it.

"What's the best way to ketch a fish, Meggie?" That's how Rabbit greeted me after not seeing me for two months.

"Have somebody throw it to you!" came my reply.

"Dad-blame it, girl!" he snorted with delight. "I'll fool you one of these days."

Wiggling his ears and nose simultaneously, he lifted the stove lid and sent a stream of brown juice sizzling into the fire. Angus grimaced and turned away. I laughed and picked up my grip and headed upstairs to my bedroom.

In the corner of the room by the door, all strapped and buckled, sat a big leather suitcase. It hadn't occurred to me that Angus would stay in the room I stayed in. It gave me a funny turn — a sort of dispossessed feeling.

I lay down on top of the starburst quilt for a minute to reclaim my territory. The felt mattress seemed to sag in the middle, so I hung my head over the side and looked underneath. Sure enough, one of the wooden slats was broken.

With a sigh I got up and tidied my hair, cleaned my specs and changed my dress. Then I put some lip rouge on.

Eva had given me a stick for my last birthday, but I hadn't used it yet. Most of the girls in high school used lip rouge — in addition to cheek rouge and face powder. They were always sneaking their puffs out behind their books to powder their noses. But I hadn't bothered yet.

"*MEGGIE!*"

Dora's strident voice came sailing up the stairwell.

"Supper is served!"

Supper is served?

I'd never heard Dora say that before. Her usual cry was, "Soup's on!"

The table was set with the green linen cloth, silver cutlery and white china dishes. In the centre, in a cut glass vase, the purple zinnias that Dora had been picking when we arrived added a nice touch of colour.

"How's the new job, then?" asked Uncle Herb as he helped himself to a huge dollop of mashed potatoes.

"Splendid, thank you, sir," answered Angus grandly. "The Transportation Commission chose me over hundreds of other applicants."

"It's no picnic landing a good job in these hard times," interjected Dora proudly as she served her son the choicest cut of meat. "And they gave him a uniform, and put him on the day shift straightaway."

I wondered what was so special about the day shift. My Pa worked nights half the time, and he was a boss.

"I'm drawing fourteen dollars a week," bragged Angus as he cut his meat into dainty, bite-sized pieces. "*Plus* overtime. And a week's summer sabbatical, *with* recompense."

Sabbatical! Recompense! He sounded as if he'd swallowed a dictionary.

Suddenly he turned his attention to me and what looked like a smirk seemed to flit across his face.

"What about you, young lady? With that crop of freckles, your ambition must surely be to marry a farmer."

He couldn't have said anything worse if he'd thought for a week. And I was sure I detected a sneer in the way he said farmer.

My face blazed and a sarcastic reply jumped to my lips. I had to bite my tongue to keep it in.

When I'd gotten hold of my temper, I answered coldly, "If I do get married, I *will* choose a farmer."

Across the table, Uncle Herb was straining forward, cupping his ear, so I raised my voice a notch.

"But my ambition is to become a veterinarian, and I don't think I'll have time to do both."

"Maggie's just past sixteen," bragged Uncle Herb, "and already she's going for her senior matriculation."

"She'll be the youngest scholar in fifth form," added Dora, anxious to make up for her son's rudeness.

"She's quick as a whip, that one. You won't find no flies on her."

Rabbit waggled his fork in my direction to emphasize his words and accidentally flicked gravy on Angus's immaculate coatsleeve.

"Oh, no!" yelled Angus.

Leaping to his feet, he stuck out his arm as if a bird had dropped something on it.

"You careless fool!" he snarled at his father. "Now see what you've done."

Dora jumped up like a shot, rushed over to the sink and came back with a wetted flannel. Nervously she began sponging the greasy brown splotch.

Angus brushed her away impatiently.

Rabbit just ignored the whole scene and picked up a juicy bone with his fingers. After a few chews, he put the bone down, poured tea from his cup to his saucer, blew waves across it and drank it down in one loud slurp. I'd never known him to use such bad manners before.

Angus glared at Rabbit with a look of pure disgust that distorted his handsome features.

"You shouldn't even eat with pigs, let alone in polite company!" he snapped. Then he marched out of the room.

Maybe he shouldn't, but *you* should! I thought to myself.

I didn't say anything out loud because poor Dora was upset enough already.

A few minutes later, Angus came back with another suit-coat on. He sat down and proceeded to eat a huge meal in outraged silence.

Phew! talk about a mean streak, I thought. Beside him, I'm as sweet as cotton candy.

When he'd finished eating, he suddenly glared at me and snapped, "I've never even *heard* of such a thing as a female veterinarian."

"You will!" I retorted immediately.

A pained expression crossed Dora's face, so I changed the subject.

"Where do you live in Toronto?" I asked in as friendly a tone as I could muster.

He dabbed at his perfect mouth daintily with the corner of his napkin before replying.

"I have excellent accommodation with a very refined family in the Beaches," he answered haughtily.

"Oh, I know where that is. We often have picnics down at Kew Beach. My family — my city family, that is — live in the east end, too. On Rose Avenue."

"Never heard of the place," Angus said huffily.

I don't know what would have come out of my mouth after that remark if fate hadn't intervened in the form of the train's warning whistle.

Angus had to run to catch it, his mother puffing behind him, lugging his heavy suitcase.

* * *

When Dora and I had finished the washing up, we all went into the parlour to listen to the gramophone. Rabbit wound it up and put on a record. Eddie Cantor began to sing "If you knew Susie like I know Susie."

Rabbit wiggled his ears in perfect time to the music. He didn't seem the least bit perturbed by what'd gone on earlier, and that really puzzled me.

Rabbit and Uncle Herb enjoyed an after-supper chaw. Then at the end of the third record, Uncle Herb said, "Well, I'd best be shoving off. It's darkening down and one of my headlamps is out."

He thanked Dora for the good grub and said goodbye. Then he and I walked hand in hand to the pickup.

"I don't understand, Uncle Herb," I said.

He chawed away and didn't answer.

"Angus is so different from either of his parents. He's so mean and disrespectful. Gosh, our Elmer is about Angus's age and my pa would knock him flat if he dared to talk to him like that."

Uncle Herb sent a jet of tobacco juice sailing over the pickup. We heard it splat on the other side.

Still he didn't say anything. He could be stubborn too when he felt like it.

"And another funny thing. I can't for the life of me figure out whose side Angus favours. He's not the least bit like his father, he's so darned handsome! No offence intended to Rabbit, of course."

"Climb up in the cab there, Maggie," interrupted Uncle Herb. "You choke and I'll crank."

It was the perfect foil. Uncle Herb knew how I loved to get my hands on the steering wheel.

He swung the crank around twice and the engine rumbled into life. I revved it up, then shoved over to make room for Uncle Herb behind the wheel. We sat there for a minute without speaking, jiggling with the rhythm of the motor.

Finally I could contain myself no longer.

"It's just that I feel sorry for Dora and Rabbit," I persisted. "Imagine having an only child as mean as that Angus."

Then at last Uncle Herb spoke.

"Well, Maggie, I reckon you're old enough to know. Roger Hare ain't the boy's real father. They're no kith or kin at all. But Rabbit's been a good father to Angus ever since the boy was knee-high to a grasshopper."

I was dumbfounded at the revelation.

"Who *is* his real father then?" I asked incredulously.

"Don't know. Never asked. Me and Mag figure it's none of our business."

He looked me straight in the eye when he said that and I knew he was warning me that it was none of mine either.

"I'll keep it under my hat," I promised.

Then I kissed him goodbye on his stubbly chin, hopped

out of the cab and waved until the truck disappeared around the corner of Main and Rail streets.

* * *

That night, Rabbit went to bed early.

"Well, what did you think of my lad?" Dora asked, blind mother love shining from her eyes.

"He's handsome as all get-out."

At least I could say that and mean it.

But in my mind I could hear my mother saying, "Handsome is as handsome does!"

"I'll bet he could get into pictures if he went to Hollywood," I continued.

Dora beamed at my praise. I should've left it at that, but my curiosity got the better of me again and I couldn't resist adding, "I can't help wondering who he looks like."

Dora held a spoonful of sugar very still over her tea. Instantly I wished with all my heart I'd kept my mouth shut.

Dora's voice was strangely quiet when she answered, "He gets his good looks from his pa. And his orneryness too."

I tried to cover up quickly.

"I sure know what it's like to inherit orneryness. Ma says I'm my Grandma Marshall all over. She had a mean streak a mile wide."

The more I said, the worse it got.

But to my relief, Dora just laughed. Then we spread the newspapers on the table, set out the breakfast dishes and went to bed, too.

Angus's father was never mentioned again.

Chapter 15

Fifth Form High

When I began my senior year, I quickly found that everything — textbooks, teachers, friends — was new and exciting. Not only that, but in fifth form there were lots more boys than girls in the class. This was because senior year was preparation for college, and not many parents encouraged their girls to go to college. Times were hard. Some kids even had to drop out of school to help support their families.

If folks could afford to send one of their offspring to university at all, boys tended to get preference. After all, reasoned their parents, educating a girl was a waste of money in the long run, because girls only became housewives and mothers — or old maids. How much learning did you need for that?

I was one of the lucky few. Aunt Marg and Uncle Herb not only encouraged me, they put up the money when the time came — eighty-five dollars for every term! It sounded like a fortune, so I offered to help by getting an after-school job. Uncle Herb turned thumbs down on that idea.

"You're my right-hand man on the farm, Maggie. Ain't nobody deserves an eddication more'n you do."

* * *

The problem was, not everybody agreed with him.

For instance, our principal and science teacher, Mr. Bannister, was dead set against higher education for women. Every time I raised my hand to answer a question, he'd look right through me and ask the boy behind me.

"I just know I'm going to lose my temper and tell him off, Dora," I complained one day after a particularly humiliating experience. "And if I do, I'll be in trouble for sure. Once my tongue gets loose, there's no telling what might come out of my mouth. Even I don't know until it's too late."

Dora was rocking briskly to and fro as she knitted a red woollen square. She was making an afghan this time.

"Why don't you try a new tack then?" she suggested.

"Like what?"

I sat down at the table, opened my exercise book, sucked the oil off my new pen-nib and dipped it in the inkpot.

"Just pay him no mind, Meggie, no mind at all. Don't even give him the time of day."

She squinted through her downstairs glasses and picked up a dropped stitch.

"Just you do your level best on your own. Then when exam time comes, he'll get his comeuppance and you'll earn an extra feather in your cap."

Dora chuckled as she rolled up her skein of yarn and spiked her needles through it.

"He's an old-fashioned stick, and that's a fact. Why, he didn't even approve of women getting the vote in 1920. Said the Lord never intended the female mind to deal in politics. But for all that, he's not a mean man, Meggie. Just ignorant. There's a world of difference."

She wagged her finger at me to make her point.

"There's a good side to Dusty Bannister," she continued while she filled the kettle. "I should know. He sure stood by me when I was left alone with Angus. Wouldn't hear a word against me. And he took care of his widowed mother to her dying day. Fair worshipped the woman, he did. That says a lot for a man."

"Dusty! What a cute name!" I laughed. "Why do you call Mr. Bannister that?"

"Oh, it goes way back to our school days. His real name is Durward. Well, no matter how clean and paid for Durward got sent off to school, he'd scuff his feet along the dirt road and arrive at the schoolhouse door covered in dust. Then the schoolmarm — Miss Teasey was her name — would make him jump up and down and shake himself off before she'd let him in the classroom. So that's how he came by his nickname. He'll always be Dusty to me."

From that day on, every time I looked at scowling Mr. Bannister I'd get a picture in my mind's eye of the dusty little boy he used to be, and somehow that softened my feelings towards him.

After all, I wasn't so prim and proper myself. My favourite get-up even at the age of sixteen was still my overalls, especially when they smelled rich and horsy.

* * *

I made a brand-new friend in fifth form. Her name was Phylis Carpenter and she lived across town. Her folks had just moved to Shelburne from Orangeville.

Phylis and I hit it off right away because we were so

much alike. Not only were we similar in personality, but we were also both tall and skinny with dark curly hair and freckles. The only difference was that Phyllis didn't wear spectacles.

"My brother Willard says I'm mean as a skunk," Phylis confided cheerfully as we sat on the girls' side of the school steps, eating our mashed potato sandwiches.

When I heard that, I told her then and there all about the nasty streak I'd inherited from my Grandma Marshall.

"I practically hate Willard," she said, blowing up her lunch bag and bursting it with a loud bang. "You know why?"

"No, why?"

"Because the other day I was in the kitchen when he came in the front hall with a boy named Bert Stromberg. Do you know Bert Stromberg?"

"Oh, you mean Philbert the nut," I replied maliciously.

Bert had had to repeat fifth form because he'd failed last year. Served him right, I thought, for wasting his time lolly-gagging after Belinda.

"Sure, I've seen him around."

"Well, they didn't know I was home.

"I heard Bert say, 'I hear you've got a sister. What's she like?'

"Then that rotten brother of mine said, 'Oh, you mean old freckle-face. You wouldn't be interested in her. She's as mean as a weasel, and she's got a figure like a tableleg.'

"It was that last remark that made me see red, so I bounded through the kitchen door and surprised the lights out of them.

"Well, at least Bert had the decency to blush, but that rat

Willard laughed his head off and said, 'See what I mean?'

"So I screeched at him, 'While you're at it, did you tell him you still have to have a rubber sheet on your bed, and that you're a typhoid carrier?'"

I almost choked on a crust and Phylis had to thump me on the back to save my life.

Phylis was a barrel of fun. We got on like a house afire. The only problem was Eva. I knew she was jealous of Phylis and I hated to hurt her feelings. I still considered Eva and Matt my best friends, but Eva was boring compared to Phylis, so I was torn between the two.

Chapter 16

Help!

The *CRASH* could be heard for miles around.

Eva said Mrs. Stromberg woke up screaming that the world was coming to an end. And Phylis Carpenter, whose house was on the outskirts of town, said she was sure her roof was going to cave in. So you can imagine how it sounded to us — because our roof *did* cave in.

I woke with a shock to find myself trapped under the collapsed ceiling. Only the sturdy iron bedstead posts had saved me from being crushed flat as a pancake. As Rabbit said later, by rights I should've been killed.

The horrendous crash still echoing in my ears, I began to scream. I'd been sleeping on my stomach, so I turned my head sideways — and saw what looked like a huge, craggy arm in a tattered sleeve poking through the broken beams. Giant, shadowy fingers seemed to be snatching at my hair.

"Dora! Dora!" I shrieked at the top of my lungs. But my voice was drowned out by the sound of grinding metal and groaning rafters and a strange assortment of noises coming from outdoors — loud shouts and wild hysterical cries.

"Meggie!" Dora screamed. "Are you alive?"

"I think so," I yelled back. "But I'm trapped in my bed. What happened?"

"Train got wrecked . . . jack-knifed right behind the house . . . split the old elm tree . . . cattle car's smashed to smithereens."

"*That's* what I can hear. It's the cows. I'm scared, Dora."

"Rabbit's gone for help, Meggie. Don't move a muscle."

I tried not to, but I was shaking from head to toe by now and bits of wood and plaster kept falling all around me. Then as my eyes adjusted to the moonlight slanting through the broken roof, I saw to my relief that the craggy arm was a limb from the elm tree in the Hare's yard, and the phantom fingers were autumn leaves plucking at my hair.

At last I heard Rabbit's voice.

"Meggie!" he called. "What's grey and wrinkled and carries a trunk?"

That Rabbit, I thought, he'll be asking riddles at Armageddon.

"An old grey mouse going on holidays," I answered, trying not to laugh.

Then I heard Rabbit say, "She'll be all right, that one. Now hang on, Meg, and we'll get you outta there afore you can spell Jack Robinson."

"Please, God, help!" I prayed fervently.

Then I heard a man's voice saying, "We'll prop the wall up with our backs while you get her out."

The voice sounded familiar, but at that moment I didn't know or care who it was.

"I've got ahold of you, girl."

Suddenly Rabbit had a tight grip on my ankles. "You'll have to wiggle out on your belly. There ain't no room to turn over."

I started squirming backwards as Rabbit pulled me by the feet. My long legs scraped over the iron bedrail.

Glancing quickly over my shoulder to check my progress, I saw in the moonlight two pale mounds.

Oh, no! My behind! My bare behind! My nightdress had worked its way up to my waist, leaving my bottom naked as a jay bird.

"Rabbit! Stop! My nightdress!"

Then I heard Dora's fierce voice.

"You men, shut your eyes or I'll blind you with a red-hot poker."

"Yes, ma'am!" I heard them answer.

Minutes dragged by like hours as I worked my way backwards.

The combination of the huge branch and the collapsed wall trying to close in on me gave me a horrible, stifling feeling.

"Talk to me, Dora," I begged.

So she did. Over and over again she assured me that everything was going to be all right.

Suddenly there came a grinding, rending *CRACK*, and the wall shifted ominously.

Grunting and straining, one of the men holding up the wall gasped, "Hurry up before our backs give out."

"Meggie," Rabbit's tone was dead serious now, "our eyes is all shut and Dora's got a quilt ready to throw over you, so wiggle outta there before the whole dern place falls in."

I made one last desperate effort — and all of a sudden I was free.

Dora wrapped the quilt around me and led me downstairs.

Just as we got to the parlour door, there was another big *CRASH*.

"Roger!" Dora screamed.

"We're right behind you. Everything's under control."

The electricity had been knocked out, so Dora lit the oil lamp she kept for emergencies.

I was still shaking like a leaf as my rescuers came in through the kitchen doorway covered in plaster dust. In the flickering lamplight they looked like three ghostly apparitions. Then they went outside to check the damage.

Oddly, not a thing had been disturbed in the kitchen. Not even a pan had fallen off the wall. Dora shut both doors and I felt safe at last.

"Dora," my voice was still a bit shaky, "who were those men with Rabbit?"

"You didn't recognize them? Mr. Stromberg and Philbert."

Bert! Oh, how I wished I'd died!

"Dora, do you think they saw?"

"Saw what?" She filled the kettle and put it on to boil.

"You know."

Dora said nothing. Instead, she silently fetched the speckled teapot from the cupboard. The white enamel mugs were already on the table for breakfast.

"My *derrière*!" I yelled at last, almost in tears.

"What's a *derrière*? I never heard tell of such a thing," she hedged innocently.

"Well then, my naked bottom. You know what that is, don't you?" I was getting mad.

Her back was to me, her salt-and-pepper braid swinging at her waist.

Then I noticed her shoulders jiggling. She was laughing! The silly article was laughing at me.

"Dora! How can you laugh. I nearly get killed, and lose all my dignity in the process, and you stand there guffawing."

She swilled hot water in the teapot and dumped it down the sink.

"Margaret, my dear, we'll probably never know who saw what. Just thank your lucky stars that their backs were strong enough to hold the wall up."

She began to mash the tea.

"That's all right for you to say," I grumbled, "but I'll be plagued by it for the rest of my natural life."

"Well, if you are, my girl" — she poured strong, steaming brew into our mugs — "then more fool you!"

* * *

The train wreck and my miraculous escape were the talk of the town, but no one snickered when they saw me, and no rude remarks were ever made, so I knew that Bert had had the decency to keep his mouth shut. Either that, or the threat of Dora's red-hot poker had scared the daylights out of him.

Anyway, when I met him on Main Street a few days later, all he said was, "Are you okay, Marg?"

I'll always be grateful to him for that.

Chapter 17

Opportunity Knocks

My bedchamber was the only room in the house that was completely demolished, so I went back to the farm until Rabbit rebuilt it.

Uncle Herb took me in to school each day. One crispy, autumn morning, as we were driving through a shower of falling leaves, I had an inspiration.

"Uncle Herb," I said, "why don't I drive myself in. Then you wouldn't have to be bothered."

"Because you ain't got no licence."

"Neither have you."

"That's different."

"Why?"

" 'Cause I'm a growed man."

"Well how do I get a licence, then?"

"You got to take a driving test in Barrie. But first you got to have lots of practice."

"Then this is my chance. If you let me drive back and forth every day, I'll soon have lots of practice. Besides, I've already practised in our lane. I can back up and change gears and stop on a dime."

That last bit was an exaggeration. The brakes of the pickup were so bad I had to stand up on them to make them work.

Uncle Herb looked pretty skeptical.

"I got a feeling Mag ain't going to like it," he said.

"Well let's not tell her until I'm ready to try my test. Then if I pass and she agrees, will you let me drive myself to school?"

"I'll think on it," he hedged.

Rolling down the window, he let a stream of tobacco juice fly with the leaves.

"I don't see how we could keep Mag from getting wind of it. More'n likely some busybody would see us and spill the beans."

"We'll leave early and take the back roads. That old road north of Potter's place is hardly ever used any more. And Mr. Potter couldn't tell if he wanted to, because he's blind as a bat."

"By rights we should discuss it with your aunt first," Uncle Herb said.

But I could feel him weakening, so I persisted.

"Let's keep her in the dark until I'm ready to try my test. Then we'll surprise her. Is it a deal?"

After chawing and spitting and contemplating for about five more minutes, Uncle Herb finally nodded and we shook on it. I think he secretly got a kick out of the idea of trying to put one over on Aunt Marg because it was so darn hard to do.

Every day for a month we took Potter's old road with me

at the wheel. I clashed gears and made the truck leapfrog up hills, and stalled it about a dozen times. And every time I stalled it, Uncle Herb made me get out and crank.

It was hard work, cranking, but he insisted that if I was going to be a driver I had to know how. I was improving every day and getting as confident as all get-out when I had my first accident.

A hedgehog ran across my path and I swerved violently to miss it — and landed us in the ditch. We were both shaken up, but not really hurt.

"I'm sorry, Uncle Herb," I said, fearful that I'd ruined my chances. "What should I have done?"

"Well, Maggie," he rubbed his head where it'd bumped on the roof, "in a case like that, it's either him or us. Just think what might've happened if we were on a busy highway and you'd swung out into the path of another veehickle."

I twisted my neck to get the crick out of it. "I won't do it again," I promised.

We climbed out of the truck to survey the situation. As luck would have, right at that moment along came Barney Slinger in his tow truck.

When he saw us, he rolled his cab window down and hollered, "What in blazes are you two doing out in this neck of the woods, Herb?"

Then Uncle Herb said the strangest thing.

"I'm fine Barney," he replied. "How's yourself?" We both looked curiously at Uncle Herb, then I jumped into the breach.

"I'm learning to drive, Mr. Slinger," I explained.

Barney laughed and said, "You're supposed to drive on the road. Need any help?"

It was a joke, not a question.

"You're lucky I took this short cut today or you'd be walking into town. You'd never drive outta there."

He hopped out, inspected the depth of the ditch, hooked us up and towed us out in no time flat, simple as that. Uncle Herb tried to pay him for his trouble, but Barney wouldn't hear of it.

"What's neighbours for?" he said. "But you better be more careful, Maggie. You two could've got banged up pretty bad. Or worse yet, broke an axle."

"I know," I answered ruefully. "But, Mr. Slinger, could I ask you one more favour?"

"Depends on how much time it'll take. I'm a busy man."

"Oh, it won't take any time at all," I assured him. "I just want to ask you to promise not to tell anybody about my driving lessons so it doesn't spoil the surprise for Aunt Marg."

He laughed when he heard that.

"I'd like to be a mouse in the corner when you surprise her. You can count on me."

He twisted his thumb and finger across his mouth three times.

"My lips are buttoned up."

By the time another couple of weeks had gone by, I was nearly an expert, so I asked Uncle Herb if I was ready.

"Ready as you'll ever be, Maggie," was his reply. "Now all we got to worry about is telling your aunt."

That night after supper we confessed.

"Herbert Alfred Wilkinson!"

Aunt Marg was furious.

"You did what? You taught our Margaret how to drive.

You did that behind my back?"

"I had no choice, Meg. She made me do it, didn't you, Maggie?"

"Made you, indeed!"

She didn't give me a chance to defend him. "You both deserve a good hiding."

"Shall I find a switch, Aunt Marg?" cried Gracie gleefully.

Gracie wasn't too thrilled about sharing her bed with me again, so she wasn't sorry to see me in trouble, even if it did include her beloved uncle.

"Oh, Aunt Marg," I pleaded, grabbing her hand. "Come for a ride with me and let me prove how good I am."

"Good or bad has nothing to do with it, Margaret. It's just the idea that the two of you would deceive me."

"We're truly sorry, aren't we, Uncle Herb?" Uncle Herb nodded his fuzzy red head vigorously.

"C'mon, Aunt Marg."

I got her coat down from the hook on the door and held it out for her.

She gave a short, impatient huff and shrugged into it. Reluctantly, she climbed into the cab of the truck. Uncle Herb had already started the engine, so I threw it in gear and took off. I drove for about five miles with the utmost care. Aunt Marg didn't say a word until I'd glided to a smooth stop back in the barnyard.

I glanced at her anxiously. To my relief I saw she was smiling. In fact she was grinning from ear to ear.

"You drive just like me!" she declared proudly. "We'll go straight into Barrie tomorrow."

We took the car instead of the pickup because it had better brakes.

I could've passed that test with one hand tied behind my back.

"You're a pretty good driver for a girl," the tester had to admit.

"You're a pretty good tester for a boy!" I retorted.

I was glad I had my licence safely in hand before I said that, because it made him mad as hops.

For the next month I drove myself triumphantly to and from school in Shelburne.

Aunt Marg laid down some hard and fast rules: no boys in the car except Matt — what a pain that was, but I'd have agreed to anything for the privilege of driving. No speeding — twenty miles an hour was my limit. And keep both hands firmly on the steering wheel.

Eva was my daily passenger. At first, Jessie didn't take to the idea of two girls driving alone back and forth on country roads. What if we ran into problems? The car might develop engine trouble or blow a tire. But Matt assured his mother that I could handle such emergencies as well as he could. I was pleased as Punch when he said that! And Zach said it would be mighty fine having Eva home every night for a change, so Jessie finally relented.

"Isn't it wonderful, Marg. Just the two of us again," remarked Eva as we bounced along the bumpy side road to Shelburne.

I knew what she meant. We hardly ever saw each other alone any more because Phylis was always there.

And it *was* wonderful. It made me appreciate Eva's genuine loyalty and her quiet intelligence. Phylis was fun — she was always saying goofy things to make me laugh — but if I ever had to choose between them, there'd be no contest. Eva would win hands down.

And of course I was the envy of my schoolmates. After all, who else had an almost brand-new Model A Ford to park beside Mr. Bannister's Whippet in the schoolyard?

Chapter 18

My Dear Uncle

One night while I was doing my physics homework by the white light of the Coleman lamp and Aunt Marg was recording the day's events in her journal, we heard sleet pinging on the windowpane.

Aunt Marg got up and peered out between cupped hands.

"I think it'll be risky driving tomorrow, Margaret," she said anxiously. "The piazza steps are already coated in ice."

Uncle Herb folded his newspaper.

"What's that you said, Mag?" he asked. So she repeated her forecast.

"Mebbe I'd better run you and Eva into school tomorrow, Maggie," he suggested.

My instant protest was drowned out by the jangling of the telephone.

"For mercy sakes, who could that be at this hour?" wondered Aunt Marg. "Answer it, will you, Herb?"

"Can't! No time."

He jumped up as quick as a jack-in-the-box. "I got chores to do in the barn."

Grabbing his coat and cap from the doorhook, he high-tailed it out through the woodshed.

The telephone rang again — two longs and two shorts.

"I'll get it," I said.

I lifted the receiver and tilted the flared mouthpiece at the bottom of the box up to my mouth. I was now so much taller than Aunt Marg that we couldn't talk on the same level.

It was Dora on the phone telling me in an animated voice that my room was ready. Her excitement was contagious, so I promised that I'd come the very next day.

Rabbit had forbidden me to set foot in their house after the catastrophe — because, he explained, he wanted to surprise me.

Well, did he ever! The room was brand-new, not just Angus's old room done over, but brand, spanking new.

Rabbit had installed a bay window with a hinged window seat that you could sit on and store things in, and he'd lined the walls with flawless pine.

Dora had sewn blue dotted swiss curtains and a matching counterpane.

To top it all off, they'd bought a new bed and washstand from the Eaton's catalogue. The washstand had a pink china pitcher in a matching bowl on top, and an oval looking glass that could be tipped to any angle. A pink chamber pot was hidden behind a door lower down.

The crowning glory was a bearskin rug beside my bed. Now I wouldn't have to step out onto cold linoleum!

"Well, Meg?"

Dora was all atwitter, waiting for my reaction. "Out with it! What've you got to say?"

For once in my life, I was almost speechless. "It's a dream

come true, Dora," I managed at last. "I've always wanted a room like this."

"Oh, and just you wait till you see the closet!" she cried.

She flung open the door of a new corner wardrobe. "There's room enough for all your things in here, even your winter coat. You won't have to hang it on that old hall tree any more. It'll hold its shape lots better on a clothes hanger."

"That reminds me, Meggie."

Rabbit had been leaning on the doorjamb, silently taking it all in. He hadn't said a word, but his ears and nose were wiggling a mile a minute, so I knew there was a riddle coming on.

"What kind of coat do you put on wet?"

Quick as a wink I answered, "A coat of paint!"

"Shoot!" he hooted.

Then he gave his knee a slap and went clumping down the stairs laughing his head off . . .

That night, Dora prepared a special welcome-home supper and served it on the tablecloth. There were potato pancakes, fried turnips, stuffed baked rabbit and apple pie.

After supper, Rabbit started singing in his funny nasal voice, "*Leave the dishes in the sink, Ma.*

"*Leave the dishes in the sink.*

"*Each dirty plate will have to wait.*

"*Tonight we're going to celebrate.*

"*So, leave the dishes in the sink!*"

"That's a dandy idea," laughed Dora. "And just like the fine folk that we are, we'll take our tea in the parlour."

The parlour had also changed a lot since the last time I'd been in it. It wasn't cluttered any more with Dora's precious gewgaws because they'd nearly all been smashed in the catastrophe.

And something else was different. Rabbit had traded in his gramophone for a brand-new electric radio. It had eight tubes, he said, and he could tune in at least four stations — five on a good night — just as clear as if they were coming from down on Main Street.

That night, we listened to a marvelous story called *The General Died at Dawn*. Dora and I sat spellbound, but halfway through it Rabbit stretched and yawned and said he was going to hit the hay. Dora and I stayed glued to the radio until the final awful moment when the general passed bravely away on the new Philco.

Then, sighing with sad satisfaction, we went into the kitchen to do the washing up and have our bedtime repast.

"How come Rabbit went to bed in the middle of such a swell story, Dora?" I asked, really mystified.

"Well, Meggie, just between you, me and the lamppost," she paused, mashed the tea and poured it through a sieve into our cups, "my Roger's got his good points" — she always referred to her husband by his correct name when she was being serious — "but a long attention span isn't one of them. He gets restless quicker than you and me."

We were just polishing off the last of the pie when the telephone rang.

"Who in the world could that be calling at this hour?" declared Dora, sounding just like Aunt Marg. "You get it like a good scout, will you, Meg?"

It was Aunt Marg.

"How d'you like your new bed chamber, Margaret?" she asked excitedly.

"It's just gorgeous, Aunt Marg. I can't wait till you see it."

"Well, Dora gave me a sneak preview a week ago, so I couldn't wait to hear what you had to say. By the way, your father phoned tonight."

"He did!"

Instantly I saw my pa in my mind's eye, tall and lanky, black curly hair like mine and big dark eyes behind thick horn-rimmed spectacles.

"What did Pa want, Aunt Marg?"

Cold shivers ran over my skin at the thought of anything wrong at home.

"He wanted to speak to you, but I told him you were back in Shelburne."

"Why did he want to speak to me especially?" The hair on the back of my neck prickled with anxiety.

"Oh, he was just checking to see if you'd suffered any ill effects to your nerves after what you went through in the catastrophe. I assured him you were fine and dandy."

I felt a wave of relief, then a backwash of disappointment.

"I wish I'd been there," I said.

"Well, never mind, dear. I promised him you'd phone home on the weekend. Then I had a chat with your mother. She sends her love and says to tell you they're all in the pink."

"Thanks, Aunt Marg. Can I speak to Uncle Herb for a minute?"

I heard her call him from wherever he was.

"Your uncle says he's too tuckered to talk, Margaret, but Gracie's pestering at my elbow, so I'll put her on. Good night, love."

"Good night, Aunt Marg. Tell Uncle Herb good night."

I talked to Gracie for a while, but it was long distance, so I rang off before too much time went by.

I hung up slowly, a feeling of apprehension creeping over me. Dora stood in the doorway, arms folded, a look of consternation puckering her brow. She'd overheard enough of the conversation to put two and two together.

"It's not like Uncle Herb," I said, following her back to the kitchen. "He always wants to talk to me. I hope Gracie hasn't completely replaced me in his affections."

"No, no, Meggie. Herb's not like that. He's got his faults, but his heart's as big as all outdoors. There's plenty of room for the both of you, and some to spare."

"Well, why the heck wouldn't he talk to me, then?"

"Maybe he's sick, Meg, and just won't let on. Remember last winter when Roger had the quincy and he wouldn't admit it until he was flat on his back?"

"No, Uncle Herb's not sick."

I was sure of that because I knew Aunt Marg would've said something. You couldn't pull the wool over her eyes where sickness was concerned. I'd tried it often enough myself. Something else was nagging at me.

Suddenly I knew.

"He can't hear well on the telephone any more, Dora. He runs a mile every time the phone rings. Come to think of it, he doesn't hear anything like he used to."

Then I told her about Barney Slinger's question when he found us in the ditch and Uncle Herb's strange answer.

"Matter of fact, I quizzed him about it later and he said if folks would stop mumbling and speak up he'd hear them just fine."

We sat silently at the kitchen table finishing our tea.

"Dora," I just had to say it out loud, "I think Uncle Herb's going deaf."

With downcast eyes she absently wet her finger on her tongue and dabbed at the crumbs on the table.

"Well, don't fret yourself until he's seen Dr. Tom, Meggie," she said. "He'll know what to do."

I decided to discuss it with Aunt Marg on the weekend. But the very next day, something unexpected happened that sent me flying home.

Chapter 19

Chip Off the Old Block

"Peggy!" Gracie screamed hysterically into the telephone.

My heart gave a wild thump.

"What is it, Gracie?"

I was terrified of the answer. Visions of Aunt Marg lying stricken on the floor or Uncle Herb pinned helplessly under the tractor out in the field flashed through my mind.

"It's a fawn! A baby deer! It's all tore open and bleeding. Uncle Herb carried it into the house and wrapped it in flannel, but now we don't know what else to do."

"Call the vet!" I shouted into the mouthpiece.

"He doesn't answer."

"Where's Aunt Marg?"

"She's at Delmer Dandy's. Clarrisa Dandy took a bad turn yesterday, so Aunt Marg said she'd stay all night. They haven't got a phone. Please, Peg, please come home!"

Suddenly I was very calm.

"Is the fawn still bleeding?"

"I think so. The flannel's all soaked."

"Tell Uncle Herb I have to speak to him."

She told him and I heard him say, "There's been enough talk. Tell Maggie I'm on my way in to get her."

"Gracie, listen to me carefully."

"I am, Peg."

Her voice was a fearful, childish whisper.

"Get some towels. Fold them into a big pad and press down firmly on the wound. Talk to the fawn softly to keep him quiet."

I hung up and looked at Dora.

"Will you come with me, Dora?" I asked as I climbed into my overalls.

In answer, she got my bag out of the closet. Over the years I'd put together a doctoring kit like Aunt Marg's — disinfectants, wads of cotton and rolls of gauze, a razor-sharp knife, long pointed tweezers, needles and thread.

"I'll just leave Rabbit a note pinned to the kitchen curtains where he'll be sure to see it," she said.

Oh, how I wished I'd driven the car in. But Aunt Marg had needed it because she'd several patients she had to see.

By the time Uncle Herb came racing down Rail Street, Dora and I were waiting impatiently at the door.

We made it back to Green Meadows in record time. Uncle Herb flew along the bumpy roads at forty miles an hour.

I leapt out of the pickup before it came to a full stop and ran with my bag into the house.

There sat Gracie on the floor, her round face smeared with blood and tears. Dark brown blood was drying on her chubby outspread fingers.

"Oh, Peg," she looked at me with swimming, tragic eyes, "I think I've let her die."

The long-legged little creature lay perfectly still. I snatched the looking glass off the wall above the wash-bench and held it close to the fawn's mouth and nostrils.

Slowly a patch of mist appeared.

"She's alive!" I cried. "Dora, you help Gracie while I scrub my hands. Uncle Herb, I'll need more light."

They followed my orders like soldiers.

Cautiously I lifted the blood-soaked pad, expecting to have to deal with a sudden red jet, but none came.

"The bleeding's stopped," I sighed. "Now all I have to do is patch the wound up."

It wasn't as easy as it sounded. There was a terrible, jagged hole, big enough to bury my fist in. I could see vital organs laid bare, but miraculously the main blood vessel hadn't been severed. I could actually see the artery pulsing as the fawn's lifeblood ran through it.

Using the tweezers, I began picking out bits of rusty metal and strands of twisted steel.

A barbed wire fence, I thought. She got caught in a barbed wire fence and tore herself free.

Then I spied something that made my blood boil — a tiny lead slug buried in her flesh.

A bullet!

I knew it was hunting season, but what kind of sports-man would shoot at a baby deer? Apart from anything else, it was against the law.

Watching intently over my shoulder, Uncle Herb said gravely, "I'll take care of that, Maggie."

I grasped the slug with the tweezers and nipped it out

clean as a whistle and dropped it into Uncle Herb's hand.

Blood spurted and I stanched the flow with a wad of cotton.

When I was finally satisfied that I'd taken out every last piece of foreign matter, I carefully sponged the area with disinfectant while Dora sterilized a needle and thread.

I tried to pull the skin together with my thumb and finger, but the torn edges wouldn't fit.

"Boil the scissors from Aunt Marg's work basket, will you, Dora?"

The little animal began to stir.

"Quickly, Gracie! Get the bottle of chloroform from my bag."

Uncle Herb handed her a clean handkerchief folded into a square pad.

"Put a few drops on it, Gracie. Then be ready to give her a whiff."

Gracie carried out my instructions like a veteran.

After what seemed like ages, the scissors were sterilized and cool enough for me to handle. I snipped the ragged skin away and pulled the edges neatly together. Then I took my first stitch.

Suddenly the fawn stirred again and opened its eyes. They were large as saucers and dark as midnight — and filled with terror. Bleating a wild, terrified cry, she began to struggle.

Uncle Herb dropped to his knees and pinned her front legs down while Dora grabbed the flailing back ones. Gracie, without being told, hugged the head tight to her body and administered more chloroform.

Slowly the little beast relaxed and lay still. I worked as fast as I could, stitching and knotting, stitching and knotting the same way I'd seen Doc Wiley do on a wounded dog once.

At last the gaping hole was closed. I'd sewn a nice, neat seam shaped like a wedge of pie.

Uncle Herb got an old quilt from the cupboard.

"Easy does it," he said as all four of us helped lift the sleeping baby onto the clean bedding.

Then he wrapped the bloody flannel in newspapers while Dora hunted up Aunt Marg's pail and string mop and went to work on the stained floorboards. We'd hardly glanced at each other throughout the whole ordeal. I turned to tell Gracie how brave she'd been, only to see hero worship glowing from her big green eyes.

"You did it, Peg!" she said in an awestruck whisper. "You saved the fawn's life."

"Not me, Gracie," I smiled at her, smoothing her dishevelled red hair behind her shoulders. "You did. If you hadn't controlled the bleeding, the little creature would've been dead long before I got here."

"Really, Peg? You're not just saying that?"

"Really," I nodded solemnly. "And since you saved her life, she belongs to you. That's the rule isn't it, Uncle Herb?"

"Yep. Them's the rules, patootie," he said as he pinched Gracie's round cheek. "It'll be up to you to take care of her until she's strong enough to go free."

He knelt and examined the V-shaped gash.

"By that time, it'll be dead of winter," he murmured anxiously. "She'll never survive out there in the bush at that time of year."

His words made Gracie gasp. Then her face lit up with an idea.

"We can keep her in the barn until spring. She'll be my pet, like Starr is Peggy's pet. Is there enough hay to feed one more animal, Uncle Herb?"

"More than enough," he replied. "But deer don't eat hay like horses, patootie. It cramps them up and gives them the scours. No, she'll have to have corn and cedar."

"Where'll we get corn and cedar?" worried Gracie.

"We can buy corn from the feed store in Shelburne, and we can bring cedar boughs in from the bush. They got to be fresh every day."

"I'll get the cedar, Uncle Herb," volunteered Gracie.

"No, Gracie, you ain't to go near the bush by your own-self. You might get turned around and get lost. Don't you worry your head about the cedar. I'll take care of that chore. Now you and Maggie go wash yourselves. It's a messy job being a vet."

After we'd tidied up and Dora had put the kitchen back to rights, we all squatted on our haunches around the groggy fawn, stroking and comforting her. The glossy reddish-brown coat shimmered under our touch.

At last the curled eyelashes fluttered open, and this time she stayed quite calm.

Just at that crucial moment, when we were winning the fawn's confidence, who should come bustling in the door but Aunt Marg.

"Well, for land's sake," she cried, dropping her bag with a thud on the floor. "What are you doing home, Margaret? And what in the world are you all on your knees for?"

The fawn jerked and bleated pitifully.

"Hush!" we all said at once.

When Aunt Marg saw what lay on the blanket, she knelt down between Gracie and me and whispered, "What happened?"

In a breathless voice, Gracie told her all about it.

Gingerly Aunt Marg lifted the gauze padding and peered at the stitchwork.

"You did this, Margaret?" she asked in an admiring whisper.

"Yes, Aunt Marg. But Gracie deserves the credit. She's a real trooper."

Then Dora piped up, "She's a chip off the old block, if you want my opinion."

"What block?" asked Gracie curiously.

"This one right here."

Uncle Herb put his arm around my shoulders. "It looks to me like we got two up-and-coming vets in this here family, Mag."

Turning to Gracie, Aunt Marg gave her a fierce hug and covered her beaming face with kisses.

"I'm ever so proud of you, old sweetheart," she declared.

We were pleased as Punch with ourselves, Gracie and me. Especially me. It was the first time since my little sister had come to live with us that I hadn't felt the slightest twinge of jealousy when Aunt Marg called Gracie by my special pet name.

Maybe, just maybe, I was growing up at last.

Chapter 20

The Culprit

Uncle Herb lost no time in ferreting out the culprit who'd shot Petunia, as Gracie called the little creature.

First he made inquiries of all our neighbours for miles around. He took a notepad with him and a pencil stub that he licked before each entry. Then he wrote down everything they said.

He tracked down every clue like a detective, checking out every strange car in the area that day and finding out the name of every person who'd been seen carrying a gun.

Bit by bit, he sifted through the evidence until he'd narrowed it down to two possible suspects. One of the two had an airtight alibi.

The other was Matt.

"Well, Matt didn't do it," I said with finality.

"It's probably just hearsay," agreed Aunt Marg.

"I'm sorry to have to put the kibosh on that surmise, but I've got a mighty reliable witness. And you know how that boy loves to hunt. He's been toting a gun around these parts ever since Collie was a pup."

"But he wouldn't shoot a baby deer," I insisted. Uncle Herb continued as if I hadn't spoken.

"He was seen on old Joe Boyle's place, and that's where I found the fawn. Do you remember old Joe Boyle, Maggie?"

"Sure I do. He was that squatter that shot himself."

"That's the fella," agreed Uncle Herb. "And his shack's been deserted ever since. The barbed fence was down and gone to wrack and ruin and the fawn was all tangled up in the rusty wire. I had a deuce of a time cutting her loose 'cause she was wild with fear and pain."

He shook his head sadly, then continued.

"Harry Potter says he saw Matt prowling around old Joe Boyle's place that very day."

"Well, that doesn't prove anything. Old man Potter is potty anyway. And he's probably lying his head off."

"Harry's not potty, Maggie, and he ain't a liar," said Uncle Herb sharply.

"Well, Matt didn't do it!"

I banged my fist so hard on the table that the spoon glass jumped about two inches.

"And all we have to do to settle it is to ask Matt. He *never* lies."

I went straight to the telephone then and turned the crank. Nora Wiggins came on instantly.

"Central here!" she answered in her operator's voice.

"Nora, it's me, Margaret. Put me through to Briarwood Farm right away, please."

"Hmph!" she snorted as she rang the Muggins' phone. Nora didn't much appreciate a straight connection with no chit-chat.

She came back on the line.

"There's no answer," she reported triumphantly.

"There has to be," I insisted, almost angrily.

"Well, don't get your shirt in a knot. I'll try again."

I heard the telephone ringing off the hook, but there was still no answer.

"Are you sure you've got the right number? One long and two short?" I demanded.

"Now don't you go getting uppity with me, Margaret Rose Emerson. I know my job."

"Well, where the heck is everybody then?"

"How should I know?" Nora snapped. "I'm a telephone operator — and a good one, I might add — not a mind reader."

"Oh, gosh, Nora, I'm sorry. I'm all upset. I didn't mean to take it out on you. But I absolutely have to get in touch with Matt. I think I'll go over to Briarwood myself."

"Well, if there's anything I can do, Margaret" — my apology seemed to mollify her a bit — "just let me . . ."

I rang off right in the middle of her sentence.

Aunt Marg knew I'd hung up on Nora because she knew Nora would be dying of curiosity. Being 'Central' for twenty years had made her that way. And she was a font of information too. Anything you wanted to know, you just had to ask Nora.

"Margaret," Aunt Marg reprimanded me. "That's no way to treat Nora, hanging up in her ear. She's a good scout and she's handled many an emergency. Just you wait until the next time you need her."

"I mind the time Nora saved the schoolhouse from burning to the ground," Uncle Herb said. "If she hadn't noticed the chimney fire in time, the whole shebang would've gone up in smoke. Lives might even have been lost. We'd be in a fine pickle without Nora, and that's a fact. We'll rue the day the telephone company replaces her with one of them modern switchboards."

"Nora's nice," put in Gracie as she brushed Silky's hair backwards, trying to make him look like a Persian. "She always gives me licorice roots."

"Nora! Nora! Nora!" I snapped, exasperated. "Where's Matt? That's what I want to know."

I already had my coat on.

"Can I have the keys to the truck, Uncle Herb?"

"Truck's got two flat tires, Maggie," said Uncle Herb.

"How about the car, Aunt Marg?"

"It's up on blocks in the driving shed for the winter. You know that, Margaret."

"I forgot," I sighed. "Well, I know one sure-fire way of getting there."

I didn't have to ask permission to ride Starr anymore. It went without saying. He was mine.

I was out the door in two shakes of a lamb's tail, or maybe Petunia's little powder puff.

Then, just as Starr and I were setting off down our lane, up the road came the Muggins' horse and buggy with the whole family squeezed in on the seat.

We pulled up side by side.

"Where you off to, girl?" asked Zacharia.

"I was on my way over to your place."

Zacharia waved towards the house and I turned Starr around and took him back to his stall. He stomped his front hoofs and grumbled in his throat the way horses do when they're mad, so I took the time to give him some extra oats.

"I'll be back soon," I promised when I'd finished filling his bin — and quickly made a beeline for the house.

The second I saw all the long faces inside, I knew something was wrong. Jessie and Aunt Marg were sitting on the settle together looking agitated. Uncle Herb and Zach were muttering under their breath and Eva was standing beside Matt, her hand on his arm protectively.

As for Matt, well his hang-dog expression gave him away instantly — and Grandma Marshall's legacy started boiling in my veins.

I raced across the room and stopped right in front of him.

"You dirty, rotten coward. You make me sick," I fumed. "You always did love killing innocent animals, didn't you? You think hunting makes you a man, don't you? Well, not to me, it doesn't."

Twice he tried to interrupt my tirade and both times I cut him dead.

"I would've bet my life on you, Matt. That's how blind and stupid I am. But you did do it, didn't you? You shot Gracie's fawn."

Matt's face turned slowly from white to red. He dropped his gaze, not able to look me in the eye. "I can explain," he muttered feebly.

"Oh, no you can't, because I'm not listening. I'll never forgive you for this, Matt. Never!"

I had to leave the room then because I was afraid I was going to smack his guilty face. Slamming the woodshed door with all my might, I headed back out to the barn.

Starr whinnied joyously to see me back so soon. I leaned my head against his and he pressed a little closer. What excuse could Matt possibly have for shooting a little wild creature, especially a baby? I hated the despicable thing he'd done.

More than ever now, I was determined to become a vet. Not just a vet, but the best animal doctor in the world.

I hugged Starr's long warm nose and he nuzzled my neck with his velvety lips. His whiskers tickled my chin and made me shiver.

He tried to comfort me with little horsy sounds, even though he couldn't know what was wrong, being a horse after all. Still, more than any human being ever could have, he helped me.

When I went back into the house, the Muggins had gone.

Uncle Herb was the first to speak.

"Everybody makes mistakes, Maggie, even your best friend."

"I have no best friend," I said, and went to bed.

* * *

The next day, I stopped in at Dr. Wiley's veterinary clinic at Four Corners to get some medicine for the fawn. His small office was pretty messy. The desk and swivel chair were scratched and old, and horse hair stuffing spilled out of the leather couch. But that didn't matter. The only things I was interested in were the certificates on the walls — his medical degrees. In my mind's eye I could visualize a framed document that read, *Doctor Margaret Rose Emerson, D.V.M.*

That night after supper, Aunt Marg and Gracie and I went down to the barn to check on our patient in the temporary pen that Uncle Herb had built and lined with clean straw.

The little fawn stood on wobbly legs, her enormous eyes staring at us curiously. She didn't seem to be the least bit afraid. I think she knew we wouldn't hurt her for the world.

It was then that Aunt Marg finally made me listen to what had taken place the day Petunia was shot.

"It was a misty morning, Margaret, and Matt was out hunting before dawn. He said the fog was so thick you could cut it with a knife, and the bush was as dark as night. Then he caught a glimpse of what he thought was a coyote and he shot it for fear it might be rabid."

As she spoke she scratched the fawn's white bib and it lifted its head for more. She continued without looking at me.

"Matt says he'll bring fresh cedar boughs in from the bush every day so your uncle won't have to. He wants to do all he can to help. And Jessie says Matt's hung his gun over the mantlepiece. She says he's learned his lesson and he's given up hunting for good and all, Margaret."

"I'll believe that when I see it," I answered coldly, still angry and unforgiving.

The Conspiracy

"Aunt Marg, I need to talk to you, woman-to-woman."

"About Matt?" she asked, too quickly.

"No." I felt a twinge of pain. "About Uncle Herb."

We were in the barn gathering eggs. Uncle Herb and Gracie had gone to Four Corners for the mail. They'd taken the horse and buggy even though the pickup's tires were all fixed and the car was off the blocks. Uncle Herb was afraid to take either one in case they got stuck in the spring mud.

Aunt Marg drew an anxious breath.

"What is it, Margaret?" she asked.

I decided not to beat around the bush.

"Uncle Herb's going deaf, isn't he? You're a nurse, so you must've noticed."

She sighed and set the egg basket down.

"Yes, Margaret, I have. For a long time now I've tried to fool myself into thinking he was just getting crotchety in his old age — we're not getting any younger, you know — but I've finally had to come to terms with it."

"What do you mean, 'come to terms'? Have you decided to just accept it? Why haven't you talked it over with me?" I couldn't keep the annoyance out of my voice.

"I didn't want to worry you, old sweetheart." She reached out and squeezed my hand.

"I thought you had enough on your plate, what with algebra and chemistry and physics and all those foreign languages. Fifth form is hard enough for anybody, let alone a sixteen-year-old."

"Have you mentioned it to Uncle Herb?"

"I've tried to broach the subject, but every time I do he gets stubborn and insists he hears fine. He just won't admit anything's wrong. Not for a moment."

"Well, I think Dr. Tom should be consulted."

"I've already hinted in that direction. I said I thought we all needed a good checkup."

"What'd he say?"

"He said to go ahead, but not to make any arrangements for him. He says he's fine and dandy."

"Well, there's only one way then. We'll have to trick him into it."

"That's easier said than done. We'd have a deuce of a time hoodwinking him into that office. He'd see right through us."

"Oh, I don't know about that. We sure pulled the wool over his eyes with that fake chewing tobacco" — we both smiled at the memory — "and I can be pretty sneaky when I want to be. That's something else I inherited from my grandma. Ma says Grandma Marshall could trick a dog out of a bone full of marrow."

Just then Petunia started bleating and thumping

around in her pen. That meant she must've heard Starr coming up the lane, which in turn to her meant Gracie would soon be there to feed her.

Sure enough, Uncle Herb was just taking Starr out of the shafts when Aunt Marg and I came out into the barnyard. As soon as Starr saw me, he began prancing around like a colt. His flying tail almost swished the egg basket out of Aunt Marg's grasp.

"For mercy sakes, Starr, act your age!" she scolded, transferring the basket from one arm to the other. "Get him into the barn, Margaret, and calm him down. And make sure he doesn't step on any of my ladies. The dear little souls did a lovely job today. They laid twice as many brown eggs as white. Gracie, you go and feed Petunia before she kicks her pen into kindling wood."

"Got any orders for me, sergeant?" chuckled Uncle Herb.

"Yes. Pull your earflaps down before you catch your death of cold. It's not spring yet, you know. You sounded wheezy last night. I'll have to dose you up with spirits of camphor tonight."

He grinned his natural, happy grin and did as he was told.

Then Aunt Marg said, "Did you remember to get me a writing tablet and a bottle of blue ink and some two cent stamps from the post office, Herb? I've owed that sister of mine a letter for a week."

Uncle Herb's grin faded and he lifted an earflap and asked peevishly, "What's that you say? Speak up, woman. You're all the time muttering."

That did it. There and then I decided to see Dr. Tom about Uncle Herb as soon as I could.

* * *

The very next day, after school was finished, I marched over to Dr. Tom's office on Main Street.

Unlike Dr. Wiley's office, Dr. Tom's was new and had nice furnishings. His medical certificates lining the walls were all framed in brass. But of course not one of them ended in the magic letters *D.V.M.*

His inner office door opened and he escorted a worried-looking young mother with a crying baby in her arms to the door, earnestly giving her advice along the way. On his way back he saw me sitting there.

"Margaret. Well, and how's your old straw hat?"

I followed him into his office and sat on the big leather chair opposite him.

"I'm fine, Dr. Tom. It's Uncle Herb I've come to see you about."

"What's that rascal been up to now?" he said, leaning back in his swivel chair and clasping his hands behind his head.

So I told him all the signs Aunt Marg and I had noticed: not hearing the crystal set when it was as clear as a cow-bell; refusing to speak on the phone, even to me; pretending to understand questions by guessing at the answers; unconsciously cupping his ear to catch what was being said; acting cranky and crotchety, which wasn't like him at all.

"I think he's going deaf," I finished despairingly.

The doctor's expression was sober now. He frowned and shook his head.

"He's certainly got all the classic symptoms," he said. "Well, I'll have to get him in here and have a look at him.

Then if your suspicions are confirmed, I'll make an appointment with a colleague of mine who's an ear specialist at the Toronto General. There are some fine hearing devices on the market today, Margaret, so don't look so distressed."

"The trouble is, Uncle Herb won't admit he's got a problem. And he refuses to come to see you. The only way we'd ever get him here would be to trick him into it. Aunt Marg and I are stumped. We thought you might have some ideas . . . "

"Hmm."

He combed thin strands of grey hair thoughtfully across the top of his shiny head with his fingers.

"Let's put our thinking caps on," he said at last.

We came up with several notions and rejected them one by one. Suddenly I had a flash of inspiration.

"I think I've got it," I cried. "I'll have a terrible attack of appendicitis when Aunt Marg is off somewhere with Gracie and can't be reached."

"You're a genius, girl, or a corker, as Herb would say. That ought to work. He'll do anything for you."

* * *

The following Saturday, Aunt Marg went over to check on Mabel Raggett, taking Gracie with her to play with Luella.

Mabel was expecting a baby soon and wouldn't let anybody but Aunt Marg touch her. She said she didn't trust doctors as far as she could throw them.

Well, as luck would have it, the baby came early and Aunt Marg had to stay on.

After supper, while Uncle Herb was out doing the milking, I phoned Dr. Tom.

"Is tonight all right?" I asked, explaining that Aunt Marg was out of reach.

"I'll be right here in my office, Margaret. I won't set foot out the door," he promised.

When Uncle Herb came in, he found me doubled up over the dishpan, the dishes only half done, moaning and holding my side. He set the bucket down so hard a wave of milk slopped over the side.

"Maggie! Maggie! What ails you, girl?"

"I think it's my appendix. Oh, please, Uncle Herb, call Dr. Tom."

He didn't hesitate for a split second. Quickly, he went to the phone, gave it a crank, and barked at Central, "Got an emergency here, Nora. Put me through to Dr. Tom pronto."

Dr. Tom, of course, said to bring me right in.

After examining me and giving me some sugar pills, the doctor explained to Uncle Herb that the pills would take the inflammation down, and he assured him I was in no immediate danger.

He spoke in a normal tone of voice, but he had his back to us while he made up the prescription. Then he turned towards us.

"Would you repeat those instructions, Herb," he asked innocently. "I want them followed to the letter."

"What letter?" Uncle Herb looked puzzled.

"Didn't you hear what I said, Herb?"

He spoke louder this time.

"You was mumbling with your backside facing me. I'm not a mind reader," snapped Uncle Herb.

"I wasn't mumbling, Herb. I was speaking very clearly. Did you hear me, Margaret?"

I nodded, still clutching my side.

"Considering Margaret heard me and you didn't, and since you're here anyway, I might as well kill two birds with one stone."

In a jiffy, before Uncle Herb had a chance to object, Dr. Tom was peering into his ear with a long thin flashlight.

I continued to hold my side and look pitiful because I was determined Uncle Herb would never find out the whole thing was a conspiracy.

When he was finished his examination, Dr. Tom said, "I want you to see a friend of mine at Toronto General, Herb. He's an ear specialist and I'm sure he can help you."

"I'm not going to no hospital."

Uncle Herb got up and shrugged on his coat.

"Are you feeling all right now, Maggie? We got to get back to Green Meadows. I've got work to do."

"I think I can make it," I said weakly, keeping up the act.

Dr. Tom helped me on with my coat and ordered me solemnly to take two pills every four hours and to come back to see him on Monday.

"I'm going to Toronto next Thursday morning, Herb. I've got two patients to check up on, so I'll pick you up at eight sharp."

Before Uncle Herb could open his mouth to object, the doctor reached for his phone and waved us out the door.

* * *

Uncle Herb went with Dr. Tom and was given a hearing aid. But the minute he got home, he put it at the back of the sideboard drawer, and there it stayed.

No one could persuade him to give it a try. He swore it was the most foolish gadget he'd ever wasted money on, a piece of tomfoolery if ever there was one.

Well, at least he never found out how it was that he came to acquire that piece of tomfoolery in the first place.

Chapter 22

Atonement

As the end of the school year drew closer, my studies crowded everything else out of my mind. I was determined to excel because I knew I had to have high marks to qualify for the Ontario Veterinary College in Guelph, especially since I was a girl.

I was prepared to do all the work alone, but in the end Mr. Bannister really surprised me with all kinds of help and encouragement. I couldn't get over it.

Dora just wagged her finger in my face and said, "I told you there was a lot of good in Dusty."

I didn't go home to the farm every weekend because I found I could concentrate better in the Hares' house.

Gracie didn't mean to bother me, but she was such a natural chatterbox that she nearly drove me to distraction. If she wasn't talking to one of us, she was rattling on to Silky. Then I'd get mad and yell at her and that would upset Aunt Marg, so I decided to spend more time in Shelburne until after the exams.

Of course I still had to endure Rabbit's riddles.

"Here's one for the highly eddicated. Who invented fractions, Maggie?" he chortled, sure that he had me this time.

"Henry the Eighth!" I dropped my head into the middle of my chemistry book with a thud and a long-suffering sigh.

Undaunted, he tried again.

"What two words have the most letters, Meg?"

"The post office!" I groaned, and threw up my hands, cracking my elbow on the table's edge.

"Ow!" I yelled, and began rubbing the pain out of my arm.

"What's the trouble, Meggie?" asked Rabbit innocently.

"I hit my funny bone," I snapped.

"Then why ain't you laughing?" he snickered.

"Rabbit Roger Hare!" Dora came at him with the broomstick. "Why don't you save your breath to cool your porridge?"

Rabbit slunk away looking offended.

* * *

After several weekends of not going to the farm, I began to feel pretty lonely. So one incredibly beautiful May day I got a ride home to Green Meadows with Zach and Eva.

As we bumped up our rutted lane, I saw Starr across the meadow grazing on some fresh spring greenery. I leapt out before we'd even stopped properly and ran to the split-rail fence. Cupping my hands around my lips, I blew our secret signal — the silent whistle that only he could hear.

Starr's head jerked up like a jack-in-the-box and then he charged across the field towards me, his tail and mane flying like sails in the wind. Fifteen hundred pounds of horseflesh stopped just inches from my toes, sending clods of earth flying in the air.

I hugged Starr's head and kissed his cheek and rubbed the star on his nose. He whinnied and snorted and vibrated his lips, making that peculiar flurried sound that only horses do.

"Take him to the barn and water him, Maggie!" called Uncle Herb from the porch.

As soon as I walked into the barn I noticed Petunia's pen was empty. Quickly I put fresh water out for Starr and gave him a feed of oats before I rushed inside.

Aunt Marg was scurrying around the kitchen looking like the cat that had swallowed the canary. Gracie was jumping up and down, her red braids bobbing with excitement.

"Matt's helping me to teach Petunia how to be wild again," she cried, her eyes all aglow.

"Where is he?" I asked skeptically.

"He's perched up in a tree for the night with his gun, watching every move Petty makes. He wouldn't let me stay because he said I might go to sleep and fall off the branch, but I wouldn't. I know I wouldn't."

I didn't question her any further. Instead, after both Gracie and Uncle Herb had gone to bed, I talked to Aunt Marg.

"Do you think it's possible for a tame animal to go back into the wild?" I asked apprehensively.

"Well, I'm no judge of that, Margaret, but Matt did talk it over with Dr. Wiley, and Dr. Wiley did say it'd been successfully done before."

She stirred and creamed our nightly cocoa, then sat down beside me at the table.

"Matt's determined to redeem himself in your eyes, Margaret."

She squeezed my hand and I couldn't help but notice how small and chubby hers was compared to my long, lean fingers.

"The least you can do is give him that chance," she added.

I decided to wait and see, so I dropped the subject.

I was content just to be home again.

Green Meadows. What a terrific name Aunt Marg and Uncle Herb had chosen for their farm years ago. It fairly sang of spring!

Chapter 23

News From Home

When I got back to the Hares' house, there was a letter propped up on the sugar bowl with my name on it. Also, there was a note pinned to the curtain explaining that Dora and Rabbit had gone to see Horace and Mabel, Rabbit's brother and his wife.

The handwriting on the envelope was Josie's, so I tore it open eagerly.

> *149 Rose Avenue*
> *Toronto, Ontario*
> *May 9, 1932*

Dear Peg,

You're the one who owes yours truly a letter, but I know you haven't got time to write because you're studying for your finals. I am, too, but I'm only in middle school, so it's not so important that I get high marks. I don't know what I want to be anyway, so I don't care as long as I pass. I'm glad I didn't skip a year like you.

Anyway, that's not what I'm writing about. I've got some news that I thought you'd find interesting, if not astonishing! Remember Rodney Gallaugher who was Andrew's best man at the wedding? You know, the handsome one who had a crush on you? Well, guess what? Rodney's saved up enough money by working at the Sunlight Soap Works to pay his way through college. He's going to Guelph, just like you! He wants to be a zoologist or a biologist. Something like that. Anyway, the thing that matters is, you'll both be in the same college. Talk about coincidence! When Olive told him you were going to be there too, she said you should've seen his face light up.

By the way, since we're on the subject of boys, I am not going around with Gilbert any more. Remember I told you how much he reminded me of Matt Muggins? Well he does, but he isn't . . . like Matt I mean. He turned out to be really nasty. A couple of times I caught him giving Bobby and Davey a smack when no one was looking. I feel like smacking them myself sometimes when they act like little fiends, but I told him not to lay a hand on them because they're not his brothers. He said that if we ever got married, they would be and then he'd fix them good. So I told him I never wanted to see him again. He went slamming out the front door, making the glass rattle. Thank goodness Pa wasn't home. That's his pride and joy, that stained glass window in the front door. I thought I'd miss Gilbert, but I don't miss him the least little bit. I'm really glad to be rid of him. He even pulled my hair once!

Actually, I miss Matt Muggins more, and that's funny

because he never was my boyfriend and I don't know him all that well. But there's something special about him. Does he ever ask about me? Maybe I'll see him when I come up in the summer. Don't forget you invited me. I'm dying to meet the Hares and eat off their newspaper tablecloth. Anyway, Peg, say hello to them for me and give my love to everybody on the farm, including Starr! Also, would you please mention my name to Matt once in a while and tell him sort of casually that I'm coming up this summer?

Please write when you have a minute and tell me all the news. Is Uncle Herb enjoying his hearing aid? Does it work with the crystal set? I'll bet he's his old happy self again.

I have to go now because the little kids are fighting over the biscuits. Ma says I'm in charge when she's out now that Harry and Jenny have work after school in Black's Funeral Parlours. They don't have to go near the dead people. They just do the sweeping and dusting in the sitting room. Ma said it's a heathenish job for young folks, but Pa says it'll teach them what life is all about. And besides, the pay's good — fifty cents a day each. You should hear some of the stories they tell about eerie moans and groans coming from the coffins when the lids are shut and there's no one else around. I'm sure they'll give you an earful when you come home for your summer visit.

I really have to go now.

> Your loving sister,
> Josephine-Frances.

P.S. Do you like my name hyphenated? I do, so don't call me Josie any more. J-F

P.P.S. I forgot to ask about Petunia. Gracie told us all about her pet deer in a cute letter she wrote the whole family. It must be incredible to have a pet deer. But what will they do with it when it gets big? Pa says they'll have to eat it and he hopes Uncle Herb remembers to put some in the icehouse for him because he's very partial to venison. But I said that sounds pretty cannibalistic and you won't allow it. You'd have the right to forbid it, because you saved its life. And I'd agree with you!

XXXOOO J-F-E

I read the letter several times and blushed every time I came to the part about Rodney. One other thing about my reaction to Josie's — Josephine-Frances' — letter: I didn't feel a speck of jealousy where Matt was concerned. I used to be as mean as a dog with a bone about Matt. Now I seemed to have finally dropped the bone. Perhaps hearing about Rodney had something to do with it.

* * *

By the time I got around to writing back, I was able to include some good news about Petunia. After many weeks of patient work on Matt's part, the young buck (as it had turned out to be after all!) had finally run off with a doe into the bush and was never seen again. This made Gracie feel sad, but she knew it was for the best.

I felt badly to have to report that Uncle Herb wasn't using his hearing aid at all.

Chapter 24

On My Way

The finals were hard, but this time I was ready for them. Still, by the time I'd finished the last exam I was so tired I could hardly keep my eyes open.

Dora gave me a pitying smile as I dragged myself in the door at the end of the week.

"I've got a nice supper on, Meggie," she said encouragingly. "Pork bones plum full of juicy meat, boiled new potatoes about the size of agates and fresh water cress. I gathered the cress myself by the creek just this morning. I was down there hunting for pearls in the freshwater shell fish. Myrtle Stromberg found a lovely pink one yesterday."

"It sounds good," I said, stifling a yawn. "Is there time for me to have a bath before supper, Dora? The cold water might pep me up."

"There's plenty of hot water. I've had the Kitchen Queen on all afternoon cooking up a storm."

Dora helped me carry pail after pail of near-boiling

water from the stove's reservoir into the little chamber beside the pantry.

It was a tiny, narrow room Rabbit had made by lopping off a piece of the kitchen. The big, copper tub and the old-fashioned toilet with the pullchain water closet above it took up so much space that you could hardly turn around.

I added cold water from the faucet until the temperature was just right. Then I slid down into the warm soft water and let the weariness soak out of my bones.

That was one thing I was really going to miss on the farm. There we still took our baths in the kitchen in a corrugated washtub that I could barely fit into any more. I had to sit with my knees drawn up right under my chin. It wasn't very relaxing.

* * *

The following afternoon I began packing my things into the back seat of the Model A.

Dora stood watching me, looking downright depressed, so I said, "I'll probably be back so often I'll wear my welcome out."

"Fat chance!" she snorted.

Then she cranked and I choked, and off I went in a cloud of dust.

Aunt Marg was making a batch of raisin tea biscuits when I arrived at the farm.

"Well, Margaret," she tried not to sound anxious as she poked some extra raisins in the soft dough with her fingertip, "aren't you going to tell me how you did?"

I felt better than I did the night before, so I answered cheerfully, "Oh, all right I guess, Aunt Marg. But every single exam was extra hard." Uncle Herb came in just as I was speaking. "What's that you say, Maggie?"

He patted his round stomach and sniffed the first batch of biscuits baking in the stove's hot oven. I kissed him hello on his red-whiskered cheek — and had to lean right over to do so. I was about four inches taller than him now.

"I was just telling Aunt Marg," I shouted in his direction, "that I found the exams really difficult this time."

"Well, just put them out of your mind now, Maggie, they're over and done with. You look pale and peaked. Come away down to the barn with me and have a look at the old girl's horn. She hurt it somehow when she was out in the pasture and it's bleeding so bad I might have to ask Doc Wiley to saw it off."

Good old Uncle Herb. He knew the pungent smell of the barn would put colour into my cheeks and make me forget everything else.

I went straight to work on Flora's injured horn. It didn't look so bad once I'd cleaned it and doused it with iodine. I wrapped it in strips of flannel and hoped she wouldn't rub the bandage off before the horn had a chance to heal.

Next, Uncle Herb and I walked out into the flowery meadowland to find Fern and Fancy. They mooed softly when we approached and gazed at us with their placid, trusting brown eyes. I patted each of them on their wide wet noses. Fern, who was still a baby, licked my hand and tried to suck my finger.

"Animals are lovely, aren't they, Uncle Herb," I said as the two cows went back to their munching.

"Lovely," he agreed, and he took hold of my hand the way he used to when I was a child.

We walked quietly hand in hand over to the grove of trees where Starr was sure to be. And there he was, upside down, playing, his great hairy hoofs thrashing the air as he rolled about ecstatically in a patch of purple clover.

He was having so much fun, we got within forty feet of him before he noticed us. His long white lashes fluttered when he spied me.

Whomp! went his huge body over to one side. He gathered himself up on his strong legs, first the front and then the back, and began galloping around us in crazy circles, whinnying his head off. Finally he came to me and buried his snout in my arms.

"It's a wonder he ain't good for nothing, the way you spoil him," laughed Uncle Herb as he gave Starr's sinewy neck a long stroke.

"It works just the opposite, Uncle Herb," I shouted over the horse's loud snorts. "Animals need love just like people. It makes them better, not worse."

"Well, I'll take your word for it, Maggie. Starr sure bears you out on that. He's the best horse in the county. And you'll be the best vet in the county, that's for certain. You got more feel for creatures than anybody I know."

"I hope you're right, Uncle Herb."

We started back to the house. Just then, Gracie saw us and came racing towards us, whirling her school bag over her head.

"My gosh you're getting tall," I said, giving her a sisterly hug. "And you've run off all your baby fat."

I couldn't get over how much she'd grown in a few short weeks. She giggled at my lopsided compliment, then we each grabbed one of Uncle Herb's rough hands and, swinging our arms in unison, we all three skipped like crazy kids across the meadow.

* * *

On a balmy night early in June, the phone rang while we were all sitting around the table dawdling over our tea. I jumped up to answer it, thinking it'd be Eva.

"Margaret," Nora said, her voice sounding more important than usual, "I have a long-distance call for you from Shelburne. Hold on and I'll put it through."

After a couple of clicks, a voice inquired, "Miss Emerson?"

I recognized Mr. Bannister's voice at once and responded with a breathless, "Yes?"

"I have some news for you. Are you sitting down?"

"No, sir," I answered stupidly, and promptly sat with a thump on the chair under the phone.

"Well, now. This is unofficial. Entirely unofficial, you understand."

My heart gave a lurch.

"Yes, Mr. Bannister?"

I turned towards the table so the others could hear.

Then I listened to what Mr. Bannister had to say.

I seemed to have lost my own voice and was able to respond only with strange little grunts.

Finally I managed to say thank you, and we both hung up.

"What is it, Margaret?" cried Aunt Marg anxiously as soon as the phone was back on the hook.

"The suspense is killin' me," declared Uncle Herb.

"Peggy, Peggy, tell us what the principal said," begged Gracie.

I felt my face stretch into a huge, triumphant grin. Usually I played down how smart I was so I wouldn't sound conceited, but this time I couldn't help bragging.

"Mr. Bannister says I'm top of the class. Maybe even top of the whole county."

Saying it made the news sink in and my eyes suddenly filled with tears. My wet lashes swept up and down my spectacles, making them all smeary.

"Oh, Margaret, my old sweetheart!" Aunt Marg jumped up and hugged me and took off my glasses to wipe them on her apron.

Uncle Herb dabbed his eyes with his checkered handkerchief, blew his nose with a loud honk and said, "Maggie, girl, I'm so happy for you that if I had a tail I'd wag it."

That made Gracie screech with laughter. Then she grabbed my hands and danced me around in a circle as though she was playing Ring Around the Rosy.

"And that's not all," I cried breathlessly as we collapsed back into our chairs. "Mr. Bannister wants me to be valedictorian at the graduation ceremonies."

"Oh, Margaret! What an honour!" Aunt Marg's round cheeks flushed with pride.

"What's a valedic . . . valedictory?" asked Gracie.

"Valedictorian, Gracie. It's the person who gives the speech on graduation day."

"Oh, boy, I'll be able to help you, Peg," cried my nine-year-old sister. "I made a speech last week all about when I was young and lived in the city. The teacher gave me an E for excellent. I'm really good at composition."

She was, too. And she helped me a lot.

* * *

The great day arrived and Josie and my parents came all the way from Toronto to attend the ceremony.

In my address I thanked them all — my two families, my faithful friends and Dusty Bannister. I called him that right out loud by mistake and my schoolmates hooted and laughed and stamped their feet.

I nearly died of embarrassment at my slip, until I saw Mr. Bannister laughing too.

When it was all over and we graduates held our fifth form diplomas in our trembling hands, our families descended upon us.

My pa, looking tall and handsome in his new straw boater, his dark eyes glittering behind thick horn-rimmed spectacles, was the first to congratulate me.

"You're a credit to us all, Peg," he said in a choked-up voice, then he kissed me self-consciously on the forehead.

Ma and Aunt Marg, looking for all the world like twins with their red hair and green silk crepe de chine dresses, hugged and kissed me tearfully.

And Josie — beautiful Josie — slipped her arm around my waist and whispered, "I'm ever so proud of you, Peg."

That meant a lot to me, coming from Josie, whom I had always envied for her extraordinary beauty.

Next it was Uncle Herb's turn. He looked unusually splendid in his blue serge suit with his father's gold watch chain looped across his stomach.

He held out his arms to me as he used to do when I was a little girl and I went into them and leaned down to receive his kiss.

"That was a mighty fine speech, Maggie," he said in a hoarse voice.

"Did you hear it, Uncle Herb?" I asked incredulously.

"Every blinkin' word," he said, pointing to his ear.

There, almost hidden by his fuzzy red side-whiskers, was the hearing aid.

"Oh, Uncle Herb, thanks for wearing it," I said.

"Best danged gadget I ever had," he answered, proud as Punch of himself.

Now the Muggins family surrounded me.

Jessie and Zach offered warm congratulations. Eva squealed and hugged me. Matt looked awkward.

We still hadn't spoken since the shooting incident. Self-consciously, he wiped his light brown hair out of his pale blue eyes.

"Good going, Marg," he said.

"Thanks, Matt."

We shook hands and wordlessly mended our fences.

Then Josie came over and she and Matt smiled shyly at each other — and I didn't mind a bit.

While all this was going on, Rabbit and Dora had stayed in the background.

I saw them over Ma's head and I beckoned for them to join us.

Dora gave me an unaccustomed kiss.

"You did fine, Meg," she said. "We're mighty proud of you."

Rabbit squeezed my hand.

"Meggie," he said in a loud but conspiratorial voice, "now that you've proved how smart you are, I got a question."

Everybody within earshot stopped talking to listen,

which is exactly what he intended them to do.

"Yes, Rabbit?"

He'd caught me off guard, so I fell neatly into his trap. I should've known better by the way his ears and nose were twitching.

"Well, now, I'd be pleased to know" — he enjoyed being the centre of attention, so he dragged it out — "what come first, the chicken or the egg?"

For the first time ever, I was stumped.

Rabbit slapped his knee and shouted gleefully, "*Gotcha!*"

When the laughter finally died down, I knew I had to come up with some kind of an answer.

"I don't know what came first, the chicken or the egg, Rabbit. That's what I'm going to university for — to find out. And when I do, you'll be the first to know."

Epilogue

I finally received my Doctorate in Veterinary Medicine in 1936 when I was twenty-one years old.

I began my practice as Dr. Wiley's assistant. When he decided to retire in 1937, I took over the practice and hung up my shingle — literally.

Matthew made it for me.

On a fine sheet of pine he carefully carved my full name, and then added those three magic letters, *D.V.M.*

One year later, that same Matthew Muggins and my own dear sister Josephine were married in Toronto.

She was the most beautiful bride I'd ever seen, and he was the proudest groom.

* * *

And Starr, my wonderful four-footed friend, lived to the ripe old age of thirty-eight, a record for a Clydesdale, or any other horse for that matter.

But that didn't make it any easier to say goodbye.

BERNICE THURMAN HUNTER was a storyteller from an early age, but it was not until her children were grown that she began to get her work published. Soon she became one of Canada's favourite writers of historical fiction for children, with a dozen books to her credit, including the best-selling *Booky* trilogy, *Lamplighter, Two Much Alike, It Takes Two, Janey's Choice* and *Amy's Promise,* winner of the 1997 Red Cedar Award. In 1989 Bernice received the Vicky Metcalf Award for her contribution to Canadian children's literature, and in 2002 she was appointed to the Order of Canada.